In praise of
Denise Mina's
Garnethill
Trilogy

"Denise Mina's Garnethill trilogy is a great achievement."
—Natasha Cooper, *Times Literary Supplement*

"Head and shoulders above much of contemporary crime fiction."
— Val McDermid

"We are asked to think hard about the nature of sympathy, justice, and retribution. We ponder these questions long after the books end, and ask, How do we apply them to the world we know and the lives we lead?"
—Margo Jefferson, *New York Times*

"Denise Mina is one of the most exciting writers to have emerged in Britain for years."
—Ian Rankin

GARNETHILL

"One of the year's best books. . . . A stunning debut. Denise Mina is definitely one to watch."
—Leslie McGill, *Kansas City Star*

"A shattering first novel. . . . You can't look away from it."
—Marilyn Stasio, *New York Times Book Review*

"Like sandpaper across a delicate varnish, the novel scrapes and tears the veneer of everyone in the book, removing the grime along with the gloss."
—Amy Rabinovitz, *Houston Chronicle*

"Mina writes with a pen dipped alternately in gallows humor and rage."
— *Kirkus Reviews*

EXILE

"A powerful novel. . . . A writer of stunning talent and accomplishment." —*Publishers Weekly* (starred review)

"In Maureen O'Donnell, Mina has fleshed out a real woman, flaws and all. An absorbing read." —Judith Evans, *St. Louis Post-Dispatch*

"This is a terrific book . . . for its accurate evocation of a thoroughly convincing milieu of tenements and child benefit books, jostling family demands and scrambling survival, cafés and night buses, as well as its collection of superbly elaborated characters, all of whom are given their well-deserved due." —P. G. Koch, *Dallas Morning News*

"The poverty Mina describes cuts like *Angela's Ashes*. . . . The danger reaches a frightening pitch that is soon surpassed by a stunning twist at the conclusion." —Jane Dickinson, *Rocky Mountain News*

RESOLUTION

"A riveting story, with the outcome in doubt until the final pages." —Susanna Yager, *Sunday Telegraph*

"If you want a reason to try the crime genre, skip Agatha Christie, skip *A Is for . . .* , and get yourself a novel by Denise Mina." —Jane Dickinson, *Rocky Mountain News*

"Once again, Mina delivers a Scottish blend of Thomas Harris, George Pelecanos, and Oprah-style reading that is uniquely her own and goes down very smoothly." —*Library Journal*

"Mina's canvas is so broad, so teeming, and so relentlessly sordid that the biggest surprise in this final chapter in Mina's not-to-be-missed Glasgow trilogy is that she can pull off the climax her title promises." —*Kirkus Reviews*

GARNETHILL

ALSO BY DENISE MINA

Exile
Resolution
Deception
Field of Blood
The Dead Hour
Slip of the Knife

GARNETHILL

A NOVEL

DENISE MINA

BACK BAY BOOKS
Little, Brown and Company
New York   Boston   London

Back Bay Books / Little, Brown and Company
Hachette Book Group
1290 Avenue of the Americas, New York, NY 10104
Visit our Web site at www.HachetteBookGroup.com

Originally published in the U.S. in hardcover by Carroll & Graf, April 1999
First Back Bay paperback edition, September 2007

Back Bay Books is an imprint of Little, Brown and Company. The Back Bay
Books name and logo are trademarks of Hachette Book Group, Inc.

The interview with Denise Mina that appears in the reading group
guide at the back of this book was originally published in *LA Weekly*
on September 16, 2004. Copyright © 2004 by LA Weekly, LP.
Reprinted with permission.

ISBN 0-316-01678-0 / 978-0-316-01678-0
LCCN 2007931252

10 9 8 7 6

LSC-H

Printed in the United States of America

To my mum, Edith

GARNETHILL

GARNETHILL

1

MAUREEN

MAUREEN DRIED HER EYES IMPATIENTLY, LIT A CIGARETTE, WALKED over to the bedroom window, and threw open the heavy red curtains. Her flat was at the top of Garnethill, the highest hill in Glasgow, and the craggy North Side lay before her, polka-dotted with cloud shadows. In the street below, art students were winding their way up to their morning classes.

When she first met Douglas she knew that this would be a big one. His voice was soft and when he spoke her name she felt that God was calling or something. She fell in love despite Elsbeth, despite his lies, despite her friends' disapproval. She remembered a time when she would watch him sleep, his eyes fluttering behind the lids, and she found the sight so beautiful that it winded her. But on Monday night she woke up and looked at him and knew it was over. Eight long months of emotional turmoil had passed as suddenly as a fart.

At work she told Liz.

"Oh, I know, I know," said Liz, back-combing her blond hair with her fingers. "Before I met Garry I used to go dancing . . ."

Liz was crap to talk to. It didn't matter what the subject was, she always brought it back round to her and Garry. Garry was a sex god, everyone fancied him, said Liz, she had been lucky to get him. Maureen was sure that Garry was the source of this information. He came by the ticket booth sometimes, hanging in the window, flirting at Maureen when Liz wasn't looking.

Liz began a rambling story about liking Garry and then not liking him and then liking him again. Two sentences into it Maureen realized she had heard the story before. Her head began to ache. "Liz," she said, "would you do me a favor and get the phones today? He's supposed to phone and I don't want to talk to him."

"Sure," said Liz. "No bother."

At half-ten Liz opened her eyes wide. "Sorry," she said theatrically into the phone, "she's not here. No, she won't be in then either. Try tomorrow." She hung up abruptly and looked at Maureen. "Pips went."

"Pips? Was he calling from a phone box?"

"Aye."

Maureen looked at her watch. "That's strange," she said. "He should be at work."

Half an hour later Liz answered the phone again. "No," she said flatly, "I told you she's not in. Try tomorrow." She put the phone down. "Well," she said, clearly impressed, "he's eager."

"Was he calling from a phone box again?"

"Sounded like it. I could hear people talking in the background like before."

The ticket booth was at the front of the Apollo Theatre, set into a triangular dip in the neoclassical façade so that customers didn't have to stand in the rain while they bought their tickets. It was a dull gray day outside the window, the first bitter day of autumn, coming just as warm afternoons had begun to feel like a birthright. The cold wind brushed under the window, eddying in the change tray. The second post brought a letter stamped with an Edinburgh postmark and addressed to Maureen. She folded it in half and slipped it into her pocket, pulled the blind down at her window and told Liz she was going to the loo.

Douglas said he was living with Elsbeth but Maureen felt sure they were married: twelve years together seemed like a lifetime and he lied about everything else. Three months ago the elections for the European Parliament had been held and Douglas's mother was returned for a second term as the MEP for Strathclyde. All the local newspapers carried variations of the same carefully staged photo opportunity. Carol Brady was standing on the forecourt of a big Glasgow hotel, smiling and holding a bunch of roses. Douglas was standing in the background next to the provost, his arm slung casually around a pretty blond woman's waist. The caption named her as Elsbeth Brady, his wife.

Maureen had written to the General Register in Edinburgh, sending a postal order and Douglas's details, asking for a fifteen-year search on the public marriage register. She remembered caring desperately when she sent the letter three months ago but now the response had arrived it was just a curiosity.

The outer door was jammed open by Audrey's mop bucket. One of the cubicle doors was shut and a thin string of smoke rose from behind the door. Maureen tiptoed over the freshly mopped floor, locked the cubicle door and sat on the edge of the toilet, ripping the fold open with her finger.

The marriage certificate said that he had been married in 1987 to Elsbeth Mary McGregor. Maureen felt a burst of lethargy like an acid rush in her stomach.

"Hello?" called Audrey from the other cubicle, speaking in the strangled accent she reserved for addressing the management.

"It's all right," said Maureen. "It's only me. Smoke on."

When she got back to the office Liz was excited. "He phoned

again," she said, looking at Maureen as if this were great news. "I said you weren't in today and he shouldn't phone back. He must be mad for you."

Maureen couldn't be arsed responding. "I really don't think so," she said, and slipped his marriage certificate into her handbag.

At six o'clock Maureen phoned Leslie at work. "Listen, d'ye fancy meeting an hour earlier?"

"I thought your appointment with the psychiatrist was on Wednesdays."

"Auch, aye," said Maureen, cringing. "I'll just dog it today."

"Right, doll," said Leslie. "I'll get you there at, what, half-six?"

"Half-six it is," said Maureen.

Liz helped to shut up the booth and then left Maureen to carry the day's takings around the corner to the night safe. Maureen walked slowly, taking the long way through the town, avoiding the Albert Hospital. Cathedral Street is a wind tunnel. It's a long slip road for the M8 motorway and was built as a dual carriageway to accommodate the heavy traffic. The tall office buildings on either side prevent cross breezes from tempering the eastern wind as it rolls down the hill, gathering nippy momentum as it crosses the graveyard and sweeps down the broad street. Maureen had misjudged the weather, her thin cotton dress and woolen jacket did nothing to keep out the cold and her toes were numb in her boots.

Louisa would be sitting behind her desk on the ninth floor of the Albert right now, her hands clenched in front of her, watching the door, waiting for her. Maureen didn't want to go. The echoey corridors and smell of industrial disinfectant freaked her every time, reminding her of her stay in the Northern. The nurses there were kind but they fed her with food she didn't like and dressed her with the curtains open. The toilets didn't have locks on them so that the patients couldn't misuse the privilege of privacy for a suicide bid. When she first got out, each day was a trial: she was terrified that she might snap and again be a piece of meat to be dressed every morning in case of visitors. Her current therapist, Dr. Louisa Wishart, said that her terror was a fear of vulnerability, not loss of dignity. And every time she went to see Louisa the same fifty-year-old underweight man was sitting in the waiting room. He kept trying to catch her eye and talk to her. She cut her waiting time as thin as possible to avoid him, sitting in one of the toilets or hovering around in the lobby.

She had been attending the Albert since Angus Farrell at the Rainbow Clinic referred her eight months before. By the time she had her first session with Louisa she knew she was going to be all right, that therapy was an empty gesture to medicalize a deep sadness. She tried to stop going to Louisa but her mother, Winnie, caused an almighty fuss, phoning her four times a day to ask how she was. She went back to the Albert and said she had been resisting a breakthrough in her therapy.

Having been brought up Catholic she felt like she had always been passing her inner life in front of someone or other for approval. So she lied, changing the names and making up story lines to entertain herself. She rarely talked about her family. Louisa smiled sadly and gave her obvious advice.

She took a cutoff to the High Street and walked down to the Pizza Pie Palace, a badly Americanized restaurant destined for insolvency from the first. The walls were varnished red brick, hung with chipped tin adverts for cigarettes and gasoline. Two battered papier-mâché cacti stood on either side of the door. The bonnet of a Cadillac had been unwisely attached to the wall just above the till, at forehead level. She could see Leslie sitting at a table at the back of the room, still wearing her battered biker's leathers, with two enormous cocktails in front of her and a cigarette in her hand. Her short dark hair was kept perpetually dirty by her crash helmet and stuck out in all directions. Her nose was flat and broad, her eyes were large and deep brown, verging on black, her teeth were big and regular. The overall effect was mad and sexy. She pushed one of the cocktail glasses toward Maureen as she walked over to the table.

"Aloha." She grinned.

A shiny-faced young waiter came over to the table and interrupted Leslie's pizza order to tell her he thought her leathers were sexy. Leslie blew a column of smoke at him. "Get us a fucking waitress," she said, and watched as he walked away.

"Leslie," said Maureen, "you shouldn't speak to people like that. He doesn't know what he's done to offend you."

"Fuck him, he can work it out for himself. And if he can't, well, he'll be offended and that makes two of us."

"It's rude. He doesn't know what he's done."

"You are correct, Mauri," she said, "but I think that the important lesson for our young friend to learn is that I'm a rude woman and he should stay the fuck out of my face."

A bouncy young waitress came over to the table. Leslie ordered a large crispy pizza for the two of them to share with anchovies, mushrooms and black olives. Maureen ordered a carafe of their cheapest red wine.

Unlike Liz, Leslie was great to talk to. Whatever had happened she unconditionally took her pal's side, happily bad-mouthed the opposition and then never mentioned it again, but she hated Douglas and she was pleased now that Maureen said she wanted to finish it. "He's an arse." She fished a cherry out of her glass with her fingers. "That was abuse. You were a minute out of hospital when he nipped you."

"He didn't nip me," said Maureen. "I nipped him."

"Doesn't matter. Getting involved with a patient is abuse."

"But I wasn't his patient, though," said Maureen, instantly defensive. "I was Angus's patient."

"He met you at the clinic, didn't he?"

"Yeah," Maureen conceded uncomfortably.

"And it's a clinic for victims of sexual abuse?"

"Yeah."

"And he worked there and knew you were a patient?"

"Yeah, but—"

"Then it's abuse," said Leslie, and, lifting the cocktail, drank it far too quickly.

"Oh, I dunno, Leslie, everything can't be abuse, you know? I mean, I wanted it. I was as much part of it as he was."

"Yeah," she said adamantly. "Everything can't be abuse but that was. Do you think he could have guessed that your consent was compromised by being four months out of a psychiatric hospital?"

"I dunno."

"Maureen, four months out of the laughing academy, come on, even a prick like Douglas knows it's not right. He's with someone else, he asks you to keep it a secret, he's got a lot of power over you. It's abusive."

"He didn't ask me to keep it a secret, actually," said Maureen, blushing with annoyance.

"Did he take you home to meet his mum?" Leslie smiled softly. "What's your damage about this guy, Mauri? He's got access to your fucking psychiatric record, how equal can that be?"

The waitress brought the carafe of wine and poured it for them as if it was nice. She lifted the empty cocktail glasses. Maureen couldn't think of anything to say. She nursed her cigarette to mask her discomfort, rolling the tip on the floor of the glass ashtray. Leslie was right. Douglas was a sad old wanker.

The carafe was half-empty by the time the giant pizza arrived. They ate it with their fingers, catching up with the news and gossip. The funding to the domestic violence shelter where Leslie worked had been cut and it might have to shut in a month. She was conducting a campaign to have the funding reinstated and was getting the rubber ear everywhere. "God, it's depressing," she said. "We got so desperate we even sent a mail shot to the papers telling them that eighty percent of battered women are turned away as it is, and not one of them phoned us. No one seems to give a shit."

"Can't you ask the women to speak to the papers? I bet they'd cover a human interest story."

Leslie drained a glass of wine and thought about it. "That's a hideous idea," she said flatly. "We can't ask these women to prostitute their experience for our sake. They've been used all their lives and most of them are still being hunted down by their own personal psychopath."

"Auch, right enough." Maureen sat forward. "I can't help thinking that we never win the abortion debate at a media level because the antiabortionists coach women to cry on telly and use photographs of dead babies and we always use statistics. We should use emotive narratives and arguments."

Leslie grinned. It must be very cheap wine, her teeth were stained dark red. Maureen supposed hers must be too.

"Frothy emotionalism," said Leslie. "Best way to engage the ignorant."

"Precisely. You should do that."

"I'm sick of trying to win arguments," said Leslie quietly. "I don't understand why we don't all just band together and attack. Doris Lessing says that men are frightened of women because they think women'll laugh at them and women are frightened of men because they think men'll kill them. We should all turn rabid and scare the living shit out of them—let them see what it feels like."

"But what justification would there be for adopting violent tactics?"

"Negotiations," said Leslie, adopting a Belfast accent, "have irretrievably broken down."

"I don't accept that," said Maureen. "I think what you mean is you've lost patience."

It was unfair of Maureen to say that: Leslie worked in the shelter with women who had been systematically beaten and raped by their partners. In Leslie's world men rape children, they kick women in the tits and teeth and shove bottles up their backsides; they steal their money and leave them for dead and then feel wronged when they leave. If anyone could justifiably lose patience Leslie could.

Leslie thought about it for a minute. She looked despairingly at her glass and struggled with some thought. Her face collapsed with exhaustion. "Fuck it," she said. "Let's get really pissed."

And they did.

Maureen's head was fuzzy with red wine. She put on her softest T-shirt straight from the wash to make herself feel coddled and went to bed. She took more than the prescribed dose of an over-the-counter liquid sleeping draft and fell asleep with her eye makeup half-off and her leg hanging out of the bed.

2

DOUGLAS

DOUGLAS WAS TIED INTO THE BLUE KITCHEN CHAIR WITH SEVERAL strands of rope. His throat had been cut clean across, right back to the vertebrae, his head was sitting off center from his neck. Splashes and spurts of his blood were drying all over the carpet. One long red splatter extended four feet diagonally from the chair, slashing across the arm of the settee and nearly hitting the skirting board on the far wall.

She couldn't seem to move. She was very hot. She had been scuttling back down the hall from the toilet when the blood-drenched cagoul lying just inside the living-room door caught her eye. A trail of bloody footprints led to Douglas, tied to the chair in the dead center of the room. The footprints were small and regular, like a dance-step diagram.

She didn't remember sliding down the wall into a fetal crouch. She must have been there for a while because her backside was numb. She couldn't see him now, just the cagoul and two of the footprints, but the sweet heavy smell of blood hung like a fog in the warm hall. The yellow plastic cagoul was drenched in blood.

The hood had been kept up; the blood pattern on the rim was jagged and irregular.

He could have been there all night, she thought. She'd gone straight to bed when she got in. She'd slept in the same house as this.

Eventually, she got up and phoned the police. "There's a dead man in my living room. It's my boyfriend."

She was standing still next to the phone, sweating and staring at the handle on the front door, afraid to move in case her eyes strayed into the living room, when she heard cars screaming to a stop in the street and people running up the stairs. They hammered on the door. She listened to the banging for two long bursts before she could reach over and open it. She was trembling.

They moved her into the close and asked her where she had been in the house since coming in. A photographer took pictures of everything.

Her neighbor, Jim Maliano, came out to see what the noise was. She could hear him asking the policemen questions in his Italian-Glaswegian rat-a-tat accent but couldn't make out what he was saying. Maureen was finding it hard to speak without drawling incomprehensibly. She felt as if she were floating. Everything was moving very slowly. Jim brought her out a chair to sit on, a cup of tea and some biscuits. She couldn't lift the cup from the saucer because she was holding the biscuits in her other hand. She put the cup and saucer down on the ground, under her chair so that no one would knock it over, and balanced the biscuits on her leg.

The neighbors from downstairs gathered vacantly on the half-landing, standing with their arms crossed, telling each new arrival that they didn't know what had happened, someone had died or something.

A plainclothes policeman in his early thirties with a Freddie Mercury mustache and piggy eyes cautioned Maureen.

"You don't need to caution me," she mumbled, standing up and dropping her biscuits. "I haven't done anything."

"It's just procedure," he said. "Right, now, what happened here?"

He said yes to everything she told him about Douglas as if he already knew and was testing her. He interrupted Maureen as she tried to explain who she was. "You lot," he said tetchily to the assembled neighbors, "you'll be contaminating evidence there. Go back indoors and wait for an officer to come and see you. Give your names and addresses to her." He gestured to a uniformed policewoman and turned back to Maureen. She threw up, narrowly missing the policeman's face but hitting him squarely in the chest, and passed out.

It took her a minute to work out where she was. It was a large bed, a black-lacquered mess with small tables attached at either side. It looked like the devil's bed. Jim Maliano was third-generation Italian immigrant and proud. His house was a shrine to Italian football and furniture design. On the wall at the foot of the bed a black and blue Inter Milan football shirt was squashed reverently behind glass and framed with tasteful silver. It was wrinkled and fading like a decaying holy relic.

Her mother, Winnie, was sitting by her feet stroking them histrionically. Winnie liked to drink whisky from a coffee cup first thing in the morning and most days were a drama from start to finish. She coughed a sob when she saw Maureen open her eyes. "Oh, honey, I can't believe it." She slid up the bed, cupped Maureen's face in her hands and kissed her forehead. "Are you all right?"

Maureen nodded.

"Sure?" Winnie's breath stank of Gold Spot.

"Aye."

"What on earth happened?"

Maureen told her about finding the body and passing out in front of the policeman. Winnie was listening intently. When she was sure

Maureen had finished talking she said that Jim had left a wee brandy for her, for the shock. She lifted an alcoholic's idea of a wee brandy from the side table.

"Mum, I've just thrown up."

"Go on," said Winnie, "it'll do you good."

"I don't want it."

"Are you sure?"

"I don't want it."

Winnie shrugged, paused and sipped.

"It's good brandy," she said, as if the quality of drink had ever made a difference. Maureen would phone Benny and get him to come over. Benny was in Alcoholics Anonymous and Winnie couldn't stand to be in the same house as him.

Winnie sipped the brandy, nonchalantly taking bigger gulps faster and faster until it was finished while Maureen got up and dressed. Jim had left out a Celtic football shirt and black jogging trousers for her. She took off her sticky T-shirt and slipped them on. Just as she was tying the drawstring on the trousers she caught sight of herself in the full-length mirror on the far wall. She had one panda eye from last night's makeup and her hair was dirty and stuck to her head. She had only washed it the morning before. She ran her index finger under her eye, wiping off the worst of the nomadic mascara.

The mustachioed policeman looked around the door. The front of his jacket and shirt were wet, he had washed Maureen's vomit off too vigorously and although he had tried to pat them dry the jacket lapels were losing their shape and his shirtfront was see-through. Maureen could see an erect nipple clinging to the wet material. "Are you decent?" he said, looking her up and down.

He was followed into the room by the policewoman and an older officer with rich auburn hair flecked with gray. Maureen had seen him directing the Forensics team. His pale face was dotted with orange freckles, oddly boyish in such a serious man. He had a big gap between his two front teeth and watery china blue eyes. She remembered him for his courtesy when he moved her into the close.

"I don't usually dress like this," said Maureen, smiling with embarrassment at her outfit. "Can I get my own clothes?"

"Is that what you were wearing last night?" asked the Mustache, gesturing to the discarded T-shirt on the bed.

"Um, yeah."

He pulled a folded white paper bag out of a pocket and took a Biro from his breast pocket. He slid the pen under the T-shirt and poked it into the bag.

"We'd like you to come with us, Miss O'Donnell," said Mustache Man. "We'd like to talk to you at the station."

"You can't arrest her!" shouted Winnie, her voice a startling wail.

"We're not trying to," said the policewoman calmingly. "We're just asking her to talk to us. If she comes down to the station it'd be voluntary."

Winnie put out her hand in front of Maureen in a dramatic, brandy-induced gesture of maternal protectiveness. "I demand that you allow her to see a solicitor," she said.

Maureen shoved Winnie's hand out of the way. "Stop it, Mum," she said, and turned back to the police officers. "I'll come down with you."

Jim Maliano watched from the living-room doorway as the motley crowd walked down the dark hall. When Maureen came past him he reached out and squeezed her shoulder gently. His small gesture of empathy touched Maureen unreasonably and she vowed not to forget it.

The rest of it was a bit of a blur. She remembered Winnie crying loudly and a small crowd parting outside the close to let her through. The red-haired man got into the driver's seat of a blue Ford and the policewoman helped Maureen into the backseat, climbing in next to her. He asked if she had been cautioned. She said she had but she wasn't really listening. He recited it for her. Within minutes they were in Stewart Street police station.

It was just round the corner from her house but Maureen hadn't paid much attention to it before. The three-story concrete building sat on the edge of an industrial estate and was fronted with reflective glass. It looked more like an office block than a police station. They drove round to the back and pulled into a small car park. It was surrounded by a high wall topped with spiraled razor wire. Looking up at the back of the building from the car park, she could see small, mean, barred windows.

The red-haired man helped her out of the car, holding on to her elbow longer than he need have. She must look a bit wobbly. "Now, don't you worry," he said. "That's the worst bit over. We're only going to talk to you."

But Maureen wasn't thinking about that. She just wanted to see Liam.

3

MARIE, UNA AND LIAM

MAUREEN WAS THE YOUNGEST OF THE FOUR OF THEM. THEY ALL bore a striking family resemblance: dark brown hair, square jaws and fat button noses. Their build was the same too: they were all short and thin. When they were children, people often mistook Liam and Maureen for twins: they had been born ten months apart, both had pale blue eyes and they spent so much time together they adopted all of the same mannerisms. When they hit puberty Liam refused to hang about with Maureen. She didn't understand: she followed him around like a little dog until he threatened to beat her up and stopped talking to her. Their resemblance gradually faded.

Marie was the eldest. She moved to London in the early eighties to get away from her mum's drinking, settled there and became one of Mrs. Thatcher's starry-eyed children. She got a job in a bank and worked her way up. At first the change in her seemed superficial: she began to define all her friends by how big their mortgage was and what kind of car they drove. It took a while for them to realize that Marie was deep down different. They didn't talk about it. They could talk about Winnie's alcoholism, about Maureen's mental-health problems, and to a lesser extent about Liam dealing drugs, but they couldn't talk about Marie being a Thatcherite. There was nothing kind to be said about that. Maureen had always assumed that Marie was a socialist because she was kind. The final break between them came the last time Marie was home for a visit. They were talking about homelessness and Maureen ruined the dinner for everybody by losing the place and shouting "Get a fucking value system!" at her sister.

It happened six months before Maureen was taken to hospital, but the way Marie told it there was only a matter of weeks between one incident and the other. And that explained it. Maureen was mental and Marie forgave her.

Marie was married to Robert, another banker, who worked in the City. They had been married on the quiet in the Chelsea Register Office two years before but Robert had never found the time to come to Glasgow and pay his respects to her family. It was a shame because now he couldn't afford to: he had become a Lloyd's Name at just the wrong time, on just the wrong syndicate, and they were living in a bedsit in Bromley.

Una's husband, Alistair, was an integral part of the family. He was a plumber and couldn't believe his luck when Una agreed to marry him. He was a quiet, honorable man and, to Una's everlasting joy, had proved himself eminently malleable. She began by changing the way he dressed, then moved on to his accent, and at the moment she was trying to change his career.

Una was a civil engineer and made a right few quid. She scheduled beginning a family for 1995 and had virtually booked her maternity leave but she didn't get pregnant. She put a brave face on it but recently she had confided in them all, individually and in confidence, that she was getting desperate. Maureen went with her to the clinic when she had the preliminary tests. It turned out that Alistair's sperm count was a bit low and he was put on a course of medication. Una was happy and Alistair was if she was.

When it came time for Liam to go to secondary school, Michael, their father, had lost his job as a journalist because of his drinking, quite a feat in those days. They couldn't afford to send Liam to the private school Marie and Una had been to so he was sent to Hillhead Comprehensive and Maureen followed him a year later. It was a good school but neither of them studied very hard.

Winnie's alcoholism progressed rapidly after Michael left them. Within four years she was married again and their new stepfather, George, became the silent partner in loud, brutal arguments. Despite the atmosphere in the house Liam delighted his mother by getting into Glasgow University Law School. He dropped out after six months and started selling hash to his friends on a casual basis but he discovered a talent and went professional. He bought a big house. They told Winnie he managed bands. Maureen used to nag him about security in the house but he said that if he started to worry about things like that he'd get really paranoid.

His present girlfriend, Maggie, was a bit of a mystery. She was a model, but they never saw her model anything, and a singer, but they never heard her sing either. She was very pretty and had the roundest arse Maureen had ever seen. She didn't seem to have any friends of her own. Poor Maggie had a lot to live up to: Lynn, Liam's first and last girlfriend, was a doctor's receptionist and as rough as a badger's arse but such great crack even Winnie's snobbishness dissipated when Lynn told a story.

Maureen did well at school and went straight to Glasgow University to study history of art. She was in her final year when she began to think she was schizophrenic. The night terrors she had always suffered from got progressively worse and she started having waking flashbacks. They were mild at first but escalated in frequency and severity. Because she didn't know what she was flashing back to, she thought they were random delusions. In her more lucid moments she realized something was very wrong. She had never done acid so that wasn't it. She began to read about mental illness and found that she was in the right age group for her first schizophrenic attack. She wasn't very surprised: like many people from unhappy families she'd never assumed the future would hold anything too thrilling. She told no one, got the job at the Apollo Theatre and bought the tiny flat in Garnethill so that when she fell down the big black hole into the hands of the social services they wouldn't make her live with Winnie.

It took a year and a half of patient panic for the breakdown to come.

She was sitting upstairs on a bus. A fat man sitting behind her was breathing mucousally in her ear. The noise got louder, closer, more rasping, until it was deafening. She waited for him to hit her, a fisted slap on the side of her head. When it didn't happen she screamed for a bit and threw up. The driver came to see what was wrong and found her sobbing and trying to wipe up the mess with a single tissue. He told her to leave it. She ran off the bus. None of the other passengers came after her.

The family got worried when Mr. Scobie, the manager at the Apollo, phoned Winnie's as a last resort. Maureen hadn't been at work for three days and hadn't called. Liam went looking for her and found her hiding in the hall cupboard in Garnethill. She had been there for two days and had urinated and defecated in the corner. She remembered Liam wrapping her in a blanket and carrying her downstairs to his car. He pulled the blanket over her face and whispered to her all the way to hospital, telling her she was safe, still safe, be brave.

One month after she was admitted to the Northern Psychiatric Hospital Una's husband, Alistair, came to visit on his own. He asked to speak to her and her psychiatrist together and broke Una's confidence, telling them that this had happened before. When Maureen was ten she had been found hiding in the cupboard under the stairs. She had been there for a whole day. Her face was bruised down one side and when they gave her a bath they found dried blood between her legs. No one knew what had happened because Maureen couldn't speak. Michael packed a few things, took the checkbook and disappeared forever. Winnie told the children that Maureen had fallen on her bottom and got a surprise. It was never mentioned again.

Winnie had never forgiven Alistair for telling. She phoned him sometimes when she was drunk. He wouldn't tell Maureen what she said.

Leslie came to the hospital every day, working her visits around her shifts at the shelter. She treated the hospital stay as if it was something that was happening to both of them together. Leslie was scared at first and then settled into the routine, getting angry about the pettiness of the ward rules and making friends with the other patients. Everyone else behaved as if they were coming to view Maureen. She knew that it was her friendship with Leslie that prompted her to get angry and get better. Their relationship changed after the hospital: Maureen couldn't bring herself to lean on Leslie in even the smallest detail. She was always reluctant to phone her when she had a problem. Leslie dealt with other people's emotional crises all day every day at the shelter and Maureen knew she could easily tip the scales and go from being Leslie's pal to being her client. She found herself wishing Leslie would have a disaster sometimes, something minor and fixable, so that Maureen could save her and restore the balance between them once and for all.

The Mustache Man was waiting for them at the car-park entrance to the station. They took her into a small reception area and asked her to sign a book saying that she had come to the station voluntarily. They asked her permission before taking her fingerprints.

She still felt light-headed, her stomach ached with tense after-vomit contractions and she was having trouble with her eyes: her depth perception kept changing suddenly, shifting objects closer and farther away. She blinked hard, pressing the rims of her eyelids tight to stop it. She knew she must look pretty crazy but they weren't watching her, they were anxious to get her upstairs.

The policewoman and the Mustache escorted her up two flights, through a set of fire doors and into a windowless beige corridor illuminated with imperceptibly flickering strip lights. The pattern on the linoleum was too big for the small space. It would have been a disorienting place at the best of times and this wasn't the best of times.

"Is this corridor a bit narrow?" Maureen asked the Mustache.

"A bit," he said, worried by the question. "Are you going to be sick again?"

She shook her head. He stopped at one of the doors and opened it, waving her through in front of him. It was a bleak room. The walls were painted with mushroom gloss, the kind that is easy to wipe clean, and a gray metal table was bolted to the floor. A large clumsy black tape recorder was resting on the table next to the wall. A tiny window, high up on the wall, was barred with wrought iron. Everything about the room whispered distrust.

A tall man with ruffled blond hair was sitting at the near side of the table with his back to the door. He stood up when they came in, introduced himself as Detective Chief Inspector Joe McEwan, and asked her to sit down, motioning to the far side of the table, the side farthest away from the door. She had noticed him back at her house: while she was standing in the close she had seen him in the living room, talking to a man wearing a white paper suit. He had looked out at her, his glance lingering too long to be casual. His skin showed a fading long-term tan, the result of regular foreign holidays. He was in his forties and dressed so carefully in black flannels and an expensive blue cotton shirt that he was either gay or a bachelor. A quick look at the fading milky strip on the third finger of his left hand told her that he had shed a wedding ring one or two sunny holidays ago. He had the look of an ambitious man on his way to some bright future. Maureen's Celtic shirt glowed a strange shade of cheap green under the fluorescent light.

She sat down and Joe McEwan introduced the Mustache Man as Detective Inspector Steven Inness. The policewoman was not introduced. She took the hint and left, shutting the door carefully behind her.

McEwan pressed a button and turned on the tape recorder, telling it the time and who was present. He turned to Maureen and asked her very formally whether or not she had been cautioned prior to the interview. She said she had been. Without looking at him McEwan nudged Inness, telling him to take over.

Inness asked her all the same questions he had asked her at the house, again nodding and yessing her answers. She told them who Douglas was, about Elsbeth and that his mother was an MEP. The two policemen glanced at each other nervously. Inness asked her what her shoe size was, and why she hadn't reported the murder last night. She hadn't looked into the living room, it was to the right of the front door and the bedroom was to the left, so there was no reason for her to pass it unless she had been to the toilet. She went straight to bed because she was pissed.

Inness left long pauses after Maureen imparted each bit of information, expecting her to panic at the silence and fill in the spaces with important clues. Maureen had seen a lot of psychiatrists in her time and knew what he was doing. She found it familiar and calming, as if, among all the confusion, she had stumbled across a set of rules she understood. She did what she had always done with the long-pause technique: she sat and looked at the person interviewing her, her face blank, waiting for them to notice that it wouldn't work. The professional thing to do was stare back at her, take it on the chin and then try something else, but Inness couldn't. He looked at everything in the room, his eyes rolling around, swerving past Maureen to the back wall and over her head to the tape recorder. He gave up and flicked back and forth through the pages of his note-book, looking increasingly confused.

McEwan took over. "Who has a key to your house apart from yourself, Miss O'Donnell?"

"Um, my brother, Liam, Douglas, and that's it. Oh, I suppose the factor would have one."

"What's the factor's name?"

She told him and guessed at the phone number. McEwan wrote it down in a notebook. "I'm not sure that's the right number," she said.

"It's okay," he said, pleased at her willingness to cooperate. "We can look it up. Where can we find your brother?"

She couldn't let them turn up at Liam's house unannounced—she knew he left stuff lying around all the time. It would frighten the shit out of him if nothing else. He'd never had a scrape with the law. "Um," she said, "he's staying with some friends at the moment, I'll bring him down if you want to talk to him."

McEwan wasn't pleased. "Can't we contact him?"

"Well, the people he's staying with aren't on the phone. They're difficult to get a hold of. I'll get him for you."

"Well, okay," said McEwan, raising his eyebrows insistently, creasing his forehead into three deep parallel ridges. She thought he must make that face a lot. "But we need to see him *today*."

"I'll bring him down, I promise. Why was it so hot in the house?"

He looked at her. "What do you mean?"

"It's not usually that hot in the house."

He nudged Inness to make a note of it and turned back to Maureen. "So Douglas had his own key?" he asked diffidently.

"Yes."

"Did you let him into your house yesterday?"

"No, the last time I saw him was on Monday. He stayed the night and left in the morning before I got up."

"Did he mention anything to you about being threatened by anyone, arguing with anyone, being followed, anything like that?"

Maureen thought back over the night's conversation. He was tired when he came in, he didn't even kiss her as he came through the door. He took his shoes off and sat on the settee telling her the usual gossip, the usual moaning appraisal of the people he worked with. Nothing different. They didn't have sex. Douglas fell asleep a minute after getting into bed and Maureen lay wide-awake next to him and watched him dribble saliva onto the pillow. They hadn't had sex for five weeks. Douglas had begun to recoil when she touched him, he rarely even kissed her now.

"Not that I remember," she said.

McEwan scribbled something in a notepad. "And that was the last time you saw him?" he said, without looking up.

"Yeah."

"Except for this morning," observed Inness unnecessarily.

"Yeah," said Maureen, puzzled by his crassness. "Except for this morning."

"Now," said McEwan, "when you found the body this morning did you touch anything?"

Maureen thought about it. "No," she said.

"Did you go into the living room before you phoned us?"

"No."

"Did you go into the hall cupboard?"

"The shoe cupboard?"

"Yes," said McEwan. "The small cupboard in the hall, the one with the shoe box in it."

"No, I didn't go in there. I saw the body and phoned you immediately."

"'Immediately'? At the scene you told Detective Inspector Inness that you sat in the hall for a while."

"Well, yeah, I saw the body and sat down in shock and as soon as I was able to stand up I got to the phone and called you."

"How long were you sitting in the hall?"

"I don't know, I was in shock."

"One hour? Two hours?"

"Ten minutes, maybe. Twenty minutes at the longest."

"And where were you sitting in the hall?"

"What difference does it make where I sat?" she said impatiently.

"Just answer the question, Miss O'Donnell."

"I was sitting directly across from the hall cupboard."

"And the door to the cupboard was . . . ?"

Joe McEwan seemed to be trying to prompt her toward some meaningful statement about the state of the cupboard but she wasn't sure what it was. She shrugged. "I dunno, what? Broken?"

"Was it open?" asked McEwan. "Was it shut?"

"Oh, right, no, it was shut."

"Could you see into the living room from where you were sitting?"

"I could see some footsteps."

"How many footsteps could you see from there?"

She thought about it for a moment. "Two," she said. "I could see two but there were seven altogether."

McEwan looked at her suspiciously. "You seem very sure about that."

"I remember them because they looked odd. They weren't shuffled, there were no scuffs of blood at the heel, but they were too close together. It looked odd. Like someone had been walking funny."

"As if they were planked," said Inness quietly, looking at his notes.

His comment annoyed McEwan for some reason: he turned and looked at Inness. Inness realized his mistake and eyed McEwan a subordinate's apology.

"Why are you so interested in the hall cupboard?" asked Maureen. "Was there something in there?"

McEwan was evasive. "Never you mind what was in there."

Maureen ran her fingers through her greasy hair. "Would either of you have a cigarette I could blag?" she said.

She had come out of shock minutes before and was desperate for a fag. Her packet was in her handbag, on the bedroom floor.

Inness sighed and looked at McEwan as if to say Maureen was a chancer. McEwan didn't respond. With pronounced reluctance Inness took a packet of Silk Cut from his pocket and handed one to Maureen. He lit a match, holding it across the table. Maureen leaned over, sitting the cigarette in the flame. It crackled softly. She inhaled and felt the smoke curl warmly in her lungs, her fingers began to tingle. McEwan reached out suddenly, took a cigarette out of Inness's packet and leaned forward, lighting it from the ready flame. Inness seemed surprised. McEwan inhaled and grimaced. "Now," he said, looking at his cigarette accusingly, "I'm afraid we can't allow you to stay at your own house for a while. Is there anyone else you can stay with?"

"Oh, aye," said Maureen, "loads of places."

"I mean, we'll need the address you'll be staying at so we can find you if we need to."

"I might be able to stay with a pal in Maryhill but I'd have to check with him first."

"That would be handy," nodded Inness. "It's just up the road."

"Yeah," said Maureen, wanting desperately to see Liam or Benny or Leslie, or anyone familiar and alive. "Can I nip up the road to ask him?"

McEwan gave her a hard, determined look. "No," he said. "I'd prefer it if you stayed here."

"I really want to leave for a while and come back."

"I want you to stay. We'll be receiving information all the time and it may be important for me to check things out with you."

"I want to go," she said firmly. "I want to get some fags and something to eat and have a think."

"We can bring you food and cigarettes."

"I want to have a think."

"What have you got to think about?"

"I just want to get the fuck out of this building for a while," she said, becoming agitated. "The lighting in here is making my eyes hurt and I'm tired, all right?"

"I want you to stay," he said, leaning on the table and exhaling smoke slowly through his nose. "We can keep you here for up to six hours if we have some reason to suspect you've broken the law."

Maureen leaned forward. They sat head-to-head, each reluctant to sit back and relinquish the space to the other. "Are you arresting me?" she asked.

"I don't need to arrest you to keep you here."

"I haven't done anything."

"It's not that simple," said Inness.

Joe McEwan was getting very annoyed, his eyes narrowed and his forehead creased indignantly. He must be very unused to being defied. Maureen thought about his ex-wife and wished her well. He stood up, shoving the chair away noisily with the backs of his knees. He leaned over and opened the door. The policewoman was standing outside: he ushered her into the interview room and left, slamming the door behind him.

"Have we got to wait for him to come back?" asked Maureen.

"Uh-huh," said Inness, fiddling with the Biro, tapping it softly on the table.

"How come there's always two of you?" said Maureen.

Inness looked up. "Corroboration."

"What's corroboration?"

"We can't use any evidence that's witnessed by one person. There have to be two officers present at all times in case we hear something important."

"Oh."

After an infinity McEwan came back in. "You can go," he said, looking disgusted and angry. "But I want you back here in two hours, is that clear?"

"Yes," said Maureen, pleased to be getting her way.

He leaned over the table and told the tape that it was eleven thirty-three, that the interview was being suspended and that he was turning it off. He flicked the switch and turned back to Maureen. "You know," he said, his voice louder than it need have been, "I really think if you wanted us to find the person who murdered your boyfriend you'd cooperate more fully."

"I appreciate that," she said, gracious in victory. "I'll do everything I can to help you but right now I need a break."

He looked at her disbelievingly and motioned for her to follow him as he walked out of the room.

Coming down the stairs to the main entrance she could see Liam sitting on a plastic chair in the lobby. He looked up and grinned when he saw her, wrinkling his nose. She shook her head softly and looked away, warning him not to speak to her. If McEwan saw Liam he'd recognize him as her brother and would insist on interviewing him right away. Maureen would have to wait for him.

"I'll be back by half-one," she said, distracting McEwan's attention. "I promise."

McEwan walked straight past Liam. He paused by the reception desk and patted it with the flat of his hand, telling her firmly that this was where she should report to when she came for their appointment. Maureen gave him an insolent look and left.

McEwan watched her walk through the glass doors and saw a young man with the same build and hair color follow Maureen O'Donnell toward the main road.

Liam caught up with her in the street. "He must be used to dealing with half-wits," he said.

"Naw, I think he was trying to patronize me. He's pissed off because I insisted on leaving for a while."

Liam's Triumph Herald was parked at the far end of the street. Maureen could see the rust patches from two hundred yards away. It was a rotten car, it broke down at least once a month but Liam said it was good for business: the police tended to stop young guys in Mercs, not mugs in shitey motors.

Maureen slipped her arm through his, something she hadn't done in years. "Did Mum tell you about Douglas, then?" she asked.

"Yeah," said Liam, keeping his eyes on the road and squeezing her arm hard.

"How long were you waiting for?" she said.

"Just about three-quarters of an hour. Not long anyway."

"Liam, they're going to have to speak to you. I didn't think and I told them you had a key to the house."

He flinched. "Oh, bollocks."

"I'm sorry," she said. "Would they know about your business?"

"Dunno, maybe," he said. "Auch, actually they probably don't. Where are we going, anyway?"

"Well, I want to ask Benny if I can stay there for a while. I'm not allowed to go home until they've finished looking through everything and I can't stay at yours, obviously. How's Mum?"

Liam looked shifty. "Mm, well, Una's with her."

"You mean she's pissed?"

"Umm, she might be," he said quietly. "She's very upset. Una's comforting her."

"For fucksake, this is going to turn into something that happened to her, isn't it?"

"You know Mum, she could scene-steal from an eclipse." He opened the passenger door for her and saw that she was winding herself up. "Getting pissed off won't make a sod of difference. You should know that by now."

Maureen got into the car. The windows were opaque with cold condensation. Maggie was sitting in the backseat. "Oh, Maggie," said Maureen. "Have you been here all that time?"

Maggie smiled politely and nodded.

"Why didn't you come inside? You must have been freezing."

"I didn't like to," she said vaguely.

Liam revved the engine. "Let's go and see Benito," he said, and pulled out into the Maryhill Road. "Benito Finito."

An unmarked police car followed the Herald at a discreet distance.

Hillhead Comprehensive's catchment area covers a middle-class area and a profoundly deprived one. Benny came from the latter. He had been expelled in third year for setting fire to a toilet but Maureen and Liam stayed in touch with him because he was mental and a good laugh.

Benny drank like his father. Consequently his early life was a series of Dadaesque adventures: he woke up in a meat factory, he got engaged to a woman whose name he couldn't remember, he fell into a quarry on a Saturday night and didn't manage to get out until the men came to work on Monday morning. When he was twenty he said he was sick of getting his face kicked in all the time and started attending Alcoholics Anonymous and got sober. He was homeless at the time and Maureen let him sleep on her bedroom floor at home. He talked about nothing but the joy of AA for two months. Winnie came to hate him.

His alcoholic family disowned him when he moved in with Maureen's family and got sober. He did some exams at college and got into Glasgow University to study law. His family owned him again. He was in senior honors studying corporate law and had a series of traineeship interviews lined up with high-flying companies. His bank manager kept writing to him, asking him to take out more loans.

* * *

They drew up into Scaramouch Street. It was short, only four closes long, with bollards blocking off the end from the Maryhill Road. The street used to be a handy cutoff before the lights. When the bollards first went up several drivers, thinking they'd be cute and save a couple of minutes, swerved straight into them and wrote their cars off. They climbed the stairs to the second floor and knocked. Benny opened the door. He wasn't bad-looking: he was dark with long eyelashes and kind gray eyes, six foot something tall, and had a solid muscular frame, but his close association with Liam and the rest of her family made Maureen squeamish about fancying him. He looked Maureen up and down and burst out laughing. "What the fuck are you wearing?" he squealed. "You look like a ned!"

Maureen pushed her way in through the door. "I've had a bit of an eventful day," she said, and went into the kitchen to put the kettle on. Benny was a dirty bastard: the kitchen was filthy. Dishes, bits of food and packaging were sitting on the work tops and table, the sink was full and smelled faintly of mildew.

She could hear them in the hall, Liam mumbling the story in a monotone and Benny whispering exclamations back. Liam called to her that he was going to drop Maggie home and would be back in half an hour.

Benny stayed in the living room for a few minutes before coming into the kitchen. His face was gray. "Jesus, Mauri," he said, "Jesus. I don't know what to say."

Maureen dropped into a chair and covered her face with her hands. She wanted to cry but nothing seemed real. Benny sat next to her, putting his arms around her, holding her close and kissing her hair. He was trembling. "Oh, Mauri," he whispered, "Jesus, Mauri, it's so shockin'." She sat up and asked him for a fag. "Haven't you got any?" She explained what had happened to hers and he insisted that she take his packet.

He gave her a lemonade and an ashtray and sat at the table with her, leaning close and listening intently. She told him about the cagoul and the shoes and the rope. How could they get into the house, she kept saying, how could they get in the front door without making a noise?

"Did Douglas have his own key?" asked Benny.

"Aye."

"And there was no sign of forced entry?"

"Not that I noticed."

"Well, Douglas must have let himself in and, either then or later, let in the person who did it. Unless they picked the lock. What kind of locks have you got?"

Maureen described them.

"They'd have to know what they were doing," he said. "Chances are he let them in so ye can conclude that he knew them."

"Aye." She was impressed by the logic of his deduction. "Aye, that'll be it. You're good at this."

"This is awful. I suppose they think it was one of his clients from the clinic. Or could it be the woman he was living with?"

"Elsbeth?"

"Yeah, Elsbeth. It's kind of poetic, killing your unfaithful man in the other woman's house."

"It didn't look very poetic," said Maureen.

"Oh, fuck, I shouldn't have said that, I'm sorry, it's hard to take in."

"I know," said Maureen. "It's so shocking it almost isn't." Her bum was numb again. She stood up and rubbed it with her palms. "I've had a very fucking strange day," she said, as if the fact had just occurred to her.

"How're ye fixed? Did you leave your wallet at home too?" He took a tenner out of his pocket and pressed it into her hand.

"I don't need any money, Benny. I'll get my wallet from the police."

"Just take it in case, okay?"

"I'll give it back as soon as I get my wallet."

Benny quirked an eyebrow playfully. "Give it back to me when you give me that *Selecter* CD back."

Maureen rolled her eyes. "God, not again, Benny, I gave you that back months ago."

"Ye never did."

"Benny Gardner, I'll buy you a replacement but you're going to find that CD in this filthy house and ye'll have to crawl to me."

"It's been discontinued and, Mauri, I'm telling ye, *you'll* find it in *your* filthy house and *you'll* have to crawl to me."

Maureen finished her lemonade. "Can you think of anything else about Douglas, Benny? Any more elementary-my-dear-Watsons?"

Benny smiled, pleased at being asked.

"Not off the top of my head, no."

Maureen slumped over the table. "I'm worried they'll think I did it."

"Oh, no"—he took her hand and squeezed it tightly—"they won't think that. They won't. Anyone who knows you could tell them it wasn't you. When you went into the living room, did you see a murder weapon?"

Maureen thought her way back through the room, censoring Douglas's body out of the picture. "I dunno, um, no. But I didn't get a good look, really." She blinked and saw a blood-soaked curl of hair behind his ear, and below that his poor broken neck, sliced open like a raw joint. She got up, washed her hands over the dirty dishes in the sink and tried to blink away the image.

"I'm just asking because it'd be good if they didn't find one," he said.

She splashed cold water on her face. "Find one what?"

"A murder weapon."

"Why?"

"Well, if you were in the house all the time and the weapon's found somewhere else that means someone came in, did it and then went away again. That'll be good for you."

"Okay," said Maureen, having trouble seeing how any of this could be good for her. She sat back down at the table. "It turns out they were married, after all. I feel like such a mug."

"Douglas was married to Elsbeth?"

"Yeah."

He touched her forearm and spoke softly. "I thought ye'd decided he was an arse anyway."

"Yeah," she said miserably, "but he was my arse."

Benny scratched his head and looked at her shirt. "You look mental. Let's find you something to wear."

They went into the bedroom and Benny dug out a red T-shirt with "The Broad Left Anti-Capitalist Dynamos F.C." printed on the front. The Anti Dynamos were a football team Benny used to play for. Maureen had been openly coveting the shirt for years and she appreciated the gesture. Benny was over six foot and Maureen was only five two so they couldn't find her any trousers.

"You'll have to keep those joggers on."

"I hate these things," she said. "They always make me think of fat guys with free-range bollocks."

He gave her a key to his house. Maureen could sleep on the sofa bed in the front room until she wanted to go home. The arrangement was perfect: Winnie would never come here.

"Can I ask another question about it, Mauri?"

"God, please, Benny, anything you can think of . . ."

He bit his lip and looked at her. "It's a bit of a rough one, though."

"I can take it."

"Sure?"

"Positive."

"Did you notice whether there were a few cuts or just one?"

"What, on his neck?"

"Yeah, were there a few cut marks and then a big one?"

She blinked. "Naw, from what I saw there was just one big one."

He exhaled slowly. "Fuckin' mental," he muttered.

Maureen asked him what he meant.

"It means whoever killed him just tied him up and did it, no threat to do it, no first go. It means they didn't hesitate."

4

ELSBETH

AS SOON AS JOE MCEWAN APPEARED AT THE TOP OF THE STAIRS
Maureen could tell he was still pissed off with her. He held her
eye as he walked steadily down the steps and came straight up to
the desk, standing too close to her, looming over her so she had to
bend her neck to look him in the face. "Did you contact your
brother?" he said abruptly.

"Yeah," said Maureen. "And here he is."

Liam stepped forward and smiled. McEwan recognized him as
the scruffy man who had been waiting in the lobby, the man who
had driven Maureen O'Donnell up to Maryhill in the red Triumph
Herald. He glowered at her. A double door next to the stairs opened
and Inness and the red-haired man appeared, greeting McEwan
with conspiratorial nods.

McEwan looked out of the glass doors. "You go with them," he
ordered. Neither Maureen nor Liam knew which of them he was
talking to. The red-haired man tapped Liam on the shoulder
and jerked his head to the doors by the stairs, signaling for him
to move. Liam looked back at his wee sister, still standing at the

desk, looking underfed and brittle in the shadow of the tall police-man. He gave her a nervous thumbs-up and she waved him a silly cheerio.

"You come with me," growled McEwan, and stomped up the stairs, taking her back to the narrow corridor.

The high midday sun shone in through the miserly window in the interview room, hitting the wall inches above the tape recorder in a glowing yellow smear. A gangly young officer was sitting at the table waiting for them. He smiled up at Joe McEwan as he came into the room. McEwan grunted back. Disconcerted by McEwan's filthy mood, the young officer turned shyly and introduced himself to Maureen. He spoke so quietly that she couldn't make out his name. It sounded like Something McMummb. His hair was mousy brown and he had a matching mousy brown mole on his left cheek. Three coarse hairs stuck out of it like the legs on a tiny milking stool. He was dressed in a brand-new suit.

Maureen took her seat at the other side of the table, away from the door. McEwan sat down and took a slim leather-bound note-book out of his pocket, placed it on the table and slid a skinny pen-cil out of the spine. He turned on the tape recorder and leaned into it, telling it who was present this time. She listened for McMummb's name but McEwan's intonation dipped at the end of the sentence and she was left none the wiser.

"Did you check the heating in the house?" she asked.

McEwan lifted his notebook and began to look through it. "The heating switch was on a timer," he said.

"Yeah, but it wasn't set for—"

McEwan interrupted her. "Were you drunk when you came home last night, Miss O'Donnell?"

"Well, yeah," she said, surprised by his adversarial tone.

"You don't seem very sure now. You were sure this morning when you said you didn't see the body because you went straight to bed. Were you or weren't you drunk?"

"What has me being drunk got to do with the central heating?"

"Is it possible that you came home and put it on?"

"I know I didn't," she said meekly.

He ignored her and wrote something in his pad. She decided to try again. "When I come home drunk I've got better things to do than fiddle about with the heating."

"Like what?"

"I dunno." She smiled, trying to get them onto a friendly footing. "Like pass out."

McEwan looked at her, thinly masking his disapproval. "You were that drunk, were you?" he asked.

They weren't going to have a friendly conversation, she could tell that now. McEwan leaned his arms on the table and meshed his fingers together. He looked her in the eye as he worked the tip of his tongue into his wisdom tooth. "You said Douglas worked at the Rainbow Clinic," he said suddenly. "Was he your therapist?"

"No," said Maureen, emphatically, defensive at the implied slight on Douglas's honor. "Never."

"Well," he said, a petulant edge to his voice, "your mother said you have received psychiatric treatment in the past."

"Um, yeah," said Maureen, uncomfortably. She knew he was launching straight into the psychiatric questions to disarm her and it was working. Most people with no experience of mental illness don't see it as part of a continuum, it's them and us, the nutters and the whole people. "I was in the Northern for five months in nineteen ninety-six," she said, "and I've seen a psychiatrist. Not for anything special, really, just in case."

McEwan wouldn't speak or break eye contact. He was much better at it than Inness. Maureen focused on the bridge of his nose.

"In case what?" asked McEwan finally.

"I had a breakdown. That's why I was in the Northern. The psychiatrist was just a follow-up thing, in case it happened again. Not that it's likely . . . just in case . . . you know."

"No, I don't know," said McEwan unpleasantly. "What were you being treated for?"

Maureen looked at them. Something McMummb seemed impressionable, probably just out of training. He watched McEwan intently, his face reacting to Maureen's answers as if he were conducting the interview himself, glancing at McEwan every so often, desperate for some sign of approval. And McEwan sat there between them, his hands clasped together, his face smug and confident, a fight looking for a venue. Fuck him, she thought, if he's so fucking smart he can find out for himself. "Depression," she said. It wasn't a lie, exactly, it was more of a half-truth, and holding information back from him made her feel empowered and confident, as if it was still her life even if McEwan was legally entitled to rake through it. She put her hands on the table, playing with an old bus ticket she had found in the pocket of Jim Maliano's jogging trousers.

"And who is your current psychiatrist?"

"I don't have one," she said, enjoying the sense of control.

McMummb looked surprised.

"Your mother said you had a psychiatrist," said McEwan.

"My mother drinks too much too often. She's in tune with the moon a lot of the time."

A hint of a smile floated across McEwan's face. "How would you know if you were having a breakdown?"

"I'm not having one, if that's what you meant. When depressives have a breakdown it's pretty obvious. We can't function or get ourselves out of the house. If I was having a breakdown you'd be able to tell."

McEwan looked at McMummb, who must have done a two-day course in psychology. He nodded his confirmation and McEwan turned back to her. McMummb sat back and blushed with delight at McEwan's deference.

"So," said McEwan, oblivious to his protégé's glee, "you said Douglas worked at the Rainbow Clinic?"

"Yes."

"And you've never been there?"

"I went a couple of times to meet him but never as a patient."

She had been to the Rainbow to see Angus, Douglas's colleague, for two sessions before being referred on to Louisa at the Albert but she knew the lie would hold up. When she first came out of the Northern they had referred her to an arse of a psychiatrist at a small clinic in the Great Western Road. He sat across a desk from her, looking unhappy and bored as he asked her leading questions about the most painful events in her life. He took the pause-and-prompt technique too far, refusing to accept that it wouldn't work with Maureen. They spent most of their sessions staring at each other in a gloomy, adversarial silence. Maureen began to phone other clinics, looking for someone else.

She found the Rainbow's number in the Yellow Pages. The clinic ran an outreach scheme for victims of sexual abuse and they let the patients use an assumed name if they wanted to. Maureen had called herself Helen and no one but Douglas knew her real name. The only way Joe McEwan could find out she had been to the Rainbow was from Louisa Wishart at the Albert.

Maureen got talking to Shirley, the receptionist at the Rainbow, the first time she went there, and Shirley introduced Douglas to her when he came into the waiting room to check his appointment times. Maureen didn't give it a second thought. She was four months out of hospital and was afraid she was losing it again. Her mind was full of other stuff. After her last session with Angus Farrell she was standing at a bus stop across the road from the clinic when Douglas stopped his car and offered her a lift back to town. She was upset, stuck in the middle of nowhere with an hour to wait for the next bus. They got talking in the car and went for a drink. She topped herself up with triples while he was in the toilet. She woke up at ten past four in the morning, her face in a puddle of hot moonlight, just in time to see Douglas struggling into his trousers at the end of her bed.

"Now," said McEwan, reaching down to a brown cardboard file box at the side of his chair and lifting a clear polyethylene bag onto the table. "Is this yours?"

The yellow plastic cagoul was folded neatly inside the open-ended bag. Most of the blood had been washed off but the white drawstring on the hood was stained an uneven pink. A long number was typed onto an envelope address label and stuck on the corner of the bag. McEwan muttered something into the tape recorder.

She didn't want to touch it—she didn't even want to touch the bag. She took her hands off the table, resting them on her lap. "Not mine," she said.

McEwan sensed her discomfort. He pushed the bag across the table to her with his fingertips. "Sure?"

"Certain," she said.

"Have you ever seen it before this morning?"

"No."

He put the cagoul back into the box at his side, pulled out a smaller bag and dropped it on the table. Four strands of bloody rope were tucked inside. "Any idea where these came from?"

Maureen looked at them. The rope was made of a shimmering nylon material and was stained pink like the drawstring on the cagoul. It was far too thick to come from the clothes pulley in the kitchen. She thought her way through the flat. "No," she said finally, "I can't think where they might have come from. Are they from the house?"

"It's not a trick question," said McEwan. "We want to know if you can identify them before we start tracing them. Have you ever seen them before?"

"No."

He put the bag away and pulled out another one. "Are these your slippers?"

Maureen looked at the bag. Her slippers were tagged and sealed inside. She turned the bag over. The soles still showed traces of dried blood. "Yeah, they're my slippers, but I don't see how they could be covered in blood. I left them in the cupboard, I haven't worn them for days."

"But they are your slippers?"

"Yeah, they're mine."

McEwan dropped the bag back in the box and fitted a cardboard lid on it. She put Benny's packet of cigarettes on the table, took one out and lit it.

McEwan watched resentfully as she inhaled. "I want to ask you again," he said. "Did you go into the living room when you saw the body?"

"No. I definitely didn't go in there."

"Did you go into the hall cupboard?"

McMummb looked excitedly from Maureen to McEwan and back again. The question was clearly significant.

"No. I didn't go in there either."

"Okay," he said slowly, and jotted something in his notebook, stabbing a full stop at the end of the sentence. "Right, next thing, do you have any idea where Douglas's key to your house might be?"

She thought for a moment. "He had it, I dunno, wasn't it in his pocket?"

"No. Was he in the habit of putting it down somewhere in the house when he came in, say, on the hall table, somewhere like that?"

"No, he kept his keys in his pocket. Are you sure it wasn't on him?"

"No. We've been pretty thorough."

"It wasn't in his jacket pocket?"

McEwan sneered. " 'Thorough' would usually include his pockets."

She thought about it with a rising sense of panic. "Could the man who killed him have taken it?"

McEwan shrugged. "We don't know where it is," he said.

Maureen slumped back in her chair. "My God, he's got a key to my house."

"You're very sure it's a man, Maureen."

"I'm guessing."

"Of course, he may not have had the key on him." McEwan spoke slowly, watching for a reaction. "He could have got into the house some other way."

"I didn't let him in, if that's what you're hinting at," she said. "I would have remembered."

"Yes," said McEwan, tip-and-tailing the skinny pencil noisily on the table. He smiled up at her. "Do you know Douglas's wife, Elsbeth Brady?"

"No."

"You've never met her?"

"No."

He asked her to go through her movements yesterday morning and afternoon. She repeated the details she had given Inness at the house that morning: she went to work at nine-thirty and didn't leave until six o'clock. McEwan asked her carefully whether she had been out of the office for longer than a few minutes, say for lunch. She definitely hadn't. She'd been in the office with Liz all day, they could ask her if they liked.

"We will," said McEwan, and closed his notebook. "Incidentally, your mother has been phoning here all day. She keeps demanding to speak to you. I suggest you phone her. She's been getting more and more . . . upset."

"Right." Maureen knew full well what Winnie had been getting more and more. "I'm sorry if she's been bothering you."

McEwan brushed over it. "Talking of mothers, do you know Douglas Brady's mother?"

"I've seen photos of her in the paper."

"But you've never met her?"

Maureen shook her head.

"Well," said McEwan, "we'll try to keep this out of the papers for as long as possible but there is going to be a lot of interest in it because she's an MEP. I don't want you talking to the press."

"Right," she said, her heart sinking at the thought of Drunk Winnie's propensity to talk and talk and talk. She couldn't be with her all the time and Drunk Winnie's very favorite subject was family secrets and how shitty her kids were.

She gave him Benny's name, address and telephone number. They wouldn't allow her into her own house unescorted; if she wanted to go home to get anything she would need to phone in advance and they would arrange for an officer to be present.

"Why?"

"In case you disturb any evidence we haven't collected yet."

"You surely don't suspect me?"

"We don't know who did it yet," he said, looking at his pencil in a manner that strongly suggested he did.

As he was showing her out they ran into Elsbeth in the lobby. She was petite with a sharp blond bob, sharper features and a tidy figure. Her eyes were red raw. Poor Elsbeth had been the focus of gut-gnawing guilt over the past eight months: Maureen's sense that they were doing a very unkind thing indeed had snowballed as her feelings for Douglas changed. Seeing the picture of Elsbeth in the newspaper had made it worse: she had a face to put to the guilt. Douglas didn't seem to think about it. He didn't flinch when Maureen reproached herself; he acted as if she was making a big something out of nothing; it was as if Maureen was being unfaithful to Elsbeth and not Douglas. Seeing Elsbeth in the flesh for the first time made Maureen feel sick and hot. She tried to slip past her but Elsbeth caught her arm. "Did you do it, Maureen?" she asked.

Maureen was startled. Elsbeth shouldn't know who she was. "No," she said, guilty and uncomfortable.

"Neither did I," said Elsbeth. Her face sagged suddenly and she shuffled over to Joe McEwan, who was standing at the foot of the stairs. Panicked and shaky, Maureen turned stiffly toward the door.

"Maureen?" Elsbeth's voice was fraught and cracked. "Will you wait for me?"

"If you want me to," said Maureen, resisting the urge to scream and run away.

McEwan smiled at her but when Elsbeth turned her back he frowned and motioned for her to leave. She watched them climb the stairs together. Elsbeth was wearing the Aran jumper Maureen had bought for Douglas's last birthday.

She left the police station and crossed the main road, walking two blocks to the shops. She'd decided to cook a meal for Benny as a thank-you for letting her stay. She chose some baby corncobs, zucchini and a green pepper to pad out a tomato sauce. The garlic looked old and sprouty. She asked an assistant if they had any more at the back of the shop and looked through it slowly. Her heart began to palpitate at the checkout. She abandoned her trolley in the queue and ran the two blocks, darting across the main road and getting into Stewart Street just in time to see Elsbeth coming out of the main entrance of the station. Elsbeth didn't seem surprised that she was there: she assumed people would do what she asked and Maureen resented her for it.

"Let's go to my house," she said, without looking up, and Maureen followed her into a waiting black cab.

The driver turned onto the broad Great Western Road and headed west. The traffic was heavy for early afternoon and the taxi got caught at three red lights in a row.

Elsbeth and Maureen sat as far apart as the backseat would allow, looking out of their respective windows in silence, watching the pedestrians going about their business.

"How did you know who I was?" asked Elsbeth, her sharp voice shattering the heavy silence between them.

Maureen turned to her and tried to catch her eye but Elsbeth was looking out of the window. "I saw a picture of you in the paper," she said softly, "at the last election. It was you and Douglas in front of a hotel."

Elsbeth looked at her lap and ground her jaw. She lifted her head and stared out of the window again.

"How come you recognized me?" asked Maureen.

"I saw a photograph of you," said Elsbeth. "It was in Douglas's briefcase. You were wearing a party hat."

Jesus Christ, the party-hat photo. Douglas had borrowed it because he thought it was so funny. Maureen was pissed and spliffed and guffawing and wearing a purple pointy hat with streamers coming out of it. The thick string of elastic was under her nose, pulling it back into a piggy snout. It must have been the ultimate insult for pristine Elsbeth, cuckold to a vulgar red-faced drunk.

The West End is Glasgow's student quarter and centers around the Byres Road, a broad street down the hill from the neo-Gothic university. Every third shop is a deli or bar. When Maureen was at university she worked in a West End bar and was often mistaken for an out-of-work actress. She was young at the time and thought it was a compliment.

As they neared the university the driver turned the cab off the Great Western Road into a crescent street. It was lined with elegant blond sandstone tenements on one side; on the other ornate cast-iron railings barred the steep drop to the river Kelvin. He pulled over to the pavement and stopped the meter.

Elsbeth stopped outside one of the blocks and took out her keys. She opened the security door into a close with shimmering green tiles up to shoulder height topped off with a border of pseudo-Mackintosh roses. The fancy tiling ceased abruptly on the first floor, replaced by green gloss.

They stopped on the second floor and Elsbeth unlocked her front door, letting it swing open into a huge hallway with stripped-pine floorboards. It was the biggest hallway Maureen had ever seen. "Come in," said Elsbeth, wrestling her key out of the door, relishing Maureen's surprise. "I'll show you around."

Elsbeth took her into all the rooms, pointing out unusual pieces of furniture and favored ornaments. The ceilings in the flat were high and ornate, the furniture sparse and expensive. The framed pictures in the living room were all Miró prints but Maureen suspected that this was a décor decision rather than a passion.

Elsbeth was trying hard but she was doing a bad job of covering her upset: her consistently indignant intonation was exhausting. Maureen had been impressed when Elsbeth had spoken to her and asked her back: she thought perhaps they were really going to talk to each other, but now Elsbeth was treating her like a new neighbor and she was behaving like one.

They settled in the large, bright kitchen. Elsbeth took a bottle of mineral water from the fridge and opened a wall cupboard full of glasses. For just a moment her hand hovered over the plain ones. She stood on her tiptoes and reached to the side, chose an expensive red and green goblet from a set of six, poured herself some mineral water and put the bottle back in the fridge without offering Maureen any.

Hanging on the wall next to the breakfast bar was a glass-covered montage of photographs. Groups of friends grinned across tables strewn with the wreckage of dinner parties past. The sun shone in various holiday destinations while Douglas sat alone reading or eating.

There were only two pictures of Douglas and Elsbeth together. One had been taken on a distant Christmas Day: they were sitting next to each other on a brown settee looking at a shiny new toaster on Douglas's knee. A lonely string of tinsel hung on the wall behind them. The other had been taken at their wedding. It was an informal photograph: they were standing on a lawn, chatting to an elderly man in a dark suit, he could be a vicar. Elsbeth was laughing and looked delicate and pretty in her plain ankle-length white dress. She had her arm around Douglas's waist. He wasn't holding her; his arms were hanging at his side, his expression a familiar mixture of disapproval and supercilious amusement. He looked at Maureen like that sometimes when he had a couple of drinks inside him; it made her feel as if she'd done something unbelievably stupid. The largest of the color photographs was of Douglas's mother. The plethora of surrounding dignitaries were frowning at something to the left of the photographer. She was holding a bunch of flowers and staring into the camera, her face creased into a glassy, go-ahead-punk smile.

Elsbeth saw her looking at it. "An extraordinary woman." She smiled. "I keep meaning to cut these others out, except, of course, Jacques Delors. I don't think he would take kindly to being cut out." And she laughed a tinkling, luncheon laugh. Maureen laughed too because she was sorry she had shagged this woman's husband and that woman's son.

It was becoming clear that Maureen hadn't been asked back to engage in a frank exchange of fond remembrances. She climbed onto a tottery stool at the breakfast bar and steeled herself like a good penitent. Elsbeth sat down opposite her and took a deep breath. She wanted Maureen to know that Douglas had had a series of affairs and she knew all about it. He had told her that he had taken on private work at an addiction clinic in Peebles, hence the Monday sleepover, but he had never been interested in that sort of work. They had a combined income of sixty-five K a year anyway, so it wasn't as if they needed the money. "So you see," said Elsbeth, a kindly veneer over her vindictive intent, "you're just the last in a long line of women."

"Yeah," said Maureen flatly, "I guessed. Am I the first one you've met?"

"Oh, no," she said, casually unaware of the pitiful picture she was painting of herself, "no, you're not."

And what the fuck were they doing, thought Maureen, having this petty, bland conversation, as if any of it mattered, as if Douglas hadn't been sliced up and killed hours before? She stopped herself. This is Elsbeth's time, she thought, this is her triumph. Let her have it. Be kind. Maureen tried to imagine what it would be like to be the wife of a philanderer, how likeable she herself would have been after a decade of hanging on to Douglas.

She had a sudden vision of him on the second night they had spent together. He had come over, ostensibly to apologize, but had stayed. Maureen had come back into the living room with a glass of water and had seen him lying on his side where she had left him, the image of Manet's *Olympia*, with his trousers around his knees and his shirt rumpled up around his chest, nonchalantly displaying his fervent hard-on. His dick wasn't round but strangely rectangular, like his buttocks, curiously geometric. But what she remembered most fondly was the unashamedly lewd look he had given her. She had knelt down next to him and leaned forward, pressing her face into the soft skin on his warm, hairy belly.

Sitting opposite Elsbeth, trying to retain her composure, she could feel Douglas's chest hair brushing her face, up and down, up and down.

Elsbeth had a great job. She worked in the graphics department in the BBC. She talked about the Corporation as though it was a beloved family friend. "What do you do?" she asked. The smile behind her eyes suggested that she already knew.

"I work at the ticket office in the Apollo."

"Oh?"

Maureen had smoked two cigarettes without as much as a cup of tea and her mouth was foul. A decade of petty humiliations and a faithless, murdered husband couldn't make Elsbeth sympathetic.

On her way out Elsbeth asked whether Douglas had ever given Maureen money.

"No," said Maureen quickly. She thought Elsbeth was trying to shame her further until she noticed the anxious expression on her face. There was something more behind the question. Elsbeth was looking for something. She was looking for some missing money.

"Well," said Maureen, as if she was thinking about it, "like when?"

"Couple of days ago?"

"Fifty quid," lied Maureen.

"Just fifty pounds?"

"Yeah, do you want it back?"

"No, no. Not important."

Maureen left the flat with the feeling that she had unwittingly been involved in a suburban wife-swapping circle. The thought depressed her beyond measure.

5

EQUAL

SHE WALKED THE THREE BLOCKS TO THE BYRES ROAD WITH HER MIND full of Douglas, Douglas gliding around his tasteful West End apartment, Douglas in her kitchen eating a roll and bacon, Douglas dead, tied into the chair, his neck slashed open. She stopped walking suddenly and shut her eyes, rubbing them hard with her fingers, trying to scrub away the image.

If she had taken the phone calls at work the day before he might have told her why he wasn't at work, he might have mentioned someone, something that would make sense of it. She thought about it realistically: he'd have lied and said things were fine. He'd have asked her about going to see Louisa and been pissed off at the mention of Leslie. But she couldn't dismiss it completely. It troubled her that he had called from a pay phone and it bothered her that he had phoned three times. He should have been at work.

The phone box on the Byres Road was in mint condition. It accepted three kinds of payment and the digital display had a French and a German option. She listened to the empty ring at Benny's house for a while and then, in a moment of weakness, called Leslie.

She let it ring until it cut out and then pressed the redial button, hanging up after two rings. She couldn't talk to Leslie without being needy and that would make her feel worse. Leslie had to work on the appeal, she told herself, get a grip. She phoned McEwan at the police station. The receptionist put her through to an office. A distracted man told her that DCI Joe McEwan wasn't available.

"I'm Maureen O'Donnell. Um, I was . . . A man was killed in my house and I need to get some clothes from the house."

"I'm Hugh McAskill." He seemed to think she'd recognize his name.

"Right," she said.

"From this morning. I was in the car with you. I was there when you were interviewed. I've got red hair."

"Oh, yeah," she said eagerly, "I remember you."

"The team are still at the house. You can get in okay."

"Smashin'."

"Are you going up now?"

"Aye."

"Tell them who you are when you get to the door—"

She interrupted him. "Mr. McAskill, can I ask you something?"

He thought for a moment. "Depends," he said tentatively.

"What was in the cupboard?"

McAskill didn't answer.

"It wasn't just slippers, was it?"

She could hear him exhale away from the receiver. "You don't want to know, pet," he said softly. "I'll phone your house and let them know you're coming."

"You're very kind," said Maureen, and meant it.

As she walked up the stairs in her close she looked out of the landing window. Eight or so uniformed officers were searching the back court; three of them poked around the spilled contents of the big communal wheelie bins.

A uniformed policeman was standing guard outside her front door. She told him she was expected. He asked her to wait and slipped inside, shutting the door in her face. He opened it two sighs later. Something McMummb was in the living room with two men from the Forensics team, still shuffling around in their white paper suits. He peered out at Maureen. "That's her," he said.

The officer on the door warned her that they would have to examine anything she wanted to take away and she wouldn't be allowed into certain parts of the house.

The heat had evaporated and it was cooler. The door of the hall cupboard was sealed shut with thick strips of yellow tape. She could see the first browning footprint in the living room. McMummb stepped lightly to the side, blocking the doorway, letting her know that she wasn't allowed to go in. Maureen lowered her eyes and went straight into the bedroom. McMummb hung back, talking to someone in the hall.

Everything was exactly as she had left it: the duvet was thrown back off the bed, the shift dress she had worn for work lay crumpled on the floor, half covering her handbag, and her watch was sitting on the bedside cabinet next to a lidless jar of cold cream. She stood next to her bed on the unaccustomed side. She wanted to sit down and rub her sore feet but she knew she shouldn't touch anything until McMummb came in to supervise. She reached out and touched the rumpled cotton sheet. The pillow showed an imprint where her sweaty head had been.

She looked down at the carpet and saw the cracked corner of a CD cover. She put her toe on it and dragged it out from under the bed without bending down. It was Benny's *Best of the Selecter* CD, the one she'd borrowed and was convinced she had given back. She had been so adamant. Benny'd never let her forget this.

McMummb came into the room and found her standing by the bed grinning at her feet. "I need to see the things," he said.

She watched him, waiting for him to finish his sentence, but his voice trailed away. He looked unhappily at the carpet in front of him.

"Okay," said Maureen, and handed him her watch to peruse.

She picked out a pair of jeans, her leather rucksack and a mustard cable-knit jumper. McMummb gave her the watch and looked inside the bag. He examined the clothes, held them to the light and checked the pockets. Another man in a white paper suit came into the room and checked them again.

She picked out four pairs of her most going-to-the-doctor knickers, some T-shirts, a tartan scarf and her charcoal cashmere overcoat. The two men looked them over with intense professionalism, running their fingers down the coat's silk lining. They handed them back to her. She shoved the T-shirts and knickers into the bag. "Can I get things out of my handbag?"

McMummb saw it on the floor and picked it up defensively, holding the long strap in front of him with two hands as if he were pushing a pram. "What do you want?"

"Fags."

He took out the fag packet and looked at it. He didn't know what he was supposed to be looking for. He shoved it at the Forensics man, who took the trouble to open the packet, look inside and poke the fags about with a long, bony finger. "I think we should keep these," he said, addressing McMummb solemnly.

"I think we should keep them," said McMummb.

"Okay," said Maureen. "Can I get my wallet?"

McMummb took out the wallet and leafed through the cashpoint receipts and pound notes. The Forensics man did the same and handed it to her.

"And my keys?"

"You can't come in here unless we're with you," said McMummb.

She nodded. "When will I be able to come home?"

"We'll notify you," said McMummb, as he opened the bag and took out the keys. He shook them, as if some vital clue might be hidden among them, and handed them to the Forensics man. The Forensics man held them up and shook them. He waited for them to stop jangling and handed them to Maureen.

"Thanks," she said, and put them in her rucksack.

The less the police picked up about Liam's movements the better. She went down to a battered, pissed-in call box in the next street rather than use her own phone and, finally, caught up with him at Benny's house.

At the base of Garnethill on Sauchiehall Street is a small and comfortingly grubby café called the Equal. Maureen took Douglas there for breakfast sometimes. It's a genuine sixties throwback, when fifties décor had just reached Glasgow: the tables are black Formica with a gold fleck through it and the coffee machine looks like a red and chrome prototype steam engine.

They sat down at an empty table near the window.

Liam tapped her on the forearm. "Where have you been all day, hen?" he asked, watching her closely to see how she was.

"I've just been sort of running around," said Maureen, her head bobbing nervously when she tried to relax her shoulders. "I didn't want to stop in case I couldn't get started again. I haven't eaten all day. That must be why I feel so shaky."

"It's probably got something to do with what happened, though, eh?"

"Well," she said, "yeah, that too."

"Scary day, though, eh?"

"I've had scarier."

He smiled at her bravura. "Could you eat something?"

When Maureen got upset the first thing to go was her appetite.

She had almost starved herself irredeemably before Liam found her in the hall cupboard and took her to the hospital. "Strangely enough, I'm starving today."

The surreal character of the café was enhanced by the depressed, elderly waitress with a sore leg. When she brought them the wrong order for the second time they accepted it to save her walking all the way to the kitchen again.

"Mum's been hassling the police," said Maureen, sliding her knife into the underside of an unrequested bridie and letting the excess grease run out of the pastry parcel. "She was phoning the station all day demanding my release."

"Yeah." Liam sipped his coffee. "She's gone into full Jill Morrell mode. They told me about it and I phoned home. Got Una to unplug the phone."

"What kind of things did they ask you about?"

"They asked about you and about Douglas. They didn't have a clue what I'm into so that was all right."

"Jim Maliano was dead nice to me," said Maureen.

"He's a bit of an arse usually, isn't he?"

"Total arse usually. He brought me out a chair and a cup of tea and everything. And he lent me that beautiful Celtic top to wear while I was being questioned."

Liam squeezed watery tomato sauce from the plastic bottle onto his plate of chips. "That must have impressed the polis." He watched his sister steer the oily rivulet away from her chips and beans, into a safe empty space at the side of the plate. She dabbed it off with a paper napkin. "I can see," he said, "that you're used to eating in top-class restaurants such as this one."

"Yup." Maureen smiled. "I don't like that Joe McEwan character at all."

"Yeah, he's a total prick but don't let on you don't like him."

"Why shouldn't I?"

"He's a big noise up there. It could make a difference to how they treat you. Try to seem friendly," he said, as if he'd spent his life being questioned by the police. "They asked me what I was doing yesterday afternoon."

"Yeah," said Maureen. "They were asking me about the morning and afternoon. I guess that's when they think it happened. I was at my work."

"Yeah. I had a key and I can't tell them where I was during the day."

"Why not?"

"I was at Tonsa's seeing Paulsa."

Tonsa was a courier. She traveled to London on the train once a month, bringing crack to Glasgow. She looked like a well-to-do lady in her early thirties: she had elegant bone structure, a slim figure and expensive, stylish dress sense. Liam had introduced her to Maureen when they bumped into her at the Barras market one Sunday. She looked normal until Maureen noticed her eyes: they were watery and open a fraction too little, they were a corpse's eyes, Tonsa was dead beneath the skin. Until then Maureen had thought of Liam as the Gentleman Jim of the drugs world. After meeting Tonsa she realized there was no such thing, that Liam must be a heavy guy. But he wasn't like that with her and she hung on to that. He was her big brother, she reasoned, and she was entitled to censor his life for her own consumption.

Tonsa had been in the papers recently: her boyfriend had been slashed, ear to chin, while he went about his lawful business. The local paper carried a photo of the lovely couple demanding that the police catch the evil men responsible. At the time Maureen had asked Liam why Tonsa let them take her picture, surely she wouldn't want that sort of attention. Liam had shrugged and said Tonsa was wasted, no one knew why Tonsa did anything.

"Liam," she said, nervous at asking, " 'member Tonsa's man was slashed?"

He looked up at her. "Aye?"

"Well, that wouldn't be anything to do with this, would it?"

"What d'ye mean?" he said, staring at her, daring her to go ahead.

"I just wondered if you knew anyone—"

"Am I getting the blame for this?" he snapped.

"Right, you"—she wagged a finger across the table at him—"calm down. I'm not blaming ye, I'm just asking ye. It's not an unreasonable question. You're the only person I know who deals with these kinds of people."

"Yeah, well, Maureen," he said, trying to be reasonable because she'd had a shitty day, "we're not the only people who do that sort of thing. There are other bad men in the world."

"I know that, I'm just wondering, gangsters do that sort of thing, don't they?"

Liam smirked uncomfortably at the table. "You watch too many films, Maureen, these are businessmen . . . Ye don't get much of that sort of thing."

Maureen looked unconvinced. "Someone wouldn't be trying to send you a message? A warning or something?"

"Look, how does that send a message to me? Why kill my wee sister's boyfriend in her house leaving no clue as to their identity?"

"I suppose."

"If someone wanted to send me a warning they'd walk up and smash me in the face. It wouldn't be a secret, I'd know I was out of line and I'd know it was coming. These people are motivated by greed. They don't want trouble with the police—that just makes it harder to do business."

"Right enough. I just thought, because of the slashing . . ."

"Slashing people's faces, that's something trainee neds do to show their mates they're hard, they don't even know the person they're doing it to, they just run past the person and—" He flicked his wrist in a way she found worryingly dismissive.

"You've never done that, eh?" she asked timidly.

"Don't be ridiculous." He was staggered at the suggestion. "Do you think I'm capable of that?"

"Not really."

"Mauri, do you really think I'd do that to someone?"

"Auch, no, Liam, no. But I know you're protective of me since I was in hospital."

"*Protective?*"

"Yeah, protective."

"And I'm stupid enough to think carving up your boyfriend in your own living room is going to protect you from something much worse? Like what? Like falling out with him?"

"Aye, right enough."

"Anyway." He smiled at her. "I'd hardly do it when my alibi would get me arrested, would I? I'd be smarter than that, anyway."

"Auch, I'm sorry, Liam." She smiled back at him. "I'm a bit bewildered today."

She cut a bite out of the bridie and put it in her mouth. It hadn't been microwaved properly and undissolved fat still clung to the slimy inside of the cold pastry wall. She bit down onto a lump of gristle and made a face. "That's disgustin'." She spat it out into a napkin, wrapping it into a little bundle and putting it in the ashtray. Her appetite was gone.

"I'm so fucked," said Liam. "I can't tell them where I was."

"It might have happened at night. That time-of-death stuff isn't a set science, it's just a good guess."

"Did the police tell you that?"

"No," she said. "But the heating was on in the house this morning—it was belting out. I wondered if that could change a time of death."

"How?"

"Well, they work it out by comparing the temperature of the body to the surrounding temperature. What would it be if the person was alive—say, ninety-eight point six degrees?"

"I dunno."

"Anyway, what if the surrounding temperature wasn't constant? That would change the rate of heat loss. What if the heating was turned right up and set to go an hour or so before he was found? That would heat up the house but wouldn't be enough to heat up a body. The police would take his temperature thinking he'd been in a warm house the whole time he'd been dead. They'd think he'd died earlier than he actually did."

"Maureen, what are you rambling about?" said Liam seriously.

"They could have got the time of death wrong. It could have happened in the evening."

He looked confused. "Wouldn't the police think of that, though?"

She shrugged. "Yeah, but even if they did it would still be hard to work out the times: they couldn't know what the temperature had been before the heating went on."

"And did it occur to you that if the murderer did that deliberately they'd need to know how the police work out the time of death? Where did you hear all that science stuff anyway?"

"I saw it on *Taggart.*"

Liam giggled at his plate. He could tell he was making Maureen angry but couldn't stop himself. He put his hand over his mouth. "I'm sorry, Mauri—"

"Yeah, fuck you."

"Yeah." He sniggered. "Okay, fuck me."

"I read it in the paper as well, Liam."

"So it must be true."

"What were you doing that night?"

"I was with Maggie at her mum and dad's."

"And were they in?"

"Yeah."

"Well, if I was right they could vouch for you."

He grinned at her as if she was mental. "Okay, Dr. X."

"Don't take the piss, Liam."

"I'm trying not to but you make it so hard." Maureen looked downcast.

"Did you tell the police that?"

She looked even more miserable. "I tried," she said.

He suppressed a smile. "And what did they say?"

She didn't answer him.

"Well," he said, jabbing at a chip, "I'm sure they'll find whoever did it soon enough. Buccleuch Street's always busy. Someone must have seen something."

Maureen picked at her chips. They were soggy, limp and warm. She should eat something. "I don't know why I keep coming here, the food's horrible."

"Good fry-ups, though," said Liam.

"Did they tell you anything about the cupboard?" she said, trying to catch the waitress's eye. She limped over to their table. Maureen ordered an ice cream and a coffee. They looked to Liam for an order. He was eating his chips eagerly now, spearing three at a time with his fork and swirling them around in the mess of ketchup on the side of the plate.

"Does sir want anything else?" asked the waitress.

Liam looked at her. "Nope."

As she limped away to the kitchen Liam stabbed Maureen gently with his fork. "What was that about a cupboard?"

"They found something in the cupboard."

"Which cupboard?"

"The hall cupboard."

"The cupboard I found you in?"

"Yeah."

"That doesn't mean anything."

"I don't know what it means."

He watched her. "It could just be an accident. It isn't necessarily significant that you were found in it."

"It could make it look like me," she said softly, "if they find out I was found in there. They might think I did it and then went and hid in there again. They might think I was in there all night and that's why I didn't phone them."

Liam worked the final bushel of chips into his mouth and thought about it. "Yeah," he said. "They're more likely to think it's significant if you don't tell them and they find out from someone else later."

"Who knows that except you and me?"

"You, me and any one of the mental-health professionals who've seen your psychiatric notes."

"It's not in my notes. I've seen my notes. It says I was hiding in the house, it doesn't mention that cupboard. Louisa at the Albert doesn't know."

"What about that guy at the Rainbow?"

"Naw, Angus didn't know either. I never discussed that time with him."

"So that leaves you and me."

"Yeah."

"I didn't do it, Maureen."

"I didn't mean that. I meant who knows that? Did you tell anyone?"

"Like who?"

"I dunno."

"Well, I dunno either." He looked at her. "I didn't do it, Maureen."

"I'm not saying you did. I didn't for a minute mean that it was you, Liam, I didn't mean that."

"Did ye not like the bridie?" The waitress was at her side with a portion of ice cream and a coffee. She put them on the table and lifted Maureen's dinner plate.

"I'm just not hungry," said Maureen quietly. She slid a spoonful of ice cream and raspberry sauce into her mouth, rolling it under her tongue, letting it dissolve slightly before swallowing.

Liam took the teaspoon from her coffee and started eating her ice cream. "So you were at your work when it happened?"

"Yeah," she said, frowning at her ice cream. "Someone phoned work yesterday. Liz thought it was Douglas but it might not have been. She told him I wasn't in and I wouldn't be in all day."

"So?"

"He phoned three times. Same guy."

"It probably was Douglas," said Liam.

"No, I don't know if it was. They were phoning from a phone box and he should have been at work. I don't think he'd have called back when she said I was out. Wouldn't want to seem too eager."

Liam stole another spoon of ice cream. She pushed it toward him. "You have it. I don't want it."

The sugar and caffeine were finding their way into Maureen's system. The shaky feeling evaporated like a hangover after a whisky and she felt relatively calm. She sipped her coffee. It was bitter and hot. She took out her cigarettes and lit one.

"Do you think you're being set up?" asked Liam.

"Maybe. I don't know what the cupboard thing means yet. If I could find out what was wrong with the cupboard . . ."

"Stop trying to find things out, pet. Leave it to the police," said Liam, without a hint of irony. "They'll sort it out."

"I'm just . . . I'm thinking."

"Keep out of it. You don't want to get involved in this."

"I'm already involved."

"Okay," he said. "You don't want to get *more* involved, Mauri. Don't meddle."

"I was only thinking."

"Leave it, Maureen."

"There's no harm in thinking about it."

Liam was exasperated. "Look, some scary fucker cut Douglas's throat when he was helpless and tied to a fucking chair. Nice people don't do that. These are unpleasant, dangerous people. This isn't *Taggart*. Bad things happen to the good guys."

"Bad things happen on *Taggart*."

"Maureen," he said, "there are very nasty people in the world. You're not like them, you're not fit for them. You've no idea what people are capable of doing to each other, no idea."

"But how are they going to catch the right person?"

"Do you think that's what the police are about? Catching the right person?" He ruffled her hair. "You're not fit for these people, Mauri. Just stand back and shut up and you'll be all right."

On the way back to Benny's Maureen stopped at the cashpoint and took out the last twenty quid from her account. If the bank withdrew her £100 overdraft facility before the end of the month she wouldn't be able to pay her meager mortgage.

She waited until Benny had gone to bed before she lay down on the settee and did the breathing exercises she had learned in the Northern. They were supposed to help her sleep but each time she started to relax images and phrases from the day flashed in her mind, startling her awake.

6

WINNIE

LIZ WAS REVELING IN THE DRAMA OF IT ALL. THE MUSTACHIOED policeman had been to the office and questioned her, asking her to sign a statement to the effect that Maureen had not left the office for any longer than five minutes during the previous day. The walk to the house took ten. Maureen had been in the toilet for fifteen minutes but Audrey had spoken to her. Liz said wasn't it lucky Audrey was a chain-smoker.

Maureen looked up a couple of times during the day and caught Liz staring at her with undisguised awe. She asked three times about going to the police station. Maureen didn't want to talk about it. She had woken up on Benny's settee with trembling hands, a throbbing headache and a terrible sense that the worst of it wasn't over. It felt like her night terrors. She wanted to be at work, pretending it was a normal day, but Liz was desperate to be part of the show. "I think friends should trust each other," she said, over lunch.

"I need a piss," said Maureen, excusing herself as only a lady could.

Mr. Scobie seemed more traumatized about it than either of them.

When Maureen went off to hide in the toilet during the morning she saw him walking toward her down the corridor. He looked panic-stricken and ducked into a cloakroom to avoid running into her. She thought about going after him, just for badness' sake, but decided against it.

In the afternoon he shuffled nervously into the ticket office, keeping his back close to the wall, and handed them their wages. Maureen had a tax rebate in hers and the brown envelope held £150 in tens and twenties. "I'm sorry to hear about your trouble, dear," said Mr. Scobie.

"Thank you, Mr. Scobie."

"Will you be taking any more days off?" His voice cracked mid-sentence. "Or can I leave the shifts as they are?"

"You can leave them as they are."

"Fine."

He scuttled back out. Liz sniggered when she was sure he was out of earshot.

Winnie phoned late in the afternoon. "Please come and see me," she said. "Please do. Just to make me feel better because I'm worried about you."

Maureen agreed to come over after work.

"Now, promise me, you won't get a bus or anything, just get into a taxi and come here and I'll pay it at the other end."

"You don't need to do that. I can pay it."

"I insist," said Winnie. She sounded stone-cold sober.

Maureen didn't want to go. Sober Winnie was almost as much work as Very Drunk Winnie and Very Drunk Winnie was a lot of work. She was angry and vindictive, shouting carefully personalized abuse at whoever happened to be in front of her, casting up any failure or humiliation, however petty, always going straight for the jugular. It was her special talent, she could find anyone's tender spot within minutes. Sober Winnie was an emotional leech, demanding affection and reassurance, bullying them with her limit-less neediness, crying piteously when she didn't get her own way. She shit-stirred between the children, rumormongering and passing on distorted comments. When anyone tried to stand up to her she cast herself as the victim and rallied the other children to her support, causing schisms. Liam said she had a rota written up somewhere and victimized the children in turn. It had worked better when they were younger: Maureen and Liam only pretended to buy into it all now, faking shock at Una's unkind comments about Maggie, pretending to care when Marie said Maureen would never recover from the hospital. But Una still played along fully and if Maureen didn't go and see Winnie today then, as sure as a fight at a wedding, she'd get a worried phone call from Una tomorrow, asking her why she was avoiding Mum, what had Mum done, couldn't Maureen see she was upsetting her.

There was a time when Very Drunk Winnie was the best of a bad choice for Maureen: it was a straight fight and she could take it because Winnie didn't know anything about her. She had been careful never to discuss the things that mattered to her in front of the family, Liam excepted. She told her friends that she didn't have a phone and wouldn't let boyfriends come to the house. She lied about where she was going at night, she even lied about her O grade subjects. So when Winnie went for Maureen's jugular she was slagging her about fictitious habits, friends and events. What happened between them in hospital had changed all that. Now Winnie had more to cast up to Maureen than the rest of them.

Winnie behaved strangely during the hospital visits. She brought an endless succession of inappropriate presents like earrings and makeup and fashion magazines. She monologued about the neighborhood gossip, who had died, what was on telly last night. She wouldn't acknowledge the fact that they were in a psychiatric hospital or talk to the staff. But Maureen was bananas at the time and lots of things seemed strange. Leslie had read up on familial reactions to abuse disclosure and said that it was normal for the non-abusing parent to feel incredibly guilty, maybe that's what was wrong with Winnie.

Maureen didn't have a lot of time to think about it: the memories of the forgotten years were coming back thick and fast, through dreams, in flashbacks, over cups of tea with other patients. She became a compulsive confider. Looking at the fading bouquets of flowers on the wallpaper above the bedstead, counting and counting and counting until it was finished.

Standing in the bath waiting to get out and Michael, her father, leaning over with the towel and looking her in the eye. The door was shut behind him.

Him sitting on the bed afterward, crying, Maureen patting his hand to comfort him as the pee stung her legs. His hand was as big as her face.

At the caravan in St. Andrews, the sea lapping over her black gutties. The rest of them were on the beach, out of sight, behind the rock, and Michael was coming after her. She scrabbled over the rocks on all fours, trying to get away, trying to look as if she wasn't running, scratching her knees on the jagged granite.

The panic when he saw the blood dribbling down her skinny legs. He'd slapped her on the side of the head and, lifting her by her upper arm, put her into the cupboard, locking it and taking the key with him. She could smell the blood as she sat in the dark cupboard and she knew what it was. She hoped she would die before he came back. It was his fingernail that had cut her, it was his nail.

Winnie crowbarring the cupboard door open and pulling Maureen out by her ankle. Marie standing behind her, twelve years old and already crying without making a noise, silent because she knew no one was listening.

She tried to piece it all together but some elements of the story were confusing: she couldn't remember when Michael left them or why certain smells prompted panic attacks or whether any of the other children had showed signs of abuse. Dr. Paton suggested asking Winnie but Maureen didn't feel comfortable about it. Dr. Paton said they might ask her under controlled conditions, perhaps they could organize a joint session with her.

Winnie came to it sober and apparently quite willing. The three of them gathered in the cozy office in the Portakabin in the hospital grounds, sitting in big armchairs and sipping tea. Dr. Paton said Maureen had something to ask her mother, there were some problematic details about the facts surrounding the abuse and would Winnie be willing to help?

Winnie smiled and listened to Maureen's first question: she remembered Winnie getting her out of the cupboard and she remembered Marie being there but was Michael in the house at the time? Winnie said she didn't know, she couldn't help there. Maureen asked about Michael, when did he leave? Winnie didn't know about that either. Dr. Paton asked her why she didn't know and Winnie started crying and saying that she'd done her best. Maureen rubbed her back and told her it was all right, they all knew she had done her best. She was a good mum.

Winnie got up and stormed off to the toilet and came back with the greasy-nothing smell of vodka on her breath. She told them that Maureen had been misinformed by her sister; Una remembered properly now and would come and talk to them if they wanted. Winnie said it had never happened and then she lost the script, shouting at Maureen and the doctor when they tried to speak, interrupting them with irrelevant details and crying when nothing else worked. Maureen had always been strange, she always made up stories. Mickey had never touched Maureen, he didn't even like her. He was a very passionate man and he had been devoted to Winnie. She cried again and said that she still loved Maureen and what had she done to make Maureen stop loving her?

Maureen was numb. "I love you, Mum," she said vacantly, and rubbed Winnie's back, "I do love you."

The effect on Maureen was marked. An iota of doubt grew into a possible truth. The memories seemed so tangible and the emotions attached to them were so intense, overwhelming, like a searing physical pain. If Maureen was misremembering, she was as mad as a fucking dog.

She felt more ashamed of herself than she ever had before. She would have killed herself but for the effect it might have on Leslie and Pauline, her pal from the OT classes. She had put everyone to all this trouble over a bullshit story.

She couldn't talk about it. Her meetings with Dr. Paton dissolved into hour-long sessions of staring at the floor, hot fat tears rolling down her immobile face. The doctor tried to get her to talk but couldn't. They both knew it was because of Winnie. The doctor sat next to Maureen and held her hand, dabbing her face dry with a tissue. She began to lose weight again. Her release time was revised and moved back a month.

Leslie knew something was very wrong. She kept asking about it but Maureen couldn't say it out loud. Finally, after two weeks of needling her with questions, Leslie got Maureen to tell her what had happened. She was furious. She roared up to Winnie's house on her bike and parked it on George's lovely lawn. She stomped into the kitchen, where Winnie was eating lunch with Una, and told her that if she denied the abuse again, even in her prayers, Leslie would personally kick her cunting teeth in. Winnie went off Leslie after that.

Leslie made Maureen draw up a list of facts corroborating the abuse and brought her books with firsthand accounts by other survivors, telling how their families had reacted when they told. It seemed that physical damage, DNA tests, even a criminal conviction, could be ignored if the family didn't want to believe, and Winnie did not want to believe.

On the day Maureen finally left the hospital Dr. Paton took her to one side. "I want you to know that there is no doubt in my mind that it happened," she said. "And, on a strictly nonprofessional level, I think that your mother is a self-serving bastard."

Maureen and Winnie never talked about it again, but because of Leslie's visit Winnie knew where Maureen's Achilles' heel was and there was always the possibility that she would bring it up when she was viciously drunk.

Maureen cheerioed Liz and left work with a knot in her stomach and a drag in her step. She would have given anything to be on her way out to get drunk with Leslie instead of going to do battle with Winnie.

The family had moved to the house when George and Winnie first got married. It was on a small council scheme with modest two-story concrete box houses. In front of the house was a tiny token lawn, meticulously cared for by George, and in front of that a broad pavement leading down the quiet street where the small children played together until their tea was ready. It was a nice scheme, peopled by good-living poor families who were ambitious for their children. The neighbors knew Winnie was a drunk and the O'Donnell kids were pitied for it.

She hadn't intended to let Winnie pay—she meant to pay herself and let the taxi go before going into the house—but Winnie was watching at the window and ran out of the house when she saw the taxi pull up. She shoved a tenner in the driver's window. "Take it off that," she said.

"Hiya," said Maureen, trying to sound cheerful.

Winnie looked terribly hung over. She put her hand to Maureen's face. "Hello, honey," she said, looking as if she might cry.

Maureen followed her into the house. Winnie and George were of a generation who believed in the value and longevity of man-made fabrics. The house was furnished with brown and yellow carpets, and curtains and furnishings that had survived from the seventies.

George was asleep on the settee in the dark living room; the silent television flickered in the corner. George drank as much and as often as Winnie but he was a dear, melancholic drunk whose greatest handicaps were falling asleep at odd moments and a propensity to recite sentimental poetry about Ireland.

Maureen could feel the heat from the cooker before she got through the kitchen door. "I've been baking all day," said Winnie. With a great flourish she opened the oven and pulled out a loaf tin. She cut a thick slice of hot gingerbread, buttered it and gave it to Maureen along with a cup of coffee.

The gingerbread tasted exactly the same as McCall's, a famous bakery in Rutherglen—they always overdid the cinnamon. But it was a kind lie, designed to make Maureen feel cared for. "Thanks, Mum," she said. "It's lovely."

Winnie sat next to her, clutching an opaque mug with a dark glaze on the inside. Maureen tried surreptitiously sniffing the air to work out what Winnie was drinking. It wasn't coffee, anyway. Winnie wasn't exhaling after each sip so it wasn't a spirit. It might be wine. Her tongue wasn't red. White wine. She had drunk just enough to get morose but not enough to be aggressive. About two cups. Maureen guessed that she had at least half an hour before Winnie started to get difficult.

Winnie sat next to her at the table and offered Maureen her old room back. "You could stay for as long as you want," she said.

When Maureen said she'd be fine at Benny's house, Winnie asked her if he was in the phone book. "Yeah," she said, before she had time to think about it. She was cursing her own stupidity as Winnie tried to give her some money. "I'm fine, Mum, really, I don't need anything."

"I've got some cheese in the fridge, I got it from the wholesalers, it's from the Orkneys."

"I don't want any cheese, Mum, thanks."

"I'll cut you a block to take home." She stood up and opened the fridge door, heaving the six-pound block of orange Cheddar onto the work top.

"I don't want any cheese, Mum, thanks."

Winnie ignored her, opened the cutlery drawer, pulled out a long bread knife, and began slicing a one-pound lump from the block. She paused, slumping over the cheese.

"Are you all right, Mum?"

"I worry about you," said Winnie, turning back to Maureen. She was on the verge of tears. "I worry about you so much."

"But you shouldn't, Mum."

"But you're a . . . I never know . . . . if only you couldn't . . ." She abandoned the giant brick of cheese and sat back down at the table, lifting her cup and drinking out of it. "I think I've got flu," she whispered, crying thin tears.

"You should go to the doctor's, then."

Winnie looked helpless. "I'm a bit depressed," she said pointedly.

Maureen sighed. "Mum," she said, "I can't comfort you just now."

"I don't want you to comfort me," Winnie said, crying fluently. "I just want to make sure you're all right."

"I *am* all right."

"I worry so much," she whimpered.

"You shouldn't."

She sat bolt upright, suddenly in control. "Maureen, I'm your mother."

"I know who you are," said Maureen, trying to cheer herself up. The wine must be kicking in: her moods were changing rapidly. Maybe more than two cups, maybe three.

"I just want to know," Winnie said softly. "Did you do it?"

"Did I do what, Mother?"

Winnie bowed her head. "Did you kill that man?" she muttered, and bit her lip.

Maureen pulled away, exasperated by Winnie's capacity for melodrama. "Oh, Mum, for God's sake, you know fine well I didn't."

Winnie was offended. "I don't know fine well . . ." She turned away as if she'd been slapped.

"Yes, you do," said Maureen. "You know I didn't kill him. You're so camp, I swear, you're like a bad female impersonator."

"I don't know you didn't do it," said Winnie solemnly. "You've often done things I didn't think you were capable of." She stood up and walked over to the sink, taking her cup with her, standing with her back to Maureen as she rearranged the glasses on the draining board.

"Like what?"

"You know . . ." And she whispered something under her breath, something that ended with "Mickey." Maureen hadn't heard her say the name since the hospital. She could feel herself shrinking in the chair.

"Don't worry," Winnie said, lifting her mug. "I'll stand by you, whatever you've done." She finished off her wine.

It was a low blow, hinting at the abuse. It was the meanest thing she could have brought up. "You drink too much, Mum," said Maureen, returning the compliment. "You wouldn't be on the verge of hysteria all the time if you drank less."

Winnie turned and looked at her, furious at the mention of her drinking. "How dare you?" she said, tight-lipped. "I paid for your taxi."

"I didn't want you to."

"But you let me."

Maureen pulled ten quid out of her wage packet and slapped it on the table. "There's a tenner, Mammy. That's us even."

Winnie screamed at her, *I don't want money!*"

Maureen rolled her eyes just as George appeared at the kitchen door. "Oh," he said quietly, "I didn't hear you come in."

"Hello, George," said Maureen.

"Hello, pal," said George, and frowned. "Heard about yesterday. Nae luck."

He didn't talk about it much but Maureen suspected that George's early life hadn't been a bundle of laughs either. He had a charming talent for minimizing grief and, living with Winnie, he often had cause to use it.

"Aye," said Maureen, suddenly tired. "It wasn't good."

He patted the back of her head gently and turned to Winnie. "Any bread, doll? The seagulls are at the window again."

Winnie gave him some from the tin and he wandered off, ripping up the slices into uneven lumps, leaving a trail of crumbs through the hall. She came back to the table and shoved the tenner at Maureen. "Take the money back," she said. "I was just feeling a bit uptight. I'm sorry for shouting at you."

"Well, you shouldn't try to pay for things if you don't really want to."

Winnie sat down at the table. "I know. I just . . . I get nervous . . . and now this."

"Don't worry, Mum, the police'll find them soon."

She looked at Maureen and brightened. "Do you think so?"

Maureen nodded. "I know they will."

Winnie sat up and looked at the huge block of cheese sitting on the work top. "What the hell am I going to do with that much cheese?"

Maureen looked over at it and giggled. "Mum, why in God's name did ye buy that?"

Winnie shrugged, confused by her own behavior. "It seemed like a good idea at the time. We were using it as a garden ornament until we ate enough off it to get it through the door."

They sat together and laughed at the industrial lump of cheese. Maureen looked at her mum. Winnie was happy to laugh at herself, neither sad nor angry, demanding nothing: this was old Winnie, Winnie from before the drinking got really bad. And then she stopped laughing and looked at her empty cup and old Winnie was gone. She lifted her hand and brushed back Maureen's hair, but she was pressing too firmly against Maureen's head and some caught on her engagement ring. She tugged it hard. Maureen tried hard not to react in case Winnie thought she was rebuffing the kindly gesture.

"How are you coping?"

Maureen rubbed her bruised scalp. "Okay."

"If it all gets too much for you," said Winnie, "I want you to promise me that you'll go back to hospital."

"Mum, for God's sake, I'm not the maddest person in the world, they don't keep a vacant bed just for me."

"I know, but I'm sure they'll take you if you say you were in before."

Maureen shrank farther into the chair.

When she got outside she walked a couple of blocks and stopped at a bench in front of a Baptist church. It was dark and spitting rain. A man on the other side of the road was walking a tired old dog. He talked to it, whispering encouragement, calling it by name. The dog stopped, panting for breath, its legs almost buckling under the weight of its body. The man tapped its back and the old dog moved off.

She smoked a couple of fags, imagining herself at home, in her cozy wee flat, before any of this had happened. She took a bath in her blue and white bathroom and sat butt naked on her settee, watching the telly and eating biscuits and letting the answerphone catch the calls.

She took a cup of tea in to Benny in the bedroom. He was sitting on the side of the bed, a shallow table in front of him with textbooks open on it. He had been sharpening his pencils into the muddy dregs in a coffee cup. He must be frantic about his exams. He put down his book and asked earnestly if she wanted to talk about yesterday.

"No, not just now. I can't even think about it yet."

"Okay," he said, looking solemn and nervous.

"Are you all right about it, Benny?"

His expression melted with relief. "God, it's a bit freaky, isn't it? You don't think of these things happening to people like us, do you?"

"I guess not." She gestured to the books. "You got an exam tomorrow?"

"No," he said. "It's next week but I haven't done nearly enough."

"You always say that and you always pass. Try and put Douglas to the back of your mind just now and concentrate on your exams." She lifted the dirty cup with the sharpenings in it. "I'll take this filthy item away."

Out in the hall she could hear someone scratching quietly on the door. She looked out of the spy hole. Leslie was standing in the close holding her crash helmet and slowly brushing her hair off her face with the other hand. She had dark circles under her eyes and looked knackered. Maureen threw the door open. "Leslie." She grinned broadly.

Leslie stepped into the hall, reached out to Maureen and squeezed her arm. "All right, hen?" she said. Her voice sounded as if she had been smoking heavily and/or had just woken up. "How ye doing?"

"Yeah," said Maureen. "I take it Liam phoned and told ye?"

"Naw, the police came to see me."

Maureen pointed into the bedroom and Leslie kicked the door open a little and stuck her head in. "Right, Benny, man?"

Maureen heard Benny "aye" from the other side of the door. Leslie pulled the door shut and pointed at it. "Working," she said. "Why the fuck didn't you call me, Mauri?"

"Auch," Maureen shrugged uncomfortably, "you've got enough on."

"For fucksake, I'm not running the world, Maureen."

"I know, I just . . . . I'll be all right."

"You're pathologically independent."

"Anyway," said Maureen, heading for the kitchen, "d'ye want a cup of tea?"

"Coffee"—Leslie put her helmet on the settee—"I need a strong coffee." She went to sit down and caught herself. "Let me get it," she said, almost staggering into the kitchen.

Maureen went after her. "Fucksake, Leslie, go and sit down."

"No," said Leslie, shaking her head adamantly, "I should get it."

"It wasn't me that was killed, Leslie. Go and sit down."

Leslie looked dismal. "I'm so fucking sorry, Maureen. I didn't like him but I'm so sorry."

"Yeah, well."

They stood close to each other, looking over one another's shoulders for a moment. Maureen said, "I feel as if we should hug each other or something."

"D'ye want to?"

"No," said Maureen. "Not really."

"I wish ye'd have phoned me," said Leslie quietly.

"If I need ye I'll phone ye."

"Don't leave it until you need me. I'm your pal, not the fire brigade." Leslie exhaled loudly and opened her eyes wide with surprise. "This is a mental thing to have happened."

"Jesus fuck," said Maureen, "I know."

Leslie said that the police had questioned her about Maureen's relationship with Douglas. They seemed more interested in that than in finding out the times of the dinner at the Pizza Pie Palace. And then she asked Maureen to tell her what had happened. The knot in Maureen's stomach tightened. She couldn't talk about it tonight: it would make it seem real.

"Ye want to hang on to the shock for a bit longer?" asked Leslie, sympathetically.

"Yeah," said Maureen. "Yeah, shock's good."

Leslie said that she was exhausted because she had been working on the appeal submissions, they had to be completed for Tuesday morning and she was having trouble understanding the law books. She asked Maureen not to tell Benny—he'd insist on giving her a hand and he had his exams to study for. Maureen told her she was pathologically independent.

They smoked a cigarette together, Leslie ripped the filter off hers to make it stronger, trying to wake herself up. Her lips and teeth were covered in bits of tobacco after every draw. Maureen laughed at her and leaned over the table. "Go home, ya daft bastard."

Leslie gave up and squashed the fag out in the ashtray. "Mauri, hen, I can't just leave you."

"Leslie, I'll see you on Tuesday afternoon. My life'll still be crap on Tuesday afternoon."

Maureen showed her out, warning her to drive carefully on the way home.

"Look, phone me if you want to talk about Douglas before then."

"Go away now," said Maureen, shooing her down the close.

Feeling strangely cheerful, she turned the television on in the living room and went into the kitchen to make herself a sandwich. The midevening news came on. Carol Brady, MEP for Strathclyde, was coming back from an ecology conference in Brazil after hearing the tragic news about her son, Douglas Brady. Maureen stepped into the doorway and watched the footage. Carol Brady was walking very fast through a large crowd of baying newsmen at the airport, walking with great purpose, and Maureen had a definite feeling that she was coming to get her.

The statement from her press office said that the family were very upset about Douglas's death and would appreciate the consideration of the press at this difficult time. They had every faith that the police would find the person responsible very soon.

A senior police officer was shown at a press conference saying that everything was under control and could anyone who had seen anything please phone and tell them about it. They gave out a special number.

7

JOURNOS

SHE WENT TO HER WORK THE NEXT DAY SUSPECTING NOTHING. IT was a miserable damp Saturday and the ticket booth wasn't busy; even the phones were quiet. Liz was on better form. She told Maureen a funny story about a long-dead uncle's nervous alopecia.

Mr. Scobie was out so they took turns using the phone and wandering off to the toilet for a skive. Liz went off to the loo with a newspaper and Maureen lifted the phone. Liam wasn't at home so she left a message on the machine. She had barely hung up when he phoned back. The police were talking to everyone they knew, he was worried someone would let something slip about him.

"Did they speak to Mum?"

"Yeah," said Liam. "She was as pissed as fuck. I was waiting downstairs for her. I dunno what she did but they couldn't wait to get her out of there. She kept shouting 'Habeas corpus!' I could hear her downstairs."

"*Alcoholism— the Secret Disease,*" giggled Maureen, quoting the name of a pamphlet they had been given at school. A well-meaning guidance teacher, Mr. Glascock, had called them out of class and took them to the counseling suite. He told them about a support group for the families of alkies called Al-Anon and gave them pamphlets. They thanked him for his concern and said yes, they would definitely come and see him if they needed someone to talk to. They ripped the piss when he left.

The school had found out that Winnie was an alkie when the headmistress phoned her about Liam's disruptive behavior in class. Winnie staggered up to the school, told the school secretary she was a wanker and fell asleep in the waiting room. She couldn't be wakened. George had to come and get her, carrying her out of the school and into the car, still snoring her head off. The teachers stopped giving them a hard time after that, they looked on them pityingly and made allowances when they didn't do homework. It was insulting, the way they spoke to them, as if their lives were pathetic and always would be, as if they couldn't help themselves. Maureen would rather have been treated as a bad child than a sad one. Liam's defiance was more ambitious: he strove to be.

"I saw her yesterday," said Maureen. "She actually asked me if I did it."

"I think you should stay the fuck away from all of them," said Liam soberly. "For a while, at least, until this is over."

"Do the police know about your business—"

He interrupted her. "No. That's not for the phone really, pal," he said.

She apologized. "Did you think about what I said, the time thing?"

"Yeah, Mauri, it's garbage."

"What about the cupboard thing?"

"I'd tell them about that. Ye don't want them finding that out from someone else. How's your head?"

"Yeah, the usual. Bursting."

Liz came back and it was Maureen's turn for a skive. She locked herself into a toilet and smoked a fag, thinking her way around her flat again, sitting in her bed drinking a coffee, standing in the morning sunlight looking out of the window in the living room. She was coming back into the office by the side door as Liz took the "back in five minutes" sign down and lifted the blinds.

Two men were standing outside, waiting. Maureen stopped. There was something wrong with the picture: they were too close to the window, bending down, looking under the blind as Liz lifted it. The nearest man was wearing a lime green woolen suit under a black overcoat. The second was dressed in a multicolored ski jacket and holding a camera with a long lens. He lifted it slowly to his face, as if he were stalking a nervous bird, and pointed it at Liz. The man in the lime suit shoved a fist holding a dictaphone under the window and barked at Liz, "How do you feel about your boyfriend's murder, Miss O'Donnell?" The photographer was snapping pictures of her. The man with the dictaphone shouted again, "Did you murder him, Miss O'Donnell?"

Liz came to life. She rammed the change tray hard into the soft skin on the journalist's wrist. He yelped but held on to the dictaphone. She slammed the tray quickly backward and forward, cutting bloody parallel ridges into his hand as he tried to pull it out. The second man took photographs of her doing it. She stuck out her tongue and made a mad, angry face at him.

Gathering her wits, Maureen slid along the wall to the window, leaned over, and pulled down the blind. She stood still and Liz sat silently, listening together, afraid to move, as the men cursed and banged on the window and the side door. After a while they stopped.

"They won't really be away," whispered Liz. "They'll be across the road or something."

At Maureen's suggestion they shut up the office, left by the goods entrance and pissed off to the pictures for the afternoon. They saw a miserable film about a man who ran around shooting people.

"That was fucking rubbish," said Maureen, when they got outside.

"Oh, I liked it," said Liz, "I think he's dishy." Liz offered to cover Monday for Maureen, she owed her a shift anyway.

"That'd be great, Liz, I need a couple of days off in a row."

It was getting dark already and the streets were Saturday teatime quiet, when families gather together to watch crap telly and unpack the shopping. Even Benny's close was silent, she couldn't hear any of the usual noises of TVs or children shouting. It felt dead.

Benny had left a note on the coffee table saying that he was at an AA meeting and would be back later. Maureen turned on all the lights in the flat, put the television on in the living room and tried to think about anything that wasn't Douglas. The house began to close in on her.

She started to make something to eat, not because she was hungry, just to keep herself moving. She found some bread but couldn't see any butter in the fridge.

The phone rang. She dropped the slices of bread and galloped over to it. It was Winnie. She was trying to disguise her drunkenness with a posher accent. Some journalists had been telephoning her.

"Don't say anything, Mum, please, and for God's sake don't give them any photos."

"I did not say anything," said Winnie. "And don't you talk to them either."

"I'm hardly going to, am I?"

"Well, sometimes people do things, things they wouldn't usually do, when things get . . . a wee bit . . ." She forgot what she was talking about.

"You're pissed, then?" said Maureen.

Winnie couldn't summon the energy for a fight. "How dare you," she said, and dropped the receiver. She mumbled something about Mickey. Maureen could hear footsteps and then George asking a question in the background.

He picked up the phone. "Hello?"

"Hello, George, it's me."

"Oh, did you phone her?"

"No, she phoned me."

"Oh. She's a bit . . . a bit tired. She was trying to phone you at work this afternoon but couldn't get an answer."

"Oh, there's something wrong with the switchboard. She'd have been put through to the back office," said Maureen. It was a good lie, made up on the spur of the moment, but her voice was too high, she was talking too fast.

"All right, then," said George irrelevantly, and hung up.

She ate some dry bread dipped in milk, the best cure for an acid stomach, and sat in front of the television, flicking from station to station, trying to find something engrossing. The programs were so asinine that not one of them could hold her attention for longer than thirty seconds.

If Benny would come home they could watch telly together. She could phone Leslie but she would have to talk about everything; she couldn't face that right now.

Maureen jumped when she heard the door. It was a polite rat-rat-rat, not a familiar knock. She walked apprehensively into the hallway, hoping to fuck it wasn't the police, and peered out of the spy hole.

She had never seen him before. He was in his midtwenties, dressed in a green bomber jacket and jeans with his hair greased back off his face. He was standing casually at the door, *contrapposto*, looking directly at the spy hole, as if he knew she was there looking out at him.

Her hand was on the latch when the letter box opened slowly.

"Maureen," he whispered, his voice a smug, nasal drawl. "I know you're there, Maureen, I can hear you moving."

Suddenly terrified, she flattened herself against the wall and slid away from the door.

"I can still hear you moving," he said. "Are you going to open the door?"

"Who are you?" breathed Maureen, a thin film of sweat forming on her upper lip.

"Open the door and I'll tell you." He tried the handle.

"Fuck off."

"Go on."

She heard him stand back and snort. He must be able to hear every move she made: the door was very thin. He tiptoed down the stairs and out of the close. Maureen tried to breathe in properly. She heard steps in the close and he tiptoed back up the stairs.

He leaned into the letter box again. "Still there?" he whispered.

She looked around the bare hall for a weapon and lifted a framed photograph off the wall. She could smash it and shove a bit of glass through the letter box, into his face, into his eye maybe, and then she could phone the police.

"Are you still there?" He tittered and let the letter box snap shut. Maureen dropped the picture. It landed corner down on the carpet and the glass fell out of the frame intact. It was Perspex. "Carol Brady sent me here."

The name took a minute to register.

"She wants to meet you tomorrow."

"Where?"

"Anywhere you like. Why not make it over lunch? That's nice and civilized."

Maureen thought for a moment.

"The DiPrano," she said. It was an expensive seafood restaurant in town. She'd look like an idiot if she suggested somewhere small-time.

The letter box opened again. "What time?"

Maureen didn't know what time it opened. She didn't want to be in the middle of lunchtime rush.

"Two o'clock."

The letter box slid shut.

Maureen could hear him walking lightly down the stairs. She waited in the hall in case he came back. She waited for a long time.

Moving very slowly, she made up the settee bed and climbed in, closing her eyes and pretending to be asleep. It was only after Benny had come home, made himself something to eat and gone to bed that Maureen moved. The right side of her body was numb.

She dreamed of breakfast served after Sunday mass. It always felt like a treat because they were hungry: they couldn't eat before taking Communion. Hot, sweet tea, back in the days when everyone took sugar, bacon-egg rolls and the short-worded papers the children could read, the ones with the sex scandals in them. The family were sitting around the front room the way they used to, half-dressed for mass, with the fragile and uncomfortable bits of clothing taken off and put in their rooms: velvet jackets that would stain with the bacon fat, itchy tights and stiff shoes. They were all adults now, except for her father, who was just as she remembered him, thirty-four years old and twice as big as any of them, sitting in the best armchair, next to the window.

Maureen was lying on her back by the side of his chair. Only Michael knew she was there and he didn't look at her. She was wearing a prim flannelette nightie with a high neck, buttoned right up, tight around her throat. It had been rolled up carefully from the hem, leaving her naked from the waist down. She couldn't get up because her back was stuck to the floor. Without taking his eyes off the paper he reached down to touch her. She tried to get up, flailing her arms and legs wildly like a dying spider, but then her gut split open and a pain seared through her abdomen, making her lie still and shut her eyes.

She woke up at eleven-thirty feeling more tired than when she had fallen asleep, threw on her jeans and the Anti Dynamos T-shirt and went to the newsagent's to buy some cigarettes. A blurry photograph of Liz was on the front page of a dirty Sunday. She was looking straight into the camera and pulling a face. Maureen's name was underneath the picture. She could see herself, from the neck down, in the background, reaching over to pull down the blind.

8

MCEWAN

SHE MADE HER WAY BACK ALONG THE SHORT ROAD TO THE CLOSE mouth, reading the front page of the paper as she walked. Both doors of a shiny red hatchback opened simultaneously and two men stepped toward her. They wore dark suits and raincoats. One was tall, balding, chubby-faced, and looked seedy. The shorter of the two stepped toward her and flipped some ID. "Miss O'Donnell?"

"No," said Maureen, folding the paper the wrong way and wondering where the camera was. "My name's McQuigan. Katrine McQuigan."

The men looked at each other. If she bolted now they'd know for sure she was O'Donnell.

"Miss O'Donnell, I know it's you," the short man said. "I've met you before. I was at the locus."

"Where's 'The Locus'?"

"I was at your house when you were taken to the police station."

"I beg your pardon," said Maureen. "I've never been taken to a police station in my life."

The men looked at each other, puzzled at her lie. The tall man stepped forward and wrapped his fat hand around her upper arm. "Joe McEwan wants to see you," he said, and squeezed hard, letting her know that he wasn't going to be fucked about.

"Oh, you're *policemen*," said Maureen. "I thought you were journalists. I didn't see your badge properly."

They didn't believe her. The seedy fat man capped his hand over the top of her head, pushed her down roughly, shoved her into the back of the car and got in beside her. The other officer got into the driver's seat and caught her eye in the rearview mirror. They definitely didn't believe her.

"I did think you were journalists," she said, addressing no one in particular.

They parked on the curb outside the Stewart Street station. The seedy man held her arm as they led her up to the front door. She noticed that the other man was walking on the outside, boxing her in from the main road in case she tried to leg it. Inness, the mustachioed policeman she'd vomited on, was standing by the desk.

"Hello," he said. He had a triumphant gleam in his eye and she guessed that this interview was not going to be an easy one. The raincoat men led her through the now-familiar series of staircases and corridors to the interview room on the second floor.

Joe McEwan was not pleased to see her. The seedy officer sat her down at the table and whispered something into his ear. Without looking at her McEwan sat down, turned on the tape recorder and told it who was there. He looked at her with overt disgust. "Right, Miss O'Donnell. On Thursday you told me that you had never been to the Rainbow Clinic for any kind of treatment, is that correct?"

"Yes, I did say that."

"You 'did say that.' Was it true?"

"How do you mean?" she said, fishing for clues.

"I think the meaning's quite clear. Did you tell me the truth when you said you hadn't been to the Rainbow for treatment?"

Maureen tried to look sad. If she didn't look sorry they'd know she was trying to be clever. She thought about the dream. "No," she said, picking it over for the painful element. "It wasn't true. I lied to you."

"Why did you lie, Miss O'Donnell?"

"Because I was ashamed."

"You were ashamed of having an affair with your psychiatrist?"

It was being stuck on her back, it was the feeling of being so small and being trapped. She remembered the sensation and her eyes filled up. "I was ashamed because of the reason I went there."

"We don't care about that, Miss O'Donnell, it's not important."

"But it's important to me," she whispered.

"Look," said McEwan, "we know about your father. I'm not interested in that. You lied to me." This clearly upset him. "Do you lie all the time, Maureen? Do you know when you're lying? I spoke to your psychiatrist today, Louisa Wishart, remember her? The woman you see every Wednesday at six o'clock. Remember?"

"Louisa? How did you find out about her?"

"It was in your notes at the Rainbow."

"How did you find out about the Rainbow?"

"You were seen, in the paper."

"How could they see me in the paper?"

McEwan's face flushed very red very suddenly. He bent forward, his voice was staggeringly loud. "STOP ASKING ME QUESTIONS."

The seedy officer cringed. The color drained from McEwan's face as suddenly as it had risen. He flipped over a couple of pages in his notebook. "Let's see," he said, completely composed, "you were referred to her in February from the Rainbow Clinic and have attended the Albert ever since. Is that a bit closer to the truth?"

"Yes," said Maureen.

McEwan paused and looked at her. "I want to know why you lied to me," he said.

Maureen took out the packet of cigarettes she had bought at the shop and held it up. "May I?" she said.

McEwan nodded.

"Want one?"

He shook his head firmly but watched the cigarette as she lit it and inhaled. Her throat closed against the rough cigarette smoke, choking her momentarily, feeling like the strangling nightie in the dream.

"I lied because of the cupboard."

McEwan was intrigued. "Did you go into the cupboard?" he said softly.

Maureen got smoke in her eye. She rubbed it hard with her fingertips. "No, when I had my breakdown I was found in that cupboard."

He looked disappointed. "So?"

"Well, I didn't know what was in there, you kept asking about it, I thought it might be something that tied in with my notes, something that made it look like I did it."

"What do you think was in the cupboard?"

"I dunno. A note or something?"

"Guess again."

"Something of mine?"

He smiled enigmatically. "And that's why you lied?"

"I didn't want you to see my psychiatric notes because I thought it might make it look like me."

She watched McEwan's face. He was giving nothing away.

"Don't lie to me again," he said, gesturing for her to leave. "It makes my job much harder."

Maureen stood up. McEwan told the recorder that he was ending the interview and turned it off. He pointed at her. "And don't give my officers a false name if they come for you again."

"Yeah," said Maureen, and walked out, taking the newspaper with her.

9

CAROL BRADY

MAUREEN HAD NEVER BEEN HAPPIER TO SEE A BOTTLE OF WHISKY. She ordered a large Glenfiddich with ice and lime cordial. The barman asked her if she was joking. She had to give him step-by-step directions. "Put a large Glenfiddich in it, that's it, now fill it up with ice, now put the lime cordial in it."

"How much lime?"

"Same again."

The barman looked at the drink as he put it on the bar. "If the bar manager came in and saw me serving a malt whisky with lime juice I just—I don't know what he'd say."

"Aye, right enough," said Maureen, drinking it in three gulps and wishing Leslie was with her.

The whisky slid down her esophagus, kissed her stomach lining and sent a radiant wave rolling up her spine. The warm glow nestled in the nape of her neck. She put a tenner on the bar. "And again, please."

The barman made the simple drink with elaborate gestures. He put it down and asked what the drink was called.

"Whisky with lime in it," said Maureen, and moved to a table.

The interior of the DiPrano was original art nouveau, the décor was organic and slightly haphazard, the way art nouveau is supposed to be. The lighting was warm and the space snaked through the concave chrome-lipped bar, around a convex walnut reception desk and into a restaurant decorated with muted peach seashell frescoes.

Maureen was underdressed for the restaurant. The other customers in the oyster bar were in wools and linens. She had on the Anti Dynamos T-shirt and her black jeans. She picked up her drink and moved nearer to the ubiquitous German tourists, unabashed in their Day-Glo casual wear.

Carol Brady was two large whiskies late. She swept straight through the bar and walked into the restaurant. The greasy-haired man trotted at her heels. Brady walked up to an empty table, waited for her assistant to pull out the chair for her and sat down facing the bar. The maître d' smiled at her from behind his desk and bowed slightly.

Brady's sniggery messenger was much shorter than Maureen had supposed. He was dressed in a cheap blue suit and slip-on brown shoes with white socks. He looked out at the bar and saw Maureen watching them expectantly. He motioned for her to join them.

"Hello," said Maureen, standing uncertainly at the edge of the table clutching what was left of her whisky.

Brady gazed up at her. "Yes," she said. "Hello." She looked Maureen over. Her displeased eye settled on Maureen's chest. She read the T-shirt. "Won't you sit down?" she said.

Maureen did.

Carol Brady didn't have an attractive face. She was very wrinkled but didn't look like she'd got that way having fun. Her eyelids were drooping, resting on her stubby eyelashes and pushing them down. Behind the little curtains of skin her eyes were raw with the shocked despair of a recent death in the family. Her brown hair was thinning and meshed together with hair spray like a lacy crash helmet.

The waiter brought them leather-bound menus and Mrs. Brady ordered a large bottle of mineral water. When he had gone, Brady said that Douglas had never spoken about Maureen. "How did you come to know him?" she asked.

"We met in a pub," said Maureen weakly, feeling that her presence here was enough of a blight on Douglas's character.

Brady pretended to read her menu. "Not through his work, then." She said it as if it were a statement of fact but waited, wanting Maureen to say no.

Maureen looked uncomfortably at her menu. Joe McEwan might tell her if Maureen didn't. "He wasn't my therapist," she said.

"He wasn't your therapist then? Or ever?"

"Never."

"I see," said Brady quickly, turning a page.

Maureen closed her menu and put it on the table. "Mrs. Brady," she said, "I'm so sorry about your son."

Carol Brady ground her teeth as her eyes turned a sudden shocking pink and filled up. She blinked quickly, trying not to cry. For a tense moment Maureen thought Brady was going to start sobbing uncontrollably.

"I'm sorry," said Maureen again. "I shouldn't have said I'd meet you here. You could have come to the house."

Brady inhaled unsteadily and her grief subsided. "I'm glad we met here," she said, dabbing her nose with a linen handkerchief. Maureen waited for her to say why she was glad or why this was better than an alternative venue but she didn't.

"Let's order some food," said Brady finally. "Why don't you have the langoustine? It's very good here."

"Okay," said Maureen, eager to please. She ordered langoustine and Brady chose the finnan haddie, and the mussels for her silent PA.

"I heard that you were in Brazil," said Maureen.

Brady made a nippy face and launched into a speech about the bad flight. Both the climate and the food were too hot for her. The conference was a waste of time. She talked about her trip, detailing dull events and characters all the way through the arrival of the food and most of the way through the meal. She didn't tell the stories very well and judging by the PA's glazed expression she had told them several times before. But the purpose of the speech was not to enthrall her audience, it was to calm Carol Brady. As she talked she managed to pull herself back from a chasm of grief and got lost in a series of petty annoyances.

Maureen wasn't required to speak: all she had to do was eat and listen, but her mind kept wandering back to the bottle of Glenfiddich at the far end of the gantry. She could see it in her mind's eye, lit up from behind like a holy vision.

They were finishing the meal when Brady moved on to the press. They had hassled her mercilessly at the airport and had called her office repeatedly. "Jackals," she said angrily. "Bloody jackals, most of them."

Maureen told her about the cameraman at her work and the phone calls to her mum. Brady looked at her. "I heard that your mother is . . . unwell," she said.

"Yeah, she is unwell," said Maureen, grateful for the euphemism. "There's a thick streak of Celtic melancholia in our family. It's the Irish blood."

"Celtic melancholia?" Brady looked at her blankly.

"Alcoholism."

"I see," said Brady. "They said you were from an unsavory family."

Maureen dropped her fork. It clattered onto her plate. "Who said that about my family?"

"The police," said Brady, and smiled at her in a way that was oddly insulting. "What is an 'unsavory family'? Are they all drunks?"

"The police told you that?"

Brady placed her cutlery on the plate and dabbed at the corners of her mouth with her napkin.

"Did the police tell you I was staying with my friend in Maryhill as well? Is that how you found me?"

"I needed to see you," Brady said, as if that explained it.

"They had no business telling you about me," said Maureen, feeling picked on.

"Keep your voice down, dear," said Brady, and motioned to the waiter. "I'm assuming you want coffee?" She gestured to Maureen's glass. "Or would you rather have more whisky?"

The question was laughable. Maureen couldn't go home, her boyfriend was dead, she was having a shitty fucking lunch with his snotty mother and it was Sunday lunchtime. Of course she'd rather have a fucking whisky.

"Coffee would be fine," she said. "Thanks."

Brady gave the order and tapped the PA on the arm. "Go to the bar and wait." When he was out of earshot she leaned forward. "How could you seduce Douglas knowing he was married?"

"I didn't know he was married."

"Were you planning to take Douglas away from Elsbeth?"

"I didn't 'plan' to take him away. Douglas was an adult, he made his own decisions."

"Douglas was a child. If you knew him better you would have known that," she said, hinting at a familial subtext that was none of Maureen's business.

They regained their composure while the coffee things were placed on the table.

Brady poured a touch of cream into hers and stirred it quickly, rhythmically. "Did Douglas pay for your flat?"

"No," said Maureen indignantly.

"I suppose he gave you money?" continued Brady. "Is that why you never bothered to get a decent job?"

"Look, I'd only known Douglas for the past eight months. I've had that job for three years."

"But you have no ambition," said Brady disparagingly. "You've never sought promotion."

"It isn't everyone's ambition to become an authority figure."

Brady looked skeptically at her. "Oh, come on now." She sipped at her coffee with a tiny drawstring mouth.

Maureen was tired of Brady's relentlessly genteel hostility. She put her coffee cup down, shoved it away and lifted what was left of her whisky. She took a generous mouthful, watching over the rim of the glass as Brady sneered at her. "I can understand that you're angry, Mrs. Brady," she said softly, "and I'm sorry for what you've been through, but that doesn't make me responsible for Douglas's behavior."

"Did he give you money?"

"Why do you keep going back to that?"

"Why won't you answer *that?*"

"He didn't give me money," she said. "He never gave me money."

Brady looked across the table with her sour eyes and Maureen suddenly wanted to get the fuck away from her and never see her again.

Brady softened her voice. "You're lying to me. You've lied to the police and now you're lying to me. Were you drunk the night Douglas was killed?"

"Is that why you're so angry with me?"

"Did you kill him?"

Maureen sat back in her chair and stared at Brady. "Do you think I killed him?"

"Yes," she said certainly, meeting Maureen's gaze. "I do."

"How could you sit here with me if you thought that?"

"I wanted to meet you, just once, to see."

"Do you think I'd come here if I did it? Do you think I could eat food with you if I did it?"

Brady broke off eye contact. "People don't always remember what they do when they're drunk."

Maureen put down her glass. "I think I should leave," she said.

Brady grabbed her by the wrist, pulling her closer so that their faces were inches apart. "They'll catch you, you know," she said. "They'll get you, and if they don't get you, I'll get you."

"Are you threatening me with something?"

"What do you think?"

"Look," said Maureen, "I'm nobody and I have nothing. There's nothing you can do to hurt me." She twisted her wrist and freed it, threw some money on the table and walked out of the restaurant.

She went straight to a phone box in Buchanan Street and phoned around for Liam but she couldn't find him anywhere. Finally she left a message on his machine telling him to clean the house from top to bottom and take the rubbish out because his father-in-law might come for a visit. If he didn't he'd be in a lot of trouble. It was urgent. She hoped the message was obtuse without being obscure.

She bought an overpriced bottle of whisky from a pub near the station, went back to Benny's house and fulfilled Carol Brady's worst expectations by drinking it neat from the bottle and passing out on the settee in front of *Songs of Praise*. She woke up at three in the morning with a spinning head and had to sit in an armchair for over an hour, sipping milky tea and wishing the nausea away before she managed to fall asleep again.

10

BENNY'S LUMBER JACKET

SHE WAS DREAMING A VAGUE DREAM WITH LOUD BANGING IN IT.
Someone was banging on the front door. She tried to open her
eyes but the sunlight scratched them like sandpaper. She waited for
a minute, hoping Benny would answer it or they'd stop it and go
away but he didn't and they didn't and she couldn't sleep through
the noise. She pulled the duvet around her and felt her way along
the wall to the front door, keeping one of her eyes shut. It was Una,
with Alistair in tow. "Mum phoned me last night. She was as drunk
as a lord, and she said you were missing." Una's voice was louder
than most people's. She didn't shout but her voice had extraordinary
natural projection.

"Well, you've found me now," said Maureen, wishing she was
anywhere other than here now, feeling anything other than this.

"I can see that," said Una.

Maureen raised her hand. One of her eyes was stuck shut with
sleep and when she spoke she could feel dried drool cracking on
her chin. "Una," she said slowly, "I am hung over today. If you need
to speak, please do it quietly. If you can't speak quietly please leave."

She dropped her hand and went into the kitchen. Alistair and Una followed her in. Maureen poured a pint of water from the tap and drank it. A note from Benny was sitting on the table. It said he had gone to the university and that Maureen was a drunken bum.

"I can't believe it," said Una, making a bad job of keeping her voice down. "What are you doing here alone? And look at the mess in here. Where's Benny?"

"He's out," said Maureen, with great effort.

"Maureen, you look terrible. I've been trying to get in touch with you but you've been out all the time."

Maureen's mouth flooded with salt water. She bombed it down the hall to the bathroom and threw up across the cistern. Una was at her back. "Dear God, Maureen, go to bed."

She fussed Maureen back down the hall and put her in Benny's bed. The room smelled strongly of Benny's Brylcreem. Una pulled the curtains against the ferocious sunlight and shut the door quietly.

When Maureen woke up again the radio in the kitchen had been tuned to a pop station and was making an irritating, upbeat noise. Testing her head, she slowly pulled herself upright and opened her eyes. She wouldn't be able to eat for a while but her stomach felt strong enough to take a cup of tea.

Una and Alistair were sitting with their coats on drinking tea in the kitchen. They had cleared a space on the table.

"Sit down," said Una, and turned off the radio. She made Maureen a cup of tea. "Have you been to the doctor?"

Una lived an ordered life, she believed in medicine; doctors were the lieutenants of absolute good. When Maureen was found in the cupboard she had had a terrible shock and wanted her put away immediately and for a very long time.

"I went on Friday," said Maureen. "I'm off work but she said I'm coping wonderfully. She's given me some medication." This didn't seem to be enough to assuage Una's fears. "And she's scheduled extra sessions for me."

"Good. Have you seen Mum?"

"Aye, I saw her on Friday."

"Did she say anything?"

"Anything about what?"

Una blushed.

"Look," said Maureen wearily, "if Mum's starting fights with me behind my back I don't want to know about it. Rope me in later, okay, Una?"

"Okay, then," said Una. "The police came to see me."

"Did they ask about Liam?"

"No, just you."

"That's good. I don't want him involved."

Una shifted in her chair. She knew what Liam did for a living but she didn't like to hear it said out loud. "The papers have been phoning everyone about you."

"I know. They came to my work."

"Oh dear."

"Mum actually asked me whether I'd done it," said Maureen. "I couldn't believe it."

Una stood up suddenly. "We'd better be going now," she said.

"Oh, come on, Una," said Maureen, as emphatically as she could manage, "what has Mum been saying about me?"

"She said she's your mum," said Una, and sat down, "and she'll stand by you, whatever you've done."

"But I didn't do it, I told her I didn't."

Una coughed, politely.

"Una, what did she say?"

Una spoke quietly, like a child caught in a lie and made to finger her co-conspirators. "She said you might not remember properly." She paused awkwardly, waiting for Maureen to lose her temper.

Maureen thought about it with the tired, apathetic calm of a bad hangover. "Mum's nuts," she said.

Una laughed loud and high with relief.

By the time Una and Alistair left it was six o'clock. Maureen phoned Liam.

"Mauri? What the fuck's going on? I came looking for you and Benny let me in and you were crashed out on the settee with an empty half bottle on the floor."

"Have you tidied up?"

"Yeah, totally. Are you all right?"

"God, aye, I suppose. I'm hung over."

"What was the message about?"

"I saw Carol Brady yesterday. She said the police called our family unsavory and I just thought . . . you know, it might be about you. I might have panicked but she was pretty scary."

"No, it was good thinking."

"She asked me to go for lunch yesterday. She thinks I killed him."

"*You?*"

"I don't feel too good, Liam," said Maureen. Her voice was trembling.

"I'll come over. I'll get videos out and you can forget about it for tonight."

Benny came back just in time to catch Liam skinning up on the coffee table while Maureen watched the trailers to *Hard Boiled,* a kung-fu movie with lots of shooting in it. He had his good brown leather jacket on, the one he wore when he went to clubs looking for a lumber. They teased him about it for a while but he wasn't up for it. He was fractious and worried about his exams. He said he'd seen the paper and Liz could sue for defamation because they'd called her by Maureen's name.

"Yeah?" said Maureen. "Why's that defamatory?"

"Because you're a notorious character," said Benny.

Benny wasn't allowed any mood-altering substances because he was in AA. He insisted that he didn't mind them smoking hash in the house but he kept waving the smoke away from his face. Liam told him not to be such a tight-arse and his tense mood deepened.

When the films were over Liam went home and Benny hurried off to bed. Maureen sat in the dark on the edge of the settee and tried to cry but her eyes just stung and burned.

The next morning they were puffy and sore. She stared at herself in the bathroom mirror. She looked mad. Anyone with an ounce of wit would think she had killed Douglas. She washed her face, splashing cold water on her eyes, hoping to soothe them. She wanted to go to work, she was missing Liz, but she comforted herself with the thought that it was Tuesday and she'd be seeing Leslie later.

She phoned Liz to tell her she could sue for defamation. Liz said that the booth was besieged by journalists and sensation seekers coming for a peek at her. Mr. Scobie kept trying to shoo them away but the minute he went inside they came back. He told her to shut the ticket office until he could find someone to take her place. So she was sitting alone in the dark booth, answering the single daily call for the hypnotist-show tickets because he wouldn't let her go home without docking her pay. She said that the photograph in the paper made her look as if she had a double chin. "He's dead pissed off with you, Maureen."

"Yeah, well, he's gonnae be more pissed off, because I'm taking a couple of days off."

Liz inhaled sharply. "Shall I tell him?"

"Yeah, go on. I'll see ye later, yeah?"

"See ye, Maureen."

11

SHIRLEY

IT SEEMED TO BE OVERCAST AND RAINING EVERY TIME MAUREEN WENT
to the Rainbow Clinic. She got off the bus and crossed the empty
dual carriageway, following the ten-foot-high wall around to the
driveway.

The clinic operated out of a converted creamery, built as part of
the Levanglen Lunatic Asylum estate. It consisted of a long, single-
story building with Portakabins at the back, where the admin was
done. Maureen walked in the front door, went straight past the pay
phones, through the main foyer and down the short corridor to the
waiting room. The walls were painted yellow and covered in posters of puppies and kittens and monkeys. When it was full of patients
the maniacally cheerful room looked like a sarcastic joke.

Straight across from the entry door, beyond Shirley's desk, a
set of fire doors led through to the corridor where Angus, Douglas
and Dr. Murray's offices were. Douglas had spoken of Murray often,
usually in a less than loving manner. They had had a fight over ex-
tending the Rainbow's client group to include patients being moved
back into the community from a long-term hospital to the east of

the city. Douglas thought that they didn't have the resources to deliver the service but Murray was determined to spearhead the development and get his name on all the letters. Douglas said he was disgustingly self-promoting.

The waiting room was empty except for a young girl sitting in the corner, pretending to read a battered copy of *Good Housekeeping*. She was wearing a leather jacket, combat trousers and big boots. She seemed to have cut her hair herself: it was chewed short and uneven with long lumps sticking up at the back. Her left jacket sleeve was deliberately pushed back to display an angry grid of slash scars on her inner wrist. Visible scars are a good way to stop casual approaches from the happy and content. Maureen turned away and sat down in a plastic chair against the other wall.

She had met many depressives in hospital. They were interesting company when she could coax them to talk: they seemed more in touch with reality than most people. Depressives, in full flight, can correctly estimate their chances of getting cancer, being the victim of a sexual attack or winning the lottery. They don't dilute to taste.

The fire door to the offices opened and Dr. Murray bustled into the waiting room carrying a sheaf of files. He put half of the bundle on Shirley's desk and walked out to the main foyer with the rest. The combat girl watched him leave. Maureen hoped she wasn't waiting to see him. He hadn't even acknowledged her presence. The foyer door opened and Shirley came in, carrying a tin tray with steaming mugs and cream and sugar set on it. She put the tray down on the desk before looking up and seeing Maureen. "Helen?" she said, surprised to see her. "What are you doing here?"

Maureen motioned for Shirley to follow her out to the foyer corridor. "Shirley, my name isn't Helen, it's Maureen O'Donnell."

"*You're* Maureen O'Donnell? But there was a picture of her in the paper yesterday."

"I know. I know. They took a picture of the wrong person."

Shirley didn't bother to mask her incredulity. Maureen wasn't particularly offended, Shirley must have seen some sights in her time and an ex-patient posing as the most recent city saddo wouldn't be beyond the bounds of possibility.

Maureen took out some ID. "It really is me. Look."

Shirley glanced at the library card and Maureen's cashpoint card, turning them over and looking at the back for extra clues.

"Okay, right, you might not believe me, but assuming I am who I say I am, will you answer some questions for me?"

Shirley thought about it. "I dunno. It's not about anything sick, is it?"

"No, no, I just wanted to know who could get to see my file here."

"Well . . . I'll go along with it but I'm stopping if you ask me anything weird, and I don't want to talk to you about Douglas. If you are Maureen O'Donnell then you probably know a lot more about him than I ever did, and some journalists have been hanging around and asking about him. Okay?"

"Tops, Shirley."

Shirley relaxed, resting her back against the wall in the dimly lit corridor.

"Okay," said Maureen. "First thing, how did the police find out I was here for treatment? I didn't tell them."

Shirley paused, forming her answer cautiously. "All I know is that the police phoned security early on Sunday morning and got them to let them into the offices."

"Did they know what they were looking for?"

"Yeah, they logged into the system, called up the right file and printed it out. I checked. It was the only file they called up."

"What would the file be called?"

"Name and date."

"Would it have been filed under Helen?"

"Yes."

"They couldn't have used a different field to call it up?"

"No, it's the old DOS system. Those are the only fields we use. We were sold the system before any of us knew what it was like."

"So they not only knew I'd been here, they knew what name I used when I was here?"

"Yes."

"I didn't tell a soul what name I'd used," said Maureen, putting her ID cards back into her wallet. "What sort of information would be on that file? Would it have notes from the therapy sessions?"

"No," Shirley said definitely. "It's just an admin file. It's only got the appointment times, who saw you, where you went, things like that."

"How could they know I was here, Shirley?"

"I assumed that someone working here had seen the picture in the paper, remembered the girl's face and telephoned them, but I suppose it couldn't be the case if you're the Maureen they're talking about."

"I am, Shirley, honestly."

"Well, that makes more sense," said Shirley. "I couldn't understand how the girl in the picture could have been attending the clinic last January without me meeting her."

"Yeah, well, she wasn't."

"Was she ever here?"

"No, never been anywhere near." Maureen picked her lip. Someone already knew her but they were pretending they'd recognized her picture in the paper.

"I heard that someone was having an affair with a patient," Shirley murmured.

"Who told you that?" said Maureen, feeling embarrassed, as if she had disgraced Douglas.

"One of the cleaning staff."

"Right," said Maureen, anxious to move the conversation on.

"Said she walked in on them. They were at it." Shirley suddenly noticed how uncomfortable she was making Maureen. "Sorry," she said, "it's not important now, I suppose. I just thought it was someone else."

Maureen was incredulous. "They were fucking in the clinic?" she said. "She walked into them in the clinic?"

Shirley bit her thumb and thought about it. "I thought her name was Iona but that could have been a false name."

"That wasn't me." Maureen snorted.

Shirley stiffened and stood up straight. "Actually, I don't really know who you are, I don't want to talk about this anymore."

"Okay, whatever," said Maureen, surprised that Shirley wasn't more shocked by the story. "Um, how many people work here?"

Shirley thought for a minute. "About fiftyish, including job shares and cleaning staff."

"God, fifty people?"

"Yeah. Could be more, actually, I'm just guessing."

"Another thing," said Maureen. "The police seem to think that I saw Douglas instead of Angus. Do you know how they could have got that idea?"

"Well, they questioned nearly everyone here. To be honest, everyone was looking at the paper in the staff room and remembering the girl in the picture. One of the nurses said she'd tried to hit her once."

Maureen smiled. "So, basically, God alone knows what they've been told."

"Basically, yes."

"Surely it would say I saw Angus on my file?"

"Well, yes, it would, now you mention it. I don't know how they got that idea."

"And would it say who I was referred to in the file?"

"Yes, it would."

"Cheers, Shirley, you've been a great help."

"Would you go in and see Angus? He's been hit terribly hard

by this. He'd be delighted to see you. You could take his coffee in to him."

"He'd be delighted to see me now that I'm involved in a murder investigation?"

"Helen, you left here and never came back or ended up across the road in Levanglen. As far as we're concerned you're a success."

They went back into the waiting room. The combat girl looked up. "Won't be long now," Shirley said to her. "The doctor's just finishing off his lunch." She stirred three sugars and a drop of cream into one of the mugs of coffee and handed it to Maureen. "I take it you can remember where the office is?"

"Sure."

Maureen walked down the corridor, passing Douglas's door and feeling slightly guilty, as if he might step out any minute and give her trouble for coming back here. She knocked on Angus's door and he called for her to come in. "Hello," he said, looking at her. He didn't seem to know her. He stood up and came over to greet her. "I haven't seen you for a while," he said, fishing for clues, "have I?"

Maureen said he hadn't.

The room was dark and comfortable and stank of fags. It should have been bright but was kept in perpetual dawn by the pall of smoke and the half-closed vertical blinds. Against the near wall stood two leather armchairs with high backs, a rickety coffee table between them with an ashtray and a box of tissues on it. Behind the farthest armchair stood a six-foot rubber plant.

Angus was in his midforties. His hair was graying and receding pleasantly, just enough to make him look a little weather-beaten. He dressed like a down-at-heel laird, in worn tweed jackets and balding corduroys. He chain-smoked and his love of tobacco had created an immediate bond between them. During their sessions they'd sat in the armchairs, leaning forward, huddled together, puffing hard as Maureen talked him through the worst of her childhood, giving one another lights and passing the ashtray to and fro.

Angus held his fag between his teeth, pushed his steel-framed glasses back up his nose and smiled a confused, expectant little smile, waiting for her to introduce herself.

Maureen grinned and handed him the mug of coffee. "Shirley asked me to give you this."

He took the mug and put it down on the coffee table, turning back to her and shaking her hand.

The tall rubber plant had been flourishing when she had been here before but its leaves were speckled with ominous crisp brown patches. "Your lovely plant's not well," she said.

"Oh, I know, I can't think what's wrong with it. I've tried pruning it back and everything. I thought it might be the cigarette smoke but I wash it once a month. I suppose they just die sometimes." He stroked one of the healthy leaves with his forefinger and suddenly looked up her. "Helen!" he said.

She laughed. "You couldn't place me there for a minute, could you?"

"No, no, I couldn't, but I remember you now!" He put out his fag in the ashtray and held her hand in both of his, shaking it warmly. "Helen, how are you?"

"Not bad." She smiled.

"You look fantastic. Hey, look, sit down, sit down." He bustled her backward into one of the armchairs. "I'm embarrassed, I wouldn't have forgotten any other time but just now . . . Did you hear about Mr. Brady from across the hall?"

"He was murdered."

"He was."

She could see baby tears nestling on the rims of his eyes. He sat down and lit another fag, inhaling deeply. "It's been a nightmare," he said softly.

"Were you close?"

He nodded. "We've known each other for years and years. It's unthinkable. Even for his clients . . . The last thing the long-term patients need is to have to go over their case histories to a locum . . . We're trying to cover them ourselves but we're not exactly at our operational best . . . None of us can take it in." He smiled unhappily. "We had to cancel the grief-counseling group Dougie used to take. We didn't want to tell them what had happened but we had to."

He saw that her hands were empty and pushed his packet of cigarettes across the table. She took one out and looked up as she was lighting it. Angus was watching her. "You see," he smiled, "I do remember you."

"Actually, that's why I'm here. Because of Douglas."

He looked at her, not quite understanding.

"My name isn't Helen. That was an assumed name I used for coming here. My real name is Maureen O'Donnell. Does that mean anything to you?"

"God's sakes, I read the papers. But there was a photograph."

"Yeah, it's a girl I work with. They took a picture of the wrong person."

He gave a wry smile. "It's not like the papers to get things wrong, is it?"

"I didn't know they were that incompetent."

"They've been harassing the staff *and the clients*," he said indignantly. "The bloody clients."

"They're wild, aren't they?"

"So, you're Maureen. I wanted to see you about this affair you were having with Douglas. It was highly unethical of him, it was very wrong. I wanted you to know that."

"Well, it was kind of mutual, really."

"Did you meet here?"

She told him the story about waiting at the bus stop and Douglas picking her up, leaving out the vigorous sex and skewing the story so that Douglas seemed guilt free.

Angus shook his head. "No, you were vulnerable. We had a duty to care for you and Douglas breached that." He squeezed her hand. "It was wrong."

She could smell the smoke on his breath. He let go of her hand and leaned back. "They found him in your house, then?" he said. "How are you coping?"

"I'm invincible since I saw you."

He blushed a little and tapped his fag. "No one's invincible to the shock of something like this," he said sadly. "Are you still seeing Louisa Wishart at the Albert?"

"Yeah."

"She treating you well? Can you talk to her?"

Maureen nodded. "Fine, fine. Listen, Angus, can I ask you something?"

"Fire away."

"The police seem to think that Douglas was my therapist. Do you know why they might think that?"

"Aye," he said. "They asked whether you were my patient but I didn't recognize the picture from the paper so I said you weren't. The files aren't always complete and they're kept on computer now so we can't even go by the handwriting on the notes the way we used to. I hope you told them it was me."

"No, I didn't, but I will."

"Good. That'll make a difference to the way Douglas is remembered."

"Angus, do you have any idea who could have done this?"

"Do you know something," he said, sighing heavily as his eyes brimmed over, "I haven't got the first fucking idea who'd do this." She'd never heard him swear properly before. He looked at her and paused.

"Do you know who did it?" His voice was higher than usual: it sounded like an accusation.

"I've no idea either," she said quietly.

They finished their cigarettes quickly and in silence. Maureen wished she hadn't come here.

"I'll have to get on," said Angus. "I have a patient coming in ten minutes and I haven't been over her notes yet."

He stood up, moved to the door and opened it for her. "Any time you want to come and see us again phone Shirley, okay?"

She wanted to shout at him or cry or something but she couldn't think of anything to say. As she slipped past him into the corridor she muttered to him, "I didn't do it, Angus."

"I know," he said unconvincingly. "I didn't mean that."

He stepped back into his office and shut the door, leaving her alone in the corridor.

The bus stop to the town was directly across the dual carriageway facing the main hospital gates and the long, high wall. Concrete blocks of flats loomed at the top of a grass embankment behind it. It was the bus stop Douglas had picked her up from on the first night they had slept together. A sweet old lady in full makeup was waiting in the shelter. She caught Maureen's eye when she came in and smiled pleasantly. "Oh, this rain," she said.

"Aye," said Maureen, hoping it wasn't going to lead to a full-blown conversation. " 'S miserable."

The dual carriageway was deserted in front of them. A figure appeared across the road at the gates of the hospital, a fat, bespectacled woman with short, dirty, flat hair. Her blue plastic jacket flapped open, showing a glittery gold halter-neck top worn without a bra. She needed one. Her large breasts washed fluidly around her middle. She was trying to get across the road but was stuck at "look left, look right."

Maureen stepped out of the shelter and called to her. "Suicide, come on!"

Suicide Tanya stared across at her.

"Come over the road now," shouted Maureen.

Tanya walked halfway across and began to look left and right again.

"It's clear, Tanya, you can come over."

Tanya came to life, belted across the road and stopped on the grass verge behind the bus stop. She turned, looked at Maureen through her rain-speckled glasses and pointed a tobacco-stained finger an inch away from her nose. "I know you," she shouted. "Helen!"

Suicide Tanya was an ageless, grizzled woman with, as her nickname suggested, a habit of attempting suicide. She was known as Suicide Tanya all over the city: all the emergency services knew her, or of her. She was forever being dragged out of the Clyde at low tide, having her stomach pumped clean of bizarre substances and being made to get off the railway tracks at main-line stations. They met in the yellow waiting room at the Rainbow. Maureen was in a state on her second visit to the clinic. She had been having panic attacks all morning, had misread her watch and turned up an hour early. Tanya came in and sat next to her, shouting her life story. She was unhappy and kept doing bad things, so they gave her pills that made her simple and fat, but she preferred it that way because *they can't arrest you for being fat, Tanya.* It was one of her many strange habits of speech: she repeated things other people had said to her without having the wit to plagiarize properly and change the wording or the intonation. She had to come to the Rainbow once a week to see Douglas and get her medication from the psychiatric nurse—she couldn't be trusted with more than a week's supply at a time.

She huddled into the shelter and spoke to the waiting lady. "I couldn't see right," she shouted, "because my glasses got rain on them."

The lady realized that Tanya was a bit mental—it wouldn't have taken a hardened professional to spot it: she had a booming voice and the concentration span of a spliffed goldfish. The lady turned away and walked, as if casually, out of the shelter to stand in the drizzling rain.

"Did you see that?" shouted Suicide, pointing at the nervous woman through the glass. "Snobby!"

"Just leave it, Suicide," said Maureen.

"You rude cunt!"

"Don't shout at her, she might be very shy."

Tanya processed the idea for a minute. "Hello. Are you very shy?"

Maureen tugged at her sleeve. "Don't, now, Tanya. Leave it, eh?"

"It's a shame if she is shy. She'll get lonely. *You have to make your own fun, ya fat mug, ye.*"

The bus into town pulled up out of nowhere. Tanya got on and showed her pass to the driver, explaining that she got a pass because she didn't keep well. The driver said he could see that and she was to go and sit down. The lady from the bus stop declined the offer when Maureen stepped back to let her on first. She waited until they were seated and chose a place as far away from Tanya as possible.

Tanya spotted the lady as the bus pulled away. "She's her from the bus stop."

"Aye, right enough, Suicide."

"Hello!"

"Aye, leave it now, Tanya. You've already said hello."

"Have I?"

"Aye."

"Sorry!"

The lady looked out of the window, her neck stiff with alarm. Tanya arranged herself next to Maureen, straightening the rumples out of the gold lamé top, pulling it over her flat breastbone and down over the large breasts sitting on the roll of her belly. She scratched at some food stuck on the front.

"I like your top, Suicide. Where did you get it?"

"In a shop. Douglas is dead," she said.

"I know."

"His mum is an MP."

"MEP."

"Yes, and I couldn't see him."

"When you went for your appointment?"

"Yes. He was gone."

"What time is your appointment?"

"*Tuesday at eleven, Tuesday at eleven, new time, try to remember.*"

"What time was it last week?"

"It's always the same because I can't remember."

"Yeah, I know, but what was the old time, before the new time?"

"*Wednesday at one, Wednesday at one.*"

"So you didn't get to see him last week, then?"

"Yes. The police said it was because he was dead. I was there for ages because Douglas didn't come."

"That's a shame, Tanya."

"My neighbors banged on the wall all weekend and I needed to tell him that."

"That's a shame. Did you get to tell someone?"

"I told the police. They don't listen. They asked me about Douglas but they don't listen."

"How don't they listen?"

"They just don't. They think I'm daft. He said thank you but I saw him laughing at me. He had a mustache."

"I know that policeman. He was rude to me too."

"Yes. I don't like him . . . My pal seen him."

"Your pal saw the man with the mustache?"

"No. She seen him. She seen him when he was dead."

"She saw Douglas?"

Tanya nodded frantically.

"When he was dead?"

"Aye," said Tanya. "Then."

"Was he a ghost?"

Tanya looked at her askance. "There's no such thing as ghosts."

"No, sorry, you're right. There's no such thing."

"There's no ghosts. Only on the telly."

"How did she see him when he was dead, then?"

"Eh?"

"Your friend who saw him, how did she see him?"

Tanya looked at her as if she was daft. "With her eyes."

"He was standing in front of her?"

Tanya opened her eyes wide and stuck out her lower jaw at Maureen, angry at being asked so many pointless questions. "He was standing in front of her."

"When he was dead?"

"Aye, when he was dead."

Maureen was still confused. "I'm sorry, Tanya, I don't understand."

"He was dead and she seen him."

"When?"

"When they asked me about—"

"No, when did she see him?"

"When he couldn't see me because he was dead."

"Wednesday at one?"

"*Wednesday at one.*"

"What's the name of your friend, Tanya, the friend who saw Douglas?"

"Siobhain. I meet her at the day center. She's fat now too."

"What's her surname?"

"Why are you asking me that?"

"I thought I knew her."

"Oh."

"Do you know Siobhain's surname?"

"McCloud."

Maureen wrote the name on the back of her bus ticket. "Is that the day center in Dennistoun?"

"Yes."

"Does Siobhain go there a lot?"

Suicide snorted. "*She practically lives there!*"

On the way into the town Tanya made rash comments about the other passengers at the top of her voice. Not a soul looked back at her. She told Maureen a complicated story about an Alsatian on top of her telly that smashed. Maureen thought she was describing a hallucination until she realized that the Alsatian was a china ornament. When they got off the bus Maureen took her to a fancy-goods shop and bought her a replacement. "That's a better one," bawled Tanya at a frightened man in the shop. "That's got a chain on it."

Tanya wanted to go with Maureen. Maureen had to explain several times that she was going to the university library and she needed to have a ticket to get in.

"I can't get in because I don't have a ticket."

"That's it, Tanya. You need a ticket."

"Buy me one."

"You can't buy them."

"No?"

"No, they have to give them to you."

"Will they give me one?"

"No."

"Why?"

"You're too tall."

Tanya insisted on waiting with Maureen until the bus came. Maureen got on the bus and waved eagerly through the window but Suicide ignored her.

In the library basement she asked an assistant for some help finding the salary scales for clinical psychologists. The assistant gave her a professional publication from behind the desk. He would have been on about forty-five K. She thanked the woman and caught the lift up to the top floor.

She pulled out the past papers and skimmed through them for news of the ecology conference in Brazil. It had been opened officially on Wednesday morning by the president. The story was accompanied by a picture of Carol Brady and some other people in expensive clothes.

Glasgow University library is eight stories high and built at the top of Gilmorehill. The walls are floor-to-ceiling smoke-tinted glass, giving the sprawled city below an unreal quality. She sat down at a table and looked out over the neo-Gothic university building, down to the river, past Govan to the airport, looking for the lightbulb factory far to the west, next to the motorway. It's possibly the most beautiful building in Glasgow. She couldn't see it.

Angus was the only therapist she had ever felt understood her properly, the only one she had ever connected with, and he thought she'd killed Douglas. He wasn't even angry with her. He must think she was very mental. She folded the newspapers carefully and shoved them back in the pile. She left the library and caught the bus back to Benny's house, hungry for the sight of him and his casual kindness.

12

MAGGIE

THEY HAD NEVER SEEN LIAM SO ANGRY. THE POLICE HAD RAIDED HIS house. He had been lying in bed with Maggie when they kicked the front door in and four officers stormed upstairs into the bedroom and found them naked, covered with a sheet. They pulled the sheet away, made them get out of bed, watching as they dressed, and took Liam downstairs.

Because of Maureen's timely warning there was nothing incriminating for the police to find, but they had brought tracker dogs with them and found the scent everywhere. They gutted the house, pulling up floorboards and digging up bits of the garden. Liam said the house was un-fucking-inhabitable; it looked like 25 Cromwell Street.

Maggie sobbed hysterically for half an hour and then phoned her mum in Newton Mearns, begging her to come and fetch her. Until this point her mother had believed that Liam was a music-business entrepreneur. Maggie didn't mention the police on the phone, her mum thought they'd had a fight. Good mother that she was, she dropped what she was doing and drove all the way across town to get Maggie. Nearing the house she saw the police cars and, good citizen that she was, pulled over, asking them what it was about and could she help. They told her. She took her daughter home and forbade her to see Liam again.

"They can't trash my fucking house and just leave it like that," said Liam aggressively. He turned on Benny. "Can I sue them for compensation?"

"There must be some way," said Benny, trying to placate him, "given that you didn't commit a crime, but I can't think what it would be."

"Those fuckers can just rip my house apart and walk away? That's fucking outrageous."

"Why don't you write to your MEP?" said Maureen, trying to lighten the prickly atmosphere.

"That's not fucking funny!" shouted Liam.

"Don't shout at me!" shouted Maureen. "It's not my fault."

"Well, if you hadn't—" Liam realized how bad he was being and corrected himself. "I won't be able to work for ages."

"I have to tell you," said Benny authoritatively, "it'd be stupid for you to deal now." He said that because the police had found the scent everywhere, they would be back time and time again until they caught him out. Even if he moved house they'd still be on his back. "I wouldn't even pass a spliff at a party now if I were you."

Liam dropped onto the settee and covered his face with his hands. "Jesus Christ," he said, his voice muffled, "what the fuck am I going to do now?"

Maureen sat down beside him. "Come on, now," she said. "You're a bright guy, you've got loads of capital in the house and you've saved some money, haven't you?"

"A bit."

"It's a big bit, isn't it?"

He shrugged. "S'pose."

"Well, we'll think of something."

"Shite, I've got a big deal coming off next week as well."

"Don't do it, Liam, eh?" Maureen pleaded.

"That would be really stupid," said Benny.

Liam shook his head. "If Joe McEwan and that mob hear about it I'll be completely fucked."

"But they didn't find anything in the house," said Maureen.

Benny and Liam glanced sidelong at each other. "That's fuck all to do with it, Maureen," said Liam. "If they find out I'm dealing there's no way they'll believe that Douglas's murder had nothing to do with me. The police think all professional criminals are capable of anything."

"Oh," said Maureen. "Sorry, I didn't think."

"*You* even thought it was me."

"I didn't think it was you, I just thought you might know something about it."

"God," he said. "You're a stupid cow sometimes."

"There's no need for name-calling," said Maureen.

Her comment struck Liam as profoundly funny. He laughed and kissed the top of her head. "You're precious," he said warmly.

He got Maureen to phone for him. When Maggie's mum answered she asked for Maggie and handed the receiver to Liam when she came on the line. He took the phone out to the hall and shut the door. Benny caught her eye and made a panicked face. Maureen stood up. "I know, I know," she mouthed.

She kept her eye on the door and snuck over to him. "Mr. Mood Swing, eh? How long's he been here?" she whispered.

"About an hour," Benny whispered back. "He was going mental when he first got here. I had to calm him—"

They could hear him ringing off. Maureen darted back to the settee. Liam came back into the living room and slammed the phone down on the side table. He looked furious. "She's gutted," he said. "She told her mother she'd smoked hash once and now she thinks Maggie's a drug-soaked gangster's moll."

Benny was puzzled. "Why did she tell her mother that?"

"Because she asked," said Liam with a superior air. "And Maggie's family don't lie to each other all the time."

"My God," said Benny. "They must hate each other."

Maureen offered to make Liam a cup of tea but he refused it, saying if he wanted a fucking cup of fucking tea he'd make it his fucking self.

"It'll be okay," she said.

"Stop fucking saying that!" shouted Liam.

"I've only said it once!" Maureen shouted back.

Benny gave her a look. She wasn't good at defusing Liam's temper, she always ended up shouting back at him. Benny said he was welcome to sleep on his floor for a while, until the house was fixed up. Liam flatly refused. Benny said he was going out for some milk anyway and slammed the front door behind him.

"You've pissed him off now," Maureen said.

Liam didn't reply but he sat down next to her on the settee. It was as close to an apology as she would get. "Did you see the picture in the paper yesterday?" she said.

"Yeah," said Liam, "I saw ye."

"It wasn't me."

Liam looked worried. "Aye, it was," he said. "You were in the ticket booth and everything, Mauri."

"Did you buy it and get a good look?"

"Well, naw, I wouldn't give them my money."

"It wasn't a picture of me, it was a photo of Liz."

Liam shifted uncomfortably and avoided her eye. She stomped across the room to her rucksack and pulled out the folded front page of the newspaper. She opened it out and handed it to Liam, sat down and watched him as he examined the picture. "Is that me?" she said.

Liam handed it back to her. "It's not you."

"Yeah, and I'm not responsible for you getting busted either. I want that one nipped in the bud."

"I know that. I'm sorry, pet, I was angry."

"Everyone I meet thinks I did it," she said.

"Everyone *I* meet thinks *I* did it," said Liam. "It's like being at school again."

"Yeah, we're a pair of wrong 'uns."

They looked at each other. Liam reached out solemnly and took her hand in his. "I'm gonnae go about saying you did it and put myself in the clear."

Maureen laughed and Liam grinned back.

"Do me a favor." She held up the newspaper. "Look at this picture again and tell me, if you didn't know me all that well, could you mistake Liz for me?"

Liam glanced at it. "No. I thought it was you because of the booth."

"Liz doesn't look like me?"

"No. Her hair's the same length as yours but that's about it."

She folded the picture away and slipped it back into her bag. "How's Mum?"

Liam's face wilted with a despondency familiar from childhood. "You don't want to know, Mauri."

Benny opened the front door and stepped into the hall. Leslie was standing behind him. She looked into the living room and saw Maureen and Liam sitting close by one another on the settee. "All right, Mauri?" she said, skipping past Benny into the living room. "You're in the paper."

"What, again?"

"Yeah."

Leslie had the *Evening Tribune*. The headline picture was of Maureen on holiday in Millport. Liam and Leslie had taken her there just a month after she got out of hospital. The weather was sunny and they had hired tricycles for the day. Maureen was standing next to hers wearing cutoff shorts, a "Never Mind the Bollocks" T-shirt and shades. She was grinning. The picture was grotesquely inappropriate next to Douglas's murder story. She looked very different in the picture, her hair was long and straggly, she had dyed it darker since then, and she was painfully thin: she hadn't been able to swallow comfortably when she was ill.

She avoided looking at the photos from that time because they reminded her so sharply of the aftermath of the breakdown, when she had had to keep smiling and telling people she was all right, when she struggled to assimilate all the things that had happened to her in the recent and the distant past. She had left the bundle of holiday photographs facedown in a box at Winnie's house.

"Who gave it to them?" asked Leslie.

"My mad cunt of a mother."

"Oh, okay," said Leslie, arching an eyebrow at the carpet.

"You look a bit less tired," said Maureen, trying to get off the subject.

"Yeah, I got a sleep last night."

Liam took the paper from Leslie and excused himself.

Maureen grinned up at Leslie and Leslie grinned back. "You ready to talk to me now?" asked Leslie.

"I am, pal. How'd the appeal go?"

"Bad." She frowned, put her crash helmet down on the settee and took off her leather jacket. "They won't make their decision until next week but I think we're fucked. I talked to the CAB lawyer and we've missed out loads of stuff."

Liam came back and threw the newspaper down on the coffee table. He dropped heavily onto the settee and waited for someone to acknowledge his dirty mood. Leslie caught Maureen's eye.

"I could do with a shower," said Maureen, and stood up.

"I'll make ye a cup of tea," said Leslie innocently. "D'ye want one, Liam?"

"Huh." He snorted. "Actually, no. Tea happens to be the last thing on my mind at the moment."

* * *

Maureen was standing under the shower, washing the shampoo out of her hair, when she felt a familiar shiver. The ghost of her father was in the bathroom. She was very small and was standing in the bath, waiting to get out. He bent down and put his face level to hers. She rinsed her hair quickly and opened her eyes but he was still there with her, she could almost smell him. She turned on the cold water and stood underneath it, sweating. Change the ending, Angus had told her. Change the ending. Keeping her eyes on her father, she reached purposefully into the bath water and pulled out a sawed-off shotgun. She aimed it at him and squeezed the trigger. His head blew off. His blood was all over the bathroom. Just like Douglas.

"You look fucking terrible," said Leslie, as Maureen came into the living room.

"Yeah."

"Benny and Liam have gone out for a pint, fancy it?"

"Liam's being a prick. Have you got your bike with you?"

"Yeah. Why?"

"Can we go to yours? I want to get away from him."

Leslie gave her the spare crash helmet from the carrier box and Maureen climbed onto the pillion, wrapping her arms around her friend's waist, and nuzzled her face into her shoulder. Leslie sat back a little as she kick-started the bike, pressing into Maureen, letting her know she was all right. The cold rain nibbled Maureen's legs numb as they rode to the northern outskirts of the city, to the Drum, the scheme where Leslie lived.

As they hit the lip of the hill overlooking the scheme a sudden burst of sunshine from the west lit the rain as it fell. In the deep valley below, the high-rise blocks stood like giants paddling in a shallow sea of bungalows.

13

LESLIE

LESLIE LIVED ON THE FOURTH FLOOR OF AN OLD-FASHIONED BLOCK of six flats. She was lucky: her neighbors were good-natured and elderly; they were at home most of the day and asleep most of the night. They put net curtains, plants and bits of carpet in the close to give it a homely atmosphere.

She pulled up outside the close, dragged the bike through to the back court and chained it to a large metal ring attached to a block of concrete. Three tiny girls were playing at skipping ropes out the back. They stopped and stared at Maureen. The wee-est girl had a square head too big for her body and thin, wispy baby hair, pulled up into a ponytail at the top of her head. She was dressed in a pale pink skirt and a red woolly jersey with bleach scars on the sleeve. Her mouth was stained with orange juice. Maureen made a silly face at her. She blushed, giggled and pulled her skirt up to cover her juice-stained face.

"That's wee Magsie," said Leslie. "She's three and a half. Aren't ye, wee teuchie?"

Wee Magsie kept her skirt over her face and giggled shyly, rocking from side to side.

"Yes," said the biggest girl, who could only have been seven. "I'm her big sister and I've to look after her today."

Wee Magsie ran away.

"Don't be fuckin' stupid, wee Magsie," shouted her big sister, running after her and dragging her back. She spat into a tissue and wiped at the orange stains on wee Magsie's face. Magsie held on to her sister's jersey with both hands and grinned as her face was roughly scrubbed.

"See that?" said Leslie. "They're wee mammies before they stop being kids."

Leslie made some coffee and listened as Maureen told her everything that had happened.

Two hours had passed and they were both tired. Leslie poured them a glass of beer each and heated up a pot of stew made with slices of onion and fifty-pence-shaped carrots.

"It's not like you to cook, Leslie," said Maureen, buttering four slices of bread and putting them on a plate.

"Mrs. Gallagher across the close made it."

"And how did you get it? Did ye steal it from her?"

"No," said Leslie, "she brought it across. She always does that, makes too much and gives ye some."

"Una does that sometimes, when she bakes."

"How is Una? Up the duff yet?"

"No, it's a sin. She was over the other day. Mum's telling everyone I'm crazy. She said I might have killed Douglas and not remembered."

Leslie ladled the stew into bowls. "I think you should stay the fuck away from her. No offense, I know she's your mum and everything, but she's—"

"I know, Leslie, you don't have to say it out loud."

"You should, though."

"I know, but she's the only parent I've got and you need at least one."

It was a fine night and Leslie liked eating hot food in the open air so they put their jackets on and took the stew out onto the veranda, sitting in the dark on old stained deck chairs, knee-deep in a forest of dead plants. The stew was thick and salty. The veranda over-looked a patch of waste ground with irregularly undulating hillocks, bald and strewn with litter. Children were shouting and chasing each other around, apparently without purpose, as a flamingo pink sunset bled into the navy blue night.

Maureen finished her stew. The waste ground was emptying, most of the children going home to their tea. Three or four hung around, silhouetted against the dying light, kicking at the ground and talking to each other. She huddled inside her big overcoat, wrapping her hands around the glass of beer as though it would warm her, and lit a cigarette. "What are you going to do about the shelter, then, if the appeal fails?"

Leslie dunked a folded slice of buttered bread in the hot gravy in her bowl. "I have not one fucking clue," she said. "We've got a meet-ing with the subcommittee next week. We should've got a lawyer in the first place but the action committee were against it, said we'd save a week's running money if we did it ourselves. What are you going to do about Douglas?"

"I dunno either," said Maureen. "The police don't seem very sharp. They totally missed Suicide Tanya and the photograph in the paper. They must have missed other stuff too, things I didn't stum-ble across."

"Yeah," said Leslie, combing through the thick gravy with her fork, looking for the meat. "I bet they did."

Maureen sipped her beer and watched Leslie biting a lump of meat off her fork. "Do you think I should leave it to the police?"

Leslie chewed a space in her mouth. "No, I don't. They'll charge you and if they don't get you they'll get Liam."

"That's what I think."

Leslie swallowed. "The police don't have an infinite amount of time to spend on anything. They just go with the most obvious answer. You're both so dodgy-looking. Think about it, the two people who could get into the house. You've got a psychiatric history which you've already lied about, you were his mistress—"

"I wasn't his *mistress*."

"That's what they'll call it and they probably can't conceive of a woman who doesn't want to get her man and keep him. And Liam, heavy guy, dealer, public enemy number one, wee sister seeing married older guy. Gets protective and kills him."

Maureen slumped in her deck chair. "They'd planted footprints with my slippers and they did something in a cupboard. It's the cupboard Liam found me in before he took me to hospital."

"In the same cupboard?"

"Yeah, same one."

"Who the fuck knew that? I didn't even know that."

"No one did. Just me and Liam."

"Which means one of you told someone else. Did Douglas know? Could he have told someone?"

"Not that I remember. Christ, I'm really fucked. Whoever did this really knew how to pick a winner."

Leslie wiped her bowl clean with a slice of bread. "He's not daft, is he? You need to find him in case he finds you first. You should carry something in your bag to protect yourself."

"What, like a knife?"

"Oh, for Christ sakes, no. The police could arrest you if they found it." She lit a cigarette. "Hair spray, you can spray it in his eyes, or one of those metal combs, you know, the ones with the pointed ends. I've got one."

She collected the dirty bowls and clambered over Maureen's legs to get into the house. When she came back she had the comb with her. She handed it to Maureen. It was stainless steel, with a long tapered handle ending in a rounded point. "Once you've sharpened that end rub it with oil to make all the metal the same color."

Maureen took it. "I think I'd freeze."

"No, you won't," said Leslie. "Just remember what he did to Douglas. He's a vicious bastard so don't flinch and don't wait for him to hurt you first." She climbed back over Maureen's legs, the tip of her cigarette leaving a glowing crimson trace against the dark sky, and sat down in her deck chair.

"I don't understand why they'd plant footsteps with my shoes and maybe even fix the timer but do it while I was at work."

"Yeah. Maybe it was just a mistake."

"It's a bit of a big mistake."

"Yeah, that doesn't mean it isn't one. Remember Benny told us that story about the gangsters who killed the guy in the woods? They burnt the face off to stop him being identified, cut off his hands and took a hammer to his teeth. When the police found him the guy had his rent book in his back pocket. Remember that?"

The night and the punch line floated through Maureen's memory like a warm breeze. It was Benny's first AA birthday and they didn't know how to help him celebrate. They couldn't take him to a bar. It was in the height of the sticky summer and they drove up to Loch Lomond with the roof down on Liam's Herald. The sun was setting and Leslie built a fire by the water as the sharp night came on. They ate Marks and Spencer's sandwiches, drank ginger and told their best stories as giant, glistening dragonflies hummed and swooped between them.

"I was thinking about the three phone calls to my work. Liz doesn't know Douglas's voice particularly well. It might've been them trying to see if I was there."

"And she said you weren't there?"

"Yeah. But, then, just because I wasn't there doesn't mean I wasn't anywhere that would give me an alibi."

"Yeah." Leslie drew on her fag and looked out over the waste ground, surveying her land. "Like I said, the guy could have made a number of daft mistakes. Why do they all think he was giving you money?"

"Some money's gone missing, I think, and they're assuming he gave it to me."

Maureen sat forward in the deck chair and drew deeply on her fag, flicking the ash over the edge of the veranda. Leslie leaned over and pulled her back into the chair.

"Don't do that," she said. "Sometimes the weans hide under here."

"Why?"

" 'Cause they can't go home."

"Sorry."

" 'S all right. So why's your mum talking about Michael?"

"Fuck," said Maureen slowly, scratching her scalp hard enough to hurt. "I don't know, I don't want to think about what Winnie's been up to. That makes me more nervous than the fucking murder."

"Fair enough, doll," said Leslie, patting her on the knee. "We'll not talk about that. I'm freezing."

Maureen stood up, eager to change the conversation. "I'll get the whisky out, then, yeah?"

"Aye."

She went into the kitchen and took the bottle from under the sink. None of Leslie's glasses matched. Maureen lifted a stolen half-pint glass and a plastic Barbie doll tumbler from the draining board. She poured four fingers into the half-pint and swallowed it in two gulps, the warm whisky aftershock floating up her nose. Back out on the veranda she gave Leslie the Barbie glass and poured a generous measure. "There you are, in your favorite glass as well."

"Great, Mauri. I hope you'll be getting me another one for my birthday this year."

"By the time ye retire I promise you'll have the whole dinner set."

They settled down in the deck chairs, sipping their whisky and smoking cigarettes. "I'm drinking all the time," said Maureen.

"I don't think alcohol abuse is a bad way to cope with short-term traumas."

Maureen laughed with surprise. "That's the worst advice you've ever given me."

Leslie thought about it. "Oh, well, fuck it, then."

The kitchen gulp hit Maureen's head and she felt a wave of purposeful clarity coming on. "I don't want to sit about holding a comb and waiting for them to come for me. How would you go about finding the person who did this?"

Leslie puffed the last of her fag and thought about it.

"You're doing all right so far," she said. "It's just a logic problem."

"But suppose their behavior isn't logical. If the murderer's mental it isn't a logic problem, is it?"

Leslie dropped her cigarette into a space between the dead plants and stepped on it, twisting it with her foot, scattering fiery red sparkles among the plant pots. "He can't be a maniac, it's all too carefully organized. He brought the rope and the cagoul, he got in and out of the flat without being seen, all that stuff. It's not the work of a crazed mind, is it?"

"No, I suppose, but that might mean they're really crazy."

"Uff." Leslie sat forward. "People talk about murder as if it's nothing to do with anything else that happens in the world. It's just part of the big picture. Sometimes killing someone is rational, sometimes it's the most rational thing to do. What about all the crazy people you've met, were they all capable of murder?"

Maureen thought her way around her ward mates in the George III beds in the Northern. "Naw," she said. "Most of them weren't capable of anything very much."

"I've met more sane people who were capable of murder than nutters." Leslie downed the whisky in her glass and poured herself some more. "Doing a shitty thing doesn't make you mental, it just makes you a shit, and Douglas wouldn't have opened the door to a psychotic nutter, would he?"

"Well, I can't see Douglas answering my door and letting anyone in. He shouldn't have been there in the first place. He wouldn't even answer my phone when he was alone in the house." Maureen sat forward, deeply glad to be sure of something. "I bet you that's what happened. They came in together. They must have."

"So who would he bring to your house?"

Maureen thought about it. "Uh, no one, actually."

"If he wouldn't bring anyone to your house," said Leslie, "someone else might have brought him to the house. They might have threatened him somewhere and made him take them to your house."

"Right."

"See?" said Leslie. "It is a logic problem. Why wouldn't he answer the phone?"

"I dunno, he was just, sort of . . . secretive, you know."

"Yeah, sort of married?"

Maureen rubbed her neck uncomfortably.

"Anyway," said Leslie, "I still think this was a rational action by a rational man. We can work it out."

"But I don't know half of the facts, though. I don't even know what was in the cupboard."

"Then we'll have to find out somehow," said Leslie, with the reassuring certainty she brought to everything she did.

Maureen ran her fingers hard through her hair. "I'm frightened, Leslie."

"He's just a guy, Maureen."

"It might be a woman, right enough."

"Nah," said Leslie. "Women don't do things like that. It's men who do that sort of shitty, vicious stuff. With us it's about important things like love and kids and not getting your face kicked in. With them it's for big motors, younger birds or a bit of a tug."

"It might be about love or kids, we don't know. The woman at the Rainbow said someone was fucking a patient in one of the offices."

"*In an office?*"

"Yeah. She didn't even seem shocked about it. She thought it was me."

"Could he be having an affair with someone else at the same time?"

"That's what I thought," said Maureen. "We hadn't shagged each other for weeks."

"That's it, then. God, men are pigs."

"Anyway," said Maureen, "I don't think men and women kill for different reasons. Logically, it could have been a woman who murdered Douglas."

Leslie pulled her collar up around her neck. "But I bet you it wasn't," she muttered.

They defied the cold and stayed on the veranda until midnight, kicking the facts backward and forward, huddled in their coats, watching their smoky breath in front of them.

14

SIOBHAIN

LESLIE SHOOK MAUREEN OUT OF A HEAVY SLEEP AT NINE. HER SHIFT AT the shelter started at ten and Maureen would need to get up now if she wanted a lift back into town.

They pulled into a lane next to the shelter. The reserve funding was running out rapidly now and the house looked shoddy in comparison with its neighbors. It stood out in the elegant street of terraced houses like a meatball in caviar. Leslie let Maureen in and pointed her to the pay phone in the front hall.

She dialed the number for the Dennistoun day center and asked the receptionist if Tanya was there. Without replying to her question the receptionist lowered the phone and spoke to someone. "Hello?" said Maureen, conscious that her money was running out and she didn't have any more change. "Hello?"

"Yeah?" said the bored receptionist.

"I asked if Tanya was there."

"She's here."

The pips went and Maureen put down the phone without bothering to thank her.

The walk only took twenty minutes but it felt like an hour. One week ago none of this had happened and Douglas was still alive, smooching about the city, lying to his wife, listening kindly to his patients and making silly jokes.

She thought about the two of them tumbling over each other in bed. Douglas had a smell about him, the smell of many women past. At first she didn't notice particularly, but gradually she began to see the unfocused look in his eyes when he spoke about his feelings for her, like an invisible shutter coming down. His lines were empty and overrehearsed. Latterly, when they had sex, she longed for the ghosts of the other women to come and keep her company because Douglas was so far away.

She remembered an evening a month ago: she had asked him calmly why he didn't want her to touch him anymore. He wouldn't answer. She got more and more angry and ended up shouting at him to fuck off back to Elsbeth. He left the house and came back four hours later, as drunk as she had ever seen him, declaring his love for her with slurred hyperbole. If he had left it for a little longer her annoyance might have subsided but it hadn't. All she could think was what an arse he was, how he was looking for comfort and not for her. As he stroked her face softly with his big hands, paying attention to every line, every detail, as though mesmerized, she noticed that his fingers smelled of fags and piss. She plied him with drink until he fell asleep. She watched him as he lay snorting and twitching in her bed and realized that she'd be disappointed if she spent much more of her life with him.

After that night they no longer argued and Maureen avoided mentioning Elsbeth. Douglas misread it as a good sign: he thought it meant they were getting on better, but Maureen was storing her grievances for a time when she was ready to be without him.

The Dennistoun day center was in a small converted kirk built before the Second World War in a narrow space between two tenements. The front was a squat rectangle with a triptych of arched windows. An acute triangular roof sat on top like a party hat. The proportions and shape of the façade were echoed in the little doorway, sitting on the side like an afterthought. Inside, the floor and ceiling had been covered in yellow pine, and the sloping roof had been inset with windows, making it bright and cheerful. Behind the high reception desk sat a miserable young woman.

Maureen walked up to her. She didn't move. Maureen drummed her fingers on the desk. The girl inhaled a "tut." "Yeah?" she said.

"Oh dear," said Maureen sympathetically. "You're not having a very good day, are you?"

The girl tutted again. "I don't even know what you're talking about," she said obnoxiously.

"Please yourself," said Maureen, tutting back. "Tanya about?"

"Tanya who?" said the girl, pulling a form out of a half-open drawer and picking up a pencil.

Forms mean time and Maureen couldn't be arsed. She rubbed her nose. "Toilets?" she said.

The girl lifted her hand slowly and pointed to the signboards hanging overhead.

"Thank you very much," said Maureen warmly. "But for you I might have got lost in this labyrinth." She followed the signs into the dayroom. A middle-aged Down's syndrome man with dark panda circles around his eyes was standing in a doorway smoking a fag. He was listening to a football match on a red plastic tranny pressed tightly against his ear. She asked for Suicide Tanya. He turned round quickly, nearly scratching her face with the retractable aerial, and pointed to the television room.

The chairs were plastic in case of incontinence, and a thick, greasy cloud of smoke sat an inch above the residents' heads, blocking out the natural light from the skylights. The chairs radiated around a loud television against the back wall. A small bare kitchenette had been built just inside the door.

Suicide Tanya spotted her from across the room. She stood up and screamed her hellos. No one paid any attention. She beckoned Maureen over. "You sit with me and we can watch the telly. This is Siobhain."

Siobhain was beautiful. For a fleeting moment Maureen wondered if Douglas had been having an affair with her too but when Siobhain smiled her eyes were so sad that Maureen knew she was depressed and had been for a long time. Douglas didn't go for that sort of thing. Siobhain's eyes were pale blue, framed in dark lashes, and she had high soft cheekbones. Her nose was arrow-shaped, pointing downward to her rounded pink lips and perfect white teeth. Her dark hair was speckled with swatches of frizzy gray and was matted at the back. She was overweight but looked as if that was a recent development: her body was still adjusting before the extra flesh settled and became watery; the fat sat in pockets on her frame, her skin taut over it.

Someone very busy had dressed Siobhain. Her red nylon trousers and brown jumper were ill-fitting and didn't match. Every so often she would reach up slowly and pull at the elasticized waistband of the trousers or the neck of the jumper, but mostly Siobhain just sat and watched the television with the dignity of a pietà, her quiet hands sitting in her lap, palms upward like dead birds.

Tanya told Maureen that she had seen her the day before and her name was Helen. Maureen agreed that this was the case.

"You gave me a dog."

"I did, Tanya."

Tanya talked about the dog for a while, then stopped suddenly and announced that she was going. She left without saying goodbye. Maureen slipped into the empty seat next to Siobhain. She waited for a moment before she spoke. "Are you very sad, Siobhain?"

Siobhain turned her head slowly and looked at her without surprise. "I am," she said. She spoke slowly, in a soft Highland accent, with the perfect diction of someone using their second language.

Without a flicker in her expression Siobhain's eyes overflowed and Maureen wept with her. They sat watching the television and crying for a while.

"Would you like me to brush your hair?" asked Maureen.

"I would."

Maureen took the metal stabbing comb out of her handbag and gently eased the tangles from Siobhain's hair, starting from the ends and working her way slowly up to the crown so as not to tug and hurt her. By the time she had finished they had both stopped crying.

"Why are you sad?" asked Siobhain.

"Oh, I dunno. A lot of reasons. Someone died. My family, you know."

"A friend of mine died too," said Siobhain.

"Was that Douglas?"

"No," said Siobhain. "He died, I heard that. I met him but he wasn't my friend. My friend died a long time ago and life was spoiled for me."

"Who was it?"

"My brother." She paused. "Who was your friend?"

"Douglas."

"I am sorry for your grief," said Siobhain, as if repeating an ancient consolation in translation.

Maureen thanked her.

"I saw your Douglas. He came to see me the day he was killed. That's why you have come to see me here, isn't it?"

Maureen nodded. "What time did he leave here?"

"About the end of the old cartoons. About half past three."

It was later than lunchtime, the time the police were particularly interested in.

"How did you know Douglas? Was he your doctor?"

"Oh, no," said Siobhain. "I didn't know him."

"Why did he come to see you, then?"

"Because my name was on the list." She pointed to the television. "This man is getting everyone else into trouble. He's telling lies about the other characters." She was watching a banal Australian soap. "Do you watch this program?"

"No, not really. Shall I give ye peace until it's finished?"

"No," said Siobhain, keeping her eyes on the screen. "They put the same one on again in the evening. I watch it both times."

"What list was your name on?"

"Your Douglas had a list of us."

"Of who?"

"Of the women. He said there were others, I thought I was the only one. He knew about the hospital. I don't know how. I have never told. He gave me this."

She reached down by the side of her chair and pulled a handbag onto her lap. It was an old-lady-style handbag, red patent leather with hoop handles and a gold clasp. She snapped it open and showed Maureen the inside. It was empty except for a brown envelope and a bundle of new twenty-pound notes rolled up with an elastic band. Maureen couldn't calculate how much was there: she had never seen so many. The roll was as thick as a man's fist. Siobhain shut the bag and dropped it carelessly onto the floor.

"What was the money for?" asked Maureen.

"He thought giving me the money would make him feel better."

Maureen was confused. "Had he harmed you in some way?"

"No, he didn't harm me. He was upset about the hospital. I can't tell you. I never told."

"Can you tell me where and when you were in hospital?"

"Yes, I can tell you that."

Maureen wrote as Siobhain told her that she had been in the Northern for three years, between 1991 and 1994. "I was in the Northern," said Maureen, "nineteen ninety-six. George III ward. I hated it."

Siobhain looked miserable. "It was finished by then," she whispered.

"What do you mean?"

Siobhain's face flushed with panic and her breathing became sharp and shallow.

"That's fine," said Maureen, patting her hand. "Don't tell me. Don't think about it."

The blood drained slowly from Siobhain's face and she began to breathe regularly again. If the police came to see Siobhain they'd ask about the hospital and the money and they wouldn't stop just because she lost her breath. "Have the police been to see you yet, Siobhain?"

"No. Will they come?"

"I don't know. I expect they will. I'd like you to avoid talking to them."

Siobhain lifted her hand slowly and stroked the back of her hair three times. She laid her hand in her lap again and looked at Maureen. "Then I will," she said. "They say I'm sick but I'm not. My heart is broken."

Maureen smiled warmly. "You're living in the wrong time, Siobhain," she said. "Broken hearts are a bit too poetic for doctors to understand."

"That's it," said Siobhain. "It's the poetry they can't understand."

They bent their heads close and looked one another in the eye, as intimate as lovers.

"Can I come and visit you again?" said Maureen.

"I would like that."

"We could go to the shops," said Maureen, as she stood up, "and you could buy some nice clothes with the money in your bag."

"I don't want nice clothes," Siobhain said flatly, and turned back to the television. "I got that money because I wore nice clothes."

The receptionist had evidently decided she was all right. She took the trouble to lift her head and say cheerio as Maureen passed on her way out.

15

DIRTY

THE TRIUMPH HERALD WAS PARKED OUTSIDE THE DENNISTOUN DAY center. Liam was sitting inside with the window rolled down, watching the door and smoking a fag. He hooted anxiously and waved her over, opening the passenger door as she walked up to the car, letting it swing wide over the pavement. Maureen bent down and looked inside. "Hello," he said coyly, "I's a bit pissed off last night. I thought I might have annoyed you."

"No, no," she lied. "How did you know I'd be here?"

"Leslie said. Joe McEwan's looking for both of us. We've to go down to the station again."

"Did he seem annoyed?"

"I don't know, I didn't see him. Benny said he phoned this morning."

Maureen threw her bag into the backseat and got in, shutting the door behind her and taking his fag off him. "What's happening about Maggie?" she asked, and took a draw.

"I dunno," he said, and half smiled. "I bumped into Lynn yesterday."

Lynn was Liam's ex-girlfriend. They had dated each other adamantly for four years and then split up suddenly after a petty fight. Two months later Liam was going out with bland Maggie. At the time Maureen and Leslie gave the relationship a month, tops, but that was over a year ago now.

"Did you bump into her by accident?"

"Yeah."

"Is that the first time you've met her since ye split up?"

Liam grinned. "Aye."

"So . . . what?"

"So nothing," he said innocently, and started the car. "You hungry?"

"Starvin'."

"What do you want to eat?"

"Any variation on the theme of red meat."

It was a brisk, sunny day. The light in Scotland is low in the autumn, gracing even the most mundane objects with dramatic chiaroscuro. Deep hard shadows from the tall buildings fell across the streets, litter bins stood on the pavement like war monuments, and pedestrians cast John Wayne showdown shadows as they stood at the traffic lights, waiting to cross the road. They drove west up Bath Street, passing alternately through withering puddles of shade and warming blasts of sunshine, heading up to a drive-through burger place at the poor end of the Maryhill Road.

Maureen hadn't been there for a few months and the area had suddenly become desolate. Subsiding buildings had been bolstered up or else abandoned, their windows and doors boarded up with fiberglass. The city surveyors had always known there was an ancient mine there; they thought it was safe, but the medieval miners had left weaker struts in it than they had supposed. Maryhill was falling into a five-hundred-year-old hole.

The drive-through was busy with thrill-seeking lunchtimers. Liam parked and Maureen ran across the road into the burger bar.

When she crossed back to the car Liam had nodded off. She knocked on the window. He opened his eyes and sat up slowly, grinning as if he'd had a dirty dream, and opened the door for her.

"Nothing happened with Lynn, then?"

"Ahh, well." He rubbed his red eyes.

They ate with the windows down and the radio on. Maureen asked him what time he'd left Paulsa's house. "About two-thirty."

"Where did you go then?"

"Went to Maggie's to pick her up and we went to the town to get flowers for her mum. Why?"

"Were you with her all day?"

"Yeah. Why?"

"Because," said Maureen, "I met someone who saw Douglas alive and well at three-thirty that day."

"Very good," he said, and nodded. "Very good indeed."

"I'd prefer it if the police didn't speak to her, though. She's a bit vulnerable."

"We'll keep her as a last resort, then," said Liam.

He tried to squash her burger into her face every time she went to take a bite. They ended up throwing chips at each other and giggling childishly. Whatever it was he and Lynn did when they were alone it suited Liam well. With Maggie he had been precious and moody but when he was with Lynn he recovered his gleeful spontaneity. They went for a coffee in a nearby shopping arcade to calm themselves before going to the police station.

Given that arcades are the poor precursor to shopping malls, this was a poor arcade: it was full of fancy-goods stores, 99p shops, with window displays of discount toilet rolls, and frozen food shops. Many of the units were empty or to let. A small central space was furnished with benches and fake trees stuck in large pots. The pots had been used routinely as ashtrays and were full of cigarette ends and greasy ash. Above, a clear Perspex roof lit the resting shoppers in an unflattering splat of light.

Liam needed razors so they went into the supermarket, then walked back to a baker's shop with a café. It was a grimy, self-service joint. The pile of trays at the counter hadn't been washed properly and the cups were stained. Dirty dishes sat uncollected on all the tables.

They picked a tray from the bottom of the pile and shuffled sideways along the counter. Maureen bought the coffee and began the search for the least dirty table. She stacked up the used dishes and moved them to an empty table before she sat down. The tabletop was strewn with crumbs and sticky patches of what appeared to be jam.

"I don't really want to drink out of that," said Liam, pointing at his cup. It had ring stains on the inside and a chip on the handle.

"It's good for you," said Maureen. "If you eat germs you get immune to them."

Liam wiped a space on the table in front of him with a paper napkin. "That sounds like an excuse for bad housekeeping to me."

"Aye, right enough, I'd never thought of it that way." She turned her cup round to a chipless part of the rim. "Mum used to say it to me. What's she up to?"

"What d'ye mean?" said Liam.

"What's Mum's new thing? She's said Dad's name twice in the past week and Una was looking well shifty."

He raised his eyebrows. "It's nothing, Mauri," he said. "I wouldn't worry about it."

That meant it was bad. Normally she wouldn't have asked Liam. They had an unspoken rule about Winnie that they didn't discuss her except in joking, disparaging terms, and even then it was as a release mechanism so that they wouldn't take her too seriously. They never gossiped about her or told each other what she'd been saying about them: they were old enough to know that none of it mattered, it could only hurt them and she'd be picking on someone else next week. But Maureen had a feeling that Winnie's recent behavior related to something more sinister than usual, and she needed to know. Liam sipped his coffee nonchalantly and grimaced. "That tastes of tires," he said. "What's yours like?"

"Tell me, Liam."

"It's nothing."

She had to cajole him all the way through her coffee. "I'm worried that she's been talking to the papers about me, that's why I need to know."

"Maureen, it's got nothing to do with that, it's not important."

"Why won't you tell me, then?"

Liam gave up on his coffee. "I can't drink that."

"Well, leave it, then," she said irritably. "Tell me."

He frowned and shoved his cup away to the side of the table. She caught his arm. "Tell me. Right now."

Liam sighed heavily. "It's to do with Marie . . . and Dad," he said.

"Has Marie remembered something?"

"No."

Maureen stopped dead. "What about Dad?"

Liam sat back and shoved his hands in his pockets, swinging backward on his chair. "Look," he muttered, "I really don't want to tell you. I just think you should stay away from them all, at least until this Douglas thing's settled."

"What is it?"

"Maureen, I—"

"DON'T LIE."

He took a deep breath and looked at her. "Marie doesn't believe you about Dad."

"Marie doesn't believe me either?"

"None of them believe you, Mauri." He laughed nervously, trying to make a joke of it. "They don't believe anything they don't want to."

"I know Mum doesn't but Marie was there when it happened. How could she not believe me?"

"I dunno."

"Which bit doesn't she believe?"

"None of it."

"What about Una?"

"She definitely doesn't."

"But Una was the one who brought it up in the first place. She only recanted to get Mum off her back. How could she not believe me?"

He shrugged.

"Marie was there," squealed Maureen. The other customers eyed them furtively. "She was fucking *there*. She saw Mum pulling me out."

"Mauri, please."

"Those fuckers!" shouted Maureen, curling over the table with fury. "Fuckers!"

A small boy at a nearby table started to cry. Liam pulled at her arm, trying to get her to sit up and calm down. "Keep it down, Mauri, please. We could get arrested for a breach."

She straightened up and took his hand roughly, pulling him forward across the table. "You tell me everything," she said fiercely. "Everything. Why are they bringing this up *now?*"

He blinked sharp little spasms and wouldn't look at her. "Mum thinks you might not have remembered about Douglas properly."

"And where did that come from?"

He picked at his fingernails. "There's been all this stuff in the papers about memory . . ."

"This false memory stuff? They don't believe me about Dad so I make up everything all the time?"

"Kind of."

She slumped over the table, muttering curses to herself.

"I'm sorry, Mauri, I'm sorry," Liam whispered.

Maureen scrubbed at her eyes, dragging the soft skin on her eyelids back and forward, trying to get it together. "They think I'm completely mental, don't they?" she said.

"I suppose."

"Have they told the police this?"

Liam shook his head. "After the show Mum made of herself at the station the other day I don't think she's exactly got the ear of the police. I wouldn't worry about that. My God, it's not as if you're used to relying on their support, is it? I just think they'll fuck our heads if you go near them. Promise me you'll stay away from them until this Douglas business blows over."

"Let's get out of this place," said Maureen. "It's dirty."

They left the arcade and walked back to the car. Liam pulled the keys from his jacket pocket. He opened the passenger door for Maureen but she didn't move to get in. "Not one of them believes me?" she said.

Liam rubbed his hands guiltily, as if he was implicated in his sisters' duplicity.

"No," he said, "they don't."

"Do you?"

"Yes, totally, completely."

"Why?"

"Because Una told you, because it's all too much of a coincidence and I know you've questioned it so often and arrived at the same conclusion every time."

"Do you believe me when I say I didn't kill Douglas?"

"Yeah, well, I know you're really hard, Maureen."

They grinned melancholically at one another. "And for fucksake," he said, "if you had done it you'd've told everyone by now."

Maureen stepped closer to him, until she could feel the warmth of his skin, and looked over his shoulder. "Liam?" she breathed, desperate for the right answer. "You don't think I could have done it and forgotten?"

Liam held her face in his hands and looked her in the eye. "You listen to me. There's nothing wrong with you."

"But maybe—"

"There's nothing wrong with you."

"Maybe . . . my memory . . ."

"Shut the fuck up. Listen, this isn't about Douglas at all, it's about them not wanting to believe you about Dad. I want you to stay the fuck away from them all."

"You want me to let this go?"

"Keep away from them," he said, strangely emphatic, and let go of her face. "*Please.* For a while, anyway."

He walked round the car and slipped into the driver's seat. Maureen climbed into the passenger's side and shut the door behind her.

"I think they're all mental," said Liam.

"You're not just saying that to comfort me?"

"I am, a bit." He smiled, caught in fib. "But I know it happened."

"Which is more than I do," she said, heartsore with self-pity.

Liam put the keys in the ignition, pulled the choke and started the engine. "Thing is," he said, "you have to ask yourself what kind of arsehole would even question a memory like that."

16

LIAM

LIAM PARKED THE CAR AROUND THE CORNER, OUT OF VIEW OF THE police station. They walked through the front doors, telling the policeman on the desk their names and who they were there to see.

Almost immediately a gang of four appeared at the top of the stairs. McEwan, Inness, Hugh McAskill and the Seedy Man. They seemed purposeful, certain, as though the outcome of the meeting was already set.

"We were just about to come and find you," said McEwan, letting them know who was in charge.

The Seedy Man said he was going to caution both of them at the same time. He recited it in a British Rail announcer's monotone. McEwan looked smug. He kept looking at Maureen, smiling inadvertently and looking away quickly, as if she would know what was making him smile if she saw it flourish. McAskill was standing three steps back from Inness and the Seedy Man, his hands in his pockets, his eyes darting around the lobby, avoiding Maureen. Liam looked at Maureen, he seemed worried. She meant to make an encouraging face but she couldn't stop thinking about Winnie and Marie and Una. She crumpled her chin and raised her eyebrows, looking blaming and distant.

The Seedy Man finished his recital and Liam shot Maureen an abortive smile. Inness took his arm, leading him away through the double doors on the ground floor. The Seedy Man followed them. Liam didn't look back at her: he walked off with his head bent to his chest like a man about to be taken to a place, there to be hanged by the neck until he was dead.

McEwan watched the door swing after them. "You want to watch the company you keep," he said.

"How do you mean?" she said innocently.

"Your brother and that Benny pal of yours."

"Benny?"

"He's got a record, didn't you know?" He pointed upstairs. "You know the way by now."

They walked up the first flight of stairs. "Naw," she said. "Benny's studying law, he couldn't get into uni if he had a record. You're mixing him up with someone else."

"It was a no pro," said McEwan.

"A what?"

"That means they didn't prosecute."

That made sense of it: he'd have been arrested for pissing up a close or something. "Not worth the hassle?"

"He was diverted."

"I don't know what that means either," she said, tired of his smug jargonizing manner.

"He got a psychiatric referral for alcoholism instead."

"Oh, right, I didn't know about that. We must look like a right bunch of nutters to you."

McEwan smiled enigmatically and opened the door to the interview room. Maureen sat down at the far side of the table and crossed her legs, swinging her foot in manic rhythmic kicks. Something important was about to happen and she couldn't concentrate for thinking about Winnie. They had been in such a hurry to caution both of them.

McAskill slipped into the seat next to the wall and started the tape recorder. McEwan took the outside chair.

"How are you, Maureen?" said McEwan, as if for the benefit of the tape.

"I'm fine, Joe," said Maureen, wishing he'd get to the fucking point. "How are you?"

"Fine."

They paused and looked at each other. Joe McEwan was savoring the moment. Maureen shifted in her chair, sitting sideways and recrossing her legs. "Are you going to ask me questions or are we going to sit here and look at each other all day?" she said.

"Yes," he said serenely. "I do have some questions to ask you. First, I want you to tell me, in as much detail as you can, what you did from nine in the morning until ten p.m. the day before Mr. Brady was found dead."

She repeated the story, telling him the details about the Pizza Pie Palace and Leslie again, wondering why they were asking about the evening. McEwan asked her if she was sure about a couple of the times she had given them and then sat back confidently, looking her up and down.

"Anything else?" she said rudely.

"Yes," he said. "A number of things. I want to talk to you about your harassment of Mrs. Carol Brady."

"My what?" Her voice was straining high. She made a mental note to calm down.

"Mrs. Brady told me that you'd contacted her and insisted that she meet you. She wouldn't be specific about the nature of the meeting—"

"It was lunch."

"I meant what was said."

"I'll tell you what was said." She sat forward. "Same thing as Elsbeth said—"

"And that's another thing," he interrupted, "stay away from her too."

"Look, they both approached me, I didn't go looking for either of them. You were there when Elsbeth asked me to wait and you gave bloody Carol Brady the address I was staying at."

"I most certainly did not."

"Well, she told me she got it from the police. Her assistant turned up at the door and nearly scared the living shit out of me." She was talking very fast, very angry.

McEwan looked at McAskill. McAskill looked confused and shook his head.

"We'll look into that," said McEwan.

"And you told her that my family were *unsavory*." She was glad to be on the offensive, glad she had something to pull him up about. "We're as savory as any other family in this city . . ." She sounded ridiculous.

"As I said," McEwan reiterated, "we'll look into it. If someone did give her the address it was against my express orders. Anyway, I made it perfectly clear I didn't want you to wait for Elsbeth. Why did you talk to either of them?"

"Look," she said, "I'm a failed Catholic woman, I feel guilty all the time anyway. I was shagging her husband and Carol Brady's son died in my living room. What the fuck am I going to do when they ask me to speak to them? Spit?"

McEwan warmed at the mention of Catholicism. McAskill didn't look up. He might be a Protestant. He might not give a shit. Maureen hoped it was the latter.

"When did Carol Brady approach you?" asked McEwan.

"Um, Saturday night. She sent her assistant to Benny's to tell me I was having lunch with her the next day. I was freaked enough as it was. Those bloody journalists had been at my work—"

"Did you give them the picture that was in the paper yesterday?"

She moved her chair back and recrossed her legs. "No, my mum did."

"Did you tell her to do it?"

"No," she said, uncrossing them.

"Why did she, then?"

Maureen held up her hands. "The ways of Winnie are many and varied."

McEwan suppressed a derogatory snigger. "I spoke to your mum."

"Oh, yeah?" she said, wanting to slap him for implicatively slagging her mammy. "I heard she was in here. She's a bit of a live wire."

McEwan grinned unkindly. "Yeah," he said. "She is."

"*Unsavory,*" said Maureen. "Anyway, both Elsbeth and Carol were asking if Douglas gave me money."

"Did he give you money?"

She noticed that the conversation was getting faster and faster and she was wiggling about in her chair. Slow, slow, she told herself, slow. "No," she said, probably too slowly. "No. He tried to pay my mortgage a couple of times but I wouldn't take it."

"He 'tried'?"

"Yeah, but I wouldn't let him."

McEwan was perplexed. "Why?"

"I didn't want to be beholden to him."

He frowned, tried to understand for a millisecond and then gave up. "I thought that was one of the good things about being a woman," he said flirtatiously.

"But nothing's for nothing, is it?" she said, puzzled by his attitude. And it hit her. That was how certain he was: he was talking fast and flirting with her, letting his guard down every which way. He didn't give a shit what she thought anymore. They'd cautioned Liam, too, and McEwan thought he had them.

She faked calm and glanced at the tape recorder. Her eyes fell on

McAskill's hands, one on top of the other, resting on the table. He lifted a finger, signaling to her to look up. His face was sad and soft. He blinked his blue eyes slowly and when he opened them again he was looking at the table.

"Are you a feminist?" asked McEwan, acting surprised and dragging her back to the game.

"Yeah," said Maureen, feeling genuinely calm, as if she'd absorbed some of Hugh's tired dignity.

McEwan laughed. "I thought you liked men," he said.

"Yeah, feminists don't like men and Martin Luther King picked on white people. You don't know many feminists, do you, Joe?"

"No," he said, oblivious to her supercilious attitude, "but I know what they look like and they don't look like you." He pointed openly to her large tits and looked away, leaving Maureen—and McAskill—aghast. He knew he'd offended her but he didn't give a shit. "Still, your political beliefs would allow you to accept cash."

"What are you talking about?"

"He gave you cash, though. You were happy enough to accept that from him, weren't you?"

"*No*. Where did you get that idea from? I didn't take money from him. I didn't want his money. I don't make a lot of money but it's mine and I manage."

McEwan reached into his pocket and pulled out a bank statement. Maureen recognized the red and blue type on the heading. He unfolded it and pushed it across the table to her.

It was a statement of her account. The last entry was a deposit of £15,000. It had been paid in on the day Douglas died. "That's a lot of money to you, isn't it, Maureen?"

"It's a lot of money," she whispered. "I didn't know . . ."

"Did he pay you not to tell his wife about your affair? Was that it?"

"I didn't know it was there."

"But you paid it in yourself."

"No. I didn't. Why did you say that?"

"It says your name on the paying-in slip."

"I didn't pay it in."

"As I said, Maureen, your name is on the paying-in slip."

"I was at work that day. I wasn't out of the office. How could I have paid it in?"

"The slip was signed 'M. O'Donnell.'"

"I always write Maureen," she said very quietly. "Not 'M.'"

McEwan made great play of taking out his notebook and reading something, rolling his lips over his gums. He looked up suddenly. "I heard about something that happened to your brother yesterday."

"Which particular thing?" said Maureen, her heart sinking.

"A police search? I take it you know about it?"

Maureen made a noncommittal noise and looked away.

"Your brother's a drug dealer, isn't he?" His voice was low now, a happy growl.

There was no point in denying it. They'd found the scent everywhere. Maureen looked back at McAskill's hands. His nails were short and clean; deep ridges were scored into the finger joints. "I wouldn't know anything about that," she mumbled.

"He doesn't tell you anything, is that right?"

"Absolutely." She nodded emphatically. "He tells me nothing."

McEwan smiled. "I expect he wants to protect you."

"I don't know why he doesn't tell me, he just doesn't."

"Is your brother very protective of you, Maureen?"

She could smell it coming, the accusation, and she didn't know how to sidestep it. "Not especially," she said.

"Oh?" said McEwan, feigning surprise. "But when you needed to go to hospital it was your brother who took you, wasn't it?"

"How is that protective?" she said, irritated by his stupid game and witless patter. "He found me sitting in a cupboard in a puddle of my own shit. What was he supposed to do?"

"I'm not saying what he did was wrong," said McEwan, uncomfortable with the image.

"No," she said. "But you're suggesting it's evidence of pathological protectiveness and I'm saying it was just ordinary decency."

McEwan leaned back and looked at her shrewdly. "I didn't say anything about pathological anything. Why did you say that?"

"I know what you're getting at," she said, a sick, hopeless panic rising from her belly. "Right? I know Liam and I know he didn't do it."

"Why would you think I was going to say that?"

"Because you mentioned the raid and then started talking about his relationship with me."

McEwan leaned forward over the table. His gestures were so assured, so certain, that Maureen wanted to punch him.

"Don't try and guess what I'm about to say, Maureen," he said carefully.

"So, I have to wait until you've finished the pantomime. Even though I know exactly what you're going to say."

She had ruined his big moment. "You don't know what I'm going to say," he said churlishly.

"Yes, I do."

"No, Maureen," he said, enunciating the words slowly. "You don't know what I'm going to say, you just think you do. I was asking about your brother's relationship with you. He *is* protective of you."

"Oh-no-he-isn't," chanted Maureen.

McAskill snorted a laugh.

McEwan was finally getting annoyed. "Just answer the questions, Miss O'Donnell. Don't try and get smart with me."

"You're a fucking arsehole."

McAskill lifted his head.

"I beg your pardon?" whispered McEwan.

"I said, you're a fucking arsehole. You're bullying and smug and patronizing and I don't like you."

McEwan spluttered, "Well, I'm sorry you feel that way."

"Yeah, so am I," said Maureen, taking out her fags and lighting one. She saw McEwan looking at the packet. She flicked it across the table to him. "Just take one, for fucksake, you make me nervous."

McAskill kept his eyes on the cigarette packet as McEwan pushed it purposefully back across the table and looked at Maureen defiantly. "You know, I really think if you wanted us to find the person who murdered your boyfriend—"

"You already said that."

"—you'd cooperate a bit more fully."

"You're not asking me to cooperate," she blurted. "You're asking me to be servile and accept intrusions into my life and tell complete strangers all my private business and my friends' business. It's horrible. I hate it."

McEwan took a packet of ten Superdelux low-tar cigarettes out of his pocket and put one in his mouth. Maureen watched him light it. "It still counts as smoking," she said, "even if you don't enjoy it."

McEwan snatched the fag out of his mouth, stood up and threw open the door, telling someone outside to bring tea. Now. He sat down. He was very annoyed. "We have to ask you questions," he said. "How are we going to find the person who did this if we don't ask any questions?"

"I know you have to," she said. "But I don't have to like it, do I?"

"I don't care whether you like it or not. I'm going to ask you questions and I want you to answer them honestly."

She nodded impatiently, rolling the ash off her cigarette against the inside of the pie-tin ashtray. McEwan looked her in the eye for too long. "Do you think your brother is a violent man?"

"No," she said.

"Well, we have evidence from a witness who said he beat her up two years ago." He sat back and watched Maureen's face fall.

"I don't believe you."

"You'd better believe me. She's downstairs now, I could bring her up if you like."

"Who?"

"A woman called Margaret Frampton. Do you know her?"

"Maggie?"

"Is she called Maggie?"

"Liam's girlfriend Maggie?"

"No, she may have been his girlfriend at one point but she isn't now, I don't think. Her nickname is Tonsa."

"Fucking Tonsa?" said Maureen, relieved and annoyed that it was the vacant crack courier. "You must know Tonsa, she's so wasted. Would you take her word against anyone's? She can't tell New York from New Year."

"She knows when she's being beaten up. She told us all about it."

"Yeah, and what did you tell her all about? The two years she'd get in Cornton Vale if she didn't say it?"

McEwan was genuinely insulted. McAskill had a curious look on his face, like a warning that she'd gone too far. It touched her, she respected him.

"All right," she conceded. "Look, Tonsa might have said that but there's no doubt in my mind that it isn't true. Ask her if she shot Kennedy, that's all I'm saying."

A knock on the door signaled the arrival of tea. A man in a startlingly white shirt came in, put down the tray and lifted the cups onto the table. Maureen took her tea weak and black without sugar. The young man had given her sugar and milk but she took it anyway, knowing that McEwan hadn't intended her to get a cup.

Still smarting from the insult, McEwan drew heavily on his super low-tar fag and stubbed it out.

"Did your brother know Douglas Brady?"

"He met him once."

"When?"

"Four months ago, I suppose. Liam came round to my house and Douglas was there."

"How long were they together for?"

"About fifteen minutes. Douglas was late for an appointment or something, he had to go."

"Was anyone else there?"

"No. Just the three of us."

"Right." McEwan wrote something down in his notebook. "Did you know Douglas was married when you got involved with him?"

"No."

"When did you find out?"

"Just recently."

"When?"

"I don't know. Recently." She picked up the cup of tea and took a sip. The milk in it left a cheesy coating on her tongue.

"We found this in your house." McEwan pushed a letter toward her. It was Douglas and Elsbeth's marriage certificate, the copy from the General Register, still inside the creamy envelope. "It's a copy of Douglas Brady and Elsbeth McGregor's marriage certificate ordered from the General Register," he said, for the benefit of the tape. "The envelope is postmarked two days before the murder. When did you receive it?"

"The day after it happened."

McEwan slapped his open hand hard on the table. "THAT WAS A STUPID LIE," he shouted. "DON'T LIE TO ME."

The letter had been addressed to her work. She had left it sitting in her handbag on the bedroom floor and McMummb had handed her the keys and wallet out of the bag. They knew she hadn't been in the bag since she found Douglas. It had to be before she found him. She sipped her cheesy tea. "Yes," she said. "It was a lie, I'm sorry."

She inhaled the last of her fag and put it out, wondering where the fuck Liam was and what they were saying to him and why

McEwan wasn't questioning him. His boss might be questioning him, if he had a boss.

"When did you receive this letter?" asked McEwan.

"The day it happened. The day before I found him."

"Did you show it to your brother?"

"No."

"Why not?"

"I didn't see him that day."

"So you've said."

"Ye didn't find his fingerprints on it, did ye?" she said triumphantly. "Did ye?"

"We haven't taken your brother's fingerprints yet. Why would you send off for a marriage certificate, I wonder?"

It was meant to be rhetorical. She decided to get in his face. "He told me he wasn't married. I thought he was lying so I sent off for a search on the Register. I'm sure the Registrar'll have a record of the request. I asked for a fifteen-year search."

"And that's how you found out he was married?"

"Yes."

"And what did Douglas say when you told him?"

"I didn't tell him. I never saw him alive again."

"That's right," said McEwan. "You didn't see him that day, did you?"

"No, I didn't."

"You've been consistent about that one point, haven't you?"

"Yes."

"As consistent as you were about not having been to the Rainbow for treatment." He turned the page on his notebook. "How did you feel when you found out he was married?"

"I kind of knew. That's why I wrote to the Registrar in the first place."

McEwan leaned over the table and repeated the question firmly. "How did you feel when you found out he was married?"

"Well, Joe," she said loudly, "I felt a bit stupid and then I felt tired and then I felt stupid again, all right?"

McEwan pointed at her. "Don't be cheeky," he said, his voice lowering an octave. He composed himself. "You didn't feel angry, at all?"

"Uff, if you get involved with men who are already spoken for, you deserve all you get, don't you?"

McEwan sat back and looked down his nose at her with a mean, lopsided smirk. "Is that right? And you weren't expecting him to leave his wife?"

"Look, I was four months out of psychiatric hospital when I met him, I was in a state. Even I knew I wasn't fit to pick a life partner."

"What do you mean? You didn't really like Douglas?"

Whatever she said sounded incriminating. She decided to come clean. "Look, Douglas was a sad middle-aged guy who couldn't keep his knickers on. I liked him and he was nice to me. I should never have got involved with him but I did because I was lonely and horny. I didn't want to see him anymore and the wedding certificate was the final straw. I wasn't upset about it. I wasn't pleased but I wasn't angry either."

McEwan was suddenly interested. "You intended to end the relationship?"

"Aye, but I wouldn't kill him or harm him in any way or have him harmed by anyone else. He was as nice to me as he knew how to be. That's all you can ask, isn't it?"

"Did you tell anyone you were going to finish the relationship?"

"Yeah, I told my pal Leslie and I told Liz at work."

"You didn't tell your brother?"

"No. Liam and I don't talk about things like that. He knew Douglas was living with someone else and he never asked much about him because he didn't take it seriously."

"Someone thought it was a serious relationship," he said pompously, folding his arms. "Serious enough to kill him in your house."

The conclusion didn't follow from the observation. Maureen told herself just to leave it. The sooner it was over the sooner she could see Liam.

McEwan raised an eyebrow and looked at her. "Here's what I think happened, Miss O'Donnell." This was what he had been building up to, this was his trump. "I think you were very upset when you received the letter telling you he was married. I think you threatened to tell his wife and he tried to pay you off but the money wasn't enough. You wanted him to leave her and come and live with you. I think you phoned your brother and told him."

"No, I didn't—"

"You invited Douglas to the house and let him in. Your brother came to the house. Maybe he just meant to threaten Douglas, make him think seriously about leaving his wife, and it just went too far."

"Oh, fuck. You're so wrong. You've no idea."

"We'll call you in if we need to speak to you again," he said. "Thank you, Miss O'Donnell."

Maureen was surprised. She looked at McAskill but he was looking at the tape recorder, away from her. "What are you going to do to Liam?" she asked.

"We're not *going to do* anything to him, we're going to talk to him. Is there anything else you want to tell me?"

McEwan looked at her as if he knew something. He was bluffing.

"I can't think of anything," she said innocently. "Who's questioning Liam?"

"We'll go and speak to him now," said McEwan.

"Is it worth me waiting?"

"No." He stood, leaned across McAskill and pressed the Off button on the recorder.

As soon as the tape was off McEwan's face turned a livid shade of purple, swollen, throbbing veins suddenly visible on his temples.

He leaned close to her, so close she could smell the lemon tang of his aftershave. "Don't you ever speak to me like that again," he whispered.

McAskill stood up, keeping his eyes down, and put his hand on McEwan's chest as if moving him back so that he could get up from the table. But there was plenty of room behind his chair—he could have pushed it backward. He was holding McEwan back, he was reminding him not to.

Joe McEwan wouldn't be the best man to cross, she thought, not the best at all.

Maureen walked across town. She didn't notice the tall man walking a hundred yards behind, following, carefully keeping himself out of sight, varying the speed of his walk. He followed her along Bath Street and up Cathedral Street. He held back when she got to the well-lit cathedral forecourt, staying in the shadows and watching as she took the side entrance into the Albert Hospital. He waited for a few moments and skirted the bright forecourt, creeping into the lobby. The lift stopped at eight. He read the board. "Level eight—Dr. Louisa Wishart." He wrote it down in his notebook, checked the time and jotted that down too. He left the building and waited across the road for her to come out.

She locked herself into a toilet cubicle and smoked a furtive fag before going into reception and checking in with Mrs. Hardy. She was worried about setting off the smoke alarm and had to keep waving her fag about to dissipate the smoke. Fifteen thousand pounds. Siobhain said he had given her money to make himself feel better about the hospital: Maureen cast her mind back, trying to remember something about her stay in the Northern that was worth £15,000. And now they had Liam. Liam had never been in trouble with the police before. Joe McEwan seemed to have his heart set on him and, like Leslie said, the police don't have an infinite amount of time. She had known that they'd come for him eventually and she'd been fucking about, wasting time, idly guessing who did it.

She had a sudden urge to phone Leslie and ask her to come over and sit with her. She'd still be at work. Leslie had her own work to do and Maureen couldn't keep leaning on her.

She wondered about them asking about the evening: they'd seemed so sure it had happened during the day. Winnie leaped to mind. False memory syndrome, a get-out-of-jail-free for anyone who didn't fancy tuning in to the dark side.

17

LOUISA

MAUREEN WALKED INTO THE OFFICE AND SMILED AT THE RECEPTION-
ist. "Hello, Mrs. Hardy," she said. "I think I might have missed an appointment last Wednesday."

"Yes, you did," said Mrs. Hardy. "We waited for you."

"I'm so sorry, it slipped my mind."

Mrs. Hardy smiled. "Don't worry, you're here now. I'll tell Louisa."

Maureen thanked her and went into the little waiting room. The eager man who always tried to speak to her was sitting on the edge of his usual chair. He had turned it sideways to face the door and called "Hello" the minute she stepped into the room. She ignored him and walked over to the window, propping her elbows on the high ledge, bending her head forward and shutting her eyes, thinking about Liam walking off through the double doors in the Stewart Street police station, his head low. She could feel the numbness coming over her.

She scratched the back of her neck slowly with her nails, ripping long, deep welts, trying to chase it away. Numbness is worse than pain: it's like a violent wasting disease when all connection with the outside world evaporates, nothing matters, nothing counts, nothing touches or entertains or surprises; even physical sensations feel distant and unreal. It's death without the paperwork.

Her neck felt wet. She stopped scratching and looked at her fingers. The tips of her nails were smeared with watery blood. She pulled the elastic band out of her hair and let her ponytail fall over her neck, covering the rips. She opened her eyes properly, looking out over the greening roof of the black medieval cathedral.

She thought of Siobhain and the numbness pulled back. Siobhain had seen Douglas at three-thirty that day. If they arrested Liam she could get Siobhain to talk to them as a last resort. They were asking about the nighttime. Maybe someone had seen something at night.

Mrs. Hardy called both of them over the intercom. Mr. McNeil was to come to the office and Ms. O'Donnell could go into Dr. Wishart's office now. Maureen turned and saw the wee man hurry out of the door. Bad day to get your nerve up, pal, she thought.

Louisa was sitting stiffly behind the desk. She pushed the newspaper across to Maureen.

"I've seen it," Maureen said.

"So your boyfriend Davie is really Douglas Brady?"

"Yeah. You can see why I couldn't tell you. I thought you might know him."

Louisa hummed and nodded.

Maureen told her how they had come to be involved with one another and described finding the body, how red everything was and how the police had treated her.

"The police came here," said Louisa.

It hadn't occurred to Maureen that the police might physically turn up at Louisa's office: she had thought perhaps they'd telephone an underling. If McEwan saw her notes he'd think she was a compulsive liar.

"Did they see my notes?"

"No," said Louisa. "They'd need a court order to see them and they didn't think it was that important. They asked me about you."

"What did they ask you?"

"They asked me if I thought you knew the difference between a lie and the truth."

"What did you say?"

"I said I thought you did."

They made meaningful eye contact for the first time ever. Maureen wondered if she knew she lied to her all the time. Louisa's line of sight slid sideways to an empty space by the door. Maureen thought it was her turn to speak. "Did they just come to see you the once?" she said.

"Yes, just once. Do you want to ask me anything else about it?"

"No," said Maureen. It was the longest conversation they had ever had. Louisa sat back.

"What else would you like to talk about today?" she said.

Louisa's blind protectiveness had touched Maureen and she gave her the after-mass rape dream as a thank-you gift. Louisa listened, and smiled happily at the end. They talked about the dream, trying to relate it to Douglas's death.

Maureen didn't want to bare her id, it was just a token gift. She said that her friend Ailish had fallen out with her boyfriend when she found out he was sleeping with her sister. Maureen had thought Ailish would have been more supportive of her during this difficult time but she wasn't being helpful at all.

"Perhaps she has a lot on her mind," said Louisa.

They speculated about Ailish's motives for a while.

"I'm a bit concerned about the hospital," said Maureen. "I keep thinking about it and avoiding going past it. I think I'm getting phobic about it again."

But Louisa wasn't biting today. "Tell me how you feel about Douglas now," she said.

"I don't feel much about it. Often I didn't see him for a week, so it just feels like that."

"You're probably in shock. When it hits you, and I'm sure it will, I want you to phone me, day or night, okay?"

Maureen thanked her.

She said she'd write a line for Maureen to excuse her from work for three weeks.

"Louisa, you know what I said about the hospital? Well, I want to face it. Do you have any contacts there I could get in touch with?"

"What for?"

"I want to go back and have a look around. It might make me feel better about it."

"I wouldn't recommend it. I think you're under enough pressure as it is."

"I feel sort of fearless just now."

"I think that's shock. You may be focusing on that to avoid your feelings about Douglas."

"Maybe," she said. "I'd still like to go back. I don't want to go around it on my own in case I can't handle it, but I won't know any of the staff there anymore."

"Martin Donegan's still there."

Maureen opened the door and turned back to Louisa, sitting quite still at her desk with her hands clenched in front of her. "Good-bye, Louisa," she said.

"Good-bye, Maureen," said Louisa.

Maureen went back into the waiting room and sat until Mrs. Hardy called her back into the office. "Here we are," said Mrs. Hardy, holding out a sheaf of papers. "That's a line from the doctor."

Maureen took it. "Thanks, Mrs. Hardy."

"Will we be seeing you next week?"

"Aye, see you then."

* * *

It was darker in the streets now and the officer who had watched her enter the hospital followed her back through the town, heading toward the Stewart Street station.

As she walked down the hill the back of her neck stung in the brisk evening air, the razor tips of her hair switching against the raw skin. But the sharp stinging brought to mind Siobhain: she could vouch for Douglas's being alive until half-three, even if she couldn't talk about the hospital.

She could go to see Martin in the next few days. He'd been working as a porter at the Northern for twenty-something years and was a quiet, steady-tempered man. The hospital complex had developed chaotically over the years but Martin knew every corridor by sight. If there was anything she needed to ask about the Northern, then Martin was the man to see.

The officer on the desk said Liam wasn't out yet. She asked how long he was likely to be but the well-mannered officer said he was sorry, he didn't know. She waited for a bit, sitting in the plastic chair Liam had sat in on the first morning, licking her fingers and rubbing the soothing saliva onto the bloody scratches on her neck, working out how long it would take to get to Winnie's. Twenty minutes later she left, catching a bus to the South Side.

The plainclothes officer followed her, sitting downstairs on the bus, watching for her.

She got off the bus and was walking the two streets to the house when suddenly, across the road, passing below an orange street-light, she saw Michael. His walk was exactly as she remembered it, a defensive, boyish swagger. She dropped back, crossing the road so that she was walking behind him. She followed him for ten minutes before realizing that it wasn't him at all. It was just a tall bald guy. The stabbing-comb teeth left an imprint on her hand. She hadn't sharpened the handle yet: all she could have done was give him a nasty poke. She shouldn't have told Louisa her dream—it revived the sensations.

She still had her key for the house. She worked it into the lock silently, hoping to avoid Winnie altogether. The lights were on in the living room and the kitchen but the house was quiet. George often went out, he had friends in different pubs all over the city, but Winnie tended to stay close to the house. She must be crashed out somewhere, probably in her bedroom or on the settee in the living room. Maureen tiptoed upstairs to her old room at the back of the house.

Her bedroom had been a beloved refuge during her growing up. When she was thirteen she'd got a Saturday job in a fruit-and-veg shop and bought a Yale lock with her first wage, fitting it on her bedroom door to stop Winnie coming in late at night when she was pissed, reeling at the bottom of the bed in the stark stream of light from the hall, scaring the shit out of her. Winnie changed the lock one day when Maureen was at school. Maureen changed it back. Liam declared his room an independent republic.

Winnie used Maureen's as a box room now. The door still had the scars from twelve screws bored into the same three square inches. Greasy Blu Tack stains on the wallpaper hinted the outline of each of her favorite posters, and the books she no longer wanted were lined up on the shelf, Enid Blytons, Agatha Christies, an O grade math textbook, *Dandy* annuals. A pile of cuddly toys sat in the corner gathering dust: Winnie had kept giving them to Maureen for birthdays and Christmases, confusing her with Marie, who liked that sort of thing.

She found the shoe box full of photographs under the bed. They had been rifled through recently, photos were bent over and shoved down the side, still springy but resigning themselves to their new position. She stuffed her bag with them, taking all of them, even the ones from when she was small.

The last one was stuck under the fold at the bottom of the box.

She picked and picked at it but it was stuck. She had to unfold the floor of the box to get it out. It was of her and her father. She was sitting on his knee, hugging him. He seemed to be drunk, his shirt-sleeves were rolled up—he always did that when he was drunk, they used to look out for it. Maureen remembered the time. It was winter and the abuse had begun. She was adoring to him when other people were there and she knew he couldn't touch her. She thought if she was nicer to him he would stop hurting her when they were alone.

She remembered that it was taken at Christmastime. Liam wanted a chopper bike and Maureen asked for a big doll she'd seen hanging from a stall in the Barras. It had a tartan dress and a big tammy. She got the doll but the minute it was out of the packet she noticed that the stitching was rough and the doll's eyes had been painted on wrong. She cried all day. Liam got his chopper and wouldn't let her have a go on it.

She lifted a copy of *The Master and Margarita* and a battered hardback, *Keep the Aspidistra Flying,* stolen from the school library. She put them in her bag and scanned the room. A yellowing picture of Joe Strummer was lying under the bookcase. She shoved it in her pocket. There was nothing else there she wanted.

A bizarre ceramic ashtray she'd made in occupational therapy at the Northern was sitting on a table on the landing. It was round, with a target pattern painted on the face of it in red and white glaze. It was the first thing she had made in the class and Pauline had helped her with the colors and the varnish. When she presented it proudly to Liam in the hospital gardens he had said it was great: when she got out she could make a fortune designing ashtrays for badly coordi-nated smokers. She picked it up and crept out of the house.

They'd been questioning him for three hours. The officer on the desk told her that he didn't know when Liam would get out, it could be a while.

She bought a lemon tea from the machine in the lobby and was just settling down for a long wait when Liam emerged from a corridor followed closely by McEwan. They both looked exhausted and angry. Liam's expression didn't falter when he saw her. He took the steaming plastic cup from her hand and put it down on a chair. "Come on," he said, taking her hand. "We're going home."

McEwan and Liam parted without saying good-bye.

18

MR. WIG

LIAM DIDN'T WANT TO TALK ABOUT WHAT HAD HAPPENED AT THE police station. All he would tell her was that Paulsa, the guy he had been to see at Tonsa's on the afternoon Douglas was murdered, had confirmed his alibi. Liam said he definitely wouldn't be allowed to see Maggie again. McEwan had phoned her parents and made them confirm his alibi for the evening. "They asked you about the evening, then?" she said.

"Yeah."

"Me too. It was good of Paulsa to come forward."

"Paulsa needs a lot of mates right now. He's just lost a lot of money."

"How?"

"Bought a job lot of bad acid, sank all his money into it without trying it first."

"Why's it bad?"

"Unsellable. A totally sick trip and everyone knows about it."

Liam parked outside Benny's close but didn't move to get out of the car. The street was quiet, bathed in the warm orange streetlight, like a film set.

Maureen brushed his hair off his face. "You look sad."

"I'm not sad," he said, chewing his lip. "I'm scared."

She had never heard him admit to it and hearing it now frightened her. "Oh, Liam," she whimpered pathetically, "I don't want you to be."

He looked out of the window. "If we get through this in one piece I'm going to sell the house and go to university."

"That's good," she said softly. "And what if we don't get through it in one piece?"

"Then I'll need to see what bits are left over and what can be done with them. I'm never going through that again."

"I'm sorry to have brought this on you," she said, thinking she sounded like Siobhain.

Liam said he didn't want to talk about it and he knew Benny would insist. "Just tell him we've been at Mum's, okay?"

A white Volkswagen was parked on the Maryhill Road opposite the bollards to Scaramouch Street. The two officers watched Maureen and Liam get out of the Triumph and go up the number twelve close. The driver picked up the radio and called in.

The heating was on and the flat was comfortably warm.

"I've been waiting hours for you two," said Benny. He had splashed out and bought three venison steaks for dinner. He banished both of them from the kitchen.

They sat on the settee watching television until Benny brought the dinner in. The meat was sweet and tender and he gave them cream-and-butter mashed potato with caramelized onions through it and steamed leek on the side. When the dinner had gone down a little, helped along by strong coffee, Maureen went down to the Ambassador to buy some ice cream.

The Ambassador coffee bar on the Maryhill Road was famous for its homemade ice cream. Its other claim to fame was the Aquarium Wall: an amoeba-shaped window had been cut into the plywood partition wall and an outsized fish tank had been placed behind it. The tank was empty now; a layer of pebbles sat on the floor of the dry aquarium, covered in a green carpet of algae stain.

No one ever seemed to eat in the café: the tables were always empty. It stayed open late at night, selling cigarettes and chocolate to locals. Behind the counter dark wood shelves reached right up to the high ceiling; a small ladder on rollers was fitted to the top one and they all strained under the weight of multicolored sweetie jars.

The man behind the counter was something of a local celebrity: apart from organizing the under twelves' football league he had the most obvious toupee in Maryhill, possibly the whole west coast. His hairpiece sat so high on his head it looked as if he kept his sandwiches under it. He was part of a local rite of passage: boys used to tell the wee kids that his name was Mr. Wig and get them to go in and call him by name.

Trying not to look at his hair, Maureen ordered a large tub of their homemade ice cream and a bottle of Irn Bru. Mr. Wig bent down to scoop the ice cream out of the freezer and she found herself face-to-face with his matted rug. Below the thick hairs on the toupee the weaving was dirty. She deflected her gaze by staring at the jars of sweeties. When they were very small Winnie would take them to sweet shops on Sundays after mass. Each child was allowed to choose one quarter. Maureen couldn't remember her favorite, it changed all the time, but Liam chose the rhubarb rock every time, without fail. She ordered a quarter. Mr. Wig weighed it out and scooped it into a paper bag, flipping it over as he twirled the corners to close it.

Back at the flat she gave the bag of sweeties to Liam. He opened it immediately and handed them round. "Man," he said, "I haven't had these for years."

In the kitchen she made floaters, pouring the fizzy Irn Bru into long glasses and spooning the ice cream into it. They mixed together, frothing all the way up the glass, settling down slowly while she added more ginger. The kitchen smelled like sweet-tooth heaven. They ate them as floaters should be eaten, greedy and graceless, with spoons and slurps and licks.

Benny had gone to the video shop, looking for *Reflecting Skin,* but it was out. He got *L'Atalante* instead, a French movie made in the thirties about a barge captain and his new wife.

They spent the evening wrapped in the cozy comfort of old friends, talking hardly at all and attending to nothing but their comfort. They would remember it as their last happy evening together, as a gentle pause in a troubled time.

19

MARTIN

SHE PHONED BEFOREHAND, JUST TO MAKE SURE THAT MARTIN WOULD be working that day. She couldn't bear the thought of turning up at the hospital without a kind face to greet her. The head porter told her Martin was on a back shift so she waited until the afternoon before setting off.

The Victorian façade of the Northern Psychiatric Hospital looked strange because the proportions were wrong. The Doric columns were too thick, the pediments too squat. With different associations Maureen was sure she would have found it beautiful but she couldn't. It looked nightmarishly lumpen. She didn't remember seeing the front of the building until the day she left to go home for good. She sat in the taxi and waved happily as Pauline, her anorexic friend from OT, waved back. Skeletal Pauline was standing in the chubby doorway as the taxi circled a turn. Maureen didn't notice that Pauline was crying until they passed her for the second time.

After the joint session, when Maureen started slipping back into the hazy blackness, it was the thought of Pauline that stopped her toying seriously with the idea of suicide. They had both been abused by their fathers, Pauline had been raped by her father and brother, but their responses were very different: Pauline couldn't get angry and Maureen couldn't get anything else. Pauline could never bring herself to tell: she said it would break her mother and that would be harder to bear than the abuse. She was putting on weight when Maureen met her. They did ceramics together—Pauline helped glaze the target ashtray in Winnie's hall. She was the best student in ceramics, she'd repeated the course three times. She'd been in hospital longer than anyone else in the class.

Maureen couldn't bring herself to go back and visit afterward but she did phone Pauline. They didn't have much to say to each other, their closeness was born of proximity, not affinity, but Pauline was always pleased to hear from her and dragged out the phone calls, talking about how her application for a house was going, repeating gossip from the ward, who was being released and what the staff were up to. Maureen found herself reluctant to phone. She stopped questioning Pauline, trying to cut the conversation short, and the phone calls got further and further apart.

Pauline was released a few months after Maureen. She wasn't given a house: apparently she'd been told that she would have to wait another three months. She'd been offered bed-and-breakfast in a bad area and turned it down. Within a week of her return to the family home she went to the woods near her house and took an overdose. She was missing for three days before a woman out walking her dog stumbled across her body. She was lying on her side, curled into a ball under the base of a tree. Her skirt had blown up over her face. At the funeral a nurse told Maureen that until they found a good-bye note in her bedroom, the police thought it was a murder because they found dried semen on her back. Someone had wanked on her as she lay dead or dying. Months later Maureen traveled deep into the suburbs to visit the wood. It was a scraggy stretch of trees leading down a hill to a main road, cut back at one side for a playing field and at the other for a private driveway. The locals were proud of the old wood but only to the extent that it didn't interfere with their individual property. The trees were thin and ailing, so that a walker would nearly always be visible from either side. Burnt plastic and cigarette ends spoke of children from good homes coming here on summer nights to drink cider and touch each other up and set fire to things. Maureen lay down among the dog ends and looked up at the treetops, empty tears running into her hair, and apologized far too late for leaving Pauline alone.

At the cremation Pauline's kind, bewildered mother cried so hard she burst blood vessels in her right eye. The father stood next to her in the pew, his arm around her, patting her shoulder when she whimpered too loudly. There were two brothers. No one knew which had raped Pauline. She never told. The minister told them that Pauline was a well-loved and dutiful daughter. Her coffin slid noiselessly along the conveyor belt, off through a red curtain.

The handful of mourners who weren't family had met Pauline in hospital and knew about her family. They avoided the usual pleasantries that accompany a young death. Only her mother thought it was needless. The mother had been too distraught to make a funeral tea and since Pauline was the only daughter there was no one else to do it for her. She apologized to everyone for her breach of protocol as the mourners walked single file over the motorway pedestrian bridge to a dingy pub.

Liam bought the father a pint of heavy. Liam had known Pauline and liked her. He knew what had happened to her.

"How the fuck could you do that?" said Maureen, under her breath.

"Hush, hush now," said Liam, and pushed her outside. "I put two acid tabs in it. His head'll burst."

She told Liam he should learn to restrain himself.

"I did," said Liam. "I wanted to give him eight."

Weeks later Maureen heard through the grapevine that the father had suffered some sort of schizophrenic episode and had briefly been hospitalized himself.

She could feel Pauline's wan smile warm her heart as she crunched over the gravel to the side door.

She found Martin in the staff canteen. He was sitting with his back to her but she recognized him from his broad shoulders and muscular arms. The back of his neck was creased and weather-worn, as if he had worked outside for a long time. He was eating a greasy pie and chips. "That stuff'll kill you," said Maureen.

Martin looked up and smiled at her. His white crew cut sat like a tiny halo around his brown face, his eyes were set into a bundle of laughter lines.

"Hello, pet," he said.

He had begun to age in the two years since Maureen had seen him: his ears and nose looked bigger. He reached over the table for the sauce bottle and she noticed that his wrists were swollen and he was wearing a copper bangle. He had red broken veins on his cheeks and white tufts of hair had been carefully trimmed on his earlobes.

"How long's your break?" asked Maureen.

"I've got another half hour."

"Can I sit with you?"

"I'd be annoyed if you didn't."

Maureen went to get a cup of tea.

"I got a phone call from a woman called Louisa Wishart at the Albert this morning," he said when she sat down.

"Oh?"

"She phoned me in the general office and they had to call me over the Tannoy. She said that you'd be coming back to see the hospital and would I look after you."

"I hope you don't mind."

"No," he said, chewing his last forkful of pie and chips. "I got time off for it. Is she your doctor now?"

"Yeah. She told me she'd worked here, I thought you'd remember her."

"Ah," said Martin, wiping his mouth with a paper serviette, "that explains why she was so pally. They've all worked here at one time or another. She must have been young. You don't pay much attention to the young ones."

"She's got big glasses, they take up half her face and she does this—" Maureen clasped her hands together and stared hard at him in an exaggerated mimic of Louisa. "She looks a bit like a fish."

"Naw, pet, I can't place her."

"Well, she's pretty forgettable."

"She doesn't sound it."

Martin was not a warm man but his natural calmness was so soothing it felt like warmth. He didn't seem as calm as usual today. He kept glancing around the canteen as if he was looking for someone. Maureen sipped her tea with a growing sense of unease. Martin watched her. "I saw you in the paper," he said.

Maureen blushed. "Oh, yeah?"

"That's why you're here, isn't it?"

"Aye."

"It's nothing to do with your treatment, is it?"

"No."

"Why does she think it is?"

"I lie to her. About most things."

"Why?"

"I don't want to tell her. I think she's a twit."

Martin was suddenly interested. "Has she got dark hair?"

"Yeah, loads of it."

"I do remember her. She was here a few years ago, just for six months. You're right. She was a twit."

They smiled at each other across the table.

"Why do you still see her?"

"My family worry about me if I don't, you know, see someone."

"I'm going to get a cup of tea, pet. D'you want another one?"

She didn't. Martin came back with a tea cake for her. It was mallow and biscuit, covered in milk chocolate. It was a child's biscuit. She must seem very young to him, she thought. She didn't know whether he was married or had children. He didn't offer information about himself. He wasn't secretive, he just didn't seem to feel the need to justify his life by placing himself in context. Maureen hoped he was married to a nice woman, that his wife trimmed his hairy ears for him of an evening, and she hoped he was a father. She thought he would be a good one.

"I can only tell you some things, pet," he said. "I can only tell you what I actually know. I'm not interested in the gossip, so I don't know what other people are saying. Okay?"

"Yep."

"There's something very bad happening and I don't want to be involved in it, right?"

"What kind of bad thing?"

"I'll tell you in a bit, but you have to promise me you won't repeat it."

"Promise."

He gave her a hard look. "Listen, this is very important, don't just say it like that. Don't repeat it."

"Right, Martin, I promise I won't."

He looked anxiously around the canteen. "I don't know who's involved in this. They might be here right now, watching us."

"Then don't act suspicious. I'm just here to see the place again and you're a helpful porter who was asked to show me round again. I didn't ask to see you, my doctor phoned you, remember?"

Martin's face relaxed. "Aye," he said, "that's right."

"And if they called you over the Tannoy and told you in the office lots of people'll know about it."

"Right enough. Come and we'll make a show of it, then. I'll take you around the old place again." Martin tidied his tray away to the appointed place and the canteen women thanked him.

He took her to George III ward. She was so engrossed in what he had said that she didn't feel much about being back there. "You remembered which ward I was in," she said.

"Oh, aye," said Martin, as if it was nothing.

When they were standing in the lift she asked him if he knew which ward Siobhain McCloud was in. "George I," he said quickly, as if he had known the question was coming. "They were all in George I."

They visited the dayroom and the patients' canteen. On the way over to the Portakabin counseling suites they passed through the gardens. The flower beds were bare now, sunken patches full of naked lumps of frozen mud, like measles scars on the well-kept lawn. Liam liked to sit here with her. They used to bring Pauline out and give her cigarettes. She wasn't allowed them because they suppressed her appetite but Maureen suspected that the real reason was punitive. Pauline wasn't starving herself to death because she wasn't hungry enough.

They walked past the Portakabin where the joint session with Winnie had taken place and back into the main body of the building. Martin led her into the theater lift. It was big enough to accommodate three trolley beds and their attendants comfortably. Maureen looked around the stainless-steel box. "I've never been in one of these before."

"We're not really supposed to use them," he said, "but they're always free."

The doors closed in front of them and he pressed Lower Basement, taking her to a part of the hospital she had never been to before. The lift slid downward, alighting softly, and the doors opened out onto a shallow lobby. They stepped out, turned right and walked through a set of fire doors, straight into a fork in the corridor. The right-hand side led up a long, windowless ramp; the left led down, deeper into the ground. They took the left fork to a corridor running parallel to the kitchen. One of the strip lights was failing, palpitating nervously. The smell of overcooked meat and synthetic gravy wafted up the corridor in a warm stream. Maureen could feel her mouth watering. Martin opened an old wooden door on the left of the corridor. "In here," he said.

They went into a dark L-shaped room. The foot of the L was obscured by a tall dusty hillock of bin bags stuffed with hospital blankets. Martin led her behind the little hill and down the L's foot to a small door. He pushed it open and flicked a switch. A bare lightbulb lit up the little room. The low ceiling sloped sharply to the left and the walls were bare, crumbling stone. Behind one she could hear a steady, low-pitched thrumming like a ship's engine. It was a warm room, perhaps because it was so close to the kitchen. On the walls hung posters of the Partick Thistle football team dating back to the 1960s. A small hand sink stood at the back of the room with a single cold tap. In front of it was a lonely hospital chair made of metal and cloth, taking up a third of the entire floor space. A pile of discarded tabloid newspapers was stacked unevenly against the wall. Some loose tea bags, a large kettle and a transistor radio were sitting on top of a miniature set of beautifully varnished mahogany drawers, with a polished brass window on the front of each drawer to hold a label in place. Martin saw her looking at it. "They used to keep the medicine in that, back in the olden days."

"Is this your den?" asked Maureen.

"Aye. No one knows it's here except me. This is where I do all my skiving."

She motioned to the Thistle posters. "I didn't know you were a religious man."

He grinned sheepishly. "Oh, aye. Season-ticket holder for my pains."

Partick Thistle FC, known as the Jags, is one of the few Glasgow football teams not associated with either side of the Protestant/ Catholic sectarian divide. Their fans are known locally for their passive but exceptional eccentricity and the team are known nationally for being crap.

Martin motioned for her to sit down in the chair, took the tea things off the mahogany drawers, put them on the floor, and crouched down on it. He looked uncomfortable so low with his big knees tucked under his chin. His feet were an inch away from hers.

He began to talk. He said that several years ago there had been some sort of problem in George I. The women in the ward were all getting much worse. It turned out that someone was interfering with them sexually. They changed all the staff and the problem cleared up but a lot of the original patients had never recovered. Martin's voice had dropped so low Maureen had to lean forward to hear him above the throbbing hum of the engine behind the wall. "I never knew about this," she said. "Did they prosecute someone?"

"Have you been to George I?"

"No."

"Oh, God, the poor souls can hardly talk. They couldn't go to court—half of them don't know their own names."

"How did they find out, then?"

He looked at a distant place somewhere through the wall and hugged his knees to his chest. "Burn marks. They'd been tied up or something. They'd burn marks on their bodies from the rope. And they were hurt . . ." He motioned downward.

"Where?"

"Their flowers—their flowers were cut."

"With a knife?"

"I don't know. You don't like to ask questions about things like that. I always thought it might be just that they were scared and they were dry." Martin was crying, his face impassive.

"Didn't they think to DNA test the semen and compare it with possible suspects?"

"There wasn't any semen," said Martin. "He'd wore a rubber. He knew exactly what he was doing."

His voice took on a peculiar timbre, halfway between a cry of despair and a growl. "I was there every day while it was going on. I didn't even notice. I keep my eyes open now."

"Oh, Martin, who would think to look for that?"

He coughed hard and wiped his face dry with his hand. She wanted to touch him. She could reach her hand out just a little and touch his brown cheek, but she didn't think he would like it. It would be done to console her, not him. He pulled his knees tighter to his chest and looked farther through the wall. "If any of us had noticed we could have stopped it."

She reached out and touched his hand with the tips of her fingers. He looked up, startled by the intrusion, and relaxed the grip on his knees. She shouldn't have touched him.

"Anyway," he said, stretching his legs out in front of him, "it doesn't much matter what I feel about it."

"Do they know who it was?" she asked.

"No, but your boyfriend was tied up, wasn't he?" Maureen nodded. "With rope?" She nodded again. "Did you know he was here?" asked Martin.

"Douglas was here?"

"You didn't know, then? I thought that's why you came back. Two weeks ago he asked Frank in the office for a list of patients' names from George I. He said he was doing a follow-up study about how they got on. Frank's a stupid bastard. He told loads of people that Dr. Brady'd been in. Frank isn't even authorized to give out that sort of information, so he was telling on himself as much as anyone.

Brady seems to have been a bright man. I'm surprised he hadn't the good sense to use a different name."

"Well . . ."

"Anyway, those of us who've been here for a while knew what it was about because he'd only asked for the George I names and he'd only asked for that time. Was he daft?"

"Not really. He wasn't very good at being secretive. You think he was killed because he got the list, don't you?"

"Aye," said Martin.

"Did you tell the police about this?"

"No."

"Why not?"

"I don't know." He looked at his feet. "That's a lie. I do know. I don't want to be involved in this. It's finished now and I'm too frightened to get involved." He didn't try to excuse himself but left the statement hanging in the air between them. "Was Douglas Brady married?" he asked.

"Aye."

"What were you doing going out with a married man?"

"God, Martin, I can't remember anymore." She'd taken up his time, reminded him of a deep hurt and touched his hand. She stood up. "I'd better be going," she said.

Martin had to stand flat against the wall to let her by. He came out after her and turned off the light, pulling the door to.

"That's a lovely wee den. How long have you had that?"

"Years," he said, leading her through the L-shaped room and back to the kitchen corridor. "Years and years and years. Don't tell anyone. It's my secret."

He walked her down the gravel path to the road and along to the bus stop. She knew fine well where the bus stop was and said Martin needn't bother but he said that he didn't need to do any work as long as she was with him and to shut up. The pavement was littered with dead leaves from the trees in the hospital grounds, help-less little carcasses, unable to defend themselves from the breezy wash of fast-passing cars.

"I think it's kind of you to keep seeing that stupid doctor so as not to worry your family," he said.

"I only do it so they won't hassle me."

"Aye, well, lots of people do good things for the wrong reasons. It's still a good thing."

He waited with her until the bus came and bade her take care.

20

LYNN

S HE GOT OFF THE BUS OUTSIDE A LARGE CHEMIST'S SHOP IN THE town center. It was on three levels and sold everything from face cream to home electrolysis kits. Maureen had a weakness for cosmetics, even the pseudoscientific face creams that made mad claims. She knew that surgery couldn't really come in a tub, that cream would have to be sold as a medicine if it did anything but moisturize, but still, when she felt bad, a good temporary solution was a face mask and a new tub of miracle face cream or a hair dye.

She wandered up and down the aisles, pausing at displays, reading packets, and settled on a dark hair dye that would condition *and* moisturize, and a face mask she'd used before. The mask was too harsh for her skin, it left it red and sore, but the cream came out of the tube black and turned bright orange as it dried. It always gave her a buzz.

Back at the house Benny had left a note on the coffee table in the living room to say he was speaking at an AA meeting and would be back at eight. Maureen started the bath running, took two clean white towels from the linen cupboard in the hall and locked the bathroom door. She stripped off, pinned her hair on top of her head and put the face mask on, spreading the black cream evenly over her face and neck. It had a pleasing rubbery texture. She sat on the edge of the toilet seat as she waited for the bath to fill and rubbed her fingers together, gathering the residue of the face mask into a gluey lump, rolling the warm black grape into the soft hollow of her palm.

She thought about Douglas, not shoddy, lying Douglas but the kind, compassionate man she'd been training herself to forget. She could understand him giving Siobhain money because of the Northern but Maureen hadn't been raped when she was there. Apart from Winnie, nothing bad had happened while she was in there. She thought about Shirley's suggestion that Douglas had been fucking someone in his office at the Rainbow. It seemed wildly out of character for Douglas. He had been so concerned with differentiating their relationship from that of a therapist who fucked his patient. He used to talk about it a lot. But, then, he hadn't mentioned that recently either so it could have been him. The bath was full. She turned off the taps.

Her face was rubbery and orange. Rolling her fingertips up her neck, she gathered the edge of the mask and pulled it off whole. Every pore on her face was tingling. The bathroom was foggy with steam as she slipped into the deep bath, sliding down until only her nose and tits were sticking out of the water, thinking of poor Ophelia. The scratches on the back of her neck bristled as the water hit them.

She stepped out and dried herself with the crisp, clean towel. The hair dye was the darkest she'd ever used: it wasn't Goth black but it wasn't a kick in the arse off it. She was shaking the bottle when she realized that she would ruin the white towels if she used them.

She chucked some clothes on and went into the hall, looking for an old towel in the airing cupboard, but there weren't any. Benny had some scabby ones, Maureen had seen them. She went into his bedroom, knelt down by the chest of drawers, pulled open the bottom one and rummaged, feeling for a towel texture. The drawer was filled with big winter jumpers and odd socks. Her hand landed on a glossy piece of paper. She nearly pulled it out before she realized it was a pornographic magazine. She shoved it back in, bristling with embarrassment, and pushed it to the very back. She felt something hard and flat and plastic lying on the floor of the drawer. She pulled back a jumper and looked in. It was a CD: it had been set into the corner of the drawer on the floor so that it didn't get lost in the jumble. She lifted it out, recognizing the two-tone corner before she saw the front of it. It was the *Best of the Selecter* CD. It was the CD she had left on the bedroom floor up in Garnethill; it even had the crack on the corner of the plastic cover.

She put it back where she had found it, covering it over with the same jumper and odd socks, and went back into the bathroom.

She combed her hair into a ponytail and hacked through it with a pair of nail scissors.

It was half-seven.

She listened at the bathroom door. The flat was still. She left a note on the kitchen table saying she'd stay at Leslie's tonight, and made her way down to the Great Western Road, taking a backstreet route she had never known Benny use.

Liam had more or less lived there for three years so she remembered the phone number. Lynn had moved; the guy who answered gave her an Anderston number.

"Hello, Lynn?"

"Aye," said Lynn cautiously.

"Lynn, it's me, Maureen O'Donnell."

"Mauri! How the fuck are you?"

They arranged to meet, under conditions of the utmost secrecy, in a large, busy café near Lynn's house.

* * *

Lynn waved happily when Maureen walked through the door. She had naturally black hair and flawless pink velvet skin but her eyes were her crowning glory, black with a blue tinge that made them look like polished semiprecious stones. Her body was slight and wiry and if Liam was to be believed she was unusually agile. She had a deep, gruff voice from smoking twenty a day from the age of twelve. She was eating a bowl of carbonara made with cubed gammon. Expertly, she rolled a string of spaghetti onto her fork as Maureen sat down. "So what's this about, Secret Squirrel? And what have you done to your hair?"

"Cut it myself," said Maureen, sitting down.

"It's all uneven. You come to mine after we've eaten and I'll straighten it."

" 'S all right," said Maureen distractedly.

"No, it's not. There's all jaggy bits hanging down at the back. It looks like a mad wummin's fanny."

They sat in silence for a moment as Lynn chewed a mouthful of pasta. The creamy sauce gathered at the corners of her mouth; it looked like froth. Maureen looked around the room. Tourist posters of Italy had been pasted onto the wall: behind Lynn's head loomed an aerial photograph of Florence. The pictures were skirted with flags-of-all-nations bunting.

"Auch," said Lynn. "Let's just skip all these pleasantries."

"Aye," said Maureen.

Lynn looked her over. "I know about your boyfriend, Maureen. Is that why you're doing this silent, haunted thing?"

"Am I?"

"Aye."

"Don't tell anyone we've met, eh?" said Maureen.

"I'm not sure we have yet," said Lynn.

They sat in silence until Lynn had finished eating. She paid the bill. "Come on," she said, standing Maureen up and slipping her arm through hers. "Let's go back to mine and fix your hair."

Lynn was living in a big flat on Argyle Street, across the road from a twenty-four-hour grocer's. The house must have been very grand once: it had five large bedrooms and a massive communal kitchen with a walk-in larder. The ceilings were thirteen foot high with ornate cornicing. One of her flatmates kept a gang of giant, love-bombing cats. The minute they got through the door the cats started rubbing against their legs, and when Maureen sat down on one of the kitchen chairs three of them scratched and hissed at one another for the right to sit on her lap. "If you sit on that wee settee," said Lynn, pointing over to a green two-seater by the TV, "they can all love you at the one time."

Maureen sat on it and her knees were immediately covered with a carpet of purring animals. Lynn stood behind her, spraying her hair with a pump-action aerosol full of water. She combed Maureen's hair this way and that, snipping at the bottom with a pair of sharp hair scissors. "Oh, Maureen," she said. "You've hurt your neck."

"Yeah."

"It looks like scratches or something."

Maureen didn't answer. The cats writhed on her lap, purring and digging their claws into her legs, nesting her as if she were a blanket.

"It looks a wee bit raw," said Lynn carefully. "Will I put some Germolene onto it?"

"Please."

She went out of the kitchen and came back with a huge jar. "Nicked it from the work," she said, when she saw Maureen looking. She rubbed the smelly cream gently, gently, onto the ripped skin on the back of Maureen's neck. "How's it feel now?"

"Itchy."

"You should put some foundation on that, doll, or wear a scarf or something. It looks a bit frightening." She screwed the lid back on the tub, washed her hands in the sink, lifted the scissors and carried on trimming. "Now," she said, "tell us why ye phoned."

"I need a favor," said Maureen.

"Big one? Wee one?"

"It's just a question. I don't know if you'd know anyway. I want to find something out from someone's medical records."

"Is it a patient at my surgery?"

"Naw. Lynn, don't tell Liam or anyone else this, right?"

"Okay."

"I think Benny's been in my house."

"Benny? Of course Benny's been in your house."

"But I think he's been in my house recently, when the police wouldn't let me in. I think he's talking to the police or something, I dunno. I can't put it together."

She would have told Lynn about the migrating CD but she knew she looked a bit mad and Lynn would think that she gave it back and then just forgot.

"I think he might have known Douglas. The police told me he'd been arrested in Inverness a few years ago. They didn't bring the case to court, he was sent for psychiatric treatment instead."

Lynn stopped cutting. "I never heard about that," she said.

"Me neither."

"Did he get treatment in Inverness?"

"No," said Maureen. "It must have been in Glasgow. He's never been away for any length of time."

"Maureen, Benny might be a bit mental sometimes but I don't think he'd talk about you to the police."

"I don't know what to think about anything now."

Lynn started snipping at her hair again. "So what do you want me to do?"

"I need to know how to get access to his medical record. I want to find out who his psychiatrist was. I think it might have been Douglas."

"Maureen, you can't get to see someone else's record without their consent. It's illegal. You can't hardly get to see your own."

"Really?"

"Yeah, man."

She finished cutting and handed Maureen a mirror, holding another behind her so that she could see what she had done. "There," she said, "that's a nice haircut."

Maureen looked at herself. It was the shortest she'd had her hair in a long time. It made her look younger. Lynn danced around her, pretending to be a hairdresser, showing her the reflection from both sides, holding it at an angle so that Maureen couldn't see the cuts on her neck.

"It's not bad, is it?"

"I think it's lovely," said Lynn.

"Do you know a guy called Paulsa?"

"Bad Acid Paulsa?"

"That guy who came forward for Liam."

"Yeah, I know him. We went up to his house once."

"Where does he stay?"

"You know that big Unionist pub off the Saltmarket? Next close."

"Oh, aye."

Maureen suddenly realized she had been talking about herself since they met and she'd barely asked Lynn how she was. She grinned unsteadily. "Did you and Liam get it together again, then?"

Lynn looked embarrassed. "Yeah, a wee bit. What's this Maggie character like?"

"She's all right. Not much crack, though. Are ye going out together again?"

"Naw," said Lynn, picking lumps of hair off the back of the settee. "I don't think we will be either."

"How come?"

Lynn displayed a polite reticence and then told her, "Uch, you know, Mauri, I used to look at him and all I could see was sunshine. It's not like that now. He's a bit too angry for me."

"Yeah," conceded Maureen. "He's angry enough."

Lynn punched her gently on the chin. "Like all the rest of the fucking family."

Maureen pulled her coat on. "It was good of you to come and meet me there," she said. "I think I lost the place for a wee minute."

"Happens to the best of us," said Lynn. "You stay in touch anyway, eh?"

"I will, Lynn, I will."

She walked down through the town, feeling her father's breath on her neck all the way to the shelter.

Leslie met her in the hallway. She led Maureen out of the house quickly and spoke to her on the doorstep. She couldn't come home, she said. Her shift didn't finish for another three hours. "The police came to see me again, they asked me about the night we went to that pizza place. I just told them the right times, is that okay?"

"Yeah."

"Can I pick you up at Benny's?"

"No, no," said Maureen. "I'll come back."

Leslie could see that something was wrong with Maureen: she was pale and her eyes were unfocused. "Where are you going?"

"I'll just wander about for a bit."

Leslie rubbed her arm. "Look," she said, trying to make eye contact, "um, go to the pictures or something, all right? Don't just wander off somewhere."

"Naw, I'm all right," Maureen murmured, and toppled off the outside step, wandering away with her hands deep in the pockets of her overcoat.

They had been there for a picnic once. Benny took Maureen and Liam down there — he had played there when he was a wee boy. It was a track of waste ground by the river, looking over to Govan and the shipyards, surrounded by run-down warehouses. It was probably a dangerous place to come at night, the motorway cut it off from the town and it was dark, but Maureen was tired of caring and she had her stabbing comb in her pocket. She lifted the chicken wire, crouched down and scrambled under it. She climbed to the top of a ten-foot-high concrete wedge sticking out of the river wall and sat down. Across the water she could see into the shipyards through an open slide door. Sparks from the welders' tongs flew in slow, red arcs. She pulled her coat tight against the mean river wind and lit a fag.

It was much darker now. The tide was coming in and the river flowed backward, slapping against the wall far below her feet. She thought about the ships passing down the river many years ago, taking emigrants to America, whole families of Scots lost to their own people forever. Lost to drizzling rain and a fifty-year recession, to endemic domestic violence and armies of drunk men shouting about football.

When she climbed down the rock and straightened her coat she felt taller somehow, as if, without trying to, she had floated across the dividing line between fear and fury.

She got there just in time to meet Leslie coming off her shift. She hadn't noticed before but Leslie had been crying. The appeal committee had notified them that morning that they would not allow them to make additional submissions. In the afternoon a husband had found the address of the house, come round and convinced his wife to move back home. "He broke her pelvis last time," said Leslie. "They only took the pins out last month."

"How the fuck did he do that?"

"He beat her with a baseball bat."

"I suppose everyone'll be going home if the appeal fails," said Maureen.

"Don't even say it," muttered Leslie, and handed Maureen a crash helmet.

21

FRANK

NEXT MORNING MAUREEN ADOPTED AN ENGLISH ACCENT AND phoned the Northern from Leslie's house. She asked reception to put her through to Frank in the office.

As soon as he lifted the receiver she realized that she should have thought it through beforehand. She didn't know who she was going to pretend to be, she didn't even know what story she was going to tell. She asked him whether he had seen the article about the superannuation mix-up, it was in the newsletter, he had probably read it. Well, Frank said, he remembered something about that, yes. Stunned that the story was hanging together, she staggered on: obviously it wasn't her fault, she had been called in to sort out her predecessor's mistakes, wasn't that always the way? Frank agreed vehemently. Maureen couldn't imagine Frank being called in to sort piss from shit but she didn't say so.

He agreed to get her a printout of the names and national insurance numbers of the full-time medical staff spanning ten years, from 1985 to 1995, excluding agency, and Maureen would send a courier to pick it up at two that day.

She looked at the phone before she put it down. Martin was right: Frank was really stupid.

Frank finished his sticky blueberry muffin and played another three games of Tetris. This was a bit lucky. If he did them this favor they might remember if he applied for a job at the regional office. A job in a real office. An office where you wouldn't be surrounded by bloody loonies.

At ten past two she walked into the office wearing a crash helmet and Leslie's leathers. Frank handed her a brown envelope. Curious as to how far she could push it, she made him sign a receipt for a novel she had bought a couple of weeks before. She walked down the back stairs and out of the hospital with her visor down, feeling untouchable, like a movie hero. Leslie had kept the engine running and the stand up on the bike. Maureen swung her leg over the seat and Leslie turned, spraying gray gravel. The lights farther down the road changed, causing a break in the traffic, and they pulled out into the road.

Back in the Drum they broke open a quarter bottle of whisky, took a slug each and opened the envelope. Frank had printed out a single sheet from his files, all medical personnel employed at the Northern covering the years 1985 to 1995, excluding agency. It was a list of national insurance numbers. No names. Frank really was a stupid bastard.

As they finished the whisky Leslie showed her how to sharpen the end of the stabbing comb into a point. She drew the long handle of the comb across a black wedge of silicon carbide, backward and forward, turning it over at the end to sharpen both sides, dragging it on the diagonal to give it an edge. She wrapped a J-cloth over the teeth and gave it to Maureen to have a go. She scratched the handle over the block, turning it over and drawing it through. She kept going until she brought it to a neat point with an inch-long sharpened ledge on either side of the tip. Leslie rubbed margarine into it to disguise the scratches.

Maureen thought about the stabbing comb as Leslie drove her back to Maryhill and Benny's house, she thought about it and it warmed her, as the remembrance of a great love would.

Leslie dropped her at the bollards in the Maryhill Road.

Benny was in the hall, on his way out to the library. "Maureen, where were you yesterday?" he said, and hugged her. "How're ye keeping?"

She stood stiff in his arms, trying to remember how she used to react to him when he touched her. She pressed herself into his chest and guessed. "I'm fine, Benny," she said, drawing back and looking him straight in the eye, holding his cheek with the flat of her hand. She looked at him, willing her suspicions about him away, but they refused to subside.

He squeezed her shoulders. "Good, wee hen." He grinned. "That's good. You've changed your hair. It's really nice."

"Yeah, I got it cut."

"God, is that whisky on your breath?"

"Um, yeah."

"Maureen, watch yourself, it's only three in the afternoon."

"I'm watching myself," she said resentfully, and pulled away from him. "I'm just . . . I just wanted some today, that's all."

"Naw"—he pulled her back by the arm—"don't be like that." He hugged her again and she found herself more uncomfortable than the first time.

"Just see ye don't end up like me, that's all I mean," he said, and let her go. "Spending your days and nights in smoky rooms with a bunch of old alkies."

The police had phoned for her and she was to phone the Stewart Street station. He said he'd made dinner for her and left it in the oven. She shouted a cheerful cheerio after him as he shut the front door behind himself.

She slipped on the oven gloves and took out the casserole dish, feeling the warmth seeping through the cheap gloves. She lifted the lid. It was a mouthwatering cheesy pasta thing. A large portion had been sliced out of it: the fresh cliff of cheese and pasta was collapsing slowly, sliding down and filling the base of the dish. She cut herself a portion and dirtied a plate and some cutlery with it before dropping it into a plastic bag ready for the bin. She arranged the plate and fork on the draining board to look like the disregarded crockery of a happy eater. She ducked into the bedroom and checked the bottom drawer. The CD was still there, unmoved since she put it back.

Her T-shirt was covered in itchy shards of hair from the night before. She went into Benny's cupboard and found the mustard crewneck jumper she had brought from the house. She took the jaggy T-shirt off and pulled the jumper over her head, opened her leather rucksack and lifted most of her clothes from the shelf, shoving them into the bag. Her hand hovered over the Anti Dynamos T-shirt. She took it for spite and left a pair of knickers and a T-shirt on the shelf in case Benny noticed everything was gone and got suspicious.

Joe McEwan couldn't come to the phone but the officer knew who she was and told her they wanted to see her at the station as soon as possible. He offered to send a car for her but she said it was okay, she'd make her own way down. He didn't object and she took it as a good sign. She collected the bag of food from the kitchen sink and dumped it in a street bin.

She was halfway down the road to the police station when she remembered Jim Maliano's Celtic shirt and jogging trousers sitting on the floor of the cupboard among the dirty socks. She would have to go back to Benny's at some point.

* * *

Hugh McAskill came to collect her from the reception desk with Inness at his back. Inness had shaved off his gay-biker mustache. It may have been because she was used to seeing him with it or because the freshly shaved skin was a lighter color than the rest of his face but his top lip seemed odd and prominent. Her eyes kept straying to it of their own accord. Inness saw her looking at it and turned his head away to shake off her gaze.

They took her to an interview room on the ground floor. McAskill seemed to be in charge. He gave her a cheeky encouraging look, took a big chocolate bar out of his pocket, ripped the packaging down the middle with his thumbnail and broke the chocolate into squares. He put it down in the middle of the table, setting it on top of the wrapper like a serving suggestion. "Wire in," he said, sucking on a square.

Inness took two and Maureen took one. "Thanks," she said, and wondered why he was always so nice to her.

Inness turned on the tape recorder, told it who was present and what the time was.

"Now, Miss O'Donnell," said McAskill, swallowing his chocolate and addressing her in a formal telephone voice, "the first thing I need to ask you is whether or not you've ever seen this before."

He produced a knife from a crumpled paper bag and put it on the table. It was a new Sabatier kitchen knife with an eight-inch stainless-steel blade and a black wooden handle. She had seen them in shops. They were expensive. A paper tag was attached to it with a piece of string, a long number scrawled on it in Biro. It had been cleaned and polished, the blade flawlessly reflecting the fluorescent bulb above their heads, a pitiless slit of light sitting on the table.

Maureen wished she hadn't taken the chocolate. Her mouth was dry and the sticky paste was stuck under her tongue and up be-

tween her gums and cheeks. Her mouth began to water at the sight
of the knife in a way she found disturbing.

"Is that it?" she asked, staring at it.

"Is it what?" said McAskill.

"Is that what was used on Douglas?"

"Yes, I'm afraid so. Have you seen it before?"

"No," said Maureen.

"You sure?"

"Yeah."

"Okay," he said, and handed it to Inness. Inness put it back in the
bag. She thought it was a stupid way to keep a sharp knife, blade
down in a paper bag.

"Where did you find it?" she asked.

"How do you mean?" said McAskill uncomfortably.

"Where was the knife? Was it out the back of the flat?"

"We found it in the house. Why?"

"I just thought you'd have asked me about it before, that's all."

"We only just found it," said Inness.

"A week and a bit afterward?" said Maureen.

"It was quite well hidden," muttered Inness, lifting another square
of chocolate and putting it in his mouth.

Maureen wondered how well hidden anything could be in a flat
the size of a fifty-quid note with ten men raking through it.

"Can I ask you something else?" she said, addressing McAskill
this time.

"Depends what it is," he said carefully.

"Have you any idea who did this?"

"We're following a number of leads," he said, shuffling his papers.

"One more question?"

He smiled kindly. "Go on, then, try me."

"Did you talk to Carol Brady?"

"Aye," he said. "She's not your greatest fan."

"Yeah, I know that."

"She's convinced you blackmailed him for that money."

"I didn't even know it was there, honestly."

"We've seen the security video at the bank," said McAskill. "Douglas paid in the money himself."

"When?"

"First thing in the morning on the day he was killed."

Maureen could almost see the time-lag security video, blurred and gray, Douglas jolting across the floor to the teller like a bad animation.

"Can you think of a reason for him to pay that much money into your account?" asked McAskill.

"Sorry?"

"Why would he do that? It was pretty obvious the other day that you had no idea it was in there. What would he give you money for?"

"I don't know." She looked at the table and wondered, "Maybe he wanted me to pass the money on to someone else and he didn't get the chance to tell me about it."

McAskill nodded but didn't seem convinced. "Okay," he said. "We'll look into that."

"Did you find out who'd told Carol Brady where I was staying?"

"I'm afraid I can't tell you that," said McAskill stiffly, rolling his eyes and nodding at the tape recorder. Maureen didn't understand the signal. He nodded at it again. Maureen leaned across the table and pressed the Stop button on the tape recorder.

"No!" said McAskill, lurching over the table and pulling her hand away. "You have to tell us you want the tape off and we need to say we're going to, right?" He switched it on again.

Inness said, "The tape was turned off at five-thirteen by the interviewee, Miss Maureen O'Donnell. Miss O'Donnell, did you just turn the tape off?"

"Yes, I did just turn the tape off."

"Do you want me to turn the tape off before we continue the interview?"

"Yes."

"Miss O'Donnell has requested that the tape recorder be turned off at this point in time," said Inness. "I am turning it off at five-fourteen and the interview will continue." He flicked the switch and turned excitedly to McAskill.

"I don't particularly want a tape of me telling you this," said Hugh, "but a young officer's facing disciplinary action over it. We went to see Brady and she gave us his name."

"Without blinking an eye," said Inness, taking another square of chocolate. "She just said his name and shut the door." He popped it in his mouth.

"Nice lady," said Maureen.

McAskill smiled. "Lovely."

"Where did the money in my account come from?"

Inness jumped in. "Mr. Brady emptied his own account. Took out thirty-odd thousand in big notes."

"God," said Maureen. "How does anyone get that much money in their account in the first place?"

"That's none of your business," said Inness defensively, his incisors smeared brown. Maureen looked at his bald top lip. He lifted his arm stiffly, rested his elbow on the table and cupped his hand over his mouth.

"He'd saved it over a number of years," said McAskill. "His wife didn't even know he had the account until he died."

Maureen took out her cigarettes and lit one. The smoke mingled with the sweet chocolate in her mouth, turning both tastes bad.

"Where do you think the rest of the money went?"

She shrugged, mulling over the lump of money in Siobhain McCloud's handbag. The other fifteen thousand couldn't be in there:

it would take seven hundred and fifty twenties to make it up and the roll couldn't possibly have had that in it. "I dunno where it went. I suppose I'll have to give the money back?"

"No," said McAskill. "He gave it to you. It's yours."

She didn't know why Douglas had given it to her but she had a bad feeling about it. She didn't really want the money. "Does Mrs. Brady still think I did it?"

"Yeah," McAskill said. "She's not interested in any evidence, she's just certain it was you."

"Certain," echoed Inness, picking up another piece of chocolate.

McAskill nudged Inness and jerked his head toward the tape recorder. "Okay," he said, "I'm going to put the tape back on now, Maureen, if that's all right with you. I need a record of me telling you this next thing."

"Sure," said Maureen.

He turned on the tape. "Anyway, Miss O'Donnell, we have finished our examination of the house and you are welcome to return at your convenience."

"Right," said Maureen tentatively. "What happens about the mess? Do you clean it up or do I?"

"It's down to you, really. It should be covered on your home insurance. We only clean the place if the person living there can't clean it on their own, like a disabled or an old person."

"Right," she said, her heart sinking at the thought of her minimal house insurance. "I see. Is that it, then?"

McAskill looked at his notebook. "Yes," he said. "That seems to be all for now."

On the way down to the lobby she asked them if she could see Joe McEwan. Inness smirked. "I don't think he'll be too happy to see you," he said. "You weren't very ladylike the last time."

"I know. I wanted to apologize about that."

"We can tell him you're sorry," said Inness.

"Well, I'd really like to see him about something else as well."

McAskill disappeared through the double doors under the stairs. Inness gave her a dirty look, for no reason, and wandered off to chat to the policeman on reception. When McAskill came back he was smiling. "You've got two minutes," he said to Maureen.

McEwan followed him out of the door. "What can I do for you?" he said sharply.

Maureen led him away from the other two. "Listen, I wanted to ask you about something. Remember you said something about Benny's no pro case? Could you tell me what he was arrested for?"

"I certainly could not," he said, looking at her as if she'd just suggested he fuck a pig while she stabbed it. "I can't tell you what was on someone else's police record."

She should never have called him an arsehole. "Just asking," she mumbled.

"Was there anything else? I'm busy finding out about your brother."

"My brother didn't do it, Joe."

"We'll see," he said, meanly.

"Come on, he's got an alibi for the whole day."

He ignored her comment. "Was there anything else?" he asked.

"No, nothing else."

"Fine."

McEwan swanned off back through the double doors, leaving them swinging, saloon-style, in his wake.

Inness was still chatting to the officer on the reception desk. McAskill sidled up to her, looking at the floor. "No pro," he said, his lips moving hardly at all, his voice a breathy whisper. "Inverness, nineteen ninety-three. Committed a breach outside a warehouse. Demanding money from a man. Six months afterward the same guy was arrested for running a stolen credit card operation covering the whole northeast. Your friend was very, very lucky he was done for breach. His case was decided before they found out what it really meant. He must have been working with the big boss."

"Could the psychiatrist who saw him have known this?"

"If your pal didn't tell him at the time he'd know afterward. It was all over the papers."

Maureen loved nonsensical stories and when Benny first got sober he used to keep her up nights telling her about his drinking. If it was an innocent incident he would have told her about it. "Thanks for telling me that, Hugh," she said. "It makes sense of some things."

He was showing her out of the door when she turned to him. "Hugh," she said, "why are you so nice to me?"

"I'm not that nice."

"But telling me about Benny, and the chocolate and stuff."

"You could have found out about your pal, it would just have taken a long time, but it's all a matter of public record."

"No, I mean, they think I'm a mental bitch, why don't you?"

He held the door open for her and she stepped outside. "Ever thought about an incest survivors' group?" he said softly.

"Eh?"

"Tuesdays. Eight p.m. St. Francis, Thurso Street. Round the back." He let the glass door swing shut behind her.

She looked back into the station lobby. He was walking away.

She could have gone home but Douglas's key was still missing and calling out a locksmith on a Friday night would cost a fortune. She found a phone box by the main road and rang Liam's house. When he picked up the phone he sounded drunk and pissed off.

"Can I stay at yours tonight, Liam?"

"What about the filth?"

He only ever used stupid colloquialisms like that when he was pissed.

"I've just seen them, they won't come to the house, honest."

"*I haven't got anything anyway,*" he said accusingly.

She checked her pockets to see how she was fixed and hailed a cab.

The blue Ford followed Maureen's cab up the Great Western Road, passing it slowly when it stopped at Liam's house. It turned the corner and parked in a side street. One police officer wrote down Liam's address while the other turned off the engine and settled back.

Liam lived on the grubby side of the West End. The four-story townhouse had been partitioned into gloomy bedsits when he bought it. He'd been doing it up gradually, working from the attic down. He had finished the first floor now but was reluctant to start renovating the ground-floor rooms. He'd kept the partition door at the foot of the stairs to make upstairs look like a separate flat and left the lower rooms scabby so that shady visitors wouldn't think there was anything worth stealing. He rarely sat downstairs. He tended to spend his free time upstairs in the enormous room at the front of the house, painted white with a stained wood floor and nothing in it but a Corbusier lounger and the eight-foot-long utility desk with his Mac on it.

Maureen pressed the doorbell. She could hear Liam brushing heavily against the walls as he staggered to the front door. He opened it without looking out and sloped back into the front room. She followed him in. The coffee table was strewn with empty cans of imported lager.

It had been a scabby room before the police searched it but Maureen wasn't prepared for the state it was in now. The dirty beige carpet had been pulled back and floorboards had been lifted and placed back down unevenly. The black leatherette settee had been cut open along the back; yellow foam spewed out like an action shot of a bursting spot. The old television was on in the corner; the molded plastic back had been reattached badly and was open at the side. *Match of the Day* was showing: a panel of three ugly men in bad ties were laughing at a joke.

Liam walked unsteadily over to the coffee table and picked a lit cigarette out of the full ashtray. He slid more than fell sideways onto the settee, pulling at the ripped back to work his way into a sitting position. He looked her up and down as if he were sickened by the sight of her and blinked slowly. "Maureen," he stated. He lifted his fag to his mouth slowly and sucked it, dragging his cheeks inward.

"You're pissed," she said, unable to hide her disappointment, and went to use the phone on the hall table.

She found the insurance company's twenty-four-hour help-line number in the Yellow Pages. She gave her details to a woman with a plummy accent and explained the situation as simply as she could. The telephonist paused for a moment, probably wondering whether it was a hoax call, and asked her for her policy number. "No, I don't actually have it with me."

"We need it to find the policy."

"Can't you just use my name and address?"

The woman paused again and sighed. "Just putting you on hold," she said. A high-pitched reworking of "Frère Jacques" squealed across the line. Maureen held the receiver away from her ear. The tune played twice through. The woman came back on the line to tell her that she was still on hold, and was gone again.

Liam was standing in the doorway in a drunken foul temper. He was having trouble keeping upright and mumbling curse words.

"Hello?" asked the woman at the insurance company. Liam's knees buckled and he slipped sideways in the door frame.

"Yes, yes, I'm here," said Maureen, standing up and helping him back onto his feet. He spun round and fell face-first into the living room.

"Well," said the woman, "I've had a look at your policy and you'll have to do it yourself. You can be reimbursed for the cost of any items provided you keep them—"

"Cheers," said Maureen, and hung up. Liam was crawling on all fours toward the settee. "Ya fuckin' drunken horse's arse," she said tenderly, working her hands under his damp armpits and dragging him onto the settee. He pulled his T-shirt straight and sat, almost prim, crossing his legs carefully, looking eerily like Very Drunk Winnie. He coughed, thought about something and glowered at Maureen. "See the state?" he said, gesturing around the room. "See it?"

Maureen sighed. "If we're going to have a fight, can we have it tomorrow?"

Liam blinked for a month. "Who's fightin'? I never said we were gonnae have a fight."

Maureen sat down next to him. "You strongly implied it," she said.

For a moment Liam's expression quivered between furious and distraught. He started to cry. "I'm fed up," he said, covering his face with his hands. Maureen put her arm around his shoulder. "Oh, Christ, Mauri, everything's turning to shite. My business . . . Douglas. I had to let Pete down on the deal and he's pissed off at me. I lost thirty grand 'cause I crapped it."

"But, Liam," she said, "you don't need more money, you've got loads of money."

He tried to shake off her arm by jerking his shoulders up and down. It didn't work and she left it there. "My bottle's gone," he said, looking at her as if she had taken it. "And Mum's going mental, she says you're a wee shite and Maggie won't even speak to me." He sat forward, wriggling out of Maureen's grasp, and wiped his face on his T-shirt.

"When did you see Mum?"

"She said that you're a wee shite and you went back and took all your photos away."

"I did."

"And she said you're a wee shite."

"Yeah, you don't have to keep going on about that bit."

"Did ye?"

"They're my photos, Liam."

"Ye could have asked her."

Maureen was indignant. "She was selling them to the newspapers."

"Yeah, but they were in her house," he said, aware of the weakness of his argument.

"Look, Liam, I'm not having a great time right now either. Why are you picking on me? Do you want a fight?"

"I don't want a fight."

"Well, shut up, then."

They sat in an uncomfortable silence and watched *Prisoner: Cell Block H* until Maureen got up to go to the toilet. He muttered after her, "Prick."

"Hey," said Maureen, shouting back into the room, "don't you be fucking cheeky to me, son."

The toilet on the first floor had been ripped apart: the U-bends had been taken off the sink and the toilet and all the jars and bottles of toiletries were sitting in the sink with their lids off. The linoleum had been pulled up, folded over and left in the bath. She went upstairs to the other bathroom. Liam kept it fairly sparse anyway and it was more or less intact. Only the towel cupboard had been riffled through: all of the fresh towels had been opened up and thrown back on the shelves.

When she came downstairs Liam was asleep in the armchair. She put out his fag, turned the telly off and went upstairs to the spare bedroom, leaving him there, his neck bent into his chest in a way that was certain to hurt like a bastard in the morning.

22

COLUMBO

IT WAS A SUNNY AUTUMN DAY. RED SANDSTONE BUILDINGS CLASHED with a powder blue sky, and out of the front windows of the bus, in the clear, far distance, Maureen could see the rugged Campsie hills capped in snow. She got off the bus and walked round the side to the staff canteen. She knew she was taking a chance and shouldn't ask for him; she would just have a quick look. She thought about going to his secret place to wait for him but he might not come there. She was buying a cup of tea at the canteen counter when she remembered that he only worked every second Saturday — he might not even be in today.

She sat at a table on her own and drank her tea, checking the tables and watching the door. She couldn't see him. She was wearing her gray overcoat and tartan scarf. The staff were all there in their white uniforms. She saw them looking at her and knew she should take off the coat to blend into the crowd but if she took it off she'd have to take the scarf off too and then the marks on the back of her neck would be visible and they would definitely think she was a patient. Dr. Paton might come in and spot her. She should never have come. A male nurse with the same eyes as Michael caught her eye and smiled, quizzically concerned. She changed her mind and hurried to leave. Martin almost banged into her in the doorway. "What in God's name are you doing here?" he said angrily.

He took her elbow and guided her firmly down the corridor, into a theater lift. He punched the button for lower ground with the side of his fist, not speaking until the doors were shut in front of them. "Why have you come back here? I told you everything."

"Martin, I need to ask you some more questions. I'm really sorry, I didn't want to phone you, I thought I'd be less conspicuous if I just turned up and found you."

"For pity sake. Sitting in the staff canteen with your coat on waiting for me?"

He walked briskly down the forked corridor. The failing fluorescent bulb was flickering slowly, like a dying man's pulse. She followed him through the door to the L-shaped room and round the corner to his den. He turned on the light and shut the door behind her. "Right, what is it?" he snapped.

"There's no need to be short with me," said Maureen.

"No, Maureen, there's every need. I suppose you thought you were being fly, getting that list off Frank yesterday. He phoned later to see if you got it. When he found out that you didn't exist he phoned the police. He's been suspended from work and it's all over the hospital. The George I man would need to be deaf and blind not to know about it now." He sat down on the metal chair and looked up at her solemnly.

"Oh, God, I'm sorry," she said, lifting the tea things off the mahogany cabinet and sitting down on it.

"You thought you were being fly, didn't you?"

She rubbed her shins with her hands quickly and owned up. "Yes," she said.

"Well, you weren't. It was a stupid thing to do. Now, why have you come back?"

"I want you to tell me who the staff were."

"Isn't that what you got off Frank?"

"No. That's what I asked him for but he gave me the wrong information."

"What did he give you?" he asked.

"A list of national insurance numbers."

Martin thought about it for a moment. His face creased into a reluctant grin and he started laughing. His hilarity escalated until he was doubled over in the chair, emitting high-pitched silly barks and wiping tears away. Maureen smiled despite herself. Martin slapped her knee and she started laughing too.

When he finally managed to calm himself he leaned over and flicked the switch on the big kettle sitting on the floor. "Aw, geeso," he giggled, "that guy, that Frank, he's such an ijit." He tapped her ankle, getting her to move her leg aside, and pulled open one of the little drawers on the mahogany chest. A stack of plastic cups was lying inside. Still chortling to himself, he took out two cups, put tea bags in them and opened another drawer with a Tupperware sandwich box containing powdered milk. Without asking her, he poured some into both cups. Maureen didn't want to correct him in case she interrupted his mood. He put the container back and took an opened half packet of Bourbon biscuits out of another drawer.

"You're all set here, aren't you, Martin?"

"Aye," he said, still grinning. "I know how to look after myself." He saw her looking at the Thistle posters. "We're playing in France tomorrow. Metz."

"You going?"

"Naw," he said. "The bus leaves today, couple of hours before my shift finishes. Shame. All my cronies are going." He poured water from the kettle into the cups and handed her one.

She took it, holding it carefully by the rim until she realized that it was barely warm. The kettle hadn't had time to boil properly, the tea bag floated ineffectually in the greasy white water.

"Do you think you'll win?" she said.

"You don't know anything about football, do you, pet? No, we'll lose."

She tried to sip the tea but couldn't face it. She put the cup down on the uneven floor and took one of the Bourbons from the packet. Her teeth slid easily through the damp biscuit and it crumbled behind her teeth, tasting old and chalky. She shoved it over to the side of her mouth, trying to keep it away from her tongue. "Can't you tell me about the staff, Martin?"

"Why should I?" he said, serious again. "As soon as I do you'll start asking questions about them and go and see them, won't you?" He dunked the lazy tea bag in his cup. It exuded some brownness and then died.

"Well, yes," she said.

"And you'll probably be as clumsy about it as you were with Frank. Everyone'll know I've told you. I could get in a lot of trouble. It might even be dangerous."

"Everyone'll think it was Frank who told me."

Martin sipped his tea and thought about it. "Aye," he said. "Aye, well, that's true enough. But why should I give you more information to draw attention to yourself with?"

She gave up the pretense and put the old biscuit down next to the undrinkable tea. "Martin, have you ever thought that he might still be doing it?"

"No," he said, with certainty. "We would have heard. They'll have caught him out by now."

"Not if his victims are vulnerable enough. Maybe what he learned from George I was just to be more careful and not leave marks on women who are washed by other people or something."

He grunted, chewing his biscuit, and considered the possibility. His face darkened. "You're not going to let this go, are you?" he said. "You're going to keep on until you find him."

"Yeah."

"You're being stupid."

"Yeah."

"He might kill you."

"I might kill him," she said.

Martin smiled. "I remember when you were frightened of the noise the dinner trolley made."

"Please tell me, Martin."

"Why are you doing this? Why don't you tell the police?"

"Well, they think my brother did it and now Siobhain McCloud's involved. She can't talk about the ward and they'll try and make her. I can't tell them about her." She could feel herself losing the thread. "The police won't listen to me anyway. They know I was in here, they just think I'm mental."

"I remember Siobhain well," he said, "she was a teuchter. What would happen if you told the police everything you've found out so far?"

Maureen thought about it. "They'll make Siobhain talk about what happened to her on George I ward. I don't know what that'll do to her—she can hardly say the ward name."

Her head was bent low over her knees, and although her dark hair had fallen over her face Martin could still see a hollow shadow in her eyes. He slapped his open hands on his thighs. "Well," he said, "you've no choice, then. Have you a pen?"

She rummaged in her leather rucksack, found a Biro under the pile of tissues and bus tickets and gave it to Martin. He tapped her ankle again and opened another mahogany drawer containing a rolled-up writing pad. It had a medical logo on it, selling a pill for hemosomething. He headed the sheet with her name in block capitals and underlined it twice, drawing in two exclamation marks. He smiled across at her and wrote out a list, chewing the end of the pen between names. Maureen looked round the room. The humming engine noise coming from behind the wall had stopped. The room was completely silent except for the scratching of pen on paper and the occasional rumble coming up through the drain in the sink from the water pipes. The walls must be feet thick.

Martin finished off the list and handed it to her. "Those are ones I remember," he said. "There'll be some I've forgotten, but those are the full-timers who were moved after the scandal."

She folded it up and slipped it into the condom pocket of her jeans. He offered her the pen back: it was chewed and slavered on. "You can keep it," she said.

He looked at the pen. "Oh." He was puzzled. "I'm always doing that."

He wanted to walk her to the bus stop. She argued with him as they went back to the lift. It would be more discreet if he didn't, she said, she'd already been stupid enough for both of them.

He shook her hand, holding it tight with both of his as the lift took off. "I don't expect to see you again," he said firmly.

"I promise you won't, I swear." She patted her hip pocket as the lift bobbed to a gentle standstill. "Thanks." The doors opened and she stepped out. "Hope your team win," she said, turning back.

"We won't." He grinned at her and the doors slid shut in front of him.

Martin had written down a list of nurses and a separate list of doctors. Maureen read and reread it on the bus. She didn't recognize any of the names.

The sullen receptionist had been replaced by an industrious, well-mannered middle-aged woman in a white blouse and burgundy cardigan who said good afternoon as she came through the lobby. Maureen smiled at her and went through to the television room.

Siobhain was sitting in her chair watching an early episode of *Columbo*. The room was nearly empty except for Siobhain and a very old lady wearing too much red lipstick. The fierce red paste had bled into the wrinkles radiating from her mouth, making it look like a badly diseased anus. It was Saturday, and Maureen supposed that most people would be with their families. The old lady stood up unsteadily when Maureen walked in and looked at her expectantly. "Is it you?" she said. Her upper set of dentures fell, collapsing diagonally and jamming her mouth open. She tried to smile and the teeth fell out, landing on the linoleum floor.

Siobhain looked up and smiled over at Maureen. "Hello, Helen," she said. She was wearing the clothes she had had on last Wednesday but they were still immaculate — she didn't do much to get them dirty.

"My name's Maureen, actually, Siobhain."

Siobhain was confused. "Did I forget?" she said.

"No," said Maureen. "Tanya always gets my name wrong. She introduced us."

"Oh, yes. I like your new hair."

"So do I," said Maureen.

The old lady was standing between them, grinning, gumsy and confused, her teeth lying in front of her on the floor. Maureen picked up the dentures and carried them to the little kitchenette at the back of the room. The lady put her hands out in front of her and kept her eyes on the teeth as she followed Maureen to the sink. Maureen turned on the cold tap and held the teeth under the water. She handed them back. "Thank you," said the lady graciously. "Thank you very much."

Maureen pulled a plastic chair next to Siobhain's and sat down. The old lady followed her, standing between them and the television. Siobhain leaned over the armrest and carried on watching *Columbo*. The lady put the teeth in and tried to smile at Maureen again, and again her teeth fell out. Maureen stood up.

"No, leave it," said Siobhain. "She shouldn't be wearing them at all, she found them in a drawer. Gurtie," she said to the old lady, "Gurtie, dear, you shouldn't put them in your mouth."

Gurtie looked puzzled.

"What are you watching?" asked Maureen.

"*Columbo.* It's very good. I like that man."

Maureen stroked the back of Siobhain's head: her hair was knotted again. It must be where she rests her head when she is sleeping, thought Maureen, where she rubs her head on the pillow. "The knot's worse today," she said. "Shall I comb it?"

"Yes, please."

She moved her chair behind Siobhain and took out her sharpened stabbing comb. Gurtie came over and offered them a ripped *Observer* magazine. They said no, thank you, Gurtie. Gurtie sat down in a chair and stared at the side of the television for a little while before wandering off into the next room.

When the knot was combed out Maureen dragged her seat next to Siobhain and sat down. They watched television for a while, eating a bag of crisps Maureen had brought with her. Columbo solved the case and the ads came on. Siobhain turned to face Maureen. "How wicked that Hollywood lady was."

"Yeah," said Maureen.

"And she did it for the money. Terrible behavior." She settled back into her seat.

"Siobhain, I wanted to ask you something."

"What is it about?"

"You know what it's about."

Siobhain looked at her hands. "I have to tell you I can't talk about it."

"I know you can't, I don't want you to talk about it. I want you to tell me the names of some of the other women in the ward at the same time. Could you do that?"

"I don't remember very well. But I suppose . . . yes."

Maureen got out Martin's list and Siobhain wrote the names at the bottom. She could only remember four: Yvonne Urquhart, Marianne McDonald, Iona McKinnon and Edith Menzies. They were all

Highland names. "That's why I remember them. I can't remember foreign names so well."

Maureen thanked her.

"No." Siobhain stiffened in the chair. "I remember." Her voice dropped to a panicky whisper. "Iona is not—she died."

"Oh," said Maureen, surprised by how upset Siobhain was. She would surely have remembered that the woman was dead if they had been that close. "I'm sorry, were you friends?"

"No." Siobhain was losing her breath. "She took her own life. Tanya said."

"How did Tanya know?"

"At the Rainbow. Iona was at the Rainbow."

"Breathe in, Siobhain," said Maureen. "Take a deep breath."

Siobhain struggled.

"Listen," said Maureen, "tell me what programs you watch on Saturdays."

Panting, Siobhain started relating the programming schedule for Saturdays. By the time she got to ten o'clock she was perfectly calm. Maureen wanted to leave but thought Siobhain might get bad again. She sat until the end of *Howards' Way.* "I should really be going," she said.

23

JIM MALIANO

LIAM HAD A CRICK IN HIS NECK AND WAS HUNG OVER AND SORRY. HE was sitting on the burst settee and nursing a mug of strong coffee with his neck bent at an awkward angle, looking up at her, unshaven and repentant.

"You called me a prick," said Maureen.

"Sorry. Mum phoned for you." He said that Winnie was drunk and being abusive and hunting for Maureen.

"Can't we screen the calls on your answer phone?"

He turned his entire torso as he looked for his fags on the settee. "The police took it away," he said. "They only needed the tape. I think they took the machine out of spite." He spotted them on the floor, bent down carefully and took one out of the packet. He caught her eye as he lit it and threw the packet to her.

She took one. "We could go to mine," she said, "and get my answer phone."

"Will the police let you go in?"

"Yeah, they've said I can go home."

"Have you been back yet?"

"No."

"Let's go," he said, levering himself off the settee.

It wasn't raining so they left the car and walked down to Garnethill, climbing the steep hill to the flat. Liam was sweating by the time they got to the top of the stairs. "God," he said, "I'm so unfit."

She put the key in the lock and opened the door. Liam reached out to stop her going in. "I'll go," he said, wiping the sweat from his glistening forehead. "I'll check it out."

She waited outside, picking at the thick chewy gloss on the door frame. When he came back out to give her the okay his face was white with shock.

Maureen stepped nervously into the hall. Liam had pulled the living-room door shut. It was warm in the flat—the neighbors downstairs must have their heating on. The salty smell from the living room was high in the hall: she tried to breathe short shallow breaths so that it wouldn't get deep into her lungs. The paintwork on the hall cupboard was marked by sticky strips where the tape had been. A note was lying on the floor; it had been folded in half and shoved under the door. It was from Jim Maliano across the landing, telling her to knock on his door when she got back, he had made too many lasagna portions and they wouldn't fit into his freezer, did she want some? She pressed the Play button on the answer phone and handed the note to Liam. "Is that the prick across the landing?" he said.

"Yeah, but he's not a prick now. I like him."

"I didn't know you liked lasagna that much," he said, turning his upper body to her, handing the note back.

"Naw." She smiled. "Remember, he was kind."

Liz had called her, could Maureen phone her back. Someone called Danny wanted her to call him at a Glasgow city-center number. The call was followed by three put-downs. Maureen didn't know anyone called Danny. Liz phoned again, please phone her.

Another mystery caller asked her to phone him at an Edinburgh number. His call was followed by another put-down.

She rang the number for Danny and was welcomed to the Alba Newspaper Group. She hung up. The mystery caller from Edinburgh was from a news agency.

Liam listened with her. "Vermin," he said.

She unplugged the answer phone and wrapped the flex around it.

"I thought you were going to get cleaners in here," said Liam, glancing nervously at the living-room door.

"Yeah, but it's not covered by the insurance."

"Fuck, you're going to have to do it yourself?"

"Yeah."

"I'll give you a hand cleaning it up," he said reluctantly.

"You've got your own house to worry about. I think I'd rather do it alone anyway." It might have been the void left by her lapsed Catholicism but important events prompted her need for ritual. Certain things had to be done in certain ways to mark the end of the cycle of events; like secular voodoo, it helped to resolve matters, signifying and punctuating.

When she had come home from hospital she sat in the hall cupboard where Liam had found her and burned her hospital ID wristband and a photograph of her father in the grill pan. She got drunk on cherry brandy and dragged the mattress off the bed onto the floor, playing Beethoven's Ninth as loud as she dared and battering the mattress with her fists, working herself into a mindless frenzy, biting it until her teeth and jaw ached. Luckily, all the rips were on one side of the mattress. She turned it over when she put it back on the bed. She didn't tell anyone about it: to the uninitiated all ritual is laughable and meaningless. She had a feeling that it would take a lot of ritual to resolve Douglas.

"Let's get the fuck out of here," she said.

"Good idea," said Liam, and slipped into the close as soon as it was polite to do so.

Jim Maliano must have been looking out through his spy hole. When Maureen stepped into the close he threw open his door and leaped out. Liam jerked his head up in surprise and yelped.

"Sorry," said Jim, embarrassed at his unnecessarily dramatic entrance, "I didn't want to miss you."

Liam rubbed his sore neck and muttered "Prick" under his breath.

"How are you, Jim?" said Maureen.

"Fine," said Jim, wondering if he had misheard Liam. "How are you?"

"All right," she said.

Jim wasn't much taller than Maureen. He was slim except for a perfectly round belly, like a large prosthetic breast shoved up his jumper. Maureen wanted to like Jim, he had been so kind to her, but in the cold light of day he wasn't very likeable. His jumper was tucked fussily into his jeans and there was something irritatingly meticulous about the way he did his hair. It looked as if he had carefully bouffanted it over a bald patch on his crown, but he wasn't balding. And his Italianism seemed affected; like a dull man accentuating a single feature as a substitute for a personality.

He rustled them into his cluttered kitchen and filled an espresso machine with fresh coffee grounds. Maureen and Liam sat down at a pine table littered with pale hot-cup stains. They watched tiny Jim fix the coffee.

"Thanks for the offer of the lasagna," said Maureen politely.

"My mum told me to do that," he said. "She said that's what neighbors do when there's a death." He blushed vibrantly and apologized for mentioning that.

"Not at all. I appreciated the note, Jim, it was kind of you."

Jim turned back to the coffee machine, now spluttering the treacle liquid into cups. He opened a cupboard and took out a set of saucers and a side plate. "There was a policeman outside your door for days," he said, lifting a packet of amaretto biscuits out of a food cupboard. "The journalists arrived in the close the day after it happened. They were here all last week, asking everyone about you. I didn't think they could print anything about a court case that was coming up."

"There might not be a court case," said Maureen. "They haven't got anyone for it yet."

"Oh, that's great," he said, looking relieved. "I knew it wasn't you." He put the plate of amaretto biscuits on the table. They were individually wrapped in blue, red and green tissue paper, twisted at the ends like big sweets.

She was trying hard to like him, if only he weren't so affected. She asked him to describe the journalists and recognized the two men who had taken pictures of Liz. "They came to see me at work," she said. "We had to shut the office because of them."

"Yeah, those two were the worst," said Jim, handing them each a cup of coffee and standing on the other side of the table as he sipped his. "They knocked on old Mrs. Sood's door for ten minutes one night. She was terrified. I think the police should have told them to stop it, I mean, there was an officer outside your door the whole time, it wouldn't have taken much effort." He leaned forward and took a biscuit, unwrapped it delicately and bit through the middle. It wasn't big enough to warrant more than one bite. Maureen wanted to stand up and ram the rest of it into his mouth. "It's a good job you didn't come up yourself," he said, "or the journalists would have caught you."

"What do you mean?" said Liam.

"Well, the night they were banging on Mrs. Sood's door"—he gestured to Maureen—"that was the same night your pal came up and went into the house."

Maureen spoke slowly. "Which pal was this, Jim?"

"Didn't you send your pal up to the house?"

"No. Why do you think it was a pal of mine?"

Jim looked thoughtfully at Maureen as he ate the second half of his biscuit. He sat down at the table. "Listen," he said, watching his hands as he spread them on the table in front of him, "I know I sound like a nosy neighbor or something but it didn't seem right. I left the note under your door because I wanted to tell you about it." He smiled slyly. "It was a bit of a ruse. It wasn't really that I'd made too much lasagna although I've got some if you want it—"

"Just tell me what happened," said Maureen, curtly.

"Well," said Jim, "I heard a noise in the close, they were banging on her door and I was watching out of the spy hole and I saw your pal, the guy that comes up sometimes."

"What does he look like?" she said.

"Dark hair cut short, tall, about six foot. Broad on the shoulders. He had a leather jacket on."

"What did the jacket look like?"

"It was brown with a zip up the front," said Jim. "Wee collar and pockets at the side."

"That's Benny!" exclaimed Liam.

"Whisht a minute, Liam," said Maureen, and turned back to Jim. "Wasn't there a policeman at the door?"

"Yes, a uniformed officer, but as I was watching he left and your pal came up the stairs."

"Did they talk to each other?"

"No, no," said Jim. "I'll tell you what happened. I was listening to them banging, and watching through the spy hole, when I heard a couple of loud bangs in the back court and the policeman heard them too. He kept bending down to look out the landing window and I saw him talking into his walkie-talkie and go downstairs. The journalists were still banging on her door. I was waiting to see if the policeman would tell them to stop it when I heard someone walking up the stairs dead fast, like they were in a big hurry. So I looked out, expecting to see the policeman again but I saw that guy in the leather jacket and he was holding something in the jacket and looking at your door with his back to me but he was acting suspicious.

He went like this—" Jim cocked his head to the side like someone listening for something, but he was enjoying being the center of attention and smiled serenely, rolling his eyes heavenward like an ugly cherub with a stupid hairdo. "See?" continued Jim. "He was listening to my door to see if there was someone in here, so I knew he wasn't a policeman. So, anyway, he let himself in and came out again in a minute or so—"

"He let himself in? You mean he had a key?"

"Uh-huh, he had a key. I didn't know who it was but when he came back out he turned round and I saw his face."

"Okay," said Maureen patiently. "Did he have the thing in his jacket when he came back out?"

Jim thought about it. "No, he had two free hands when he came out." He waggled his hands in illustration. "Did he steal something? Is that why he was there?"

Maureen said she didn't know, she hadn't looked. "When was this, Jim?"

"Last Monday night," said Jim. "About eight."

Liam looked at her inquisitively. "What was going on then?"

"It was the night we watched *Hard Boiled*," said Maureen.

"He came in with the jacket on that night," said Liam. " 'Member?"

"It just didn't seem right to me," said Jim, trying to get their attention again.

"Are you sure he had a key?" asked Maureen.

"Aye."

"You said he had something under the jacket. What sort of thing?"

"Well, he was being careful with it, he was holding it at the bottom, like this." Jim held his hand across his body and made a fist, as if he were holding a pole upright.

"How long was it? Could you see through the jacket?"

"I could see an outline. It looked about ten, twelve, inches long. It was like he was holding a stick or something."

"Jim," said Maureen, avoiding direct eye contact in case her dislike became too evident, "you've been such a help, really . . ."

"I did think there was something wrong about it all," said Jim. He looked about to launch into another monologue.

"We have to go," said Maureen. "Thanks again."

When they left the house Jim asked her to remember to bring his Celtic top back.

"Oh, Jim, of course," she said, "and the jogging trousers."

"You take care of yourself," he said, avuncular and pitying. "I'll see you when you come home."

He gave her a peck on the cheek. His lips were damp.

The white Volkswagen got stuck in the filter lane for the M8 motorway and the policemen had to split up. One ran after Maureen and Liam on foot while the other waited out the jam.

Maureen and Liam walked back toward the West End in silence, oblivious to the minor drama unfolding behind them. It was drizzling again; Maureen's hair was stuck to her head and she didn't have her scarf with her. Swirling damp rain was getting in at the neck, softening the scratch scabs, ripening them for the rough collar of her overcoat. Liam looked normal now, as if his head was bent against the rain. Maureen started crying noiselessly, knowing that the soft rain would cover for her.

When Liam finally spoke his voice was a hoarse whisper, but he was so close that she could hear him perfectly over the noise of the fast cars slashing past. "What does this mean?" he said.

She took a deep shaky breath to stop herself crying. "Well," she said, checking that her voice sounded okay, "it doesn't mean we're cozy safe and among friends, does it?"

Liam hooked his arm through hers. "Are you crying, Mauri?"

"A bit," she said.

"What's making you cry?" His voice was gentle and she was afraid she might start bawling in the street.

"That was the worst-told story I've ever had to sit through," she said.

Liam squeezed her arm with his elbow. Maureen squeezed back. "You don't seem surprised about Benny," said Liam.

"Naw, I'm not."

"Why?"

"Auch," she sighed. "It's a bit of a long story. Benny lent me a CD and it was in my flat when I went back up to get some stuff. I found it in his house the other day so I guessed he'd been at mine."

"That was stupid."

"Well, I thought I'd given it back. Before Jim said that he was sneaking about I thought maybe he was in cahoots with the police and they'd given it to him."

"And that thing in his jacket, do you know what it was?"

"I think it was the knife. The police were in the house for over a week and they didn't find it and then suddenly it turns up."

"Did you see the actual knife?"

"Yeah, it was fucking huge, and when I asked why it took them so long to find it they acted funny."

"How did Benny get a key to your house?"

"Well, he didn't get it off me," she said, into her chest.

Liam's voice was whiny and defensive. "I didn't give it to him," he said.

"Oh, for Christ's sake, Liam, I wasn't hinting at that. I meant that he has the missing key—he has Douglas's key."

They stopped at the traffic lights, waiting to cross the busy road. Maureen let go of Liam's arm and pressed the yellow pedestrian button three times in quick succession. Liam slipped his arm back through hers. She had never known him be so tactile. "You're getting good at this, Mauri," he said. "McEwan asked me about the evening Douglas died. Ye might be right about the time as well."

Liam had more or less admitted he was wrong three times in the past week. Strange times. She poked the pedestrian button impatiently. "I don't think these things do anything," she said. "I think they put them there to keep you occupied so that you don't just chuck yourself across."

"Does this mean Benny killed Douglas?" asked Liam.

"Dunno," she said. "Douglas and Benny would need to be connected somehow."

"Yeah. There would have to be a reason for him to do it. Benny isn't mental unless he drinks."

She told him about the psychiatric referral from Inverness. "Douglas could have been the psychiatrist who saw him. It sounds as if Benny was involved with some dodgy geezers up in Inverness and he might not have wanted anyone to know about it."

"Why?"

"It was a fraud ring. It could ruin his legal career."

"So that would give him a motive?"

"Yeah, but I can't believe Benny would do that."

"Didn't think he'd sneak about and creep into your house either, though, did you? And how could he get a key—" Liam flinched suddenly and jerked his arm away from her. "God, shit, yes, Mauri, oh, fuck!"

"What? What?" she said, and tugged at his elbow, making him jerk his neck to the side. He yowled and slapped his hand to it, groaning at the sharp pain.

"I told Benny about the cupboard," he whispered, bending over with the pain, both his hands wrapped around the sore side of his neck.

Maureen was standing stunned beside him, her hands limp at her sides, the cold rain running down her face, dripping off her nose and chin. She spoke quietly. "You told him that?"

"Aye," said Liam, still cringing from the pain.

"You said you didn't tell anyone," she said.

He straightened up slightly and, looking at her, said, "I forgot."

"Did you tell him which cupboard?"

"I pointed it out one day when we were in the house. God, Mauri, I'm sorry."

She stood up on her tiptoes and kissed his cheek, slipping her arm back through his. "There's no reason for you to be sorry, Liam. No reason at all."

They walked on in silence, Liam keeping his free hand on his neck. Maureen was holding his arm too firmly, pressing it tightly against her side, pinching his skin in the cup of her elbow. He could feel her tiny walnut biceps digging into his arm and her intensity frightened him. "Why would he plant the knife?" he asked.

"Well, if it's found in the house it looks like I did it because I didn't go out, yeah?"

Liam nodded. "Right, but why leave it so long?"

"That I don't know. Maybe he wasn't working alone and it wasn't his idea to do it. Maybe someone else told him to do it and he couldn't refuse. He told me on the first day that it would look like me if they found it in the house. He wouldn't have told me if he was thinking about doing it. I think he must have mentioned it to someone else and they told him to go up there and do it."

"He's a cunt," said Liam. "Even if he didn't kill Douglas, even if he didn't put the knife there, even if he took my key or your key and just got in to get his CD, he's still a cunt."

"Aye," she said. "But he's the closest thing I've got to a lead at the moment so I don't want you to say anything to him."

"I want to batter him," said Liam petulantly.

Maureen disentangled her arm. "Don't you dare breathe a word about this. Not a single word to anyone. You'll fuck everything up. Just act normal with him and if you can't do that stay away from him."

They walked on.

"We've known Benny forever, Mauri."

"Yeah," said Maureen. "And it wasn't long enough."

* * *

When they got back to his house Liam fitted the answer phone and got clean towels from the upstairs bathroom while Maureen made a pot of tea. She dried her hair roughly and followed Liam as he carried the tray upstairs to the nice room on the second floor.

She lay down on the Corbusier chair. Liam sat on the desktop, gasping as he tried to dry his hair without jerking his head. "God, that's sore," he said. He poured out the tea and turned on his computer. "Do you fancy a game of *Doom*?" They looked at each other and sniggered miserably. "Not really, Liam, no."

The doorbell rang downstairs. "Fuck," said Liam. "If that's Pete . . ." He put the pot of tea down, walked across the room and peered out of the window. He waved down to someone on the front steps. "Fuck me if it isn't himself," he muttered.

Maureen stood up and looked out. Benny was standing on the stairs waving up at them cheerfully. She waved back.

One hundred yards farther down the road a wet policeman and a dry policeman were sitting in the Volkswagen. They recognized Benny as the third party seen leaving the Scaramouch Street residence on Thursday morning. They guessed rightly that he was the householder, Brendan Gardner. The dry officer turned to the wet officer. "This guy keeps coming up, doesn't he?"

Liam waved out of the window. "We gonnae let the cunt in?" he asked.

"Got to," she said. "Don't let on, Liam, eh?"

Liam stomped down the stairs. She could hear the front door swing open and Benny greeting Liam in a loud happy call. Liam grunted something.

Benny walked up the stairs and stood in the doorway. "All right, Mauri?" He smiled. "Just passing. I had my first exam today."

"Right. I didn't think they had exams on Saturdays anymore."

Benny shrugged. "Old-fashioned college."

"How did it go?"

"Okay."

Liam brushed past him gruffly and picked up his cup of tea.

"How are ye, Liam, man?" asked Benny.

"Fine," said Liam, picking up a bit of paper from the desk and pretending to read it.

Benny paused for a still moment and looked at him, confused by his mood. He turned to Maureen and made a bewildered face. She raised an eyebrow. "Want a cup of tea, then?" she said, walking toward the door and motioning for him to follow her. They went downstairs to the kitchen.

It was chaotic: the police seemed to have concentrated their search in there. Liam usually left it a mess anyway because it was next to the front room. The window was almost opaque with dirt, the floor was half ripped lino, half bare rotting floorboards. Fossilized dirt had turned the old cooker from white to an uneven brown. The police had emptied spice jars into the sink, the contents of the fridge and freezer were stacked on the table and had defrosted over the surface and onto the floor. The crockery, cutlery and saucepans had been taken out of the cupboards and left in piles on the work tops.

"What's wrong with Liam now?" asked Benny, unperturbed by the state of the kitchen.

"It's family stuff. Winnie's turned rabid."

"No, really?"

"Yeah," she said, and began to cry. She tried to stop but couldn't help herself. She was struggling for breath, gasping and weeping open-faced like a lost child. Benny put his arms around her and whispered consolations into her damp hair. She murmured his name, repeating it over and over, holding him tight until she'd calmed down.

"What's she done?" he said when she let go. He rubbed her back gently. "What's she done now, Mauri?"

She could see Liam over Benny's shoulder, walking through the front room toward them. She held Benny tight. "She's lost it. She went mental and threw Liam out of the house."

She caught Liam's eye over Benny's shoulder and gave him a hard look. Benny pressed his face into her neck. "You all right now?" he muttered.

"I'm all right," she said. "It's not the best run of luck I've ever had, though, is it?"

"Guess not," he said.

Liam put the kettle on. "Benny, man, how'd the exam go?" he said, smiling genially.

They brought some big cushions and the portable telly from Liam's bedroom into the upstairs room so they could watch *Repo Man* on TV. She hadn't realized but the day had worn her out. She lay down to rest her eyes during the ads and fell asleep. They covered her with a duvet.

She woke up in the middle of the night, clammy in her day clothes, and undressed sleepily as she made her way to the spare bedroom, falling asleep the moment she lay down. She dreamed that Martin was combing her hair to comfort her.

24

YVONNE

BEFORE SHE EVEN OPENED HER EYES THE NEXT MORNING SHE KNEW that it was time to move home to Garnethill.

She was going to make Liam breakfast but when she looked in on him he was still asleep. There was a large hole in the floor next to his bed: the floorboards had been lifted and left next to the empty space. Nails were sticking up vertically out of the planks, like the ragged teeth on a latent predator. The contents of his clothes cupboard had been thrown onto the floor and the black-and-white checkered linoleum in the en suite bathroom had been ripped up. Maureen shut the door quietly and crept downstairs. No wonder he was fucked off.

She picked a twenty-four-hour locksmith out of the Yellow Pages and dialed the number. They said that there would be a twenty-quid bonus charge because it was Sunday but she didn't care. The man on the phone took her address in Garnethill and said he'd send someone over at twelve with a new bolt and Yale.

She was drinking a coffee and packing her answer phone into a plastic bag when the phone rang out. "Hello," said Una. "I phoned Benny's but he said you were at Liam's."

"Well," said Maureen, "here I am."

She was intent on meeting Maureen to tell her some good news.

"I can't see you, Una," Maureen said, mindful of Liam's warning. "I'm moving back home today."

But Una was determined. She'd come over to Liam's, she said, and drive Maureen and her answerphone home. Una had driven since she was seventeen and refused to believe that anyone would rather walk anywhere.

"Well, okay, but I'm leaving now and Liam's still asleep. He's exhausted, so just knock, okay? Don't ring the bell."

When the knock came on Liam's front door Maureen threw on her coat and scarf and picked up the bag. She opened the door and stepped outside, pecked Una briskly on the cheek and turned away to lock the front door behind her.

"Aren't we going to have a cup of tea?" asked Una, sensing a strained atmosphere and preparing to be offended on the slightest pretext.

"Well, I need to get on, really," said Maureen.

Una looked aggrieved. "All right, then," she said magnanimously. "If you're in such a big hurry."

They walked down the front steps to Una's company car. It was a big green Rover with a walnut dashboard and electric windows and everything. It was Una's pride and joy. She started the engine and told Maureen the good news: Marie was coming up for a visit the day after next and the girls were all meeting up at Winnie's for a lovely lunch on Thursday.

Maureen thought about the three of them together, sitting around the kitchen table, waiting for her to arrive. Why were they having a lunch and not a dinner, like they usually did when Marie came home, and why wasn't Liam invited? He would stand up for her if he was there. They must be planning something: they were going to confront her, tell her everything she remembered was a lie and she was mental.

As they drove down the Maryhill Road Maureen noticed Una's eyes flicking to the side when she dared, checking on her wee sister, making sure she wasn't doing anything crazy. Maureen couldn't think of anything to say. They'd call Louisa Wishart if she got upset, that would be the first thing they'd do.

She was hot with worry by the time they got halfway down the Maryhill Road. Una asked why she was so quiet and she pretended she hadn't slept well. "Mum's angry with me for taking my photos away."

"I know," said Una, drawing her lips tight together and clenching her jaw.

"But they were mine and she was selling them to the newspapers."

"No, Maureen," said Una, holding her hand up. "Mum didn't sell them."

"Well, she gave them away, then."

"Yes, which is different," said Una.

They fell into an uneasy silence. The car's engine hummed quietly as they drew up to the traffic lights and stopped.

"Did Liam tell you about Mum at the police station?" said Maureen.

"Oh, dear me, yes," said Una, wrinkling her nose. "She was a bit excited."

"He told me she was screaming her fucking face off," said Maureen loudly, her voice quivering with misplaced indignation. Una didn't like swearing or screeching or untoward emotional reactions of any kind. Maureen could tell she was freaking her out.

Una pulled the car into the curb and stopped the engine. "Are you sure you're okay?" she said carefully. "D'you think you should be going home today?"

Maureen thought about confronting Una now, weighing up the pros and cons. Not yet. Not just now. She didn't want to go ballistic. "I'm fine," she said. "I'm a bit frightened about going home again, that's all."

Una leaned across and pulled her over, hugging her and pressing the gear stick into Maureen's ribs. She let go. "We all love you very much," she said kindly.

"I know that, Una," said Maureen, crying with fury.

"We all want the best for you," she said.

Maureen turned her face away, angrily swatting the tears off her face. "I know," she said, "I know."

Una had meant to suggest that Maureen go back to hospital but she seemed so unstable that it might not be a good idea. She'd phone Dr. Wishart when she got back to the office and ask her about readmission. She started the car again. "You could come and stay with us if you want," she said, pulling out into the traffic.

It would be Una's worst nightmare, herself moping around their ordered house, smoking fags all over the place and watching old movies. "You're such a sweetheart, Una," Maureen said, controlling her voice to make it sound normal. "I don't know how you do it. We're all crazy and it just seems to roll off your back."

Una smiled, pleased at being differentiated from the rest of them. "Let's have some music," she said, and clicked the radio on.

They sang along to a jolly pop song all the way up the road, guessing the words and humming the hard parts so they wouldn't have to speak to each other.

Maureen looked out of the window and told herself that very, very soon, as soon as the Douglas thing was over, she would tell Una and the rest of them what she thought of them.

* * *

Una parked the car outside the close, pulled on the hand brake, turned off the ignition and undid her seat belt.

"No," said Maureen. "You can't come up with me."

She was desperate to get away from her sister. If Una came upstairs and saw as much as a drop of blood she'd start crying and need to be tended and comforted. She'd phone Alistair and get him to come over, she might even call Winnie and George. She'd be there for fucking hours.

Una stared at her. "Why not?"

"Um, the police won't let you in, only me."

"Why are the police up there?"

"They want me to show them around the house, so you can't come in."

"But I'm your sister."

"I know that, Una, but they can't let just anyone in."

"I'm not just anyone," said Una, taking the key out of the ignition and pocketing it. "I'm your sister." She opened her door and put one foot on the pavement.

"Una," said Maureen, as firmly as she could without shouting, "you cannot come upstairs."

Una brought her foot back into the car and turned to face her wee sister. "Maureen," she said solemnly, "I am not letting you go into that house without anyone to support you."

"Una," said Maureen, copying her sister's sanctimonious tone, "I am not letting you come upstairs with me. The police are there, they already dislike our family because Mum was drunk and shouted at them and because our brother is a drug dealer, and I am not going to jeopardize what small relationship I have with them by demanding that they grant you access to the house."

Una sighed heavily and shook her head. "Why on earth wouldn't the police want me up there?"

"It's in case you interfere with some evidence they haven't collected yet."

"But I'm your sister. I don't think you should go in there alone."

"I won't be alone, the police'll be there with me."

Una rolled her eyes heavenward and muttered "Pete's sake" before shutting her door.

"It's all right," said Maureen, pulling the polyethylene bag with her answer phone in it out of the backseat. "The police are in there."

They kissed and arranged to meet at Winnie's for lunch on Thursday, when Marie would be home.

Una watched Maureen walk up the close carrying the poly bag. It was dark inside the door; Maureen's small shadow jogged up the first flight of stairs, around the corner and disappeared. She sat for a moment before picking up the car phone and dialing Dr. Wishart's number at the Albert Hospital. It was engaged. She hung up and pressed the redial button. Still engaged. She replaced the phone and looked back up the close, weighing up the pros and cons of going after Maureen. She fitted the key in the ignition, started the engine, lifted off the hand brake and pulled the car out into the steep street.

Maureen climbed the stairs with trepidation, slowing down as she neared the top floor. The sight of Jim's door reminded her that she had left his Celtic shirt sitting in the bottom of Benny's wardrobe. She wished he hadn't told her about watching through the spy hole, not that she was ungrateful for the information about Benny, but she'd never stand on the landing again without imagining Jim, with his worrying hairdo, pressed up behind his door, peering out at her with his jumper tucked tightly into his denims. She took out her keys, unlocked the front door and let it swing open.

The house smelled stale and oppressively sweet. She stepped in and shut the door behind her, leaving Jim with nothing to see. She dropped the bag in the hall, took a deep breath and turned the handle on the living-room door.

The blood had turned brown in the direct sunlight. It was hard to spot a bit of the carpet that wasn't brown. Deep puddles of Douglas's precious blood had dried into it; action streaks from jugular spurts radiated out from the four circular indents marking the position of the chair. The blue chair had been cleaned by some kind officer; it was by the window, facing it at an angle, as if someone had been sitting there, enjoying the view.

She stepped carefully across the crunchy floor, using the clear spaces as stepping stones to the window, which she opened, pulling it right back against the wall, letting the harsh wind into the room. She sat down in Douglas's blue chair because she was afraid to and smoked a cigarette by the blustery open window, waiting until the horror of it had passed. She stubbed the end of the cigarette out on the windowsill, lifted the chair by the back and carried it out into the hall.

She stacked the contents of the bookcase into piles on the floor and carried them out one at a time, resting them precariously against the wall by the kitchen door. She took the coffee table into the bedroom, then humped the portable television through, banging her legs with it. Back in the living room she folded the bookcase flat, leaving it near the bathroom door. She wheeled out the old horsehair armchair, recklessly rolling its wooden castors over the crusty brown blood.

She walked back into the empty living room and stood on the spot marked out by the indentations from the chair, looking around and breathing in the dry, bloody dust. Only the settee with the stripe of blood across the arm was left in the room. It wouldn't clean up; she didn't know what to do with it. She could throw it away but then she wouldn't have anything to sit on except the horsehair and that was uncomfortable. She didn't need to decide right away; she could work around it today. She found the hammer in the kitchen cupboard and, starting below the open window, used the forked end to lever up the carpet tacks around the edge.

* * *

When the doorbell rang she had lifted a third of the carpet around the skirting board. She shut the door to the living room before looking out of the spy hole. A young man, tanned like a tea bag, was standing at the door holding a small metal box with a handle. He was wearing a T-shirt with "Armani" written across the chest, jeans and a yellow suede jacket. His hair was striped with ill-suited blond streaks that looked green in the close light. He was two hours late and looked badly hung over. He probably hadn't been home yet. She opened the door. "Locksmith?"

"Mm," he said, stepping into the cluttered hallway and fingering the locks on the door.

"Want a cup of tea?"

"Naw."

She left him to it and went off to hide in the kitchen. She wanted to finish the living room but she couldn't get in there without him seeing the mess and she didn't feel like explaining. She put the kettle on and opened the door to the cups cupboard. The cups had all been moved around. Rarely used ones had been put to the front of the shelf and several were upside down, the way cups are meant to be stored. She opened the food cupboard and the cutlery drawer: same thing in all of them. The police had been through them and moved everything. They must have been very thorough. Flushed with a sudden shamed panic she went into the bedroom and opened the door to the bedside cabinet. Three broken vibrators had been tidied away in a little triangular pile. The one with the acid burns from the leaky batteries was on the bottom with the red screw-top lid placed neatly beside it. She kept meaning to throw it away but was too embarrassed to put it in a bin, as if all of her neighbors would find it and come to the door en masse demanding an explanation. Both of her Nancy Friday politically correct wank books had been leafed through. She sat down on the bed and tried to minimize it but couldn't. She slumped on the bed, looking at the floor. The *Selecter* CD was gone, right enough.

She went back to the kitchen, trying to convince herself that once she told Leslie it would become a funny story, and made herself a coffee.

After a long pause in the drilling the locksmith came to the kitchen door. He looked downcast and green.

"Want a cup of tea now?" she said.

"Naw." His voice was wobbly, as if he was about to spew his ring. "Finished."

She paid him in cash and he gave her two copies of the key for the new Yale lock and one for the bolt. When he left she used the new bolt and locked herself firmly in.

Back in the living room she lit a fag, holding it between her teeth as she levered up the rest of the carpet tacks with the hammer. She lifted the edge under the window and dragged it over itself halfway across the room. It was heavy. She let go of the carpet and took hold of the settee arm, pulling it over the fold in the carpet and onto the bare floorboards. The last castor stuck on the fold. She tugged the settee and the carpet started to unfurl. She was kneeling down, trying to lift the castor over the fold, when she happened to glance across the room. A tear-shaped drop of blood had dried on the skirting board, red and glassy against the white paint. She crawled over on all fours and sat down next to it, her head resting on the wall, stroking it with her fingertips, over and over, until it got dark.

She turned on the hall light and opened the cupboard door. The shoe box had been lifted and placed on the high shelf at eye level, leaving the floor of the cupboard empty. In the right-hand corner of the carpeted floor was a bloody oval stain the size of her palm. She crouched down and put her hand on it. It wasn't powdery and thin like the stains around the edge of the living room: it was solid like the space under the chair. The pile on the carpet was completely flattened because the blood spill had been so heavy. It was too heavy to be a splash and the mark was too small to have come from her slippers. Something bloody had been put there.

She stood up, letting her eyes linger on the spot as she tried to imagine what sort of thing could have caused a stain that shape. A bloody rag would have left a stain with uneven edges, so that wasn't it. She tried supposing that the Northern rapist and Douglas's murderer were the same person to see if that would shed any light on the cause of the mark. It could have come from bloody ropes being dumped there but they'd have had to be dripping with blood and, anyway, Douglas had still been tied up when she had found him. She couldn't think what could have caused it.

In the kitchen she opened the door to the boiler and checked the timer for the heating: it was set to go on at five-thirty a.m. and off again at eight. The evening times had been changed too. The little arrows on the dial had been pushed together so that the heating would be off all evening. She changed them back to the previous setting, off in the morning and on from six p.m. until eleven, and shut the door.

The list Martin had given her was still in the condom pocket of her black jeans. If the patients had been raped the only safe approach was through the female members of staff. Starting with the nurses' list, she picked out the three recognizably female names and got the Glasgow phone directory from the kitchen drawer. The first name was Suzanne Taylor. Fifteen Taylors were listed in the book. Maureen worked out that they were arranged alphabetically by the first name. The last one listed was Spen. Taylor: Suzanne had either married or moved away. The second name, Jill McLaughlin, might well have been hidden among the thirty or so J. McLaughlins.

Sharon Ryan was a godsend. She was one of three if she was there at all. Maureen tried the first one. The number had been disconnected. The second number had never heard of Sharon Ryan; the third hadn't either.

She hung up and tried to narrow the margins on Jill McLaughlin. Jill would be somewhere between Jas. and Joseph; that left eight possibles. She lifted the receiver and tried the first one, then the second, then the third. She was losing hope. Five McLaughlins and still no Jill. On the seventh a tiny voice answered: "Hello."

"Hello, could I speak to Jill McLaughlin, please?"

"Who're ye?" said the tiny voice.

It might have been habit or the child's voice but she didn't lie. "I'm Maureen O'Donnell," she said.

The little voice thought about it for a moment before shouting, "Mummy, Mummy, it's a lady."

She could hear the woman at the other end talking the child gruffly away from the phone. "Yes?" she said.

"Am I talking to Jill McLaughlin?"

"Yes," she said.

"Can I ask you, Ms. McLaughlin, are you a nurse?"

"Not now," she said bluntly.

If Jill McLaughlin had left the caring profession she'd done it a big favor.

"Were you a nurse?" asked Maureen.

"Auxiliary."

"Sorry?"

"I was a care assistant," she said. She broke off to tell the child to stop it. Maureen heard a slap and the child started to cry.

"Look, I'm sorry to bother you, I can hear you've got your hands full there."

"Yes, I have."

"Are you the Nurse McLaughlin who worked in George I ward at the Northern?"

McLaughlin paused. Maureen could hear her sucking on a fag. "Who is this?" she said suspiciously, exhaling noisily into the receiver. "Are you with the papers?"

"No, no," said Maureen. "I'm not."

The child was wailing in the background. "You are so with the papers."

"No, honest, I'm not."

"Who are you, then?"

"I'm Maureen O'Donnell—"

"I've seen you in the paper," growled McLaughlin viciously. "I seen you."

There was a click on the line and Maureen found herself listening to the dial tone.

Siobhain's list of women would be harder to trace because they were Highland clan names, and the listings were long for all of them. Siobhain had written "Bearsden" in brackets next to Yvonne Urquhart. It was the name of an upper-class suburb to the northwest of the city. Maureen looked in the phone book for the Urquharts listed with Bearsden codes. There were only three. When she dialed the second number she got Yvonne Urquhart's sister. She sounded quite old and had an anxious, tremulous voice. "My sister Yvonne has moved to Daniel House, out by Whiteinch," she warbled. "She moved there a wee while ago."

"Oh, I see."

"Are you her friend, perhaps? Would I know you?"

"Well, I knew her at the Northern. I wanted to see her again, see how she was getting on."

"Oh, dear me, I'm afraid you'll find she's terribly changed. She got much worse in the past few years. She isn't well at all now, not well at all, I'm afraid."

"I'm sorry to hear that. Could you give me the number for Daniel House?"

"Certainly, certainly. May you hold?"

Maureen phoned the number and was told she could visit Yvonne until eight o'clock but not after that. It was half-five already. She put on her coat hurriedly, straightened her makeup in the bathroom mirror and made for the door, patting her pockets to check for money and the new keys.

The phone rang out abruptly, startling her so much that she fumbled with the receiver and dropped it. The woman at the other end was giggling and embarrassed. "Um, hello, um, you rang here about half an hour ago? Looking for Sharon Ryan? I rang one four seven one and got your number because I thought you might actually be looking for Shan instead of Sharon."

The name was written down on Martin's list as Shan Ryan. Maureen had assumed it stood for Sharon. "Is Shan a nurse?"

"Yeah, but he isn't in right now."

"Um, did he work at the Northern between 'ninety-one and 'ninety-four?"

"Well, I'm not sure of the dates but I think it's definitely him you want."

"I've got him down as Sharon."

"It's a mistake lots of people make," said the helpful woman, "but he's not in just now."

"Do you know what time he'll be back?"

"No idea, I'm just his flatmate, he doesn't tell me anything. He's probably in the Variety Bar in Sauchiehall Street if you want to go down there."

"Well, it's not that urgent, really."

"Or you could call him at work tomorrow. He's in the dispensary in the Rainbow Clinic on the South Side. If you phone Levanglen they'll put you through."

"Thanks," said Maureen, and put the receiver down as if it had burned her.

She could feel tiny Jim's eyes on her back as she locked the front door behind her. Out in the dark street the policemen in the car nudged one another awake and waited until she was halfway down the hill before starting the engine and turning the lights on.

Maureen tried to come up with a good justification for wasting money on a cab instead of hanging about and waiting for a bus. If she ran out of her own money she could use some of Douglas's, but she didn't want to. It was Sunday and there wouldn't be many buses about. She might have to wait for ages; she might miss the visiting time. She walked down the hill to the main road and hailed a cab, asking the driver to take her to the far end of Whiteinch.

The driver began a monologue about his daughter's wonderful exam results and kept it up all the way down Dumbarton Road. Maureen asked him to stop at a newsagent's and nipped out, blowing more money on an unhappy bouquet of dying flowers and a box of chocolates to take to Yvonne.

Daniel House looked like any of the other detached brownstone houses in the street. Only the economy-model cars in the driveway marked it out: the other houses had Mercedes and BMWs parked outside. A discreet brass sign screwed into the low garden wall identified it as Daniel House Nursing Home. The storm doors were open and folded back against the porch; the doorstep had been replaced with a short ramp. The inside door was enormous and had a four-foot-tall glass panel, etched with an elaborate Grecian vase design.

Maureen pressed the white plastic doorbell and stepped back. A young nurse opened the door. She wore a white pinny over a blue candy-striped uniform. "Hello?" she said.

"I phoned earlier, about Yvonne Urquhart."

"Oh, yes," she said, and opened the door wide, welcoming Maureen in.

Maureen felt the heavy-duty nylon carpet squeak and drag on her rubber-soled boots. The heating in the nursing home was very high and she started sweating as soon as she stepped through the door. Twin oak doorways on either side of the hall led into large communal rooms. Directly opposite the front door a broad oak staircase swept up to the second floor. A stainless-steel rail had been screwed onto the elegant balustrade and a folded lift chair nestled idly at the foot of the stairs. In the shadow of the graceful staircase stood a gray medication trolley with the lid down.

The nurse saw the box of chocolates in Maureen's hand and flinched. "It's a while since you saw Yvonne, isn't it?"

"Yeah," said Maureen.

"I don't think you should give her those," she said, pointing at the box. "She could choke."

Maureen put them in her bag. The nurse smiled apologetically and led her up the staircase to the second floor. She pointed to a half-open door with a brass number five screwed onto it and trotted off down the stairs. The doors marked three and four were firmly shut, so Maureen guessed this was the right one. She pushed it open with her fingertips.

The room was smaller than the big door suggested. It had been partitioned badly: the window consisted of a two-foot offcut from next door's window, the ceilings were too high and the new walls looked patched on and flimsy. The only light came from a pink-shaded lamp sitting on top of the chest of drawers, giving off a dull pink glow—it was a nightlight for a frightened child. There didn't seem to be any personal effects in the room. The pictures of flowers on the wall had been chosen because the red plastic frames matched. On top of a locker next to the sink sat an unopened matching set of soap and talc and a glass of weak orange squash with a toddler's feed lid on it.

A painfully thin elderly nurse was dressing a woman sitting in a chair. She was wearing the striped uniform, and thick support tights over her varicose veins. She kept her back to the door as she wrestled Yvonne's limp body into a washed-out nylon nightie. The nightdress was frantic with static and clung to Yvonne's face and arms. It was split up the back like an incontinence dress. The nurse muttered soft words of encouragement as she popped Yvonne's head through the neck and buttoned it up. Maureen coughed notice of her presence and the nurse turned on her heels. "Who are you?" she said, annoyed and surprised.

"I've come to visit Yvonne."

"Will you wait outside until she's dressed, please?" she said crossly.

Maureen stepped out and stood like a scolded child on the landing until the nurse came out. "You may go in now," she said, as she passed on her way downstairs. Maureen held the flowers in front of her and went into the room.

Yvonne's hair was honey blond, turning brown through lack of sun and cut into a short, manageable hospital style. She was sitting in an orthopedic armchair; cushions had been placed between her hips and the chair sides to stop her slipping over. A freshly puffed pillow in a transparent plastic cover lay in front of her on the table attachment. She was slumped over it, her hands in her lap. Her glassy blue eyes were half-open, her cheek was resting on the plastic-covered pillow in the slick of warm saliva dribbling horizontally out of her mouth. She was forty at most. The skin on her face was loose, sagging to the side, folding against the pillow but devoid of wrinkles. It was a long time since Yvonne had had an expression on her face. Both her hands were curled shut like a stroke victim's and swatches of heavily talcumed cotton wool had been worked between the fingers to stop her getting contact sores.

Maureen put the flowers in the sink and pulled a chair round to Yvonne's left side so that she could see her face as she spoke to her. She asked her whether she had been at the Northern, did she remember Siobhain McCloud, had she seen Douglas, Douglas with the dark eyes and the low voice? Maureen found herself describing him slowly and softly, her voice dipping so low that she could only have been whispering to herself.

She waited with Yvonne for ten minutes to make it look good.

When she stood up to leave she noticed Yvonne's feet. They were curled over the arch like a ballerina's point. Someone who cared about her had knitted little pink booties with a white drawstring around the ankle. The light from the hall shone under the table, illuminating the dry, flaky skin on her skinny legs. An inch above the ankle the skin color changed. It was a ribbon of pink shiny skin, like snakeskin, running all the way around her calf. And then Maureen realized it was a scar. From a rope burn.

She went back downstairs. The young nurse was sitting in the dayroom, watching TV and holding a woman's hand. The patient was nodding and twitching in a vain attempt to resist medication-induced sleep. The nurse saw Maureen standing in the hall and waved her in. The color on the TV set was turned up too high: the actors' faces were orange and their red lips were blurred and undefined. Six or seven empty identical brown orthopedic armchairs were arranged around the television. A folded wheelchair and a Zimmer frame were tidied away against the wall. There were no pictures on the walls and the glorious windows were defaced with beige nylon curtains. It was a desolate, functional room. Maureen sat down in a chair. The nurse reached over with her free hand and touched Maureen's arm. "Are you okay there?" she said, whispering so as not to disturb her sleepy companion. "You look a bit shocked. You haven't seen her for a while, have you?"

"How long's she been like that?" Maureen whispered back.

"Long time. Where do you know her from?"

"From before she went into the Northern."

"Oh, dear," said the wee lassie. "She went downhill there, apparently. She had a bit of a stroke."

"What's that mark around her ankle?"

"No idea. She's had it since I've known her."

"Did a guy come to see her recently? About five ten, in his forties, soft voice?"

The nurse's face lit up. "Yeah," she said. "Guy called Douglas. He was a relative of Yvonne's. He came on business."

"On business?"

"Yeah," said the nurse. "He saw Jenny in the office and paid Yvonne's costs for the next six months. Do you know him?"

"Vaguely," said Maureen.

The sleepy patient gave up the fight and slumped sideways. "I better get Precious to bed," whispered the nurse.

She couldn't face the bus. She hailed a cab and got the driver to drop her at Mr. Padda's, the licensed grocer's around the corner from her house. Mr. Padda had been questioned by the policemen: they'd asked him whether he had seen anyone covered in blood walking down the road a week last Wednesday. "Did you, Mr. Padda?"

"No, dear," he said, and smiled. "Saturdays, yes, often, Wednesdays, no."

She bought a half bottle of whisky and some fags.

When she got into the kitchen she unscrewed the lid of the whisky bottle and then shut it again without taking a drink. She didn't want it.

Back in the living room she levered out the few remaining carpet tacks and rolled up the carpet, wrestled it upright and leaned it against the wall. Even the underlay was covered in Douglas's blood. She took two black bags from the kitchen drawer and filled them with bits of underlay, ripping it up in raw angry handfuls.

It was eleven o'clock before the floor was bare. She brought the whisky and a glass in from the kitchen and sat in the dark living room with her back resting against the wall, looking at all that was left of Douglas: a ten-foot stretch of blood-soaked rug.

She drank the whisky too fast and dipped into Yvonne's box of chocolates as she held a maudlin, solitary wake to the memory of

Douglas, chronologically recalling all that she knew of his life. She celebrated his first day of school, when he cried for three hours until Carol took him home again, his exchange trip to Denmark in fourth year, where he met a German girl and fell in love for the first time, his father's death, over which he felt nothing, his first degree and his place on the coveted clinical psychology course, his marriage to Elsbeth, his first night in Maureen's bed, when poor Elsbeth would have been lying awake alone, wondering where her husband was until four in the morning, guessing right and crying to herself, his lost weekend in Prague, his petty dislike of the people he worked with and his numerous illicit affairs.

She poured the last of the whisky into the glass and held it up, toasting the rolled-up carpet against the wall. "To Douglas and his miserable, grasping life," she said, and cringed. In polite company talking like Bette Davis always means it's time to put the glass down and go to bed.

She did.

25

THISTLE

THEY PUT HER THROUGH TO THE BACK OFFICE. "LIZ?"

"Maureen! God, you're in so much trouble, why didn't you put the sick line in?"

Maureen had forgotten. She'd been off her work for a week and a half without remembering to send the note from Louisa.

"He's going to sack you," said Liz. "I kept phoning you to try and tell you. If you've got a line you can still put it in."

The last time she had seen the sick line was in Benny's house, the night he cooked the venison steaks. "I've left it somewhere," said Maureen. "I'm not even sure whereabouts."

"Well, find it," said Liz.

"Right, I will, Liz. How are you, anyway? Are you going to sue the papers?"

Liz said she couldn't be arsed. She'd phoned the paper and they had printed an apology on page twelve. "Listen," she said, "put the sick line in. If you get the sack because of something you've done they won't let you sign on for ages."

Someone banged heavily on Maureen's front door. "Fuck, really?"

she said, holding the receiver between her ear and shoulder and leaning over to look out of the spy hole. McEwan and McAskill were standing in the close. McAskill was frowning and shaking the rain off his mac, flapping the front panels open and shut. McEwan was wearing a full-length black woolen overcoat and a black trilby.

"Tell you what," said Liz, "I'll tell him you're mental again and we'll see what he does, okay?"

"Good one, Lizbo."

She checked her trousers were done up and straightened her hair before opening the door. McEwan took his hat off and told her officiously that Martin Donegan had gone missing from the Northern Hospital in the middle of his shift on Saturday. A security breach at the hospital was under investigation, they thought Martin's disappearance might have something to do with it and Maureen had been seen there.

She opened the door wide, letting them into the cluttered hall. Something must have happened to make Martin disappear. Something must have frightened him. Or worse. She tried to remember what Martin had told her and what she had promised not to repeat.

McAskill was actively avoiding her eye. He stepped carefully across a pile of books and took up the space in the living-room doorway.

"You've taken the carpet up, then?" said McEwan, looking past McAskill into the living room. His eye fell to rest on the indulgent still life sitting on the floor, an empty half bottle and the box of chocolates.

"Yeah," said Maureen, "I just lifted it out."

"You'd have to do that anyway," said McAskill timidly. "It doesn't come out very well. Usually leaves bad stains." He shuffled past McEwan in the hall, keeping his eyes down and his back to the wall. He was aware of Maureen watching him and blushed a little.

Martin was missing and she didn't know what to do. If she could just be alone for ten minutes she might be able to work it out.

"Will you have to keep the carpet until the insurance see it?" asked McAskill, pointing back into the living room.

"No," said Maureen. "It'll take too long, I'll just chuck it out."

"We'll carry it downstairs for you, if you like, get it out of the way."

"Thanks, Hugh," said Maureen, and touched his elbow, but he still wouldn't look at her.

McEwan was less eager to help. "But I've got my good coat on," he said.

"I'll help you to take it off," muttered McAskill. They looked at each other for a moment.

"Come in here," she said, breaking it up and leading them into the kitchen. Martin had been so adamant when he made her promise not to repeat the stuff about the George I ward. The only reason he'd discussed any of it was because she insisted it would be safe to. She shook the kettle to check the water level and turned it on, praying to a bleak void that nothing bad had happened to him, that he was sitting in his little den reading the paper and listening to a football match.

McEwan sat down on the most comfortable chair, splaying his meaty legs around the little table and taking up more room than he need have. Maureen's kitchen was even smaller than Jim's: it was cramped with three in it and McEwan and McAskill were big people. She gestured for McAskill to sit down on the only other chair at the table. He shook his head and remained standing behind McEwan, leaning his backside against the work top. For a terrible moment the image of the wank books came into her mind, but he would have been embarrassed before now if that was it. The incest survivors, of course. She kicked him discreetly and winked when he looked up, letting him know it was all right. He looked at his shoes and grinned with relief.

"Why were you there?" asked McEwan.

"At the Northern?"

"Yes," he said, blinking slowly with forced patience. "At the Northern." He seemed to feel the need to be particularly unpleasant to Maureen when they were in her house, as if his authority was threatened by being on her patch.

"I went back as part of my therapy and Martin was asked to show me around again. You can check with Louisa Wishart. She phoned the hospital and asked him to meet me." She picked her cigarettes up from the table and lit one.

"Worst time to smoke, in the morning," said McEwan.

"Then don't," said Maureen. "What time did Martin go missing?"

"He was last seen at two o'clock on Saturday. He wasn't seen for the rest of the shift and he hasn't been home."

"His wife's worried sick," added McAskill.

His wife hadn't seen him, he hadn't been home. He couldn't sit in his den for twenty-four hours, no way. "Two o'clock . . . That was a couple of hours after I left."

"What time did you leave?"

"About noon."

"Where did you go afterward?"

"I went to visit a pal."

The kettle boiled and she took a mug down from the cupboard, filled it with water and shook in some coffee granules straight from the jar. She had assured Martin that it would be safe to tell her. She had talked him into it. She swirled the mug around to mix the coffee with the water and sat down opposite McEwan.

"Did Martin say anything to you about going away?" he asked.

Of course, the Jags. "Oh, God, he was talking about a Thistle game in France yesterday—Meatis? Meatpiss?"

McAskill corrected her. "Metz," he said, and smiled the fond way men do when they're talking about their team. That's why he didn't give a shit when she said she was Catholic. McAskill was a Thistle fan.

"That's it," she said. "Martin said the bus left two hours before his shift finished so he couldn't go. Maybe he changed his mind."

McEwan used his mobile and got the number off Directory Enquiries. He phoned the Partick Thistle office, asked for the secretary of the supporters' club running buses to Metz. They gave him the guy's work number and he phoned, looking out of the kitchen window as he waited in a telequeue for his call to be answered.

It was a gray day outside the window. The cloud was so low that Maureen could see above little puffs of mist clinging to the roofs below.

"It's quite a view you have from here," he said.

"Yeah, 's nice," said Maureen, sipping her coffee happily.

The secretary said he'd check the passport list for Martin's name and phone McEwan back.

Maureen smiled to herself. Martin could be sitting on a bus in France somewhere, singing Jags songs, surrounded by old friends and red and yellow scarves and hats and jerseys. She sketched the image in detail, trying to convince herself that it was a possible explanation, maybe even a probable explanation, but she knew it wasn't. Martin had made her promise not to tell anyone.

It was lunchtime for McAskill and McEwan, and Maureen's breakfast time. At her suggestion they agreed to go down the hill to the Equal Café for something to eat. She wanted to stay near McEwan until the call came through from the supporters' club. "Let's get that carpet downstairs then," said McAskill, pushing himself forward from the work top. He stepped carefully over the piles of books in the busy hall and went into the living room. "You get that end," he said, wrapping his arms around the roll and letting it slide horizontally onto the floor.

McEwan's defiance was underspoken. "No."

"It'll only take a minute."

"I've got my good gear on."

McAskill held on to the end of the roll and dragged it across the living room and out to the front door, leaving a brown trail of blood dust. Maureen nipped into the bedroom and put on her boots. She dropped her money and the new keys into her overcoat pocket, handing the coat to McEwan as she stepped over the rolled carpet and lifted the free end in the living room. McAskill opened the front door and stepped out into the close. "*You* shouldn't have to do it," he said.

McEwan muttered a curse and moved to take off his coat. "Let go," he said to Maureen.

"I can manage, Joe," said Maureen.

"Let go of it," he said firmly.

" 'M fine," said Maureen. "I've lifted things before." But the carpet was much heavier than she thought it would be. It was rolled up loosely and was difficult to get a hold of.

McAskill was standing pressed up against Jim Maliano's door and still the end of the carpet was inside the front door.

"Can we bend it?" said Maureen.

"Aye," he said, bracing himself. "Give it a shove."

Maureen pushed hard, getting the carpet to bend slightly in the middle. She moved sideways onto the first step.

"Look," said McEwan, following them out onto the landing, "I'll get it."

" 'M fine," she said, trying not to sound breathless. "Lock the door after ye. The key's in the pocket."

McAskill and Maureen struggled down the stairs, negotiating the landing turns by bending the roll and shuffling sideways. McEwan locked the door and followed them sullenly. The carpet was beginning to buckle of its own accord, the belly sagged downward, dragging on the ground, making it heavier, and Maureen was losing her hold on it. The weight was bending her fingernails back.

They turned slowly on the bottom landing and carried it out of the back door. They were both sweating when they got outside. A cool rain speckled Maureen's hot forehead as she staggered the last few steps to the midden. McAskill's face was blotchy and red. He bent over to put the carpet down and his head inclined close to hers; his eyelashes were dark and long, the pores on his nose were open.

"I found a stain in the cupboard," said Maureen, shaking her sore hands.

"Yeah?" puffed McAskill.

"Yeah."

He brushed off the front of his coat and rubbed his hands together.

"What was it, Hugh?"

"What was what?"

"What was in the cupboard?"

"I can't tell you that, Maureen."

"Why?"

"We'll need it to identify the killer. If it leaks it's useless."

"There must be other facts you could use. I wouldn't breathe a word. I know how to shut up, hand on heart."

McAskill looked at her suspiciously. "Why's it so important?"

McEwan appeared in the doorway carrying Maureen's coat. "Come on!" he shouted.

"It's important because I live there," she said.

McAskill sighed and wiped his hands clean.

"Because it's my house," she said.

He turned to the close. "I can't tell you," he said under his breath. "I'm sorry."

He walked back to McEwan, head bent against the damp weather, leaving Maureen standing next to her bloody carpet, both of them growing soggy in the spitting rain.

McEwan peered out at her. "Come on," he shouted unpleasantly. "We haven't got all day."

"You are a fucking arsehole," whispered Maureen to herself.

* * *

Maureen and McAskill both ordered the all-day breakfast and McEwan asked for a salad. When the waitress brought the wrong things he sent her back for the right things. Her limp and her depression got visibly worse every time she returned to the table and McEwan got more and more annoyed. When it finally arrived it was a very Scottish salad: limp garnish stepped up to the size of a meal. McEwan looked at it miserably for a long moment before attempting to eat it.

His mobile phone was sitting on the table, swaddled in soft black leather. Maureen kept looking at it, willing it not to ring and tell her she was wrong, tell her that Martin wasn't sitting on a coach with his pals, drinking lager and laughing his head off.

The all-day breakfast consisted of a runny fried egg, a potato scone, black pudding, Lorne sausage, mushrooms, fried tomato and bacon. Maureen worked her way silently through various combinations, egg yolk over sausage, scone and crumbling black pudding, egg white and mushrooms, but nothing sat comfortably in her mouth or her stomach. Martin's wife was worried. He hadn't phoned to tell her he was going to Metz. It felt like a long time since she'd enjoyed a meal.

The call came through as they were finishing off. Martin hadn't been on any of the four buses. He had genuinely disappeared.

Maureen relented and told them about the George I ward and what had happened there. McEwan was furious. "I thought you said you'd tell me anything as and when you came across it," he said.

"Martin said he didn't want me to repeat the story. He's got a wee den in the hospital basement."

"I don't give a fuc— monkey's what he told you to do," said McEwan, correcting his language midsentence. "You should have told me about this the other day."

"You wouldn't talk to me about anything the other day. Can we go and look there?"

McEwan leaned heavily on the table and stared at her, his blood pressure showing in his eyes. "I would have spoken to you about this," he said slowly.

"Yeah," said Maureen, a lot less interested in McEwan's mood than he was. "Well, I'm telling you about it now. See, there are parallels between the way Douglas was killed and the way the women were hurt. He was tied up like the women and he had been asking people about the assaults on the women. It was all over the hospital, everyone knew."

"Why was Douglas asking questions about it?"

"I dunno," she said, putting her overcoat on, anxious to get to the Northern. "Maybe he was outraged."

McEwan put his cutlery carefully on the half-empty plate, balancing the fork on top of the knife, and dabbed tiny touches around his mouth with his napkin. Maureen hadn't noticed how anal he was until she saw him eat. He caught the waitress's eye and motioned for the bill. "And what has this got to do with Martin Donegan disappearing?"

"Martin knew about it. He was the one who said there were parallels."

"Let me get this straight," said McEwan, narrowing his eyes and sitting back to look at her. "You went back to the Northern as part of your therapy and, quite spontaneously, Martin Donegan tells you a potentially vital piece of information about Douglas Brady's death."

"Aye. Can we go and look for him?"

McEwan sat forward. "Miss O'Donnell," he said quietly, "if I find out you're messing about and interviewing witnesses before we get to them I will be very, very angry, do you understand me?"

"Yeah," she said impatiently.

"You could face criminal prosecution."

"Aye, I know." She stood up. "Please, can we go?"

McEwan stared at her for a moment. "Where do you think Martin Donegan went?"

"Dunno," she said impatiently. "He's got a secret place in the hospital. I think he'll have left me a note."

They took the passenger lift down to the lower basement. Maureen turned left when they stepped out of the lifts and they ended up in the cavernous hospital kitchen. Ten women in blue hairnets and white coats were arranged around a moving conveyor belt with plates on it. As each plate came past the women took an individual portion of food from metal tubs and slapped it on. They looked over as Maureen and the two burly policemen came in through the double doors. The two groups stared at each other for a moment. Trays of empty plates skimmed past; only one woman was paying attention, frantically throwing boiled potatoes at the belt.

"I took a wrong turn," mumbled Maureen, backing out.

She retraced her steps to the lift and took them down the sloping ramp. She found the right corridor, recognizing it from the direction of the breeze carrying smells from the kitchen. It was dark, the failing strip light had given up. Only the overspill of light from round the corner split the blue dark. Guessing, she opened a wooden door and found herself in the L-shaped room. She could hear the humming engine behind the far wall. "This is it," she said.

McAskill followed her as she felt her way over to the little hill of bin bags at the back. McEwan was standing uncertainly in the doorway, watching them.

"Come on," she called back to him. "Come on, it's quite safe. There's a wee door here."

McAskill waved him over and they followed her around the bags, their eyes adjusting slowly to the damp dark. She tried to push the den door open but it wouldn't give.

"It wasn't locked before," she said.

McAskill pushed the door hard with the flat of his palm. The top of it opened four inches, springing back as soon as he let go, but the bottom didn't give at all. It seemed to be bolted from the inside. He shoved with both hands and felt it give. "Something's stuck behind it," he said, and kicked the bottom. He pushed hard but the door jammed half-open. Maureen stood at ninety degrees to the door and slid her arm along the wall; it felt warm and powdery, like talcum-covered skin. She found the light switch and flicked it on.

Martin was lying on the floor. His feet had been barring the door and McAskill's shoving had pushed them to the side, making his legs lie at a crazy, broken angle. She thought he was facedown, that she was looking at the back of his head, until she saw his copper bangle. His left hand was resting on his stomach, the fingers rolled back into a fist except for the casually extended index finger. His face and upper chest were unrecognizable, a mess of rips of skin and dark red contusions. Martin's face had been ripped apart. The concrete floor was black and silver, awash with syrupy blood.

Maureen's eyes went into spasm, opening wide, making her stare at the worst of it. She rasped, struggling to breathe until McAskill grabbed her roughly by the back of her neck and pressed her face into his chest.

She couldn't stop crying. Someone had given her some pills but they just paralyzed her face and made her mouth hang open. Tears spilled from her eyes like fruit from a cornucopia. They weren't going to let her go until she spoke again. She sat behind the desk in the miserable ground-floor office at the Stewart Street station, with the wall plans and gray filing cabinets, and stared at the door. Hot air was being pumped noisily through a vent by her chair, warming her calves, she could hear it hissing into the room. The skin on her legs began to get angry. She waited until it stung before moving out of the path of the heat.

She didn't know how long she had been there but gradually the tears slowed down and she thought she could talk. She stood up, shaking slightly, and walked across the room, opening the door and looking outside. A uniformed policeman was sitting in a chair just outside the door.

"McEwan?"

McEwan came in, ashen and angry. "Come," he said, and gestured for her to follow him out of the office. He walked in front of her, leading her up the stairs and through the fire doors to the disorienting corridor with the hideous linoleum. The uniformed officer followed at her back. McEwan opened the door to an interview room and stepped back. "In," he said, and Maureen went into the room.

Something McMummb was sitting next to the tape recorder. McEwan nodded at him and he started the tape rolling. "Where were you on Saturday after two p.m.?" asked McEwan.

It took a tremendous effort for her to speak. The words swirled endlessly around in her head before she could summon the energy to move her mouth and say them. "With a friend," she said finally.

"Who was it and where are they?"

"Siobhain McCloud. At the Dennistoun day center. I'll need to speak to her first, I asked her not to talk to the police."

"Oh," said McEwan, "she'll talk to us."

"She won't."

"I think she will," said McEwan, and Maureen started to cry again.

Inness came into the gray office. He wouldn't look at her. "You'll have to come and tell her to talk."

He took her up to the narrow corridor again and into an interview room she hadn't been in before. It was identical to the others but the window was bigger. Siobhain was sitting on the far side of the table. She looked enormous out of the day center: she was wearing the red nylon slacks that cut into her waist and a Mr. Happy "Glasgow's miles better" T-shirt. Her eyes were open wide and she was grinning. She seemed strangely present: Maureen had only ever addressed the back of her head or the side of her face. It was the first time they'd met without being chaperoned by a noisy television.

"Hello to you," said Siobhain.

Maureen sat sideways in the empty chair, pressing her knees into Siobhain's fleshy thigh. Siobhain reached slowly into her pocket and pulled out a packet of Handy Andys. She folded one around her finger and dabbed the tears from Maureen's face, barely touching her skin with the tissue. Maureen shut her burning eyes and felt Siobhain's milky breath on her lids.

"There," said Siobhain. "Now I can do you a good turn." She lifted her hands slowly to either side of Maureen's head and took hold of her ears, shaking her head softly from side to side, and grinned at her again.

Maureen smiled despite herself, but her eyes began crying again. "Tell them where I was on Saturday afternoon." She sniffed.

Siobhain turned to McEwan. "She was visiting me."

"What time did she arrive?" asked McEwan.

"She came to see me while *Columbo* was on the television, just after the Hollywood star had ruined the party. She stayed until *Howards' Way* was over."

McEwan sent Inness to check it out. Maureen noticed that he hadn't turned off the recorder.

"This is the most interesting thing that has happened to me in many years," said Siobhain to a thoroughly uninterested McEwan.

Inness reappeared and McEwan ordered Maureen back downstairs to the grim office.

She had been there for what felt like an hour when McEwan came in for some papers. He still wouldn't look at her.

"Could you eat something?" he said.

"No."

"We'll need to talk about protecting you, Maureen. There's every chance that you'll be targeted now. I'd like to offer you a panic button. You can—"

"Why am I still here?" she said.

"We want to talk to you after we've questioned Miss McCloud."

"Why are you still questioning her?"

"She was a patient in the George I ward at the Northern Hospital."

"You can't ask her about that, Joe."

"Why?"

"You just can't. She won't talk to you, will she? She can't talk about it. It'll make her sick."

"Well, she seems to be talking. I'm not questioning her, Sergeant Harris is. Harris is a woman."

"You don't understand. It doesn't matter that it's a woman."

McEwan was impassive. "Why don't you just leave it to us. Are you hungry?"

"No, I'm not fucking hungry."

26

ACID

THE STATION NOISES DIED DOWN AND THE OFFICE BECAME STILL. The hissing stopped and the heating was turned off. As the oppressive heat of the afternoon seeped away the wooden desk and chair contracted, creaking low groans and snapping loudly. It was growing dark outside the window.

The door opened suddenly and McEwan came in. He stood at the edge of the desk playing with part of a broken pencil, picking at the frayed end. "You can go now," he said, his voice low and slow. "I want you to cooperate with us. We need to provide some protection for you. This is a panic button." He put a small gray box the size of a cigarette packet on the table. "It operates like a beeper. If you press this button it alerts us and we can have a patrol car there in a few minutes. Take it." He pushed it across the table toward her.

"What did Siobhain say?" asked Maureen.

"And I want you back here first thing tomorrow morning."

"Where is she?"

McEwan worked a strip off the pencil with his fingernail. He looked upset. "She's in the foyer." He said it as if it were a question.

Maureen lifted the beeper and brushed past him.

The sparkle in Siobhain's eyes was gone and she was trembling. She was walking slowly, shuffling tiny geisha steps. Maureen got her as far as the main road and hailed a cab. She walked Siobhain to the door and opened it but Siobhain just stood, staring at the pavement in front of her feet. Maureen asked her if she wanted to get the cab home but she didn't answer. The driver leaned over and slid the window down. "Come on," he said impatiently. "You hailed me."

Maureen walked Siobhain forward two steps and got her to hold on to the leather strap inside the cab. She tapped the right leg and, holding her ankle, stood it on the taxi floor. She tapped the left leg and shoved Siobhain's bum with her shoulder as she placed the left foot next to the other. Siobhain was frozen in a crouch in the cab door. Maureen pushed Siobhain's hip gently, working her around to the seat, and climbed back out. The red patent-leather handbag was sitting on the pavement. She rummaged under the roll of twenty-quid notes and found an envelope with Siobhain's address on it. "Fifty-three Apsley Street, please, driver."

But the driver refused to take Siobhain alone. "No way," he said. "She's jellied."

Maureen climbed into the cab beside her.

A blue Ford followed the cab at a less than discreet distance.

The address on the envelope was the second floor of an old tenement in Dennistoun, just two blocks from the day center. The close was dark and miserable, littered with free newspapers and flyers for takeaway dinner shops. An acrid blend of piss and cat spray loitered by the back door. They climbed the stairs to the second floor slowly. Maureen found the door key in Siobhain's pocket, a lone Yale on a chipped Shakin' Stevens key ring.

When she shoved the door open, a wall of heavy heather scent wafted out at her. A large jar of it was sitting on the hall table. The sweet smell crept all through the house, hinting at a landscape, broad and brutal, a hundred miles away from the poky flat with low ceilings and cheap fabrics. The furnishings were goodnik castoffs; the walls in all the rooms were painted mushroom. The only personal item in the living room was sitting on top of the television, a small framed watercolor of purple and yellow irises. Tucked into the corner of the frame, obscuring the picture, was a photograph of a small boy. He was wearing shiny red plastic Wellingtons, long gray shorts and a sky blue jersey. He was standing on a windy green hillside, self-conscious in front of the camera, smiling sadly a long time ago.

Maureen sat Siobhain in an armchair and lit the gas fire. She made two cups of tea in the galley kitchen and took them through, turned an armchair round and sat down opposite her. Siobhain wasn't moving.

"Siobhain," said Maureen. "Siobhain, can you speak?"

Still she didn't move. Maureen touched her hair. Getting no response, she waved her hand in front of her face and Siobhain blinked. "Siobhain, I'm so sorry, I didn't know they'd ask you about the hospital. I'm so sorry."

Siobhain sighed the deepest sigh Maureen had ever heard, like all the Mothers of Ireland breathing out at the one time. Maureen's resolve snapped. She couldn't find a telephone in the house so she took the Shakin' Stevens key ring and went to look for a phone box.

"Leslie," she said, when Leslie answered. "Leslie, I've done a terrible thing."

Leslie tried to introduce herself but she couldn't get a response either. Maureen pointed her through to the kitchen. "Why are you here with her?" whispered Leslie urgently. "She should be in hospital."

"No, Leslie, I can't take her to a hospital, that's her worst nightmare."

"Why didn't the police deal with it?"

"If I'd left her in the station they'd have sent her to hospital for sure."

They stood in the kitchen and Maureen explained what had happened.

"Let me call her a doctor," said Leslie. "She might need some medication."

Maureen wasn't sure but Leslie swore on her mother's life that she wouldn't let them take Siobhain to a hospital.

Maureen searched the bathroom and Leslie looked through the drawers in the kitchen but they couldn't find anything with a doctor's name on it.

"Try the bedroom," suggested Leslie.

They opened the door and, past the bed, saw an old-fashioned lady's dressing table with three angled mirrors. In front of them, on the surface where the cosmetics should have been, sat an army of pill jars arranged into squads of five. The three mirrors reflected them, swelling their numbers. The same doctor's name was printed on all of the labels.

Leslie went down to the phone box. She came back up and said that Dr. Pastawali didn't want to come out. He had told her that Siobhain had these turns sometimes and she'd be fine in the morning. Maureen took the number and went down to the phone box herself.

She had been so short with him on the phone that she expected Dr. Pastawali to be annoyed with her but he was sweet and courteous. "Good evening to you, ladies," he said when they opened the door to him. "Where is Miss McCloud, please?"

He was a tall Asian man in his fifties, with dark sad eyes. He crouched down next to the armchair and took Siobhain's pulse and blood pressure. He muttered to Siobhain all the time he did it, explaining what he was doing and why, asking her little questions about her health, moving on to another query when she didn't answer. Eventually, he managed to get her to look at him.

Maureen hung about in the doorway as he got Siobhain to move her hands and wiggle her toes. He held her hand and muttered something unintelligible.

"I'm very tired," murmured Siobhain.

He took Maureen into the kitchen.

"You're not going to send her to hospital, are you?"

"No," said the doctor. "I'm sending her to bed."

Siobhain wouldn't help Maureen undress her. After half an hour of asking and cajoling and finally trying to wrestle her out of her trousers Maureen gave up and put her to bed fully clothed. She turned off the light, shut the door quietly and crept back into the living room.

Leslie had turned on the television to the evening news. Douglas and Elsbeth's wedding photograph flashed onto the screen. The picture had been treated so that the vicar and Elsbeth were in a dark shadow and Douglas's face was highlighted. The supercilious expression on his face made him look smug and unkind. "Bad picture," said Leslie, as Maureen sat down next to her on the settee.

Carol Brady was being interviewed outside the front door of a house. She was chalk white and quivering with fury. She complained about the Strathclyde police force's incompetent handling of the investigation, saying they should concentrate on bringing charges against the person who had killed her son. They knew who had done it and so did she. She read out a prepared speech about the disastrous consequences of Care in the Community and the danger of it, not only to the public but to those people released into the community and unable to cope. Anyone familiar with the case would appreciate the implication that Maureen had done it.

Leslie leaned over and turned it off.

"Nae luck, Mauri," she said.

"Do you mind if we stay here tonight?" asked Maureen. "I just want to be here in the morning in case she's the same."

"No," said Leslie. "I don't mind."

They took the cushions off the settee and armchairs and made beds on the floor. Leslie turned out the light and they settled down to sleep in the drafty living room. Maureen put the police buzzer on the floor next to her, touching it when she lay down to make sure it was within easy reach.

Leslie had her leathers on but Maureen only had her overcoat for cover. She took the place nearest the gas fire and left it on but it just accentuated the damp cold creeping over any part of her body not directly in the path of the heat. A streetlight just outside the drizzle-splattered window suffused the room with a warm orange glow. Maureen lay on her back, watching the light dance on the ceiling as the steady rain fell. "If I hadn't been to see Martin he'd never have been killed and if I hadn't told them about Siobhain they'd never have questioned her. I'm fucking up people's lives."

"Shut up, Mauri," Leslie murmured sleepily. "It's nothing to do with you."

"Yes, it is, it's my fault. I'm playing at this and I don't know what I'm doing. I could be putting you in danger, or Liam, or anyone. Or even Siobhain."

"Maureen, please, shut up and go to sleep."

"I can't, I feel like such an arse. I was there just a couple of hours beforehand. I was the last person to see him alive—"

"You can't have been, Maureen," said Leslie, her voice irritated and loud. "They wouldn't have let you go if you had been."

"D'ye think so? D'ye think someone else saw him after me?"

"Yeah. Why's that important?"

"Dunno. Do you think I've got a good memory?"

"What, for details and stuff?"

"Aye."

"It's fine, Mauri. Can we go to sleep now?"

"I should never have gone to see Martin in the first place, and going back a second time, I don't know what I was thinking about or why I was trying to find the person who did this. There's nothing I can do even if I do find them."

"Why?"

"Well, if it has got anything to do with the Northern the police'll want to talk to Siobhain and all the other women about it, and look at what this afternoon did to her. It could kill her."

Leslie rolled onto her back and stared at the ceiling.

"So you're giving up?"

"Fuck, I'll have to. Everyone at the Northern knew about the list from that Frank guy. I mean, I might have been just as clumsy about other things."

"He isn't coming after the people the police are talking to, is he? He's coming after the people you're talking to. That means you're on the right track."

"But even if I do find out who did it I can't take them to the police. They'll need witnesses and they'll have to question the women. God knows what kind of damage they could do."

Leslie rolled onto her side and looked at her. "You can't just stop." She sounded angry. "It doesn't matter a toss that you can't take him to the police, Maureen, for fucksake. We have to take responsibility about this and do something to stop it."

"But the police—"

"Never mind the fucking police. The point is, you know more about this than anyone else now. We can't just throw our hands up and walk away, for Christ's sake. We have to stop him from hurting other people."

"But I wouldn't know what to do."

"Well," she said sarcastically, "let's mount a poster campaign or something. How about letters to the papers?"

"Auch, Leslie—"

" 'Auch, Leslie' nothing. This is it, Maureen, this is the big crunch. Do you genuinely give a shit or do you just like fighting about politics?"

"No, but—"

"If you do give a shit we have to find this man and put him out of action."

"I'm not killing anyone."

"I'll do it if you don't." Leslie rolled onto her back again, crossing her arms and tucking her hands under her armpits, grunting with annoyance.

"We still don't know it's a man who did it," said Maureen carefully. "We don't know that the rapes at the Northern were done by the person who killed Douglas or Martin. For all we know those murders could have been done by a woman."

"Of course it's a fucking man," snapped Leslie. "You just don't want to be wrong."

"Maybe we'll never know . . ."

Leslie sat up impatiently. The back of her head was in a shaft of light from the street, obscuring her face. She pointed her finger at Maureen, poking it aggressively. "You have to find this fucker, not just for yourself but for that Martin guy and Siobhain in there and all the other women, 'cause you can bet your arse the bastard wasn't caught out every time. Do you think he got this brutal at a knitting bee? He's been working up to it, practicing on other people, he's been busy and I'll fucking bet you any money that there are women all over this city who can't live in their skin because of what he did to them. And when we find him we need to stop him, not try and educate him or get the police to sort him out, just fucking stop him."

She took her finger out of Maureen's face and tugged at the pockets in her jacket. She found a packet of cigarettes, flipped it open, and shoved one in her mouth.

"Christ, Leslie, man," said Maureen, holding tightly on to the edge of her coat/blanket and pulling it up a little. "Calm down."

"I'm sorry," she said sharply, rummaging in her pocket for matches.

"You should be," said Maureen. "What was that about?"

"I hate that, I hate it."

"You hate what?"

"Just that when we act so powerless, like there's nothing we can do, they smack us and we say please stop, they smack us and we say please stop. We should smack them fucking back."

"But if we use violence how are we different from them?"

"Morally?"

"Yeah, morally there'd be nothing to separate us."

Leslie shook her head. "God Al-fucking-mighty, Maureen, have you thought about this at all? It's all right for you and me to worry about our moral standing—neither of us are getting our faces kicked in every night in the week. These women are treated as if they were born on the end of a boot and we set up committees and worry about our moral standing. It's a fucking joke, the movement's turning into the WRVS, it pisses me off. We're not fucking helpless, we're fucking cowards."

She lit the cigarette and Maureen saw her face in the match's flare. She was frowning angrily, her eyebrows knitted tightly together. "Specifically in what context does it piss you off?" said Maureen, now sure that it was nothing she'd done.

"It just does, okay?"

"Tell me the story, though."

She drew heavily on her cigarette. "I don't really want to," she said and exhaled.

"All right, then," said Maureen.

The smoke swirled above Maureen's head.

"Do you remember the woman who was raped by the three men in the West End?" asked Leslie quietly. "They threw acid in her face afterward."

"I read about it in the paper. It was a while ago."

"It was two and a half years ago. She was called Charlotte. She'd been in the shelter for a while."

"I didn't know that."

"Yeah." She puffed at the cigarette.

"Give us some," said Maureen, holding her hand out for the fag. As Leslie passed it to her their fingertips touched momentarily and Maureen felt how cold Leslie was.

"Her husband had been beating her and she came to us. She had these facial scars—you know, the kind that make you shudder when you first see them. Her nose was flattened and one of her eyes was higher than the other. Ina said it was a cheekbone fracture that hadn't been set, it'd just been left. You could see the bone sticking out sometimes when she was eating. She'd scars all over her cheek, there." She gestured to her left cheek, drawing a circle on it. "The really vicious ones cut across cuts so that the doctors can't sew it up. There's nothing to sew it onto, just bits of skin hanging off. They can't patch it up, they just have to let it scar. That's how out of control these fuckers are, they've got the presence of mind to go over the cuts a second time." She took the cigarette from Maureen and sucked it hungrily.

"Anyway," she said, "she started getting it together, really together. She went on a course and got a job doing landscape gardening. She was going to set up her own business, once she'd saved some money, went to see the bank manager with a business plan and everything. She got herself a wee flat and moved out.

"Four months later I read in the paper about a rape. They dragged this woman off the Byres Road in the early morning and took her to a house and raped her for eight hours. Then they threw acid in her face. She crawled out into the hall after they left and managed to get into the close. They said she was in a critical condition. We were all talking about it in work and Annie came in and said it was Charlotte."

Leslie paused uncharacteristically and rubbed her eye hard with the ball of her palm. Her long slim neck was bent and the wispy hairs and bumpy vertebrae were lit in stark relief by the streetlight.

"She was on her way to work out in Lanarkshire when they got her. I knew it was the husband, we all fucking knew. He used to rape her, he'd dragged her off the street and everything—he'd even got his pals to rape her before. So we phoned the police and told them we thought it was him. Anyway, Charlotte died and the police said they couldn't do anything about it, no evidence or witnesses to any of it.

"The husband knew we'd told them and he started coming by the shelter and d'you know what we did? We hid. He was out there every day for fucking weeks. We phoned the police and they picked him up and gave him a doing but he came straight back, standing across the road at a bus stop with a black eye and his arm in plaster, staring in the window, looking at everyone who came out of the house. Three women left the shelter because they couldn't take it anymore. We hid and I'm never fucking doing that again."

"But that was the responsible thing to do," said Maureen. "There was nothing you could do without harming the shelter."

Leslie wasn't buying it. "Yeah. Right."

"What happened then?"

Leslie slumped. "It gets worse. One of the women used to wait at the bus stop across the road and he started talking to her. We warned her about him, we fucking told her. Then she left. The last time I saw her she had scars on her face." She motioned to her cheek again. "Same mark, like he was branding his cows or something. Her eyes were empty, way past scared. I tried to talk to her but she ran away from me."

Leslie stared into the dark room for a few moments. "You can't just stop now because he's getting closer and scarier, Mauri. This Martin bloke, he was a good man, wasn't he? He'd want you to get the guy."

"Yeah, he was a good man but he didn't want any trouble and I brought it to him."

"I'll be there, Mauri, I promise."

Maureen lay down next to Leslie, her hand resting on the beeper, and tried to sleep.

Leslie was right, she couldn't walk away. Whoever it was knew she'd been to see Martin, they'd been following or watching or something. Any one of them could be killed at any time and Maureen couldn't be ready for it always. If she could flush out the killer, make him come to her when she was expecting it, when she was ready.

She couldn't have blood on her hands, not a rapist's, not anyone's. And yet when she thought of Yvonne's snakeskin anklet, she knew that she didn't just want to stop the man who'd put it there, she wanted to hurt him, to make him feel a little of what the women had felt. It wasn't enough to stop it happening again. She fell asleep with the image of Martin's hand resting on his stomach, pointing at nothing.

She woke up at nine and went in to see how Siobhain was doing. She was lying on her back with her hands and chubby arms resting on top of the bedspread. Her head was sunk deep into the pillow, her mouth and eyes were open but she wasn't moving.

Maureen sat down softly on the side of the bed. "Siobhain?" she said.

Siobhain didn't move. Maureen reached up and brushed a hair off her face. "Did you sleep?"

Still Siobhain didn't move. Maureen had a sudden surge of adrenaline and grabbed Siobhain's shoulders, shaking her and shouting into her face, "Wake up! Siobhain, wake up!"

Siobhain raised her hand slowly. "Stop doing that," she said, lowering her eyes and looking at Maureen. "Help me out of the bed."

Maureen pulled the blankets back and lifted Siobhain's feet onto the floor.

Siobhain got out of bed and took off her clothes slowly, stripping down to her pants and vest. She took a gray V-neck jumper out of the chest of drawers and put it on. It was washed-out and flared at the bottom. She put on a pair of purple nylon trousers and a blue windcheater. The sleeves were elasticized at the ends and dug into the fat on her wrists.

"Where are you going?" asked Maureen.

"The center," replied Siobhain. "It's where I want to be."

"I'll come with you," said Maureen. It was said out of a sense of duty: she had no real desire to spend a day sitting on a plastic chair in a smoky room.

"No." Siobhain was very firm. "I can't get on with my business if you're there." She shambled down the hall, as purposeful as a golem, and went into the kitchen. She opened the fridge door, took out a carton of milk and filled a pint glass, spread margarine on five slices of bread, stacked them on top of one another and carried the lot through to her bedroom. She sat down at the dressing table and began opening jars of pills, taking out her medication and laying it in front of her.

Leslie was stirring in the living room. She rolled onto her back and saw Maureen standing in the dark hall. "All right, Mauri?" she said, rubbing her face and stretching. Her eyes were red and puffy.

"Maybe you should get up, hen," said Maureen. "Siobhain's on the move. She's going out."

"Oh," said Leslie, sitting up. "She's okay, then?"

"Seems to be."

Siobhain had finished taking her pills. She had replaced the lids on the jars and was working her way through the slices of bread and margarine. Maureen went into the living room and helped Leslie put the cushions back on the settee. Siobhain appeared in the doorway and Maureen looked up. "Are you off, wee hen?"

Siobhain nodded and walked down the hall. They could hear the front door opening. Maureen picked up the beeper and they grabbed their coats, scanning the living room to make sure they hadn't left anything. They followed Siobhain out of the house, down the stairs and onto the street, catching up with her at the corner. Leslie touched Siobhain's arm. "Where are we going?" she asked.

Siobhain didn't seem to register the touch.

"Siobhain's going to the day center," said Maureen, adding, "we'll just walk round with ye," to Siobhain, in case she thought she was talking over her.

They got to the main door and Siobhain walked in without looking back at them.

"Is she all right, Mauri?"

"I don't know," said Maureen. "She seems better but I don't know what she's like normally."

She waited for a minute and slipped into the day center after her. The sullen receptionist was behind the desk again. Her face lit up a flicker when Maureen walked in. "Heya," said Maureen. "See that lassie that just came in?"

"Fat lassie?" said the girl disparagingly.

"Aye. She's had a bad shock and I was just wondering if you could keep an eye on her. Just see she doesn't get ill or something."

The girl sighed. "Well, okay," she said reluctantly.

"I'll phone later and check up on her," said Maureen when she got outside.

"Listen," said Leslie, "I've got a few days owing. I could skive off and drive you about a bit if you like."

"Naw, I've got to go to the police station. I might be a while."

The blue Ford followed Maureen to the bus stop and cruised around the block, waiting for her bus to arrive.

27

GURTIE

MCEWAN STOOD AT THE TOP OF THE STAIRS AND GESTURED FOR HER to come up. He was wearing a white T-shirt under an expensive blue silk suit.

"*Miami Vice*," said Maureen, pointing at his outfit, knowing before it was out of her mouth that the comment was a mistake.

She followed him upstairs to their interview room. Face-to-face McEwan seemed just as domineering and confident as ever but as they walked along Maureen caught him watching her a couple of times, seeing how she was, as if trying to gauge how she was going to be with him. It was disconcerting. The McEwan she had known to date didn't yield to other people's moods: he decided where he wanted to go and just crashed on through like Godzilla in a suit, certain always that he was center stage and the world was full of extras.

He opened the door to the interview room and stepped back, letting her go in without being told to.

Hugh McAskill was standing unassumingly by the radiator. He nodded a hello. McEwan sat down in his usual chair and turned on the tape recorder. "Right, Maureen," he said quietly. "I want you to tell me everything you know about George I ward."

He took out a packet of twenty Superdelux low-tar cigarettes and offered them to her. She didn't like them but took one to be genial. "I've told you everything I know," she said.

McEwan lit his cigarette with a disposable lighter, which he put down in front of her. He exhaled and got smoke in his eye. "No, you haven't," he said calmly, looking at her as he rubbed his right eye with the tips of his fingers.

Maureen lit her cigarette and placed the lighter back on the table near McEwan. "Yes, I have."

He pulled a photocopy on A4 paper out from under his notes. "We found this," he said, pushing it toward her.

It was the list Martin had written for her but the writing wasn't in Biro, it was written in a grainy charcoal. A couple of the names were indistinct, words and letters trailed off in various places. "Shan Ryan" read as "Sno Ruom."

"We found this imprint on a pad he kept in a drawer," said Mc-Ewan. "It's a list. He's written your name at the top. What is it a list of?"

"It's a list of the staff who worked in the George I ward during the trouble."

McEwan smirked unhappily. "Why would he give you that?"

"He wanted me to pass it on to you," she said.

"Why didn't you?"

"I didn't get a chance."

"Maureen," he said, glancing at her with a tired, desperate look in his eyes, "we're not after your brother now, okay? And we know it wasn't you. I know we've had our differences in the past but you really need to cooperate with me now. Do you understand?"

Maureen paused and looked at her cigarette. It would be wonderful to hand it over and step back, to relinquish responsibility and let McEwan do all the work, let him be responsible if anyone else was killed. But she thought about Yvonne with the rope burn on her leg, about poor dead Iona and about Siobhain, and knew she couldn't hand them over to the police, that it would be an act of cowardice, that they would damage the women even more. McEwan hadn't even asked how Siobhain was today.

"Your neighbor in Garnethill phoned me."

"Which one?" She watched his face, trying to anticipate what he knew.

"The man who lives across the close from you," said McEwan. "The Italian guy."

"Right," said Maureen. "Why?"

"Your friend Brendan Gardner has been seen acting suspicious near your house. Did you send him up there for something?"

"Today?"

"No, a week ago yesterday. You didn't send him?"

She shook her head. "No, I didn't."

"Does he ever drink?"

She didn't want this: whatever Benny had done she didn't want to be here, dubbing him up to the polis as if he was just a guy she knew. "No," she said. "He doesn't drink anymore. Hasn't had a drink for three years." She must have looked upset because McEwan took it upon himself to lean across the table and pat her hand.

"He's not in the frame yet," he said. "We're just asking. We have to ask."

"What does 'in the frame' mean?"

"He's not a suspect, he just keeps coming up."

"Siobhain didn't tell you anything, did she? She didn't tell you who raped them?"

McEwan sounded utterly exasperated. "Why protect him? I don't understand why she'd protect him like that."

"She isn't protecting him, she's protecting herself."

He thought about it. "I don't understand."

"Well, there are different reasons why people can't tell." McEwan was watching her, listening intently. "Siobhain could have been threatened during it. Some people feel that if they say it out loud it becomes real or they'll make someone else dirty if they tell them about it, and other people have other reasons. She isn't trying to outsmart you."

He puffed his cigarette and looked sadly at the table. He seemed to be taking Siobhain's inability to discuss her brutal rape as a personal reproach. "Well, we'll try again later," he said.

"I don't think you should do that," said Maureen. "You have no idea what you're putting her through."

He ignored her objections and sat upright, regaining his distance. "What I was saying before is you don't need to be defensive with us now. You can tell us everything you know."

"I have told you everything."

McEwan tapped the list. "Why didn't you give me this?"

"I just didn't get a chance, Joe. You haven't been overfriendly and I wasn't going to rush down here with the list so that you could call me a twat."

He seemed hurt. "*I've* never called *you* anything," he said.

Maureen looked at him. McEwan was like a different man. He was being thoughtful and kind, comfortably displaying genuine emotions, and he was asking her to help him without trying to bully her. He had been unbearably adversarial but now that he wasn't suspicious of her Joe McEwan was almost likeable.

"I'm sorry," she said. "I am sorry for calling you that. You were being very aggressive to me and I wasn't on top form."

"Where is the list?"

"At home."

"We'll go and get it when we've finished here. Now, why were you getting lists off him and why were you visiting someone who was on the George I ward?"

"I'm just stuck in the middle of this," she said. "Honestly, Joe, I'm

not interviewing people before you get to them. I've known Siobhain for years and Martin gave me the list to give to you."

McEwan seemed genuinely upset. "Let's go and get the list," he
said heavily, and stood up, stepping behind her and lifting her
coat from the back of her chair. He held it out for her and helped
her into it carefully, lifting the heavy coat up her back and fitting
the collar around her neck. She swung back to the chair to get her
bag and saw McEwan out of the corner of her eye. He was smiling
to himself, a sly, private smile. Joe McEwan was at it.

The sullen temp was back for another eight hours sitting on the
uncomfortable chair. Their full-time receptionist, a middle-aged
woman with gray hair, had ME and kept having to take days off. The
next time the agency phoned her with this job she'd tell them to get
someone else. If she wasn't saving up for the fortnight in Corfu she'd
never have come here in the first place, never mind for a second
time. The lobby was drafty and the whole place smelled of the stale
smoke from the TV room.

And there was another thing. When she was taking her coat off
that morning the Mongol man with the tranny came straight up to
the desk and tried to touch her on the chest. She wasn't a nurse, she
wasn't trained to deal with maddies like that. She'd reported him to
the back office but she heard them laughing when she walked away.
When she went to get a cup of tea she saw the woman social worker
holding his hand and the two of them were talking away, quite the
thing.

At lunchtime she put the machine on, not that anyone phoned
there anyway, and went around to the shops to buy a Wispa and a
can of ginger to cheer herself up. The Weight Watchers said she
could have a Wispa anyway as long as she took diet drinks and not
the real ones. She bought a magazine as well because she had a
plan: the desk in the lobby was high enough for her to hide a maga-

zine under the shelf and read it when she was supposed to be working. If she saw someone coming she could shove it under as they walked over to her and no one would be any the wiser.

The Wispa didn't even last back to the day center. She opened the can of diet ginger when she got back behind the desk, took a big mouthful, and turned the answer phone off. She opened the magazine and put it down, walked round the desk quickly and leaned over it from the other side. The magazine was invisible under the shelf. Feeling very clever, she skipped back round and sat down. She started reading a true story about a dog burial service who used the same coffin the whole time and charged all the clients £200 for it.

The phone rang. "Hello," she said apathetically. There was no answer on the other end but she could hear a strange, loud clicking noise. "Hello?" she said. "This is the Dennistoun day center." The caller hung up. Confused, she put the phone down just as another call came through on the same line. "Hello," she said. "Dennistoun day center."

She listened but no one spoke. All she could hear was the strange clicking noise on the other end. She was so engrossed she didn't notice the figure coming through the farthest entry door, one hand tucked into a bulky pocket, scratching the receiver on a mobile phone. It slid unnoticed through the lobby, heading straight for the dayroom, where Siobhain was sitting in her chair watching television, alone.

The temp turned the page. The police exhumed the dogs after a disgruntled groundskeeper got the sack and reported them. The dog widow was gutted. She wanted the police to charge the company with fraud. She knew she could never replace Scamper but she was looking at puppies and wanted to tell her story to as many people as possible so that they would be spared—

"What do you want?"

The woman's cardigan was buttoned up wrong and she had disgusting red lipstick all over her old mouth. She smiled and her teeth fell out onto the desk, rolling over the edge and tumbling onto the magazine. They were covered in spit and lippy and bits of chewed digestive biscuit.

"Go away," spat the temp, standing up and grabbing the old lady's arm tightly. She spun her around and pointed her at the dayroom. "Go. Go in there."

The old lady looked back at her, confused. "Shoo," said the temp, waving her hand.

The old lady shuffled away, one arm out in front of her.

The temp picked up the magazine at the edges and dropped the teeth into the bin, ripping out the pages they'd landed on. The spit had seeped through to the next effing pages as well. It better be a good holiday anyway.

He had only taken one step toward her when the toothless old woman walked into the room and said hello. Siobhain turned her head slowly, the bud of a smile flowering softly over her pretty face until her eyes fell on him.

Maureen opened the front door to her flat and stepped in, knocking over a pile of books with the swing of her overcoat. McAskill bent down to pick them up. "It's all right, Hugh," she said. "The place is a mess anyway."

He stacked the books into a tidy pile against the wall.

"Where did you leave the list?" asked McEwan kindly.

"Oh, Joe, it's in the kitchen somewhere," said Maureen, putting her bag down on the floor. "Listen, you go on, I'll just nip to the loo."

"Whereabouts in the kitchen?" asked McEwan.

Maureen gestured to the mess in the hall. "I'm not the sort of woman who has a special place for storing lists." She smiled at him and walked down the hall to the toilet.

She sat on the side of the bath and took the list out of her pocket, folding it carefully between the staff names Martin had given her and the list of Siobhain's ward mates. She put the toilet seat down and leaned the list on it, scratching the fold with her thumbnail until it was crisp. She opened it out and put a hand flat on either side of the fold, pulling it apart from the top down, ripping Siobhain's list off the bottom. She licked her fingertip and ran it along the ripped end of Martin's list, flattening the minute telltale hairs. She flushed the toilet and washed her hands.

Back in the kitchen McEwan was looking through the piles of newspapers on the window ledge and McAskill was sifting a pile of bills Maureen kept in the toast rack. She turned her back to them and opened the plastic-bags drawer, pretending to rummage through it. "Found it," she said, and held out the list to McEwan. He took it off her and held it up to the window. "What ye looking for?" she said innocently.

"Nothing," said McEwan thoughtfully, running the ripped end between his thumb and forefinger. "Was this bit of paper longer? I remember the pad as longer than this. Was a bit ripped off the bottom?"

Maureen shrugged. "Not that I know of."

"It's a bit damp."

"I just washed my hands."

She was seeing them out of the front door when she noticed the answer phone winking at her. McEwan caught her eye as he followed McAskill into the close. "Carol Brady was on TV last night," he said. "I don't know if you saw it?"

"No," said Maureen.

"Well, I think the press'll be hanging around again. Just watch your back, okay?" He smiled at her.

"Thanks, Joe." She patted his arm. "I will." She shut the door and waited until the policemen had walked down a couple of landings before she pressed the Play button on the answer phone. It was Lynn, she was off today, could Maureen call her at home.

A man with a Belfast accent answered and said he'd see if she was in. He put down the receiver, walked away two steps, knocked on a door and shouted something. Maureen could hear the cats meowing intermittently in the background. A door opened, two footsteps, and Lynn lifted the phone. "Hello?"

"Lynn!"

"Mauri! What's the crack? How ye feeling now?"

"Oh, I'm much better now, Lynn. Thanks for the other day."

"Liam said you'd cut your hair and it looked dead nice. I didn't let on I'd seen ye."

"Good woman."

"Look, he told me about Benny going to your house and him having a key and everything."

"God, I told him not to say anything. He's an awful arse."

"Yeah, he's that all right," said Lynn fondly. "Anyway, I might be able to do that wee thing you asked about."

"Which thing?"

"Can't say, really."

There must be someone in the background. "The medical file?" guessed Maureen. "Do you know how I get to see it?"

"I might be able to do more than that. I might be able to get it for you."

"How can you do that?"

"Inverness's files are networked and my cousin works there."

"Can you get the name of the doctor from that?"

"Patient name, address, condition, treatment and doctor's name."

"Oh, Lynn, would you? All I need is the doctor's name."

"If it's there she'll get it. Not one word, Secret Squirrel, not even to Liam. I could get my books over this."

"When could you get it for?"

"Couple of days? Phone me at work on Thursday. If ye phone in the morning I'll definitely be there."

They whispered their cheerios.

She dialed the number of the Dennistoun day center. A man answered. When Maureen asked about Siobhain McCloud the man hummed and hawed in a manner so forcefully nonchalant that Maureen was terrified. "Are you a relation?" he asked.

"I'm her cousin. Tell me what happened."

"Miss McCloud's been . . . I'm afraid . . ." His voice trailed off, as if he had turned his head away from the receiver to look at something.

She demanded to speak to the female receptionist. The girl picked up the phone. "Hello?" Maureen was halfway through reminding her she'd been in that morning when she heard a watery, tearful sniff on the other end of the phone. The receptionist had been crying.

Maureen threw down the phone and ran out of the house, hailing a cab to Dennistoun.

She ran through the reception area. Old Gurtie with the falling teeth was crying by the desk, her hand to her face, the red lipstick smudged over her cheek and nose. A woman in a smart navy trouser suit was standing by the door to the dayroom. "You can't go in!" she shouted as Maureen bolted toward the door. Maureen skipped past her. The woman lunged forward and caught the back of Maureen's overcoat, dragging her back into the lobby. Maureen slipped her arms out of the coat and ran into the dayroom.

Siobhain was sitting in the chair, still facing the television. Behind the television the fire exit was lying open, a bitter draft blowing into the room from the back alley. A dark-haired man was sitting on a chair next to Siobhain, holding a paper bag over her face. She was breathing into it. He looked up as Maureen ran over and said something about a bad turn. Maureen crouched down in front of Siobhain. She couldn't speak because of the bag over her face—she was hyperventilating—but she was awake again. Her eyes were wide with terror.

Maureen hunkered down in front of her, stroking her knee and inhaling in time with her. Siobhain's breathing slowly returned to normal and the man took the bag away from her mouth. "I saw him," mouthed Siobhain. "Him."

The man told her that Siobhain had been watching TV and one of the other clients had walked in, giving her a fright. She began to scream and lost her breath. "She worked herself up into a right old state," he said, holding her hand. "Didn't you, pet?" He gestured to the reception area. "Nearly scared the life out of poor old Gurtie."

Maureen took Siobhain's hand. "Do you want to go home and have a lie-down?"

Siobhain shut her eyes and nodded.

The dark-haired man yanked her into her windcheater. Maureen took her own coat from the suited woman and held Siobhain's arm, leading her out of the day center and into the street.

It could have been a flashback—a rapist would hardly walk into a day center in broad daylight. The staff hadn't seen anyone else in the room except Gurtie. From her own experience of flashbacks Maureen knew how difficult it is to tell them from reality and she knew they were triggered by stress. Maybe this was an aftereffect of the interview with Joe McEwan. Maureen looked around the street for pedestrians or occupied cars. The only car in the street was a blue Ford but two people were sitting in it and they were chatting to each other quite casually.

They walked slowly around the corner. "Not Gurtie," whispered Siobhain.

"I know it wasn't Gurtie you saw, hen. Can you say his name to me?"

Siobhain jackknifed stiffly forward, squeezed her eyes tight together, and vomited stringy white lumps of bread and spit onto her shoes.

Maureen tried to help her upright. "I'm sorry, Siobhain, I'm sorry."

Maureen stopped at the edge of the pavement, waiting for a pause in the traffic so that they could cross to the phone box, but Siobhain tugged her sleeve. "I was going to phone Leslie," said Maureen.

"Home," said Siobhain. "Home."

"But I can't stay here all day and I think you should have someone with you."

Siobhain ignored her, tugging her sleeve. "Home," she said, walking on and turning into her close.

A small boy with a wedge haircut and a football was standing in the close. He had a Man United shirt on. He flattened himself against the wall to let them pass, watching Siobhain shuffle up the stairs. When they had passed he began his game again, headering the ball against the inside wall of the close. He was playing keepy-uppy, leaving round muddy marks on the cream wall. He was six or seven, too young to go out on his own.

The smell of heather wasn't as strong as Maureen remembered it: she must be getting used to it. She made Siobhain a cup of tea, listening all the while to the rhythmic thump, thump of the boy's ball game in the close below. She took the tea bag out and stirred three sugars into the cup.

Siobhain drank a mouthful. "Sugar," she said.

"It's good for shock," said Maureen, putting her fingers on the base of the cup and tilting it to Siobhain's mouth.

Siobhain drank quickly as she stared at the carpet, taking big gulps, leaving a brown smile at the corners of her mouth. Maureen took the cup and put it on the floor. "I really think you should go to Leslie's house, Siobhain, you shouldn't be on your own. The only thing is you'll need to go on the motorbike—"

"No," whispered Siobhain, shaking her head slowly. "No."

"Siobhain, I can't stay here all day and I don't think you should be alone just now."

"Stay."

"I really can't, Siobhain, I have to attend to some things."

Siobhain pursed her lips and turned her head, staring Maureen out with hurt, angry eyes. "Stay."

"I can't stay here, Siobhain. Can't I take you to Leslie's house instead?"

Siobhain turned her face away. "Stay."

"Siobhain, I can stay for a couple of hours but I can't stay all day."

Siobhain's fat face turned red and convulsed with impotent fury, her neck tight, her mouth open in a terrified silent scream. She stood up and shuffled forward, pushing and slapping at Maureen's arm and making her stand up. Tugging and pushing and nudging, she hassled Maureen out to the hall and opened the door, shoving her over the step and into the close. She shut the door. Maureen stood still, surprised to find herself in the cold close. She could hear Siobhain breathing heavily on the other side of the door. "Siobhain, at least lock the fucking thing."

Siobhain turned the snib and leaned against the door.

"I'll wait out here, okay?" said Maureen, addressing the door. "Okay?"

Siobhain didn't answer. Maureen could hear her shuffle back down the hall to the living room. Downstairs, the wee boy stopped playing and climbed up the first three stairs. He looked through the banister and caught Maureen's eye. He grinned at her. His front teeth were missing. She smiled back and he went back downstairs and began his game again.

Maureen sat down on the top step and smoked a cigarette to calm herself. She couldn't hear anything inside the flat. She knocked on the door, slowly so as not to scare her, and opened the letter box. "Siobhain, are ye there?"

The dark hall was still. The pool of light cast onto the carpet from the living room was steady. She wasn't moving.

"Are ye there?"

The wee boy stopped playing and came back up to look at her through the banisters again. He grinned at her. Maureen nodded. "Right, son?" He held up his football for her to look at.

"That's smashing, son. Away you downstairs now and play for a wee bit."

The boy disappeared again. She pushed the letter box open again. "Siobhain?"

She could hear Siobhain saying something, speaking very quietly in the living room, whispering almost. She had to concentrate hard to hear it, pressing her ear to the letter box. Siobhain was reciting the Saturday TV schedule to herself.

She phoned Leslie at work. "Hen," she said, "'s me. Big fuck-off emergency, Siobhain's scared shitless. She thinks she saw the Northern man. I don't know if it's a flashback or what. I need a lift to Benny's and a body to stay with Siobhain while I go and do some stuff. Can you get away?"

"Where are you?"

"Phone box by Siobhain's house. She might not even let ye into the house, ye might be sitting outside her door. She chucked me out."

"How long'll it take?"

"Days, weeks, a month, I don't know."

Leslie thought about it for a minute. "I'm there," she said, and hung up.

Maureen came out of the phone box. She needed to take Leslie away for twenty minutes and didn't want to leave Siobhain alone, on the off chance that it hadn't been a flashback. She thought about the wee boy. She nipped across the road quickly and looked in the close. He was still there. "Hey," she said. "Wee fella? How long're you going to be here?"

"Till my tea," he said.

"What time's that?"

The wee boy looked blankly at her. He was six or seven, for fuck-sake, he didn't even know how to tell the time.

"Look," she said, "never mind about that." She took a quid note out of her pocket and held it in front of him. "See if a man comes past and goes up to that lady's house and tries to kick her door in. You come outside here and start shouting and get folk up there. Could you do that, wee man?"

"I'm not allowed out the close," said the wee boy, looking at the pound note.

"Can ye stand in the close mouth and shout, just here?" She gestured to the top step.

"Aye," said the wee boy. "I can do that."

"Remember, if a man goes up there and interferes with the door you've to come out here and shout like mad, okay?"

"Aye. How have I to? Is her man gonnae give her a doing?"

"Not if we stop him."

The boy looked at the pound note and back at Maureen, his eyes wide with surprise. "Can ye stop a man giving a *mammy* a doing?" He looked up at her, his face old and wondering, waiting for the answer.

"Ye can phone the police," she said. He bounced his ball once, shook his head and smiled cynically. "Ye can tell other people about it. That'll embarrass him."

He bounced his ball. "Right," he said, nodding and thinking about it. "Very good."

"Anyway, see the lassie upstairs? See if he comes and you shout loud, I'll give ye another pound when I get back."

He grinned at Maureen as though she had given him eternal life. "I'll shout dead loud," he said.

"And get people up to the door, eh?"

"Dead, dead loud," he said, and went back to playing keepy-uppy.

Maureen ran back up the stairs and held the letter box open. Siobhain was still whispering times and programs to herself.

* * *

Leslie was parking outside the close when she saw Maureen coming toward her.

"How did you get away?" asked Maureen.

"Said my mum was ill. So we're off to Benny's?"

"Yeah, I need to get my sick line and post it in or I'll be sacked. And then if you could come and wait with Siobhain—or get her to go to yours, that'd be best."

Leslie gave Maureen the spare helmet from the box and they drove up through the town, past the cathedral and up the Great Western Road, cutting up a side street to Maryhill.

28

BOLLOCKS

LESLIE DROVE THROUGH THE BOLLARDED END OF SCARAMOUCH street and stopped the bike. The usually empty street was packed with big new cars. They took off their helmets and looked around. These were company cars.

It sounded like a rumble. It was coming from one of the tenement closes. Suddenly, a belch of men staggered backward, spilling out of Benny's close, taking photos over their heads and shouting questions and instructions. Maureen shoved the helmet back on, scratching her rough tartan scarf down the back of her neck, knocking a dry scab off and making the skin throb. Leslie put her helmet back on and buckled it under her chin.

Joe McEwan was in the center of the crowd, his head down, fighting through them. McAskill was behind him, following in his wake. The journalists put their arms out, trying to hold them back, jostling and shouting at them. Maureen and Leslie stood at the end of the street and watched as McEwan single-mindedly worked his way through the journalists and headed for a blue Ford.

Maureen and Leslie jumped back onto the bike. "Follow him," said Maureen.

McEwan's car drove out of the far end of the street. Leslie put her foot down, spun the bike in the opposite direction and sped over the pedestrian dead end onto the Maryhill Road, turning a sharp right.

"No," shouted Maureen, over the noise of the bike, "*follow.*"

Leslie didn't react. Maureen panicked. They were screaming up the Maryhill Road toward a red traffic light, going in the opposite direction from McEwan. She banged Leslie on the thigh. "*The blue Ford.*"

Leslie stopped the bike sharply. The back wheel leaped an inch off the road surface, bumping Maureen high off the pillion. "The fucking Ford. Follow the blue Ford!" she shouted.

Leslie pointed to the empty outside lane next to the bike. Just then the blue Ford cruised alongside them and stopped. McAskill was driving, McEwan was sitting in the back next to McMummb. Leslie rapped on the window and pointed behind her, McEwan peeked out and recognized Maureen's tartan scarf. He pointed eagerly down the road. The lights changed and the Ford pulled off with the bike behind it.

A couple of miles up the road the car pulled into a side street. Leslie followed and parked ten feet behind it.

"Sorry," Maureen said to her. "I lost the head there for a minute."

"'S all right, doll."

McMummb and McAskill got out of the car and walked over to Maureen and Leslie, standing next to the bike. McAskill looked happy: his coat was flapping open and he was swaggering, stepping lightly, swinging his hips. He walked up to the bike and stood close, grinning broadly, showing off his gappy teeth. "He wants to see you in the car," he said to Maureen.

"What are you so happy about?" she asked, slipping off the bike and taking off her helmet.

"Had a wee bit of good news," he said, and turned away as if the conversation was over.

Maureen walked over to the car, leaving Leslie with McMummb and McAskill. McEwan opened the passenger door as she approached, waving her into the backseat with him. "I want to talk to you," said McEwan.

"Were you looking for me at Benny's house?" asked Maureen, unwinding her itchy scarf and feeling a little bloody patch on the back of her neck.

"No, we were looking for Brendan Gardner."

"Are you going to question him?"

"Maybe," he said. "We want his prints. You're not surprised."

She shrugged. "What were the press doing?"

"Brady told them you were there. They think there's a big story. She told them off the record that there was some sort of cover-up."

"I take it I'm the subject of this cover-up."

"She said it, not in so many words, but they got the message. She told them about your brother as well."

"And you're supposed to be protecting me?"

McEwan smirked. "Yeah, I'm putting my career on the line because I like you so much."

Maureen didn't smile back.

McEwan sucked his teeth while his eyes raced over the back of the driver's seat. "We found fingerprints at the locus in the Northern."

"Do they match anyone?"

"No one we know."

She looked out of the window. They were in a suburban cul-de-sac of prissy little bungalows. "The fingerprints were on the back of Martin Donegan's neck," said McEwan.

"On the *back* of his neck?"

"Aye. He had his hand looped around the back of Donegan's neck while he stabbed him. He watched, at the most, from a foot away while he stabbed Martin Donegan's face."

"Why are you telling me that?" snapped Maureen, disgusted at the details. "No one'll tell me anything for weeks and then suddenly you tell me that."

"I told you because I know what you're doing and I want you to stop it."

Maureen opened the door of the car and shouted to Leslie to give her a fag. Leslie swaggered over. She took the lit cigarette out of her mouth, handed it in through the door and went back to her bike. McEwan watched her walk away. "She picked up the list from the clerk at the Northern then?"

Maureen took a drag on the cigarette.

"I think you're trying to find the guy who did these murders and I think you're putting a lot of innocent people in danger."

"Oh, that's ridiculous," she said, and blushed. "I'm not stupid, Joe, I wouldn't do that. I'm just unlucky, that's all."

Maureen could see his jaw muscles rippling as he ground his teeth in annoyance.

"We've been following you every inch of the way, Maureen. Even if we hadn't been we'd still know what you've been up to. Does the name Jill McLaughlin ring a bell? She's on the list Martin Donegan gave you. We've just phoned her. She said that you'd phoned her asking all sorts of questions."

Maureen picked at a sticky mark on the back of the driver's seat. "I asked her about herself," she said sullenly.

"You were asking about George I."

"She didn't tell me anything, anyway."

McEwan looked at her for a moment. "And Daniel House? What about that?"

"Daniel House?"

"You were there asking about Douglas, weren't you? We saw you go in and come out. One of the nurses saw the picture of him on television last night. She phoned and told us about his visit, just in case it mattered, and she told us someone had been there asking after him, a young woman with blue eyes."

She didn't want to look at him. His voice was so soft she was sure he was building up to shouting at her.

"Maureen," he said quietly, "off the record, this guy's a vicious bastard. I haven't seen anything like this in a long time. You have to stop it. It's madness, you don't know what you're doing."

She looked at him. McEwan wasn't angry, he was worried.

"We know about the Northern now and we're tracing all the male patients and staff with access to the wards. We're keeping our eye on a very promising suspect for the murders right now, so it's all in hand."

"Is it Benny?"

McEwan rolled his eyes. "Stop it. Will you promise me you'll stop it?"

He was asking her, he was asking nicely. "Okay," she said, feigning reluctance. "Okay, I'll stop. Just tell me if it's Benny or I won't know whether to press the buzzer if he comes to see me."

McEwan nodded slowly, giving himself time to think through the implications of telling her. He wouldn't have taken that long if it wasn't Benny.

"Okay, you don't have to say it," she said. "I can tell."

"Good," he said. "Now, until we make an arrest you're in danger. I want you to stay near your house. Stay in it if possible, okay?"

"Okay."

"And lock it."

"Okay, Joe."

He leaned across her to open the car door but she put her hand out and stopped him. "I'm sorry I was so rude to you that time, when I called you . . . what I called you before, but it's hard to just stop having anything to do with your own life and hand it over to someone else to sort out, you know? I don't suppose it's something that comes naturally to most people."

He sat back and looked at her. "You're wrong about that. It comes very naturally to most people," he said, displaying a level of reflection she would never have suspected of him. "You still got the beeper?"

"Yeah." She patted her pocket. "I've got it."

"Use it, for even the slightest reason. Okay?"

"Okay."

He took the fag from Maureen's hand and drew on it.

"Joe, do you or don't you smoke?"

"Gave up." He handed the fag back and leaned across, opening the car door.

"I know you were at it this morning," she said, "I know ye were pretending to be friendly. I'd have given you the list anyway, ye didn't need to do that."

He looked startled but said nothing.

"You smiled when ye were putting my coat on," she explained. "Gave you away. This is much better, the way you're doing it now."

McEwan coughed. "I'm not doing anything now," he said, and looked out of the window. They sat in a rocky silence.

"Right," she said awkwardly. "Well, it comes over better, anyway."

She got out of the car, took four steps and dropped her scarf. McAskill stepped forward and picked it up for her. "Hall cupboard," he whispered. "His balls. Cut off and put there." He got back into the driver's seat and McMummb climbed into the back next to Mc-Ewan. The car pulled away from the curb, followed the line of the cul-de-sac and drove out to the main road. Maureen watched them as they turned. McEwan was saying something serious to Mc-Mummb.

"And tell them," said McEwan, "not to let her out of their sight. Not for a minute."

"Yes, sir," said McMummb, and wrote the order in longhand in his notebook.

* * *

"You were right," muttered Maureen to Leslie, "it is a man."

"How do you know?" asked Leslie.

"Douglas's bollocks were cut off. That's what was in the cupboard."

"And that makes it a man?"

"A woman would've cut his dick off. Bollocks aren't exactly loaded with symbolic meaning for us, are they?"

"Dunno," said Leslie. "I'm not all women. Reckon it's the same guy as the Northern rapes?"

"Yeah."

"Did you tell them?"

"No."

"What are you going to do, then?"

"I'm going to get the fucker," said Maureen, putting on her helmet and fastening it tight.

Maureen sat on the back of the bike and shut her eyes as Leslie drove her into the town. She held Leslie's waist and felt the hum of the engine beneath her, felt the cold air pushing past her, the stinging on the back of her neck, and heard the distant noise of traffic outside her helmet.

In another time her hot face lay on Douglas's damp thigh and he stroked her hair with a gentle hand, his still-wet dick lolling to the side and twitching, his balls contracted into the shape of a love heart.

29

BOY

THE FOOTBALL BANGED HARD OFF THE WALL. TEN ELEVEN EIGHT seven ten eleven eight three four, ages. The man had dear shoes on. He went past and up the stairs. In a minute the tea would be ready and the telly would be on and the house would be warm. The bang, bang on the stairs was just someone knocking.

He thought about the pound. Was it another pound if the man tried to give her a doing or even if he didn't? He couldn't remember but the chapping was coming from the second floor.

He put down his ball carefully, making sure it wouldn't roll away out of the close. He wasn't allowed out of the close and if the ball rolled away he would have to wait for Mammy to get it back. He crept up the stairs on his hands and knees, peeking around the bend just enough to see feet. The man was at her door anyway, he could hear a scratching noise and the man's legs were shaking. He moved up the stair a wee bit and saw the man's hands moving something in the lock, pushing it in and out, very fast. He wasn't kicking the door in like for a doing, though. The boy went back downstairs, looking out of the close mouth, keeping his feet inside and holding on to the wall, hanging out and looking for his mammy. People were coming past all the time but his mammy wasn't there, just other people coming back from work and messages.

It wasn't loud but he heard it. It was a woman saying a scared thing. He knew the sound very well. It was coming from up the stairs.

He hung out of the close and opened his mouth and shouted, bending over with the effort, screaming as hard and as loud and as angry as he could, until his face went red. He wasn't shouting any words.

Some women in the street came running over, holding his face in their hands, stroking and trying to quiet him but he wouldn't be consoled. He didn't stop until the man with the dear shoes walked behind the back of the women and out the close, until he went away. All of a sudden he stopped. Mrs. Hatih gave him a sweetie. His papa said not to take things from Pakis but he needed it because he was sore from shouting.

Leslie dropped Maureen in the town and drove back to Siobhain's. The eastbound traffic was at a standstill all the way up Duke Street. She stayed in the outside lane, weaving between the stagnant traffic, enjoying the sway and verve of the bike.

A wee boy was messing about with a football just inside Siobhain's close. He stopped as Leslie walked past, holding his football under his skinny arm, and watched her. "Son," she said to him, "did a lady give you a pound earlier on?"

"Aye." The boy smiled. "And I shouted dead loud."

"Did the man come?"

"Aye." He grinned. "He was poking at the door."

Leslie left him and ran up the stairs two at a time.

She hammered on Siobhain's door and shouted in at her. The boy followed her up to the landing. He watched the door, holding Leslie's leather trousers in a tight fist at the back of her knee. The lock's metal face had fresh scratches on it, as though someone had been trying to fit something sharp into the keyhole.

"Siobhain," shouted Leslie, "it's Leslie, Maureen's pal from last night. Let me in! Open the door."

They heard a nervous scratching as Siobhain took the snib off the lock. The door opened a fraction and Siobhain looked out, slumping backward when she saw it was Leslie, leaving the door to swing open. Her eyes were glazed. Leslie stepped into the hall, put her arms around Siobhain and patted her back. The boy looked Siobhain over. "No doin' then, na?" He shook his head at Leslie.

"Eh?"

"D'she no' get a doin', then?"

Leslie was disturbed by the question. "No, son, she didn't." She pushed the door shut in his face.

Leslie took a plastic bag from the kitchen and packed it with knickers, a toothbrush and a spare jumper. She held the bag open at the dresser and swept the pill jars into it. She made sure Siobhain had her house key and put a heavy coat on her. "You ever been on a bike before, Siobhain?"

Siobhain didn't answer. Leslie buttoned up the front of her coat. "Just relax and you'll be fine, okay?" Leslie put her hands on Siobhain's hips and moved them from side to side. "Just relax and we'll be fine, okay? Let them follow the movement of the bike." She led Siobhain down the stairs.

The boy was watching them. "Son, come 'ere. The lady asked me to give you this." She handed him a pound.

"I made him stop," he said, looking guilty.

Leslie kissed the top of his head. "I know you did, wee man," she said. "I know you did."

She strapped the helmet onto Siobhain's head and helped her get her leg over the seat. Her big body was rigid with fright. It would be like riding the bike with a fridge on the back.

30

PAULSA

MAUREEN PHONED LESLIE'S HOUSE IN CASE SHE HAD MOVED SIOB-
hain there. Leslie answered the phone almost as soon as it
rang out. She said that Siobhain's lock had been fiddled with,
that he didn't get in and the wee boy said he'd scared the man
away.

"Christ," said Maureen, "I thought she was having a flashback."

"Naw, he was there, all right, unless that wee boy's a clever con
man."

"Did the lock look fiddled with?"

"Yeah," said Leslie. "Judging from the state Siobhain's in he'd definitely been there. She can't talk and I don't know if she can see. I'd
come and get you, but I'm afraid to leave her alone."

"Don't worry. I'll be there in a couple of hours."

"Yeah, and bring drink."

"What kind?"

"The cheap, strong kind."

On the way to Paulsa's house Maureen stopped at a cash machine and fed in her card. She requested two hundred quid of

Douglas's money and put it in her back pocket, keeping it separate. It didn't feel like her money at all. She still didn't know why he had given it to her.

Paulsa lived in the Saltmarket. The close was next door to a Unionist pub with a Union Jack flag painted on one of the windows. Maureen had never been to Paulsa's before, she'd never been to any dealer's house before apart from Liam's and she didn't know what to expect. But people come in and out of these houses all the time, she told herself, and they don't all get killed or raped on the doorstep. And, anyway, she was Liam's wee sister and Paulsa was looking for allies.

The close had a buzzer entrance system. She guessed the dirtiest button would be Paulsa's and pressed it. The speaker crackled and a distant voice muttered a quizzing "Yeah?"

"Is Paulsa there?" said Maureen, lowering her voice and trying to sound a bit hard anyway.

"Paulsa? Who's Paulsa?"

"I'm Liam O'Donnell's wee sister," she said.

The lock on the door buzzed excitedly. Maureen pushed it open and walked up to the second floor. As she stood on the landing one of the doors opened slowly. Paulsa looked her over. His skin was a shallow yellow color—even the whites of his eyes had a yellow tinge to them. He was wearing navy blue jeans and the newest Nike trainers. A dribble of brown food had dried on the front of his orange Adidas T-shirt. He looked like the last man on earth with a need for sportswear: he didn't look as if he was going to be here for very long. A slow smile hovered across his face, his jaw hanging open so she could see all of his teeth, which were very bad indeed: specks of black rot dotted them at regular intervals. Maureen felt like a well-meaning woman of the parish come to minister to the poor.

"You're Liam's wee sister," drawled Paulsa.

"Aye," she said.

"I saw you in the paper. Smart T-shirt ye had on."

Paulsa smiled in slow motion again, his head rolling in a tiny circle. He probably meant to nod. At this rate they might stand in the close all night. She walked toward him and he moved back slowly, letting her into the flat.

The living room was nicely painted in pale green, a terra-cotta three-piece suite looked new, apart from the clusters of cigarette burns on the armrests. A glass coffee table was covered with packets of Rizlas, bits of tinfoil and matches, and ripped, empty fag packets. An incongruously twee onyx table lighter sat in the middle of the mess like a centerpiece. A couple of pizza boxes were lying on the floor next to a very large, very full ashtray.

Paulsa walked in, stepping cautiously on his tiptoes like a Parkinson's victim. He dropped onto the settee and grinned up at Maureen. "I saw you in the paper," he said again. "Your brother's a good guy."

"Yeah," said Maureen, "he is. You stuck your neck out for him, Paulsa. Cheers, man."

"No bother, man."

She didn't know whether to say it but she thought maybe no one else would. "Are you well, Paulsa? You don't look it. You're awful yellow."

Paulsa screwed up his face and giggled infectiously. " 'I'm turning Japanese,' " he sang. " 'I think I'm turning Japanese, I really think so . . .' " He held up his hands and waggled his fingers, singing the old Vapors tune and looking angelically at the ceiling. He got confused and slipped into "Echo Beach" by Martha and the Muffins. He sang for too long, way past where it would have been funny, through where it was sad, and stopped abruptly just before it got funny again. He giggled again, covering his mouth with his hand. "Anyway," he said, "what can I do for ye?"

"I want to buy something."

Paulsa weighed it up in his mind. It took a while. "Why didn't you get it off Liam?"

Maureen blushed. "I can't really," she said quietly. "It's for a nefarious purpose."

"A *nefarious* purpose?" Paulsa echoed, enjoying the unfamiliar word. "What is it you want?" She told him. "What are you going to do with it?" he asked.

She started to answer but he interrupted her after getting the gist of it. "Don't tell me about that any more," he said, looking shaken.

He tiptoed into the kitchen and came back with her order in a plastic money bag. "It might take about an hour to get going."

She gave him three twenty-pound notes from Douglas's money.

"I've no change," said Paulsa, worried that she might want to stay in his company while he got some.

"Don't worry, Paulsa," she said, moving toward the front door. "I'll get it from you again."

Paulsa tiptoed quickly around her and opened the front door, anxious to get her out of the house.

"I'm sorry I freaked you, Paulsa."

"I wish you'd never told me that."

"I'm sorry." She stepped out into the close and Paulsa shut the door quickly behind her. She shouldn't have told him: she had expected him to be less empathetic. She slipped the plastic money bag into her inside pocket and did up the buttons on her coat.

As she walked up to Argyle Street, where the buses stopped for the Drum, she passed a phone box and decided to phone Liz, just to touch down.

Garry answered. "I'll just get her," he said when Maureen said it was herself phoning.

Liz didn't bother to say hello or ask her how she was. "Did you get the letter he sent you?" she asked.

"No."

"Maybe it hasn't got to you yet. Maureen, he's sacking you."

"Oh, fuck."

"Did you send the line in?"

"No," said Maureen, "I've left it somewhere awkward. How are ye anyway, Lizbo?"

"Aye, fine."

Maureen wanted a comforting, normal conversation, but Liz could hear a strange tension in her voice and didn't want to chat about trivia with her. She was going to Tenerife in the morning and still had a lot of packing to do. They arranged to meet for lunch at some undefined date in the future. It was a more diplomatic cheerio than a final good-bye.

She stopped at an off-license and bought a bottle of peach schnapps. It wasn't until she was handing over the money that she remembered she didn't have a job anymore and that there would be no money coming in on Friday. It didn't feel right taking Douglas's money. Fuck it, she thought, I'll worry about that later, and she bought some fags as well.

The image of Douglas's balls made her throat ache as she walked to the bus stop. She stayed outside the shelter, leaning on the damp Perspex, and lit a cigarette, drawing heavily on the filter, shoving the grief downward into her belly, putting it by for later.

Leslie was sitting alone in the living room watching television, she was in an excitable, giggly mood.

"What are you so cheery about?" said Maureen.

"Oh," Leslie grinned, "I've just been with the Queen of Sadness all day. I'd shoot myself in the foot for a laugh right now."

"Yeah," said Maureen. "Where is she?"

"In bed," said Leslie. "We'll have to sleep on the floor again." She tried to rummage in Maureen's bag. "Drink," she said. "Give me drink."

"Wait, wait," said Maureen. She sat Leslie down on the settee and explained that she was going to take Siobhain to Millport in the next couple of days. "Can you come with us?"

"We're not going there for a laugh, are we, Mauri?"

"No," said Maureen. "I'm going to try and flush him out, get him to follow us and take care of it once and for all. Will you come?"

"I said I was in," she said definitely. "I'm in."

Maureen lit a fag. "I've finally been sacked," she said. "There's a letter on its way to my house."

"Because of the sick line?"

"Yeah. I don't mind not working and I can use Douglas's money if things get tight but I can't sit at home with my thoughts all day. I'll go bananas."

"Why don't you come and work voluntary at the shelter for a wee while? We're desperate for extra hands. I mean, you'd need to be passed by a committee and everything but I don't think it'd be a problem."

"That would be brilliant," said Maureen.

"We might not be working the same shifts or anything, and it might only last another couple of months, you know that?"

"Yeah, I meant it would be brilliant to do something that mattered."

Leslie looked at her thoughtfully. "I've been thinking," she said. "The budget committee meets in a couple of weeks. If we could get people to write in and protest it might change their decision."

"Yeah? So?"

"Well, remember what the Guerrilla Girls did in New York?"

Maureen smiled a long, smug smile. "You mean mount a poster campaign?"

Leslie raised an eyebrow. "Might work. What d'you think?"

"I could pay for it out of Douglas's money. I'd like to do that. I don't know what else to do with the money." When Maureen got the bottle of peach schnapps out of her bag Leslie ran away into the kitchen and brought out a two-liter bottle of lemonade and some glasses. They settled down in the living room to watch television and get pissed. The programs weren't very good so Leslie put an old copy of *Public Enemy* in the video. They watched it, sipping at the sweet schnapps, laughing at Jean Harlow's cardboard hairdo and Cagney's macho posturing. When Cagney punched his mum on the chin Leslie laughed so hard she tumbled off the settee. She crawled to the bathroom on all fours. "Oh, man," she giggled, "I'm so fucking tired."

"Want me to pause it?"

"No, I can't watch any more."

She came back with two sleeping bags.

"I haven't brushed my teeth for two days," reflected Maureen.

"You're a dirty cow," said Leslie, arranging cushions on the floor.

"And I'm not brushing them tonight either."

"That's filthy," said Leslie, and slid into her sleeping bag. Maureen stripped down to her knickers and T-shirt, laid the beeper next to her on the floor and put out the lights. She fell into a drunken, hazy sleep.

31

SHAN RYAN

MAUREEN ROLLED OVER UNCOMFORTABLY AND FELT THE STRAINS and bruises from another night on a floor. Siobhain was standing over her head like a colossus, looking down at her.

"Siobhain," Leslie called softly from the kitchen doorway. "Come away from there, hen. You'll scare the shit out of her."

Siobhain turned around and waddled into the kitchen. Maureen rubbed her face and sat up. She had a tremendous amount of crusty sleep in her eyes. Leslie brought out a coffee for her and sat on the settee watching her drink it. "So, what's the deal today, then?"

"Just hang around here with Siobhain and don't answer the door without checking it first. When we get to Millport all you have to do is sit tight and I'll take care of everything."

"Right," said Leslie quietly. "Maureen, you're not going to stab him, are you?"

"Nah." Maureen climbed out of the sleeping bag and rolled it up. "All being well I won't even touch him."

Leslie nodded soberly and patted her knees with her open hands.

"Are you losing your bottle, Leslie?"

"Yeah," Leslie said. "To be honest I think I am."

"Why?"

"Dunno. I just don't feel like attacking anyone at the moment. You losing your bottle, Mauri?"

"No," said Maureen certainly. "I'm not. I'm getting angrier."

"Maureen, what are you going to do to him?"

Maureen didn't want to tell her. It would be better if no one else knew and she didn't want to have an ethical debate about it. "I'm going to stop him," she said, picking up the phone book.

"Brush your teeth before that, eh?"

Maureen found the number and phoned the Isle of Cumbrae tourist board, asking for information about three-bed flats in Millport. The man on the other end of the phone spoke in a strange transatlantic drawl and kept trying to make personal conversation, asking her if she'd ever been there before. She said no in an attempt to guillotine the conversation but he launched off into a speech about the sights on the island. She finally managed to get contact numbers for five addresses from him. Two of the flats were in the same close—the close they had stayed in the last time they were in Millport, the time Liam and Leslie had taken her, the time of the photograph in the papers. It would be best to get the flats in the same close, in case he found them before she found him.

She called one of the contact numbers and booked the flat for a week starting tomorrow. She hadn't planned it but when the young woman at the other end asked her for a name and contact phone number she found herself making things up, lying so fluently she felt completely in control, she didn't even hesitate when the woman asked her to spell her false surname. Then she rang Liam, gave him the phone number for the other flat in the close and asked him to book it for her. "What for?" he said. "Are you trying to get away from the police for a bit?"

"Yeah."

Minutes later he phoned back to tell her he'd done it. "She asked for my number. I just made it up off the top of my head, is that all right?"

"Should be," said Maureen. "Unless they call to check it."

She wanted him to talk about something, anything, get him to tell her a long story so that she could listen to his voice for a while because there was a chance that she wouldn't come back from Millport. "Has Benny been in touch?"

"No. I had to phone him eventually. He said the police had questioned him and taken his prints. He wanted to know if they'd asked me about him."

"What did you say?"

"I said no. Listen," Liam said, "you know Marie's home this week?"

"Yeah, Una said the other day."

Liam paused. "Did you see her?"

"Yeah."

"For fucksake, Mauri, I told you not to go near them, I told you—".

"I know, I know, I'm not going to."

Someone rang Liam's front doorbell and he had to go. "Stay away from them."

"I will, doll, I will," she said. "You take care. Good-bye."

The insistent caller rang Liam's door again. "Yeah, Maureen," said Liam, bewildered by her solemn tone. "You take care as well."

She took a shower and used Leslie's damp toothbrush, scrubbing hard, making her gums bleed at the sides. She glanced at herself in the mirror. She looked rough. Her skin was gray, her eyes were pink and she had dark shadows under her eyes.

Back in the kitchen Leslie handed her a plate of buttery toast and another coffee. "And where are you going today?" she asked.

"South Side. We're going to Millport tomorrow. Can you get the time off okay?"

"Yeah, yeah, no bother. Is that where it's going to happen?"

"Aye."

"Right," said Leslie, nodding gravely. "Right."

Siobhain was sitting on the veranda, staring at the bald hills out the back.

"I haven't heard her speak yet," Leslie said.

"She's a beautiful voice," said Maureen. "You'll hear her one day."

Maureen went out to the veranda and sat down on the deck chair next to Siobhain, holding her hand and talking about the games the children were playing down below. It was rainy and they wore jackets and hats and wellies. She remembered from the hospital how important it had been to her when people took the time to talk. She explained that they were going to Millport the next day, and, although she couldn't be sure, she thought Siobhain squeezed her hand a little.

She picked up the beeper, put her overcoat on, borrowed Leslie's woolly hat and went downstairs to get the bus over to Levanglen.

Maureen pulled the hat down over her forehead and followed the signs straight to the dispensary. It was a small hole in the wall with sliding frosted-glass windows and a bell next to a handwritten sign telling her to ring for attention. She pressed it and stood away. A honey blond nurse wearing a white uniform and cerise lipstick slid the frosted window back. "Can I help you?" she said, and smiled the most uncomplicated smile Maureen had seen in a long time.

"Yeah, I wonder if you can. I'm looking for Shan Ryan."

"Shan's having his lunch."

She stepped back to let Maureen see him. He was sitting at a desk with his feet up, dressed in a nurse's white button-over jacket with a big ID badge hanging from the breast pocket, eating salad from a Tupperware container. She had guessed that he was half-Asian from his name and she was right. His skin was dark and he had shiny black hair but his almond eyes were khaki green. When he stood up to come to the window Maureen could see that he was at least six foot tall. He stood noncommittally behind the honey blond nurse and looked at Maureen expectantly. His front teeth were large and straight and white, his broad lips seemed unusually red.

"Um, listen, I just wanted to ask whether you used to know Douglas Brady?"

Shan ignored the question and let the honey blond nurse answer. "The guy who got killed?" she asked.

"Yeah. He used to work upstairs as a therapist."

"I heard about that. His mum was an MEP, wasn't she?"

"Yeah," said Maureen. "Did you know him?"

"No," she said, "I never met him myself, I've just started here, but—"

She turned to Shan Ryan. "Me neither," he said, turning and walking back to his seat at the desk. He picked a cherry tomato out of his salad and sat down, looking Maureen in the eye as he bit the tomato between his front teeth, slicing it in half.

Maureen watched him. "Did you know Iona McKinnon?"

Shan glared into his lunch box.

"Sorry," said the nurse, filling in the silence, "I didn't know her either. Shan?"

Shan looked faintly surprised and shook his head. The nurse turned back to Maureen. "Sorry 'bout that," she said, smiling her delicious smile. "Are you a policewoman?"

"I think the answer to that question is quite obvious," said Maureen.

The nurse smiled at whichever obvious answer she was going with.

Maureen caught Shan's eye once more before thanking them and stepping back from the window. He seemed shrewd, as though he recognized her from somewhere and was trying to place her.

It was only two o'clock: she might as well go back to Leslie's. She had hoped her visit to Levanglen would take longer. All she had left to do was a bit of shopping and, apart from that, it would be a straightforward wait until the next day when she made the phone call to Benny and they caught the train to Largs.

The bus took a long time to come. Maureen stood in the shelter, staring down the dual carriageway in unison with the other damp passengers. The drizzle was intrusive today, swirling into Maureen's collar and up her sleeves. A brisk wind swept under the glass wall of the shelter, freezing her ankles. When the forty-seven finally arrived she climbed on board, bought her ticket and went upstairs, sitting at the back. The bus was a little too warm. Damp rose from thick, wet coats, making the atmosphere muggy and tiring. By the time it got to the Linthouse the smell on the top deck was fetid.

A blue Mini Clubman left its parking space in the Levanglen Hospital car park and drove out of the gates, following the bus through Linthouse, through the town and up the Great Western Road all the way to Anniesland.

Maureen had to change to a sixty-two bus at Anniesland to get to the Drum. She stood up as the bus pulled under the railway bridge and carefully worked her way down the stairwell to the door.

The Clubman driver saw her get up and struggle to the door. He stopped the car under the bridge, waited for the lights to change, then took a sharp left and parked in a side street.

The smell of old damp clothes lingered in her nose and she couldn't be bothered getting straight back onto another bus. She nipped into a coffee importer's and bought a quarter pound of fresh-ground Colombian coffee. The room smelled of chocolate and warmth. Standing at the back of the shop, the coffee grinder was a huge brass monster—it dwarfed the woman who was serving. She had to climb up a three-step ladder to put Maureen's beans into the grinding funnel, Maureen took the warm paper bag from her, paid, and stepped back out the door into the damp day.

The coffee shop's pleasant chocolate smell filled Maureen's head, and she didn't want to lose it. She looked down the street and saw the army surplus sign. She would need a flask and they might have them cheap. She pulled up her coat collar and walked down to the shop. Camouflage army gear and sportswear were hung on tidy racks against the wall. A circular sale rack had been put just inside the door, as if they were desperate to get rid of the stuff.

A plump woman in her midforties was serving at the counter. On the shelves behind her were the smaller items shoplifters would favor: hats and gloves, pocket hand warmers and mini butane fires for camping. "Can I help you?" she asked in a clipped, nasal Kelvinside accent. She sounded like Elsbeth.

"I'm looking for a cheap flask," said Maureen, shaking the rain off her woolly hat.

The woman bent her legs in a bunny dip and reached into the back of the counter. "I'm afraid we only have two models in stock at the moment. This one"—she put a red plastic flask on the counter—"and this one."

The second flask had a matte silver body with a black plastic base and handle. Maureen unscrewed the cup and stopper and looked into it. The lip fanned out smoothly. She put her finger in and tapped the inside with her nail. It sounded sturdy enough. "How much?"

"Eight pounds."

"Fine, yeah, I'll take it."

As the woman put the flask back into its box Maureen glanced out of the window into the busy main street. Shan Ryan was standing outside the window, looking in at her. He was wearing a full-length black leather overcoat. He gestured down the street and disappeared.

"Eight pounds, then?"

"Oh," said Maureen. "Yes." She handed over a tenner.

The woman gave her some change and a bag with the flask in it. "Thank you for your custom," she called as Maureen stepped outside.

Shan was turning into a side street. Maureen paused in the doorway of the army shop and patted her pocket, finding the beeper. She put the flask into her rucksack, and her fingers found the cold metal handle of her stabbing comb. She relaxed a little. She slid it into her coat pocket with the sharp end pointing downward. She might need to pull it out quickly and use it.

When she got to the street corner Maureen stopped and looked around. The lights on a Mini Clubman flashed twice. She walked down the street toward it. Shan reached across the passenger seat and opened the car door for her. A bebop jazz tape was playing quietly on the stereo. She leaned down into the car and looked at Shan. He scowled at the dashboard.

He had shed his white nurse's coat and was wearing a faded pair of blue jeans and a black cotton crew-neck jumper with nothing underneath. She could see the impression of a lot of hair trapped under the front of the jumper, and black hair curled over the collar in a Hokusai wave.

He leaned over the passenger seat and looked up at her. "Get in, then," he said.

Maureen sighed and tapped her hand on the roof of the car.

"Are ye getting in?" he said, not seeming to understand her reluctance.

"Why would I get into a car with a man I don't know?" she said.

Shan frowned and looked hurt. "I'm not trying to abduct you," he said. "I thought you wanted to talk to me. I'll go away if you want me to, I didn't mean to scare you." He leaned over to shut the door but Maureen caught it with her foot. "No, really," he said firmly. "I'd really rather ye didn't get in now I've scared you."

"It's all right," said Maureen, feeling she had insulted him. "I'll get in."

"I left my work to come and talk to you. I don't want to hurt you."

Maureen opened the door and clambered into the car. Shan reached for the ignition key and paused. "You can still get out if you want," he said, watching the parade of slow-moving traffic passing in front of them.

"No," said Maureen, squeezing the comb in her pocket. "Really."

Shan pulled the Clubman into the traffic and crawled along the main street, stopping every three hundred yards at red lights. He turned the car left onto the motorway.

"Where are we going?" she asked.

"Away somewhere," said Shan. "Somewhere we won't be seen talking together."

"Why?"

He gave her a you-know look.

"Do you think I'm a policewoman?"

"I know exactly who you are," he said, and turned the music up.

They were on the motorway headed out to the flat Renfrew plain and the airport. The rain had cleared up and darkness was falling quickly, as it does in midautumn in Scotland. The big sky was a sudden pink smear.

They passed the lightbulb factory, Maureen's favorite building in Glasgow. It starts as an inauspicious concrete rectangular base with broad, square windows, and then soars into a glass-brick attic with a turret. Many of its windows have been smashed but, like one of the mystical secrets of geometry, it's still appealing. Shan saw her looking at it as they passed. "Do you like it?" he said, smiling as if it were his.

"Aye," said Maureen.

"Me too."

Farther along he took the slip road for the airport, drove under the motorway flyover and into the huge empty car park. He pulled up in a space directly across from the terminal doors. "Why did we have to come all the way out here?" asked Maureen.

"Paki guy with green eyes talking to a white lassie? There aren't many places in Glasgow where that wouldn't be noticed."

Shan locked the car and they took the zebra crossing over the empty road to the airport terminal. The automatic double doors opened in front of them and they stepped inside. The illuminated signs and posters lent the building an all-pervasive melancholy yellow light. Straight in front of them were the check-in desks, manned by heavily made-up women wearing silly hats. Above their heads the check boards told the number and destination of the next flight. A group of tall adolescent boys with Scandinavian Airlines stickers on their rucksacks were standing aimlessly in front of one of the desks. An electric cleaning cart trundled past, driven by a fat guy in overalls.

Shan veered off to the left, taking the escalator up to the second floor where the big café was, and Maureen followed him. It was a large space with about fifty tables arranged round a well-defended serving area in the middle. The tables were partitioned off into user-friendly spaces by flimsy white trestle walls with plastic vines hanging off them. At the center was an oval self-service island offering breakfast, lunch and dinner at the same time. The place was almost deserted.

Shan bought Maureen a coffee and chose a can of Irn Bru for himself. She noticed that he didn't look up at the woman tending the till.

They sat down at a table next to a glass wall overlooking the car park and the flyover. Shan opened his can and took a mouthful. "Jill McLaughlin phoned me," he said.

"Right," said Maureen.

"She said you phoned her on Sunday."

"Oh?" She blew on her coffee. It had been boiled and smelled of burnt plastic. A bing-bong overhead call announced a flight to Paris, Orly.

"I'm sorry about Douglas," he said.

"Thanks."

Shan sat back and looked at her, scratching his hairy forearm softly. His nails were long, yellowing and horny. He must play acoustic guitar. "D'you not want to talk about this?" he said sharply, bending his neck to catch her eye and bringing her gaze back up to his face. "I'm only here because I got the impression that you did."

"I do," she said formally, wondering who the fuck this guy was. "I'm sorry. Do you or Jill know why Douglas was killed?"

"I'm not spillin' my guts," he said sternly. "This is heavy stuff and I want to know who you are."

"I thought you knew who I was," said Maureen. "You said you knew in the car."

"Aye," he said. "I know your name, that's all. I want you to tell me what you know about this before I start talking about it."

"Fair enough. What is it you want to know?"

Shan sucked a tut through his big front teeth and drew a sharp breath. "I left my fucking work to come after you, yeah? I didn't need to do that."

"But you did."

"Yeah," he said indignantly, "I fucking did as well."

"Because I asked about Iona."

He nodded sadly. "Because of Iona."

Shan could have taken her to a field and slit her throat. No one had seen them, and he had no reason to bring her to the airport, where they might be seen together. There was no reason for him to talk to her, and he'd been so sweet when she didn't want to get into the car.

"I know Iona was at the Northern," she said. "I know she was on the George I ward during the incidents—"

"They were rapes," said Shan flatly. "Not incidents."

"Right, I wasn't sure about that. I know she was having an affair with someone at the Rainbow. Then she killed herself."

Shan waited, expecting more. When he realized there wasn't any more he dropped his can heavily onto the table. "*That's* what you know?"

"Yes," said Maureen, after a long pause. "That's what I know."

Shan watched his can as he turned it round on the tabletop with the tips of his fingers, tapping his long nails on the thin aluminum surface. He smiled unkindly at the can. "And you wanted to know who she was having an affair with? You were jealous in case it was Douglas?"

"No. I don't give a shit who she was seeing," Maureen said, pissed off at the suggestion that her motive was so puerile. "I just thought she might have been raped at the Northern and people seem to have known her. I thought she might have said something, given someone a clue about who did it. The rest of them can't seem to talk."

Shan looked up suddenly. "The rest of them?" he said softly. "Who have you seen?"

Maureen felt a rush up the back of her neck. She couldn't name them, she didn't know who Shan was, he might be the rapist, could be why he took the time to talk, he wanted to find out who she'd spoken to. He was sweet so she'd get into the car, that's why he was like that, he'd done this before. Her mind had gone blank, she couldn't think of a single lie. She felt inside her pocket for the beeper. McEwan said that it might take a few minutes for the police to arrive. She could be dead by then. She slid her hand into the other pocket, feeling for the stabbing comb. She found it and looked past him, scanning the third floor, looking for the café exits and ways out of the airport. No, stay in the fucking airport. She was on the bare, dark Renfrew plain with no car, little money and a comb to protect her. She looked out at the shadowy cars speeding past on the flyover, their pinprick lights leaving glimmer trails in the heavy dark, and squeezed the comb in her pocket. She felt one of the teeth break the skin on her palm. Shan was watching her. "Dunno." She clenched her teeth. "Dunno."

Shan frowned, his black eyebrows casting a dark shadow over his piercing eyes. "You won't tell me," he said. "You won't tell me their names?"

Maureen shook her head and squeezed again, breaking through another bit of skin. A Tannoy call announced the shuttle flight to Manchester. Shan leaned on the table, bringing his face close to hers. She would have moved back and away from him but she was so tense she couldn't be sure that she was capable of slipping casually backward in the chair—she might look as if she were about to scarper.

"Iona wasn't having an affair," said Shan quietly. "You heard it from the cleaner, right? Susan with the big mouth?"

Maureen nodded. It was a lie but if she tried to speak her voice would sound high and shaky and she didn't want him to know how scared she was.

"Susan saw Iona being raped. She saw it through a chink in the blinds. She was being raped in a therapist's office and because she wasn't kicking and screaming Susan decided they were having an affair." Still frowning, he jerked the can to his mouth, took a long drink and dropped it back down on the table. "You don't happen to smoke, do you?" he said.

"Um, yeah." She sounded like a chipmunk.

"Have you got some fags on ye?"

"Yeah."

She had to take her left hand off the comb to get her bag. Her palm came away from the metal surface uneasily, like bare thighs from a plastic car seat left in the sun. She lifted the rucksack to her hand, trembling with a jittery postadrenaline rush. She took the packet out, dropping it on the table rather than handing it over in case he saw her hand shake. The packet slid across the polished surface of the table and hit the side of her cup of coffee, sloshing brown liquid onto the white tabletop. Shan reached out quickly, coolly, and grabbed the packet away from the coffee spill. He took a cigarette and lit it with a new brass Zippo he produced from his pocket.

Casual smokers don't have brand-new Zippo lighters, Zippos are expensive and cumbersome to carry. Shan must have cigarettes. He might have seen her take the comb from her bag, he might be asking for the fags so that she would let go of it, so that she would be undefended. She jerked her hand into her pocket and grabbed hold of it again. He watched her.

He inhaled the first smoke and held it in his lungs, tapping the ash from the cigarette under the table, watching the cigarette as he did, being precious with it. Shan had a Zippo because he smoked a lot of hash. He looked at her and his face softened. "You don't need to be afraid of me," he said. "I'm going to tell you everything I know and then you can leave before me, after me or with me. Whatever makes you feel safe."

" 'Kay," said Maureen.

"I'm sorry if I gave you a fright, I forgot about what's happened to you. You don't even know who I am. I suppose I could be anyone to you."

"I don't know if we can smoke in here," she said, changing the subject.

"Yeah, well, fuck it," said Shan, quietly unperturbed.

Maureen took the packet and pulled one out for herself. Shan gave her a light from his Zippo. "Go on, then," she said.

"Yeah, right," said Shan, turning to the window, looking out at the motorway, following the lights of the passing cars with his eyes. "Iona and the George I rapes, it was the same person . . ." He said it in an undertone, but Maureen caught the name.

She gasped, sucking smoke so deep into her lungs that it hurt. "Are you sure?"

"Yeah," said Shan, calmly flicking the ash from his cigarette under the table. "Do you believe me?"

"Why do you think it was him, for God's sake?"

"It's a long story," he said.

Maureen squashed her fag out and stood up. "I need a drink," she said. "I'm getting a beer. D'you want one?"

Shan lifted his head and looked at her. "What, an alcoholic drink?"

"Yeah."

He put his hand in his jacket pocket. "No, no, I'll get it," said Maureen. "What d'ye want?"

"Any whisky? Auch, naw, that's bad, actually, I'm driving."

Maureen shrugged. "It's up to yourself. You're allowed one, aren't you?"

"Auch," he said, clearly gasping. "Auch, aye, get us a whisky if they've got it."

Maureen negotiated her way through the tables and around the trestle walls to the deserted island of food in the center of the café. She bought a whisky miniature and a cold can of Kerslin, an extra-strong lager with a bitter taste caused by the artificially heightened alcohol content. As she passed the till she picked up two plastic cups and four sugar sachets, which she tucked deep into her pocket under the beeper.

Shan was slumped over the table, chin in hand, watching the traffic on the motorway. He took the whisky from her, poured it into the plastic cup and sipped carefully. Maureen smiled and sat down. "You don't drink much, do you? I'd have walloped that back in a oner."

Shan looked at her can of lager. "How the fuck can you drink that stuff? It tastes like ethanol."

"Yeah," she said. "That's why I like it. How do you know this, Shan?"

"Like I said, it's a long story," he said, his head bent over the glass of whisky, enjoying the smell. He whistled a sigh and looked out of the window. "It wasn't long ago, I went to work one day and before I got changed into my uniform one of the cleaners came running into the staff room. Someone was crying in the toilets. I went in." Shan was talking quickly, quietly, as if he were giving a case report. "It was Iona. She was in a cubicle. I couldn't get her out. I climbed over the wall. She was sitting on the floor with her knickers around her ankles. She was scratching at herself, at her fanny. I got her to stop it and said come upstairs and see a doctor. She started scratching herself again." He took one of Maureen's fags without asking her and lit it, downing the rest of the whisky before he exhaled.

"When was this?" asked Maureen.

"Eight . . . ," he said, scratching his forehead and thinking about it. "Eight? No, nine weeks ago—"

"Seven weeks before Douglas was killed?" said Maureen.

"Yeah. I knew Iona from the Northern. I was working in George I when the mysterious rapes were happening, yeah? We were all moved, even the female staff. The agency nurses were sent home and never employed again. Jill McLaughlin was agency. She was up for a full-time job at the Northern. Never worked again."

"That's why she was so jumpy when I phoned."

"Yeah. Only the senior staff weren't moved, they weren't even stigmatized. We didn't know Iona had been raped then. She didn't have a rope mark on her, no one suspected. I take it you know what I'm talking about when I say 'rope marks'?"

"Yvonne Urquhart's still got one on her ankle."

"Yvonne?" His face brightened. "How is she? Have you seen her?"

"You don't want to know how Yvonne is . . ."

Shan watched her carefully. "Okay, I can imagine anyway," he said, his voice dipping to a whisper. "Yvonne had a stroke . . . after . . . So, anyway, Iona wouldn't come upstairs with me. She said she wanted to go home, that's all she would say, she wanted to go home. I decided to drive her to her house, stay with her till the panic's gone, limit the damage. She wouldn't speak. When we got to the house she told me that he hurt her then. She knew what she meant and I knew what she was telling me. I asked her if she wanted to go to the police and she started pulling at her skin again so I took her over to Jane Scoular at the Dowling Clinic, it's all female staff there, and she got an emergency admission. The next day she hung herself in the staff toilets."

"Did you tell the police?"

He looked desperate. "Tell them what, for Christ's sake? Someone's been accused of a disgusting rape by a woman who's killed herself and also had a lifelong psychiatric history? She wasn't exactly a good witness, you know."

"Yeah," said Maureen, "I know exactly. Did you speak to Douglas?"

"No, that was later. I didn't know what the fuck to do."

"How many women were there?"

"Four that we knew of, five including Iona."

"Surely one of them would want to testify?"

"Maureen," Shan said, using her name for the first time, "after Douglas got the list from the office we went to see all of them. We even went to see some that were just on the ward at the time. They either can't talk or they're terrified at the mention of his name. Most of them can't even say it."

"Did Douglas know it was him?"

"Yeah. I told him a couple of weeks after Iona killed herself," continued Shan. "I was in the Variety Bar and I saw Douglas, pissed to fuck, coming up the stairs from the toilet, so I called him over. Man, he was so drunk, he almost couldn't breathe. You know that labored way?" He mimicked someone breathing heavily. "Yeah?"

"Yeah," said Maureen, not much the wiser.

"Douglas wanted me to order a drink for him, the barman had refused him. He was behaving strangely, he kept crying and laughing, and when I asked him where he lived he'd point in different directions and wouldn't say, so I took him up to mine to crash. On the way home he started to sober up a wee bit and by the time we got to mine he was more or less lucid. We sat up with a bottle and he was acting crazy, like crazy mood swings, and then he told me that Iona had hung herself. She was a colleague's patient and Douglas knew they were having an affair. He knew and did nothing and she killed herself. He said she always seemed fine to him, he thought she was all right. He'd been keeping an eye on her."

"And he felt guilty because he knew about it and did nothing," she said, taking a cigarette out and lighting it with Shan's lighter. "Did he know it wasn't an affair?"

"No, he really thought it was consensual. I could tell by the way he was talking about it." Shan smiled uncomfortably. "When I read about you it all made a lot more sense. That's why he wouldn't report them for having an affair."

"But I wasn't his patient," she said, lowering her eyes. "I was at the Rainbow but I was Angus's patient. I didn't have a professional relationship with Douglas."

"That's a bit thin," said Shan. "Fucking a patient is fucking a patient, whichever way you look at it."

Maureen inhaled heavily and kept her eyes on the table. She needed to believe she wasn't a victim just as much as Douglas had. "It might be a bit thin . . . but it's still different, isn't it?"

"No." Shan shook his head adamantly. "It's not. Doctors and nurses shouldn't fuck patients. That's fundamental. We all know that. Douglas knew it, we all know it."

Maureen took a heavy gulp of the bitter lager. "All right, it's a fine distinction," she said. "But it is still a distinction."

"Bollocks," said Shan. "Don't fuck the patients. How complicated is that? You're either fucking the patients or you're not."

Shan was right and Maureen knew he was.

"People who do things like that," said Shan, "they always say to themselves, 'This is different because yada-yada-yada, because I'm not her therapist now, because she's better—' "

"Because she's got a big hat."

"Exactly, they've all got justifications. They don't say to themselves, 'I'm a bastard and I'm doing a fucking terrible thing.' Rapists do it. Pedophiles do it too. They say, 'They wanted it,' 'They were asking for it.' "

Maureen rubbed her head. Thinking of Douglas in the same league as a pedophile made her eyes ache. "I don't think he saw himself in the same league as them," she said, sad and disgusted. "He always drew the distinction that I wasn't his patient. I think he believed it. When did you meet him? What day was it?"

"A Monday," said Shan. "Monday's country-and-western night at the Variety. Monday, five weeks ago."

"He didn't touch me after that," she murmured.

"What—like, sexually?"

"Yeah. Never again." She lifted her beer. "Never again before he died."

Maureen drank a throatful as Shan sat back and sighed. "Well, maybe the justification stopped working the night I told him. Maybe he was crying for himself as much as anything."

Maureen looked up at Shan. "Was Douglas *crying?*"

"Yeah, big-time," said Shan. "He started crying when I told him about Iona, he was sobbing. He hid himself in my bathroom. He was in there for an hour—I could hear him crying through the door."

"Fuck," she said. "I went out with him for eight months and I never saw him crying."

"Well, he couldn't have been more upset if Iona was his own daughter."

Maureen dropped her cigarette onto the floor, stepping on it to put it out. "He withdrew the contents of his account," she said, "and paid Yvonne's nursing-home fees. I think it was to ease his conscience. He gave me money too."

"How much?"

"Too much. It feels like blood money." Maureen picked up her packet of fags. "D'ye want one?"

"Yeah," said Shan pleasantly. "Go on.

"Anyway," Shan went on when he'd lit their cigarettes, "I told Douglas who it was and I told him about the Northern."

"What did he say?" she asked, hoping that Shan would repeat something Douglas had said or say something like he would say it so that she could hear Douglas's voice again.

"He didn't say anything," said Shan. "In the morning he was very serious and we talked about it. He said we should try to prosecute through the courts, for the sake of the victims we might never find. They'd see it on TV and know they were safe. He got the list from the office in the Northern and we started going to see them all."

"But why was he so clumsy about getting the list?" she asked.

"We didn't think anyone would pay a blind bit of notice, to be honest."

"Everyone in the Northern knew," said Maureen.

Shan cringed. "Really?"

"Yeah."

"God." He shut his eyes tight. "Fuck, we thought we were being well fly."

"Maybe he only knew Douglas was involved because of the list. You weren't there when he got it, were you?"

"No. They wouldn't have given it to me."

"That's why he was killed—because he was finding out about the Northern."

"Actually"—Shan held up his hand to stop her—"I know he didn't kill Douglas. I know that for sure."

"How?"

"Well, when the police came to see us they were asking about the daytime, yeah? I was working and he was in the office all day. He didn't leave until half-six and then he drove one of the secretaries home to Bothwell and that's miles out on the South Side. He didn't even leave his office to go for lunch—"

Maureen interrupted. "They've been asking about the evening too now."

Shan was stunned. "They've been what . . . ?"

"They seem to think it happened in the evening now. It's a bit of a media myth, the time of death thing, they just have a good guess."

Shan had turned gray. "I was sure it couldn't be him because the only time he left the room was to use the pay phones in the foyer."

Maureen's heart was palpitating. "Why would he use a pay phone? Isn't there a phone in his office?"

"Yeah, but the line's only for domestic calls," Shan said. "Shirley said he was calling abroad or something."

"What time did he use the pay phone?"

"Why do you want to know that?"

"Just . . ." She shook her head.

Shan shrugged. "I've no idea."

"Can you try to remember?"

He thought about it. "Before lunch, about eleven or twelve the first time. Then after lunch. Early. Early afternoon."

"How many more times?" she asked.

"Only twice that I know of. All before two o'clock, because there was a case conference in his office after that and he was definitely there."

She ran her finger over the spilled coffee on the table, drawing a snake pattern.

"Who was he phoning?" he asked.

"He phoned me," she said. "At work. He wanted to see if I was there. My pal said I wasn't in. He thought I was away for the day."

"Why would he phone to see if you were in?"

"He needed the house to be empty during the day. He did it at night and fixed it to look as if it happened much earlier. He made a half-arsed attempt to frame me. He made footsteps near to the body with my slippers as well. He even got information about me and fitted the scene to look like something I'd done before . . ."

She shut her eyes and rubbed them hard. If the Northern rapist had killed Douglas to stop him digging up evidence, he would want to make the police think Douglas died in the afternoon. That way they wouldn't try to trace Douglas's movements during the day and they would miss Siobhain. She led straight back to the Northern rapes. And it would explain why Maureen had been left with a cast-iron alibi; the murderer wanted an empty house that Douglas could have been hidden in all day. Fitting Maureen up badly wasn't a mistake at all, it was halfhearted because it was incidental. His real concern was fucking up the time of death and keeping Siobhain out of it.

She opened her eyes. Shan was trying to mask his evident worry under a frown.

"He made it look like something you done before?" he said slowly.

"Naw," she smiled, "I didn't kill anyone. I hid in the cupboard. I stayed there for a few days and I had to be carried out and taken to hospital. It's not important but only certain people knew that. He left something of Douglas's in there after he killed him. I think he thought the police would find out and make some kind of connection to me."

Shan looked relieved. "Right, I thought it was something bad," he said, shaking his head and bringing himself back to the story. "Just wondering. What did you just ask me?"

"Why did Douglas think they were having an affair?"

"Oh, because he'd seen them together before, a long time before. He saw them in North Lanarkshire. They were sitting in a car and he was touching Iona's neck and smiling."

They looked at each other and Maureen could see a sadness creeping in behind Shan's green eyes. He couldn't fake that, she thought, not that level of empathy. De Niro couldn't fake that. "And Iona wasn't smiling?" she said.

"No," said Shan softly, putting his elbow on the table and resting his forehead on it. "Iona wasn't smiling."

"When was this?"

"Two or three years ago."

Shan was bent over the table, his head resting in his hand, his long fingernails parting the thick black hair. Douglas had thick hair, dark brown with an auburn fleck. Finally, he sat back in his chair. "What you going to do? Are you going to the police with this stuff?"

"No," said Maureen, "I'm not. They've already interviewed one of the women and nearly broke her fucking brain."

Shan nodded.

"What are you thinking?" asked Maureen.

"I spoke to the women he raped, and I'd like to start punching him but I don't think I should."

"Why?"

"Don't know if I could stop."

Shan took an early slip road and stopped outside the lightbulb factory. They got out of the car and sat quietly across the road on a concrete slab, under the lip of the motorway, looking up at the glass building, brightly illuminated by the floodlights on the motorway. Red slivers of light raced across the shimmering glass, reflecting the taillights of cars passing above. Maureen lit a cigarette. She offered the packet to Shan but he waved it away.

"Do you miss him?" he asked.

"Don't counsel me," said Maureen, without intonation.

They looked at the building again for a while.

"Let's go out and get pissed together one night," she said.

"I'd like that," he said. "I'm in the Variety most Mondays."

"I might have some lovely news about our mutual friend when I see you," she said quietly, raising her eyes and looking innocently at the glass-brick turret.

Shan turned his head and examined her face for a moment.

"I'd like some lovely news about that cunt," he said gently.

32

FAMILY

SHAN DROPPED HER TWO BLOCKS FROM WINNIE'S HOUSE. IT WAS still early. She found a functioning phone box outside a green Republican pub on the Pollokshaws Road. The long, broad road led straight to the center of Glasgow and was a major route for cars and buses. She could hardly hear the dialing tone above the noisy traffic. She called Leslie's.

"We're fine," said Leslie, shouting so Maureen could hear her. "We've been watching television all day and we had our dinner on the veranda."

"Is she eating?" Maureen shouted back.

"Fuck, aye. Everything I put in front of her. How did it go at Levanglen?"

"I don't know, to be honest. I'll know tomorrow. Can Siobhain talk yet?" The beeps started and she put another ten pence in.

"No, she hasn't said anything," shouted Leslie. "Where are you, anyway?"

"I'm on the South Side. This phone box is eating money." She noticed a blue Ford parked quite far up on the opposite side of the road, it was the only car parked on the busy street. The lights were off but two men were sitting in it looking straight ahead. It was the car she had been sitting in the morning before, with Joe McEwan.

"Why are you on the South Side?" asked Leslie.

"I'm going to see my mum. Will you be all right for a while?"

"Should be. Why are you going to see Winnie?"

"I'm going to tell her what I think of her."

"Wow, good for you! Are you going to tell her everything?"

"Yeah, fucking everything."

"You even going to say about the hospital?"

" 'Specially about the hospital."

One of the men in the stationary car looked over and caught her eye. She stared back at him. The man got flustered and looked away, he said something to his pal.

"Should you do it tonight, though, Mauri?"

"I want to do it tonight," she said, writing her name on the dirty glass with her finger. "I feel fucking ferocious tonight."

Una's big fancy car was parked outside, incongruous in front of the small council house. The lights in the front room were on and the curtains were open. George'd be in there on his own—Winnie never left the curtains open, day or night, when she was sitting in the room, she said the neighbors were nosy. The upstairs windows were dark. They must be sitting around the table in the kitchen at the back of the house.

Maureen had brought a bottle of whisky for Winnie as a sweetener. She clutched it with both hands and tramped across the thin strip of lawn and up to the door. She rang the bell and drew herself up two inches. George opened it. He seemed surprised to see her and waved her straight down the corridor to the kitchen. He looked a bit green and Maureen figured that he couldn't have developed a compound hangover unless Winnie had one too. She would be relatively cowed and Maureen was glad.

The door was propped open with an old pig-nosed bed warmer and she could see into the kitchen. Marie was sitting at the table with Una and Winnie, her hands clutched in front of her on the table. Winnie turned away her head to ask Una a question and Marie glanced anxiously at Winnie's cup. She saw Maureen and stood up, her frightened eyes belying her smile.

"I thought you were coming tomorrow," said Una.

"I couldn't wait to see Marie," said Maureen.

Marie stepped forward and hugged Maureen stiffly. Her expensive clothes were getting shabby through excess wear. Maureen hadn't thought about it before but Marie must dress up for her family as though she were coming for a difficult interview. Through force of habit Maureen asked how the flight was. Marie blushed. "I took the bus," she said, and sat down. From the nervous, guilty glances passing between them Maureen could tell they had been talking about her.

"How are you, Mum?" she said.

"I've got flu again," said Winnie, her eyes heavy and red.

Maureen leaned over to kiss her and smelled the vinegar edge from a heavy bout of drinking. She sat down at the table, hoping to mask her mood until she had said what she needed to. "I brought you a present," she said, and held out the bottle of whisky to Winnie.

Una's face fell when she saw it. The children had always moved carefully to curtail Winnie's drinking with small tricks and ways of working. Now here was Maureen feeding her bottles of whisky. Winnie was delighted. She brought four wineglasses out from the cupboard and poured a large-large whisky into each.

"Mum," said Una miserably, "I can't drink that."

"Why?" said Winnie, seeming surprised, but the girls knew her of old.

"I'm driving," said Una.

"Auch, well," said Winnie. "It's out now."

She put the glasses on the table, setting the extra one nearest to hers, and sat down, smiling at Maureen, whom she wrongly supposed to be her new friend. She downed a glass with a deft hand and smiled at Marie, holding her eye so that she wouldn't look down. "It's very nice whisky," she said, letting her hand fall to rest next to the orphan glass. "Try it, Marie."

"Doesn't Marie look well, Maureen?" said Una, eager to get the conversation off to a friendly start.

"Listen," said Maureen, "I came here because I wanted to talk to all of you together." She lit a cigarette and sipped her whisky.

"Is it about Douglas?" asked Winnie sweetly.

"Not really, Mum, no." Her voice was steady and she felt that nothing could break her resolve. For the first time in a long while she knew she was right. "I want to tell you that I know what you're all thinking about me. You think I'm mental and I don't remember properly and that I made all that stuff up about Dad." She tapped her fag on the blue-glass ashtray and drank the rest of her whisky. No one spoke. "I want to say that my memory's just as good as any of yours. You can do this revisionist shit as much as you want but it still happened. He still did it to me and nothing can change that. I wish it could but it can't. I didn't touch Douglas. It wasn't me. And you can't use the fact that you've changed your story about Dad to accuse me of something like that."

Una, who had a terror of confrontation, was shaking and changing color rapidly.

Winnie used the diversion to lift the spare whisky and drink it.

"What are you talking about?" muttered Marie. "We didn't say you killed Douglas."

Maureen could feel herself getting angry. "You fucking did, you shitty bitch," she hissed.

Marie shook her head stupidly. "I didn't."

"I know you did, so stop lying."

"But I didn't . . ." Marie's voice trailed away and she sat back, hiding herself behind Una.

"Yeah," said Maureen. "I might not have killed Douglas but I made up all that stuff about Dad for a laugh, so who knows what else I'll do, right? Who fucking knows what I'm capable of? You know, the only reason I'm not in fucking prison right now is because Mum was psychotic with drink when they took her in for questioning."

Una took Maureen's hand in both of hers and squeezed it. "We don't think you're mad, Maureen," she said. "We know you're not mad." Her frightened eyes raced over Maureen's face, looking for a telltale sign that she was. "We love you," she said, "you know that."

Maureen shook off Una's hand. "Look"—she lifted the bottle and poured herself another generous measure, letting the whisky glugglug into the glass—"I remembered before Alistair came to the hospital, I remembered the house and the cupboard and everything, I just didn't know what it meant. There's fuck-all wrong with my memory. I remember that night and I didn't kill Douglas, so if you've invited me to lunch tomorrow to tell me I did then you'd better think again."

"What the fuck are you talking about?" said Winnie, her personality changing rapidly under the influence. "Tomorrow was just a lunch. I've bought everything in for it—you can look in the fridge if you don't believe me."

"Yeah," said Una, "she's bought lots of food."

"I'm not interested in the food," said Maureen, much too loudly. "My point is, I know you don't believe me, right? I know you're telling each other that my memory's fucked and I make things up all the time and I'm living in a parallel reality."

Winnie leaned over and snatched the whisky bottle away from Maureen, pouring herself an unashamed tumblerful. "The bloody fridge is full of food," she said.

Maureen snatched the bottle back. "Can you even hear me speak? Never mind about the fucking food."

"Where did she get this crap about killing Douglas from?" said Winnie, addressing anyone at the table but Maureen.

"Yeah," said Una, overcoming her fear at the scent of a scapegoat, "who told you that?"

"Never mind who I heard it from, right? It doesn't matter—"

"Liam," said Winnie, looking at Marie. "Liam's told her a load of old shite and she's believed it as usual. Stupid cow."

"It wasn't Liam, Mum, it was you."

Winnie was stunned. "I most certainly did not."

"Don't you remember? When I came to see you two days after, ye asked me if I did it. You accused me."

Winnie didn't know what she had said, she probably didn't remember the visit, she probably didn't remember Friday. She sipped her generous whisky and raised her eyebrows. "Anyway, Maureen," she said, in a voice loaded with emotion or whisky or both, "why are you bringing your father up now?"

Una flinched and kicked Winnie's leg hard under the table. "Fuck off," hissed Winnie.

"Maureen," said Una swiftly, ignoring Winnie's curse, "I don't think for a minute that you had anything to do with Douglas's death."

"Neither do I," said Marie, sitting forward eagerly.

Maureen leaned forward and looked at Marie's face. Marie was a very bad liar.

"You're a bunch of cunts," said Maureen.

There were few words Winnie would flinch at when she was very drunk but she wasn't very drunk yet. Her jaw fell.

"Yes, Mum, even you, especially you. You've bullied me and hassled me and talked to me as if I'm a fucking idiot when I'm bigger than any of you. I can't imagine what would be in your minds when you say these things about me to each other. It happened. I can't prove it to you but I remember. And, Una, you remember it too. You told Alistair before you thought you'd have to face up to Mum with it, didn't you? And then ye buckled. Marie, I remember you standing behind Mum, watching her pull me out of the cupboard. You were standing behind her next to the old telephone table and you were crying and wearing the dress with the giraffe on the pocket."

Marie was sitting with her hands limp on her lap, her head and shoulders shaking nervously. She was near to tears. Maureen leaned over the table, bending down to look her in the eye. She stabbed the table in front of her with her forefinger. "I know you remember it, Marie. When I look in your eyes I know that you remember. You sold me out for peace with a mother ye won't even live in the same country as."

Marie covered her face and began to sob.

"Look what you've done," said Una, standing up and putting an arm around Marie's heaving shoulders. She looked at Maureen reproachfully. "She's only home for a visit."

Maureen stood up and buttoned her overcoat. "Lets all of you off the hook if I'm bananas, doesn't it? There's nothing wrong with this family and it's just my problem. Well"—she leaned over and lifted the bottle of whisky from the table, screwing the lid on tightly—"I'm getting out of here and I'm not coming back." She took the bottle and walked out of the kitchen.

Winnie followed her out into the hall. "Where are you going?" she said, inadvertently staring at the bottle.

"That's it, isn't it, Mum? That's the history of our family. You've got one child walking out of your life and another crying her tits off in the kitchen and all you're interested in is where's the bottle of whisky gone."

Winnie folded her arms and looked deeply hurt. "I've always done my best by you, Maureen, and I'm sorry if that wasn't enough."

"Mum," said Maureen, "all we do is lie to each other."

"When have we ever lied to each other, Maureen?" Winnie smiled bitterly. "I'm only asking because I haven't lied to you and I'd like to know when you lied to me."

"You don't have flu, Winnie, you've got a cunting hangover. You gave the picture to the papers, didn't you? Did they pay you?"

"There's obviously no point in discussing this," Winnie said, shutting her eyes in a long cutoff blink. "I can see that you've already made up your mind about it."

"Yeah," shouted Maureen. "There's no fucking point in discussing anything you've ever done, is there?"

Winnie spoke quietly. "I have never deliberately done anything to hurt you, Maureen. I don't know why you think I—"

"Bollocks," said Maureen, shaking with fury as she opened the door and stepped outside. "You're a vindictive, self-serving cow."

Winnie gave the bottle a last grieving look and slammed the door shut in her daughter's face.

It was an hour before the pubs shut and Maureen was the only person at the bus stop with the right to vote.

A crowd of excitable teenagers were hanging about. They were guessing at how to behave, each of them a bundle of secret terrors and paranoias. Their voices were too loud, their gesticulations too pronounced, like bad actors in a theater with rotten acoustics. The blue Ford was parked a hundred yards down the road. Maureen looked up, pretending to look past it for the bus. One of the policemen was looking straight at her. He seemed to be trying to catch her eye.

The bus came after a couple of minutes and she clambered aboard, leaving the youngsters behind. She went upstairs to the top deck, sitting down two seats from the back. It was quiet: a couple of people sat singly near the front, a woman looking out of the window, a man reading a paper. She shut her eyes and thought about

Douglas's lovely bollocks sitting in a bloody puddle in the dark hall cupboard. And she saw herself sitting in there, in the black dark, hiding from no one, not knowing whether she was ten or twenty. The two time frames seemed to blur together so that she was in one corner and Douglas's bollocks were in the other.

He wasn't a complete shit, after all, he was just a poor, bewildered bastard feeling his way, and knowing that made her feel closer to him. She thought about the last few weeks of his life, when he would have heard about Iona and started investigating rapes at the Northern. She was looking for some small clue she could have picked up on at the time. She could have tried to help. But she was part of the problem he was trying to solve. Douglas had been further away than she could ever have imagined.

She had a strong sense of coming to the end of a painful time in her life, a time riddled with betrayals and half-arsed apologies. She couldn't remember what she was like when she wasn't in a state.

She could hear Leslie moving carefully behind the door. "Yeah?"

"It's me."

Leslie opened the door a crack and peered out with one very frightened eye. She grinned unsteadily and let the door swing wide. She was holding an old wooden walking stick by the toe. It had a vicious duck's-head brass handle, the sharp beak pointing outward.

"What's happening?" said Maureen. "That looks scary."

"Yeah," said Leslie, double-locking the door behind Maureen and walking back into the living room. She was still holding the walking stick.

"Where's Siobhain?"

"In bed," whispered Leslie urgently, standing close to Maureen. "She's asleep. Someone was at the door. Half hour ago, trying the handle."

"What did you do?"

"I was standing, watching. I coughed and they let it go. I heard them belting off downstairs."

"Does Benny have your address?"

"No."

"Well, if it is Benny he couldn't have followed me, I just got here. Could have been kids."

Leslie looked relieved. "Yeah," she said, and handed Maureen the stick. "They usually work their way around a close. I'm going across the hall to ask Mrs. Gallagher if they tried her door. You stay here."

Maureen stood behind the door, listening, as Leslie knocked for Mrs. Gallagher across the landing. After a pause she heard voices. Leslie was still talking when she scratched at the door to be let back in. Maureen opened it. Mrs. Gallagher was standing at her open door in a pink nylon dressing gown and matching fluffy slippers.

"'S all right," said Leslie, grinning widely. "They tried her door. It was just some wee robbers."

Leslie came back into the house, said good night to Mrs. Gallagher and shut the door, locking it behind her. "Thank fuck for that." She took the stick off Maureen and set it down by the door. They went into the living room. Maureen took off her coat and threw it over the back of a chair.

"How did it go with your family?"

"Well, I said everything I meant to but that's all. They didn't exactly see my point of view. They seemed confused when I said about accusing me of killing Douglas. I dunno why they'd deny that, they were definitely up to something."

"Right," said Leslie, standing formally in front of her with her hands clasped behind her back, swaying on the balls of her feet. "So we're off tomorrow, then?"

"Yes."

"Right."

"Well, I brought drink again," said Maureen, pulling the opened bottle of whisky out of her rucksack.

"Fucking ace." Leslie went into the kitchen and brought out some glasses. "We're drinking too much," she said as she held out her glass for Maureen to fill it.

"I thought alcohol abuse was a good way to cope," said Maureen.

"I'm getting too old for it," said Leslie. "I'm starting to feel it during the day."

"This is a difficult time. It won't always be like this."

Maureen poured a whisky for herself and drank it like ginger. She shouldn't be able to drink it like that. She was drinking far, far too much. She wasn't even getting the rolling glow anymore. They sat down next to each other on the settee but Maureen noticed that Leslie settled at the far end, as far away as she could get. She was pale and stared at the opposite wall.

"See, about tomorrow?" she said timidly. "I . . . um . . . I've been thinking about it and, um . . . I just don't know if it's a good idea."

"What the fuck are you talking about?"

"Listen to me. The police know about the hospital and the list. They might catch up with him any minute."

"He'll come for us."

"But it seems to be dying down now," she said uncertainly.

"He'll come if the police aren't holding him." Maureen put her whisky down. "And I don't think they've got enough evidence to hold him. He doesn't need to hurry, he can come for any of us any time. He's killed two people to cover up the rapes in the Northern. If anything, we're more of a threat than Douglas was because we've got Siobhain. He needs to kill us."

"I'm a bit scared, Mauri, that's all," said Leslie. "I'm sorry."

"I'm doing it," said Maureen, and picked up her whisky again.

They drank in silence until Leslie suddenly blurted out, "Wonder why he hasn't come for you yet."

"I'd be harder to get at," said Maureen calmly. "I've been moving around the whole time. And, besides, there's a police car on my tail."

"They're following you?"

"Yeah, McEwan knows every step I've taken in the past week and I just spotted them. They'll be outside now in that blue Ford McEwan was in this morning."

Leslie's face contorted into a parody of a smile. "Then we can't do it, can we? The police'll see us and we'll get charged."

"No, Leslie, they won't see us. If they're still with us at Largs then we'll leave it and come straight home. You're really scared, aren't you?"

Leslie looked up at Maureen and her furtive expression collapsed. "Yeah, I'm fucking scared." She slammed her whisky down on a side table and turned to Maureen, shouting under her breath in case she woke Siobhain: "I've spent all day with Siobhain and I don't know what he did to her but I don't want him to do it to me. I've never been this scared. Even Charlotte wasn't as cowed as Siobhain. At least she had a shred of fucking personality left and her man'd done all sorts of surgery on her."

"But Siobhain was sick before it happened. This probably compounded it. We don't know what she's like when she's well."

"I feel like packing up my bike and getting the fuck out of here."

Maureen sighed. "You can do that if you want. I'd understand."

Leslie picked her glass up and looked into it for the answer. "But if Siobhain isn't seen getting onto the Millport ferry he won't come, will he? And you can't manage her and see to him, can you? I have to go if you go." She looked at Maureen, leaving it open for her to say she wouldn't go either.

"These women can't give evidence, Leslie, they've got no one to stand up for them but us. I can't stop now." She told Leslie what Shan had told her, about Iona, about the rapes, about Douglas crying in the toilet.

"Are you sure about this, Mauri?"

"I dunno," she said. "I heard it all from one person and I don't know how reliable he is."

Leslie huffed. "That doesn't sound very likely to me," she said. "Didn't good, kind Douglas see a hint of irony in his relationship with you?"

"I think he may have seen a shocking irony in it," murmured Maureen. "He didn't touch me once after Iona killed herself and I think that's why he paid the money into my account."

"So he fucked you and paid you off?"

"I didn't say what he did was good or right."

"It's a big change of heart to credit to such a prick."

"I think he was trying, though."

"That guy was a skank of the first order. Just 'cause he knows he's a skank doesn't stop him being a skank."

Maureen smiled up at her pal. That's how it was with Leslie. Bad people did the bad things and good people did the good things; there were no roads to Damascus, no moments of realization, no twelfth-hour conversions, just white hats and black hats. Leslie was a hanging judge.

"Well, whoever it is, I'm not stopping," said Maureen, "I'm going to get him."

"How do you know you're getting the right guy?"

"I'll know. If he comes after us it's definitely him."

Leslie sighed. "I don't want to go to prison, Maureen. I like my wee life."

"You won't go to prison. You won't even be there when it happens, I promise."

"I don't know what you're going to do to him."

"I know, I think that's for the best. If you don't know what's going to happen and the police get involved you can't be done for conspiracy to anything, can you?"

"Maybe I should know."

"No," said Maureen. "I don't think you should."

They sat silent for a minute. Leslie raised her glass. "Fuck it, then."

"Make thick my blood," said Maureen, and threw back the last of her whisky, sloshing it through her teeth until it burned her gums before she swallowed.

"I need to go to bed," said Leslie, pulling the sleeping bags out from behind the settee and unrolling them. "What time d'you want up?"

"Any time before three in the afternoon."

33

MILLPORT

MAUREEN WOKE UP WITH MORE ACHES AND PAINS THAN SHE'D HAD the morning before. Her hip bone had been digging into the hard floor and was numb. She got up quickly, glad to be off the stern floor. Outside the picture window Leslie was sitting in a deck chair on the veranda, drinking coffee and eating toast. Siobhain was standing next to her, leaning on the railing, looking down at the ground.

It was half-twelve. Maureen phoned Lynn at the surgery. "Hello," she said. "It's the Secret Squirrel here. Any word?"

"Yes," said Lynn. "For Friday? That seems to be fine."

"Can't you talk now? Shall I phone later?"

"If I could just take your name," said Lynn, and paused. "Can you spell that for me?" And then she spelled out a familiar name as though she were repeating what she was hearing over the phone. Fine. "Do you understand the arrangement, then?"

"That's the name of Benny's doctor, is it?"

"Yes, certainly."

"Lynn, I owe you a big one."

"Yes, that's right," said Lynn. "I'll see you, then. Bye-bye now."

"Bye, Lynn."

Maureen hung up and pulled on her clothes. The mustard jumper was beginning to get smelly and the crispness in her jeans was a distant memory, but she told herself that she'd be home soon and would be able to do a washing, and if she didn't get home in the next two days it wouldn't really matter whether her clothes were clean or not. "Leslie," she said, calling to her on the veranda, "have you got a wee bag or a box I could put some things in?"

Leslie looked into the living room. "What did you say?"

"I've some things I want to keep separate from the luggage. Have you a wee bag or something?"

"Have a look under the sink."

Maureen rummaged through the bags, looking for a thick one. On the floor at the back she found a navy blue hexagonal cardboard presentation box with "Boothy and Co." written on it. She pulled off the lid. Jagged bits of dusty toffee had gathered in one corner. She picked out a small, thick plastic bag, shoved the rest back into the cupboard and wandered out onto the veranda. "Can I have this box?"

"Course," said Leslie. "I've had it for ages. Can't bring myself to throw it away because it's so pretty but I can't find a use for it either."

"Good," said Maureen, and went back indoors.

She put the bag of Colombian coffee into the box with the sachets of sugar she had lifted in the airport café the night before. She took three coffee filter papers from Leslie's cupboard and found a pocket alarm clock and a bottle of Tipp-Ex in the odds and ends drawer. Leslie came into the kitchen, put down her empty mug and flicked the kettle on. "Want a coffee?" she said.

"Yeah, please."

"What ye doing?"

"Just packing some things."

Leslie took a fresh mug out of the cupboard, watching as Maureen folded the coffee filters and polyethylene bag and slipped them into the Boothy box.

"Does this alarm work, Leslie?"

"Yeah. It's got new batteries in it."

Leslie made the coffee and picked hers up. "I'll leave you to it, then?"

"Yeah, how's Siobhain?"

"Same," said Leslie, looking into the Boothy box. "What are you doing, Maureen?"

"Do ye want to know?"

Leslie thought about it. "No," she said finally.

"I'll need your handcuffs," said Maureen, "if that's all right."

Leslie looked disconcerted. "Sure."

"And your leather gloves."

"Okay," she said, and went to get them from the bedroom.

"And cream," Maureen muttered to herself. "I'll need cream."

The rain was coming down in sheets. The children had left the waste ground and Siobhain and Leslie had pushed the deck chairs back against the wall to keep themselves dry. The were sitting quietly, holding hands, watching the rain erode the little dirt hills.

"Can I take these with me as well?" asked Maureen.

Leslie looked at the stained Marigold washing-up gloves and the plastic coffee filter cone in her hand. "Take them and keep them if you want." She seemed confused and more than a little frightened.

"Yeah, I'll need to," said Maureen, and went back into the kitchen.

Leslie didn't have any traveling bags so their knickers, the Boothy box and their for-in-case jumpers were shoved into ill-chosen poly bags with precariously stretching handles. Maureen took the bags and caught the bus to the town, taking the red Ford and its two policemen with her. She got off the bus outside the Buchanan Street bus station and waited on the curb before crossing, making sure that the Ford was still with her. The car pulled up down the road a little and she crossed. The passenger policeman got out of the car and followed her on foot. She passed the narrow entrance to the bus station, ducking into the doorway of the multistory car park. The policeman jogged past her, no more than four feet away, and went into the bus station. Maureen ran round the corner, jumping down the steep stairs to the taxi rank, and leaped into the back of a cab, telling the driver to take her to Central Station.

As they drove down the road she glanced out of the side window and saw the blue Ford parked at the side of the road. The driver was examining the passing pedestrians carefully.

The taxi dropped her at the entrance. She stopped at the ticket office and, as an act of faith, bought three returns. Next door, in the station newsagent's, she picked up a Basildon Bond letter-writing pad and a Bic Biro and sidled up to a spotty clerk stacking shelves with chocolate bars. "Can I ask you something?" She smiled. He looked up. "I wondered whether you sell many of these notepads?"

"Aye," he said. "We've got them in our shops all over Britain. We sell hundreds of them."

"Great," she said. "Thanks."

She paid for them at the till and leaned on the lottery-ticket table to write the note, using her left hand so that the script would be unrecognizable. At the top of the page she put the Stewart Street station number with the full regional code and McEwan's office extension under it. "Please phone this number in case of emergency. Ask for DCI Joe McEwan and tell him that I am responsible for Martin Donegan and Douglas Brady." She folded it to the size of a credit card and put it in the back pocket of her jeans.

Leslie and Siobhain hadn't made it into the station yet. The overhead speakers were playing an easy-listening version of "American Pie." Maureen stood in the center of the vast marble-floored concourse

and tried to think straight, working out the times: the train connected with the last ferry to Cumbrae. Even if someone drove and
broke the speed limit all the way to Largs they still wouldn't get
there for the last ferry, at eight-twenty. It would be safe to send the
word.

She walked to the phone boxes by the side exit and phoned
Scaramouch Street. "Listen," she said when Benny answered, "I can't
get hold of Liam. Would you phone him and tell him I've gone to
Millport with Siobhain for a couple of days?"

"Okay," said Benny. "When'll you be back?"

"Couple of days, tops. Tell him it's the same close we stayed in
last time, only it's the top flat. I heard the police questioned ye?"

"Yeah," he said, sounding suddenly breathless. "They wanted my
fingerprints. They must have found them in your house, eh?"

"Yeah, I expect so."

"I'll see you when ye get back. My last exam's tomorrow."

"Yeah, I'll be in touch."

"Okay, have a lovely time."

"See ya, Benny," she said, and hung up.

She picked up the bags and walked slowly over to the Bullet, a
memorial of the Great War made from an upright brass shell casing.
Still no sign of Leslie and Siobhain. They only had seven minutes
before their train left.

"Cream!" she said suddenly, and ran over to the delicatessen.
When she came out she saw Leslie guiding the slow-moving Siobhain into the station through the main entrance. They had four minutes to go before the train pulled out. Maureen walked over and
took Siobhain's arm, leading her along the platform and up the step
onto the train, sitting her in a window seat near the door. Leslie followed them on with the bags. The train's engine hummed and
revved, the doors beeped and slid shut, and the train pulled slowly
out of Central Station.

The conductor came looking for the tickets as the train slipped away from the city. Maureen handed them over. He clipped all three at once and eyed their bags. "Is that you on your holidays?"

"Aye," said Maureen.

"You haven't got the weather, I'm afraid."

"Auch, well."

The dark night was behind the window, and within minutes they were in the unlit countryside. The double glazing reflected the inside of the carriage like a drunk's mirror, showing two shaky shadows of everything.

Within an hour they were at the coast, where the high hills collapse into a charcoal sea kept ever still by the proximity of the islands. The train slowed as it approached Largs, chuffing casually into the single-platform station. Leslie helped Siobhain up and off while Maureen carried the bags. They walked down the dark, deserted high street to the quay. Across the bay they could see the lights of the little ferry docked at the tiny Isle of Cumbrae.

The island consists of a jagged sandstone hill in the center with a flat skirt of land around it. It's an untouched 1950s holiday destination where the major tourist attractions are the crazy-golf course in Millport town, the freak rock formations painted to look like animals and a ring road that leads all the way around the island and can be cycled in under an hour.

Maureen left Leslie with Siobhain and the bags and went to the ticket office to buy three tickets and find out the times of the morning ferry. When she got back to the dock the clump of pedestrian passengers had shifted five feet down the concrete ramp and the queue of cars was edging forward impatiently.

Slowly, the yellow and red ferryboat made its way across the water and into the dock. The back of the hull wound gently to the floor and the disembarking passengers walked down it, past the waiting crowd. The cars and cyclists came off last.

A ticket collector wearing a fluorescent yellow anorak and big green wellies followed the cars, stood on the hull and waved the pedestrians forward. They lifted their bags and walked down to the boat. Maureen gave up their tickets. He checked them and pocketed them. "Hey, they're returns," said Leslie.

"You'll not need them," he said briskly, and held out his hand to the backpacking couple behind her.

Maureen tugged Leslie's sleeve. "'Member the last time we came?" she said. "They only sell returns. The ferry's the only way to get on or off the island."

The ferry had two high decks on either side of the car-deck valley. The view over the bay was best from there but Siobhain couldn't climb the steep metal ladder so they had to make do with the cabin. They stepped into the narrow corridor and sat down on the red leatherette bench below the windows. The ferry churned the water noisily and they moved out into the bay. The lights of the navy vessels in Dunoon slipped slowly past the window.

Maureen was confident of her timing but wanted to make sure they hadn't been followed. She left Leslie and Siobhain sitting downstairs and made a quick tour of the deck, checking all the faces and peering into cars. She didn't recognize anyone.

The ferry turned round and docked at Cumbrae. They waited until everyone else had left the cabin before standing Siobhain up again and pointing her to the door. Eventually they joined the clump of pedestrians at the top of the steep concrete incline leading from the ferry, gathered around the bus stop at the side of the road. The lights from the disembarking cars soon died away as they drove off to the left, following the road to Millport. The ferry wound up its hull and slipped away to park in the mainland dock for the night. In front of them stood a steep grassy hill. It was very dark.

A glint of light flashed over the shoulder of the steep hill on the left and they could hear the bus coming. It turned the corner, blinding them momentarily, did an expert U-turn in the narrow road and came to a stop in front of the waiting crowd. It was a very old bus, painted green and cream with a rounded roof and chrome speed lines. The door shished open and the passengers gathered around it, climbing on and handing up luggage, locals helloing the driver and being greeted in return. Leslie helped Siobhain up the steps while Maureen got the tickets, and they moved down to the back-seat. The backpackers took their time settling their rucksacks on the overhead luggage racks and under the seats. Women coming home from work on the mainland put their groceries in the luggage rest at the front of the bus.

When all the passengers had settled into their seats the driver turned and called, "Are yees all right in there, now?"

An uneven chorus of ayes and yesses came back at him from the crowd.

"All right, then," he said, and started the engine, jolting the bus away from the curb and into the empty road.

"Look," said Leslie, nudging Siobhain. "Lion Rock." A tall outcrop of sandstone on the side of the hill had eroded into the vague shape of a lion. It only looked like a lion if it was seen from a very particular angle and in a good light. It was getting dark and the bus had moved past it by the time she pointed it out. Siobhain looked out of the window. "See it?" said Leslie. Siobhain nodded but seemed slightly puzzled. Maureen thought it might be a good sign: she hadn't seemed slightly anything for days.

The bus stopped in Kames Bay to let a lady with three Asda bags off. The driver shut the door, pulled out into the road, and they drove on to Millport.

"Hey," said Leslie. "Crocodile Rock!" A long flat rock on the beach had been painted with big happy eyes and a crocodile's mouth. Siobhain saw it and smiled. "Isn't it great?" said Leslie tenderly, turning back to see it again.

"Leslie," said Maureen, "it's an auld fat rock with a mouth painted on it."

"I know. I like it."

The bus drove along the Millport seafront. It was long past

the holiday season and two months to Christmas but faded pastel fairy lights were still strung between the lampposts. The tide was out and brightly painted wooden boats lolled drunkenly in the mud, waiting.

The bus dropped them at the George Hotel, a three-story white-washed building with black-rimmed windows and a sign painted in Nazi script.

"Ah," said Leslie. "This is nice."

They were supposed to pay for the flats and pick up the keys from the man at the chip shop. Maureen went in and paid for one set. She sent Leslie in for the other.

"Give him this money," said Maureen, and handed her an envelope, but Leslie said she would pay for this one. "It's Douglas's money," said Maureen. "Take it. And keep your head down. Don't let them see your face."

No. 6, the Sea Front, was a flatted tenement built over the Laughter Emporium joke shop. The close was openmouthed and the stairs were narrow and steep. Siobhain held on to the wooden handrail and took the stairs one at a time. Maureen picked up the plastic bags. "I'll go on," she said, and ran up the stairs, taking them two at a time until she got to the top landing. She struggled into Leslie's leather gloves before fitting the key into the lock and opening the door.

The flat was small and furnished with the legal minimum of a table, beds, chairs and a settee. The hall and the living room had been decorated with hideous pink flowery wallpaper but it was cozy and the owner had left a plate of Jammie Dodgers out for them. Maureen felt a pang of guilt.

She made sure the TV worked, turned the heating on full to make it seem inhabited, pulled the curtains shut and double-bolted the door on her way out. She took the gloves off as she ran back down two flights. Siobhain and Leslie were resting on the half landing below.

"This is us," said Maureen, slipping the other set of keys into the door and pushing it open.

"It's the flat we stayed in when you got out of the Northern," said Leslie, walking up the stairs quickly, leaving Siobhain to negotiate the last few steps herself.

"The very one," said Maureen.

It had been decorated since they were last there: Maureen remembered white chip wallpaper in the hall and constantly having to resist the urge to pick at it. It had been painted pale blue since then. The living room had a new blue carpet and the walls were papered with a gray and pink swirling pattern. It was a botch job: the corners were curling up and overlapping edges were threatening to spoil.

"I remember this settee," said Leslie, flopping onto it. "We used to fight about who had to sleep on this, remember?"

"Yeah."

It was gray velour with raised diagonal stripes. A pine table with matching chairs was sitting under the window. In the bedroom there were twin beds, separated by a dark wood table with a red-shaded lamp and an ashtray on it. Siobhain came in through the front door.

"Right," said Leslie, "I don't give a shit about who's due it, I'm sleeping in a bed tonight."

"Siobhain," said Maureen, "you take the other one. I have to get up early in the morning."

She would have to be up at six to catch the first ferry coming to the island.

Siobhain seemed to be perking up a little. She looked out of the window at the fairy lights and nodded when Maureen asked her if she wanted a fish supper.

When Leslie went downstairs to the chip shop Maureen got some plates out of the cupboard in the kitchen and put the television on for Siobhain. Leslie came back with a selection of food for them to share. Siobhain ate the entire haggis supper without offering them any and then ate anything else they put in front of her, washing it down with a giant mug of sweet tea.

"You must have been hungry," said Leslie to Siobhain, looking at the front of her jumper. It was covered in bits of haggis and batter.

Siobhain blushed. "I was," she whispered, and Maureen could have cried to hear her voice.

The original *Planet of the Apes* with Charlton Heston was on TV. Leslie and Siobhain wanted to watch it so they humped the TV through to the bedroom, sitting it on the chest of drawers at the foot of the beds. They took turns in the bathroom, brushing their teeth and changing into their nightclothes.

Maureen waited until she was sure they had settled down in the bedroom before filling the kettle and turning it on. She took the flask and the Boothy box out of the Asda bag and opened the box reverently. She put the filter in the cone and tipped the coffee into it, sat it on top of the flask and poured the boiling water over it, listening as the frothy bubbles dried and cracked on the side of the paper. It was essential that there was only enough coffee for one, so she measured it, filling the screw-top cup to the brim with steaming coffee and putting the rest down the sink.

Working carefully now, she painted two tiny parallel lines on the inside of the silver lip with the Tipp-Ex, scratching at the sides when it had dried to make them as narrow and invisible as possible. It would be her marker, the part she could touch with her lips without endangering herself.

Holding the Marigolds open by the rim, she held them up to the light and looked through them to check for holes. They seemed intact. She pulled them on and took Paulsa's plastic bag from her pocket, pulling it open, ripping the bag recklessly. She folded the perforated sheet quite loosely and dropped it into the flask, watching as the porous paper floated on the coffee, soaking it in and turning brown until it buckled under the weight and slid under the black surface. She screwed the lid on tight and put the ripped wrapper and the Marigolds safely in the plastic bag.

The cupboard under the sink was full of cleaning products, put there by the hopeful owner as a reminder to the tenants. She swept them aside, put the flask near the back and washed her hands maniacally before getting into bed.

She lay down on the lumpy settee, looking out over the moonlit bay, sweating gently and listening to Leslie making comments about the film in the other room, saying substitute lines for the character in silly voices. She remembered Leslie doing the same for her when she was ill.

34

FIRE

IT WAS STILL DARK WHEN THE POCKET ALARM WENT OFF, BEEP-BEEPING her awake. She grabbed it and sat up, remembering instantly why she had set it. In the kitchen she lit a fag and made a pint of strong coffee with lukewarm water, drinking it down despite the taste. Reaching under the sink, she picked up the flask and took the Marigolds out of the bag, slipping them on, taking special care not to touch the outside of them with her bare hands. When she lifted the flask out and unscrewed the lid she could see little flecks of dissolved paper floating on the surface. She unfolded a fresh filter paper and put it into the cone. Holding the cone over a saucepan, she tipped the flask gently. Lumps of soggy paper slopped out with the coffee, catching on the sides of the filter paper. When the coffee had filtered through she warmed it gently over a gas ring, watching carefully, making sure it didn't get too hot. She didn't know whether heat could spoil acid. She added a touch of cream and poured in the three sugars.

After decanting the coffee back into the flask, she filled the saucepan with some diluted bleach and cleaned the work top. She put every trace of the wrappers and filters into the thick plastic bag, rolled it up tight and put it in the bottom of her rucksack.

She dressed in her black jeans, boots and jumper, pulled on the woolly hat, Leslie's leather gloves and her overcoat, leaving off her telltale tartan scarf. She checked her pocket for the stabbing comb, telling herself that it was him, she was right. It wouldn't come to that. The flask would be enough.

The green bus arrived just in time to meet the ferryboat backing slowly up to the concrete ramp, churning the dirty water beneath it. The crowd of waiting pedestrian passengers walked on quickly, afraid that they might miss it, bumping and jostling the few disembarkers. Three cars rolled off. Few people came to the island in the morning: most of the passengers were traveling to work on the mainland. Adjusting her eyes to the grainy half-light, she managed to get a good look at everyone leaving the ferry and waited until the last minute before getting on so that she didn't miss anyone.

She climbed the steep metal ladder up to the top deck, watching the swell and spill of the black water illuminated by the white light of the ship. Across the bay a string of lights at the power station swung steadily in the rising dawn breeze. Her nose was numb with the cold. She pulled her overcoat tight around her and lit a cigarette. It was one of Leslie's, it was a stronger brand than she was used to.

The ferry crossed the bay and pulled into Largs. There was no undignified jostling here: the ticket collector held everyone back until the ferry was empty. Maureen stayed behind the lifeboat on the high deck and looked down at the pedestrians waiting to board. If he was catching this ferry he wasn't on foot.

Only one car rolled on, an Astra with a woman driver. When the ferry was halfway back to Cumbrae Maureen clambered down onto the car deck, standing behind the metal ladder, and looked in at her. She didn't know her.

As the ferry made its way over to Cumbrae and back to Largs for the second time the sun rose gloriously over the bay, the yellow sunlight gilding the tips of the choppy gray waves. A larger crowd of pedestrians and eight cars were waiting at Largs for the second crossing. The rising sun hit the car roofs at an acute angle, casting a deep shadow over the drivers' faces as they paused to give up their tickets to the conductor. She couldn't see any of them clearly but she was ready, her hand curled around the teeth of the stabbing comb, just in case.

She had to wait until the hull had been cranked up and the ferry was entering the bay again before climbing down the ladder for a look. She was standing in the shadows, checking out the drivers, when she saw him sitting patiently in a white Jaguar, his gloved hands resting on the wheel, a cigarette in his right hand. He was wearing a green jacket and a fishing hat. The sunlight glinted off his steel-framed glasses.

Maureen let go of the comb, took a deep breath and patted her bag to make sure the flask was still with her before crossing the deck to his car.

She knocked on the passenger window. He leaned across the white leather upholstery and looked out at her. His expression didn't falter. He touched the door and the window lowered electronically. "Hello, Maureen."

"Oh, Angus, thank God. Did Siobhain phone you?"

He blinked. "Yeah," he said uncertainly, sitting back so that she couldn't quite see his eyes.

"I can't believe you came," she said. "It was so good of you. Can I get in?"

He swallowed and glanced sideways.

"Siobhain's staying with me. We came over together."

"Oh, right," he said, and smiled. It wasn't a very good smile—she had expected him to do better than that. He opened the passenger door, trailing his leather-clad fingertips on the retreating handle, as if reluctant to let it go. She put her bag on the floor and climbed in before he had time to object.

"Didn't Siobhain tell you I was with her?" she asked. Her eyes were racing around his face, she was raising her eyebrows with every second word, creasing her forehead and speaking too quickly. She slowed herself down. "I'm surprised she didn't because she knows I know you."

"She didn't mention you," he said, drawing on his fag. "Maybe she forgot."

"God, I wouldn't be surprised. I expect she was in a state when she phoned, yeah?"

"Yes," he said. "Very upset."

"What did she say?"

"Oh, just, could I come and get her immediately, you know, that sort of thing. Why are you on the ferry at this time in the morning?"

"I had to send a fax to my work," she said, off the top of her head. "I forgot to put my sick line in."

"Don't they have a fax machine on the island? You'd think it would be particularly useful for an outlying community."

He was nervous, she'd never heard him speak so formally, and knowing that he was shitting it made her feel infinitely more comfortable, as if she couldn't do wrong, as if it was destined to go smoothly. She savored the feeling and realized how tense her shoulders were. "Yeah," she said, stretching her neck to relieve the knotted muscles. "They've got one in the post office but it's broken." She reached into her bag, amazed at her bizarre sense of calm, and took out the flask.

Angus frowned and stubbed out his fag in the ashtray. "How is Siobhain, anyway?"

Maureen unscrewed the lid, balancing the silver cup on her knee. "To be honest, she's not making much sense. But, then, she's speaking dead quickly and I can't really understand her accent too well."

"Yes, it's difficult."

"I suppose you're used to the way she speaks?"

"Yes."

"Yeah, she won't talk about you but I can tell you did her a lot of good." Maureen smiled shyly. "She gets a funny look on her face whenever your name's mentioned."

Angus smiled humbly at the dashboard. Maureen used the opportunity to find the Tipp-Ex mark with her finger and keep it there so she wouldn't have to keep looking. "Did she gibber on the phone?" she said.

"A bit. She was able to get the address out, though." He reached down to his pocket and pulled out a packet of fags, lighting one for himself before offering them to Maureen.

"Just had one," she said. "Thanks." She took a firm hold of the cup and poured the coffee quickly. Out of the corner of her eye she could see him watching her with interest. The bitter-chocolate smell of hot coffee radiated out of the flask. She lifted the cup to her mouth and looked at Angus. He was watching her closely. She lowered the cup. "I'd offer you some but it's got lots of sugar in it," she said.

"I take sugar."

"Do you?"

"Yes." He nodded and smiled. "I take loads of sugar."

"Well," she said, sounding chirpy, "a fellow sugar taker. There aren't many of us left these days, are there?"

"Nope." Angus grinned.

She handed him the cup. He lifted it to his nose and smelled it before he sipped. "That's quality coffee," he said, and took another drink.

"It's real coffee." She turned the flask around until the white marker was pointing toward her. "We brought it with us." She tilted the flask forty-five degrees, hoping to fuck he wouldn't realize she was drinking air. He offered her the half-full cup back. "No, it's all right," she said, saluting him with the flask. "You finish that."

She watched him tip the cup high and drink the last drop. He held it out, offering her it back. She didn't want to touch it. She put the stopper in and held the flask out to him. He screwed the cup back on, turning it until it was tight. He smiled at her. "Nice to see you," he said.

Maureen smiled back. "Aye, it's nice to see you too, Angus."

They felt the bottom of the boat scrape the incline of the concrete ramp and the hull wound down in front of them like a drawbridge. The pedestrian passengers walked off in front of them, hurrying up the ramp to the waiting bus.

He started the car and drove over the ferry hull, up the steep concrete ramp, and turned left onto the road, following the signs for Millport. They drove around the east side of the island, passing Lion Rock, magnificent with the early-morning light behind it, through Kames Bay and on to the seafront at Millport. Angus was keeping an eye on the road and reading the door numbers. "What is it," he said. "Number six?"

"Yeah," said Maureen. "Number six."

"Top flat," said Angus, smiling to himself.

He parked the car opposite the chip shop, pulled on the hand brake, opened his door and got out. The shops were just opening, the bike-hire shop's shutters were half-up and a bearded man with a ponderous beer belly was pushing colorful bicycles and tricycles outside, arranging them in rows on the pavement. The baker's was open: the window displayed full trays of bridies and mince rounds, fresh-made bread and iced buns. The newsagent's was open. Paulsa had told her it might take an hour to work and it was only fifteen minutes or so since Angus had drunk the coffee.

Maureen stepped out of the car with her bag and shut the door. She walked around the bonnet to Angus. A Land Rover was driving slowly down the seafront, closely followed by the green and chrome bus. They stepped back against the Jaguar and waited for them to pass. Angus was holding a foot-long Gladstone bag with a flat bottom and a hinged mouth. It was made of flawless dark brown leather.

"That's a beautiful bag," she said, as the Land Rover sailed past. "You don't see many of them nowadays."

"I had it made. It was to replace an old one."

The ferry bus passed them and she held out her gloved hand to Angus. "Can I see it?" she said.

"My bag?"

"Yeah."

Angus tightened his grip on the leather-bound handle. "It's got my notes and everything in it."

Maureen smiled innocently. "Oh, come on, Angus, I'm hardly going to steal it, am I?"

"No," he said stupidly. "But I have a professional obligation."

He turned and crossed the road. She watched him walk away. His tweed jacket was ripped at the back, the seam under the arm was coming apart, ruining the line of it. His shoes were handmade.

She trotted after him. "Listen, can you hang on for a minute? I need to get something."

She meant for him to wait outside but he followed her into the newsagent's. Not wanting to be seen with him, she moved over to the magazine rack, leaving Angus standing on his own by the books. She might be able to get out of the shop without talking to him. She picked up a chocolate bar and took a pint of milk out of the fridge, wasting time by checking the sell-by date. Angus was at the far side of the shop—he didn't want to be seen with her either: he had pulled his hat down and was facing some posters. Next to him a tidy queue of pensioners waited patiently under a red sign. Suddenly the sign came into focus and she realized that they were in the post-office. She moved over to the counter quickly, paid for the chocolate and the milk, shoving the money at the bearded man behind the till, and walked out.

Angus followed her onto the pavement and took hold of her

elbow, pulling her round to face him. "They do have a fax machine," he said, looking at her with his eyes half-closed.

"Yeah, and I told you it's broken."

"It didn't have a sign on it or anything."

She thought about the day she went back to the Rainbow, how he had called her Helen and pretended not to know her. He'd recognized her the moment she'd opened the door and handed him the coffee; she could tell he had, but she'd suppressed her discomfort, mistaking it for embarrassment at being forgotten. He'd pretended not to know her when only a few days before he had been creeping around her house in a blood-soaked cagoul, planting footprints and cutting off Douglas's soft bollocks. "Do you need to send a fax?" she said, seeming confused.

"No."

They stood and looked at each other.

"So . . . what?" said Maureen.

Angus jerked his head away and looked over the bay. "Nothing," he said. "I just . . . I don't know."

She checked her watch. She had better get him off the street before it kicked in. "I'm sorry, Angus, I don't know what you mean. D'you need to contact someone? There's a phone upstairs if you need an ambulance for Siobhain."

"Okay," he said uncertainly. "That'll be all right, then."

"We're at number six," she said, and walked on. She led him up the steep stairs, not daring to look at the front door on the first landing in case he saw her. She blinked hard, willing Siobhain and Leslie to stay inside. Angus followed her up to the top flat.

She waited until he was standing on the top landing with her before she took the keys out. She positioned herself at an angle to the door, with her back to the wall, as she slid the key in, turned it and waved him into the flat in front of her. Angus stepped back gallantly and gestured for Maureen to go in first. She couldn't insist without arousing his suspicion. She stepped into the pink flowery hallway. Angus followed her in and shut the door carefully, quietly. She heard him slip the button on the lock, sealing them into the flat together. Maureen stepped forward toward the living-room door. Angus was moving behind her, standing too close. She shoved the living-room door open, banging it against the wall in her hurry to get away from him, and a burning wave of heat billowed out into the hall. "Jesus," said Angus, blanching. "What's going on in here?"

"It's very hot," said Maureen.

She walked into the living room as though she were looking for someone.

"Yeah, but *why* is it so hot?"

"It's the heating. Hello?" she called softly.

"Where's Siobhain?"

"She doesn't seem to be here."

Angus dropped his bag and hat onto the floor and took off his jacket, resting it over his arm. Two dark rings were forming under his arms, he wiped his glistening forehead with his hand.

Maureen looked at him and smiled. He smiled back, slightly confused, panting lightly in the unbearable heat. He rolled his head back a little and gathered himself together slowly, reminding himself that the bag was on the floor. "Maureen," he said, sliding toward her over a mile of carpet, "I like you." He reached for her wrist but she whipped it away from him.

His skin was burning, the heat was trying to escape from his body any way it could, he could feel blood spots bursting on his back, the size of two-pence pieces, bright, red and burning. A lava rush of sweat ran into his left eye. He pulled off his glasses and jerked his arm up to wipe it from his eyelid but something was moving on his shirtsleeve. He looked at it. He was on fire. Tiny jagged flames leaped on his arm, cartoon flames with red eyes and wicked sharp-toothed smiles. He looked more closely. They were real flames, orange at the base with blue tips, like a gas pipe. He tried to breathe in. The hot air dried his throat and mouth, burning his windpipe. His shirt was melting, sticking to his skin. He tried to lie down and roll the fire off but couldn't move properly and fell onto his knees, leaning his head and shoulder heavily against the red wall.

She was pulling his flaming hair, pulling him by his hair, dragging him away somewhere. She clicked a metal bracelet onto his wrist. He was attached to the bed now and pulled as hard as he could but the bed followed him, biting his wrist, making it bleed heat around the bangle.

"I'm on fire," he said tearfully.

She took his jacket and hat and glasses from the floor and put them on a chair. She undid his shoelaces and slipped his shoes off, unzipped his trousers and let them fall down, pulling them out from under his stockinged feet. Riffling through the pockets she found his wallet. She left the money untouched and took anything that could help to identify him—library cards, cashpoint receipts, credit cards. She slipped the Basildon Bond note to McEwan into the wallet and put it in Angus's trouser pocket, folding the trousers and laying them neatly over the chair.

"You know . . . ," he said into his chest, "you've know. Vyouv."

She carried the portable television in from the living room and put it on the floor, plugged it in and switched it on.

"Where's Siobhain? Why can't I see her?" Tears drizzled down his face. "Let me go?" he said.

"You were Benny's therapist, weren't ye? You blackmailed him about the credit-card thefts. Ye threatened to shop him and ruin his law career."

"Yes. Please stop this."

"Did you get him to plant the knife back in the flat?"

"Yes. Please . . . make it stop."

"Did he tell you about my cupboard?"

"Yea . . ." Angus was murmuring nonsense, his head lolling heavily on his chest.

"I want you to know," Maureen said slowly, so that he would remember, "this is for Siobhain and Yvonne and Iona and the others. And this is for Douglas and this is for Martin."

"I don't know who Martin is," he said innocently.

She stood still and looked at him. A little bent man sweating in his underwear. A string of thick saliva fell from the side of his open mouth, landing softly on the front of his shirt.

"Martin is the guy you killed at the Northern."

"The porter."

"Yes, the porter."

Angus raised his head. His eyes were open wide, too, too wide. "You know it!" he shouted, suddenly coherent. His face was red and his voice tight, strangled, as if he was shitting. "That's why the dreams. You said his nail ripped you but he fucked you. You know it. *He fuckt you.*"

She ran two steps forward and head-butted him. She felt more than heard the crack. She stepped back. Blood was running into his open mouth, his nose was swelling rapidly. He drawled, spluttering through the blood, "Fuckt."

She butted him again. He shut his eyes and was suddenly calm. "Are you going to kill me?"

"Yes."

"Am I on fire?"

"Yes, Angus, you're on fire."

Angus gathered his breath and let out a screeching wail. Maureen turned the TV up full and waited for a pause in the screaming. She opened the door and walked downstairs.

Siobhain and Leslie were sitting at the table by the window, eating Ricicles in milk. Behind them the bright sun shone over the bay like a picture postcard and blue and red wooden boats bobbed on the water.

"Hello," said Siobhain. "Where have you been?"

"We have to get out of here *right now*," said Maureen, and went into the kitchen. She picked up the dishcloth from under the sink and used it to wipe anything in the kitchen that could conceivably have touched the sheet of acid.

Leslie ran into the bedroom and dressed. Siobhain shuffled into the kitchen doorway.

"Why are we in a hurry?"

"Siobhain, do you trust me?"

"Yes, I do."

"Then please, move, get dressed. We need to be out of here in ten minutes."

"You have blood on your forehead," she said, and shuffled away.

Leslie appeared at the kitchen door, panting and zipping up her trousers. She looked terrified. "What do you want me to do?"

"Pack everything," said Maureen. "Leave the place spotless so there aren't any complaints. And leave a tenner on the table for a tip."

"A tip?"

"Goodwill gesture."

"You've got blood on your forehead."

35

HOME

THE TRAIN WAS WAITING IN LARGS STATION. MAUREEN HELPED SIOB-hain and Leslie into the first carriage and ran up to the conductor, who was smoking a fag on the platform. "What time does the train go?" she asked.

"Twelve-thirty," he said lethargically. "You've got ten minutes."

Her heart was beating loudly. She ran over to the phone box and called Liam at home. "Hello, Liam?"

"Maureen, I know you're in Millport, I booked the fucking house."

"Did Benny tell you, then?"

"Yeah, the fucker phoned here last night as pally as anything, asking for the address we stayed at the last time. He said he wanted to send you flowers. I was going to drive down and see you."

"Well, don't, I'm coming home. I just phoned to tell you that I've finished using Benny, you can do what you like with him."

"Fucking . . . right." Liam slammed the phone down.

* * *

Siobhain grinned at Maureen as she came along the carriage and sat down next to her. She took Maureen's hand and squeezed it. "Where are we going now?" she asked.

"We're going home, Siobhain."

"Is it safe now?"

"Aye."

"Why is it safe?"

"It just is."

"How did it get to be safe?"

"I'm awful tired, Siobhain, do you mind if we don't speak?"

"Yes, I want to speak."

"But I'm dead tired."

Siobhain's cheeks blushed pink. "Fine, then," she said, throwing Maureen's hand away and turning her face resolutely to the window.

Maureen opened the door and walked into her house. She dropped her coat onto Douglas's blue kitchen chair in the cluttered hall, went into the kitchen and turned the boiler on. She wandered into the living room. The floorboards were stained with brown blood but they could be painted over. She had a feeling that she wanted to live with the marks for a while, to walk past them in the morning and get used to them.

She opened the hall cupboard and looked at the bloody stain. Crouching down on her hunkers, she put her hand on it. It was stiff and crunchy. She stood up a little and shuffled her feet forward, moving into the cupboard, and pulled the door shut, closing herself in. She sat in the corner for a while, her fingertips resting on the dried bloody splatter, thinking about love hearts. Finally, she kicked open the door, clambered out and went into the living room, leaving the cupboard door to swing open into the hall. She binned the empty whisky bottle and the half-empty box of chocolates, went into the bedroom, stripped the bedsheets and binned them too.

She walked to the bathroom, shedding her dirty clothes as she went, dropping the jumper in the hall and losing her jeans at the bathroom doorway. She put the plug in the bath, turned on the hot tap and went for a naked walk through her little house, smoking a fag as she did. Her scalp felt rank from wearing the woolly hat against the incessant damp rain; she scratched at it, letting the air through.

It was the best bath she'd ever had. The water was deep and hot, she lay back and felt it run through her hair, warming her scalp and running into her ears. She got out and towel-dried her hair, covered herself in scented body oil and took the blue chair into the living room, sitting on it like a giant sherbet pomander, enjoying her house.

The phone rang out, disrupting her serenity. She didn't answer and the machine wasn't plugged back in yet. It rang for a long time. When it stopped she got up and dialed 1471. It was Liam, phoning from his house. She'd call him later.

She lifted the chair into the bedroom and sat there for a while, thinking about all the times the room had seen her through. Then she took the chair into the kitchen and reclaimed that room too.

She was just beginning to tire of the ritual when someone banged on the door impatiently. It seemed strange because they hadn't knocked a first time. She scampered into the bedroom and looked for something to put on. She was covered in body oil—whatever she put on would be ruined. They banged on the door again and she threw on an old summer dress with a red-wine stain down the back.

She looked out of the spy hole. It was Jim Maliano with his jumper tucked into his jeans and his spooky hairdo. He seemed annoyed.

Maureen opened the door. "Hello—"

"I've come to get my top back." His voice was high and aggressive and grated on her sweet mood.

"I beg your pardon?"

"Give me back my Celtic top."

She couldn't be bothered with this. "Jim," she said apathetically, "I've lost it, I'm sorry."

Jim's eyes widened, the bouffant over his crown started to shake. "You're sorry?" he shouted. "Do you have any idea how much that cost me?"

"Jim, I'll give you the money, I just—"

Jim pointed a stubby finger in her face, jabbing it an inch from the end of her nose. "Is this how you repay me? I took you into my house, I gave you and your brother coffee and treated you to my hospitality—"

"Auch, piss off," she said unreasonably. "I'll give ye the money."

"Piss off? Piss off?"

"Yeah, and stop spying on me through your door as well."

"How dare you? I went to the police about your friend—"

Maureen felt a bit giggly. "Jim," she said, trying not to smile, "get the fuck away from my door."

And she shut it in his face. She crouched behind it, shaking with laughter, holding her hands over her mouth so that he wouldn't hear her. She stood up and peered out of the spy hole. He stomped across the landing and slammed his own door shut.

36

DAD

MAUREEN LET THE PHONE RING ITSELF OUT AND WENT BACK TO sleep. Minutes later someone was banging on the door. She pulled on her dressing gown and staggered into the hall. Her eyes were so puffy she could barely negotiate the spy hole. Liam was standing in the close, holding bits of shopping. She opened the door.

"Have you just woken up, Mauri? It's one in the afternoon." He stepped into the hall and held out a bag of fresh croissants and a carton of orange juice. "I've been phoning you loads."

When she came back from the toilet Liam had put the croissants in the oven to warm, made a pot of tasteless instant coffee and set the table for a formal breakfast, with cups and cutlery and everything. He had tiny bloody cuts on his knuckles and a long black bruise on the side of his neck. It started as an inch-wide mark under his ear, spreading into a broad triangle as it descended to his shoulder; the edges of the bruise were yellowing. He handed her a cold glass of orange juice.

It was sunny outside. Maureen leaned against the window frame and looked out at her favorite view. "I got sacked," she said.

"Auch, well, you'll find another job soon enough," said Liam. "I expect you'll miss the cut and thrust of ticket selling, though, eh?"

"Yeah, I'll miss sitting behind that drafty wee window like a Dutch whore day after day. What's happening with you, then, Liam?"

"Well," he said, "I went to Glasgow Uni the other day. They said I could start a course this year if I wanted, as long as I can guarantee the fees."

She smiled at him. "God, that's brilliant, but will you have to pay for it yourself?"

"The first grand, yeah. I phoned the SED and they'll pay the rest but it might take a while to come through."

"What's the course?"

"Film and Media."

"Not law?"

"Nah," he said, "I'm tired of chasing money."

"I didn't even know you were interested in filmmaking."

"Neither did I."

The croissants were hot. She cut them in half and spread butter and jam on them, watching the butter liquefy into warm yellow puddles in the pastry. They ate a calm, quiet breakfast.

"What's the state of play between you and the women?" she asked.

"Uh, Maggie left home and came to stay with me. I dunno. She keeps making me dinner and that." He looked dismal.

"What's wrong with that?"

"Dunno," he said, shaking his head pensively, his chin shiny with greasy melted butter.

"Don't you want her to stay with you?"

He chewed and thought about it. "No," he said. "I want Lynn."

"Why not finish it with Maggie and ask Lynn out again, then?"

"I asked Lynn, she won't have me."

"Oh dear." She sipped her coffee and looked up at him. He was watching her, wondering. "Did you see Lynn?"

"No," she said. "Why?"

"Nothing. She said something about your hair." He drank some orange juice and looked out into the hallway. "What are you going to do with this flat, then?"

"I'd like to stay for a while. I like it here."

"I can pay the mortgage for a while, if you like."

"No need. Douglas left me some money."

Benny was being treated in the Albert. Liam drove her through the busy town, along Cathedral Street and up to the main door. "Aren't you coming up for a nice wee visit?" she said.

"I don't ever want to see that prick again," muttered Liam, picking at one of the scabs on the back of his hand. He was in a serious mood, and Maureen didn't think it was just to do with the cuts and bruises on his hands, but she couldn't be arsed holding more than one thought in her head today and her one thought at the moment was Benny.

"I'll see you in a minute, then," she said, and got out of the car.

She had only ever been through the small entrance for Louisa's office at the side of the building. This was the main entrance. It was two stories high, and more like a small airport than a hospital. A balcony with open-plan offices ran three-quarters of the way around it, a busy newsagent's-cum-florist's was open just inside the door and a Bank of Scotland cash machine was set into the wall next to it. Beyond the security desk were six lifts with stainless-steel doors, three on each side of the lobby, leading up to the wards. She read the display board hanging overhead. Ward 4B was on the fourth floor.

Maureen looked in through the double doors. It was an old-fashioned ward with sixteen beds, eight on each side of the room.

Tall meshed windows lined the walls. At the end of the enormous room stood a TV surrounded by low plastic armchairs. It was a crisis ward for accident victims. The first three beds on the left had support poles with traction ropes hanging from them like cat's cradles. The other patients had casts and dressings covering varying degrees of their body surface. She couldn't see Benny.

Three nurses were sitting in a side office eating cocktail-sized sausage rolls and drinking lemonade out of paper cups. The youngest nurse was holding an open greetings card. They were watching Maureen standing aimlessly by the doors.

"Oh, hello, I'm looking for Brendan Gardner."

The sister stood up. She was slim and glamorous, and had a bigger hat than the others. "Are you a relative?" she asked.

"Yeah, I'm his cousin." The sister pointed her down the ward to the last bed on the left.

Maureen wouldn't have known him. His eyes were swollen shut like two sets of purple lips, his lumpy swollen face was covered in blue and yellow bruises and his right arm was in a plaster cast. "Hello, Benny."

He tried instinctively to sit up when he heard her voice but fell back on the bed, lying tense and panicked, and defenseless.

"You look terrible," she said.

He nodded a fraction.

"Can't you talk?"

His lips were trembling as he pulled them back. He tried and failed, and then tried again. She could just see the thin wires holding his shattered jaw in place.

"Broke your jaw?"

He moved his good hand slightly to the left, unfolding his fist slowly and pointing a finger. A pencil and pad were sitting on top of the bedside cabinet. She sat the pad by his left hand and gave him the pencil, working it between his stiff fingers.

"So sorry," he wrote. His writing was a nervous, childish scrawl. He couldn't see the pad and was writing with his unaccustomed hand. He turned the page. "So so sorry."

She had meant to shout at him and say mean things, tell him that she'd do him a bad turn if she ever got the chance, but she sat and looked at him and knew she couldn't censor all he had been to her. Her eyes brimmed over with stinging, reluctant tears. She felt as if she were watching him die.

"Why, though?" she whispered.

He turned the page on the pad. "Bad ma uuera hurrel."

Maureen read it several times. "Bad ma uuera hurrel?"

He turned the page. "HAD ME OVER A BARREL."

"You dubbed me up for your career? He was going to kill me, Benny."

"I BEEN CHARGED."

"What with?"

"BREAKING."

"So your career's fucked anyway, eh?"

Benny lay still, his hand resting on the pad. She took the Anti Dynamos T-shirt out of her bag and put it on the bed. "I brought your T-shirt back," she said.

He turned the page. "PLEASE KEEP IT."

"Don't want it," she said, standing up and bending over the bed as if to kiss him. She forked her fingers, gave the blood-swollen flesh on his eyelids a vicious poke and walked out.

A small bald man was waiting for the lift. He wore blue overalls with "Albert" printed in white across his shoulders. Maureen was breathing in unevenly to stop herself crying. The porter flashed her a consolatory smile. "Are you all right, pet?"

"Not really." She tried to smile back but failed, disabled by her trembling chin.

The lift arrived and he stepped back, letting her get in first.

"Ground floor?" She nodded. "Is it your boyfriend?" he asked, pointing up to the ward.

"No." She sniffed. "Just a friend."

"Don't worry, pet," he said. "I'm sure your friend'll be okay. We see miracles every day in here."

The lift bounced to a gentle standstill at the ground floor. The doors opened onto a crowd of waiting nurses. The porter waved her off in front of him. "Thank you," she whispered as she got out.

She stood next to the car and blew her nose before opening the door and getting in. "Right, Liam," she said. "What's on your mind? If you've got anything to tell me do it now."

Liam took a deep breath and looked at his knees. "Are you sure?"

"Yes. Tell me now."

"They didn't say you killed Douglas."

"I gathered that much."

"Yeah, well, I had a good reason for lying."

He stopped and touched the bruise on his neck, patting it twice with the pads of his fingers. He let his hand drop into his lap and looked out of the window, squinting at the cathedral.

"Tell me."

"They do think there's something wrong with your memory."

"That's not all it's about, though, is it?"

He picked at the rotting leatherette cover on the steering wheel. "They said you've got false memory."

"Tell me the whole story, Liam."

Liam cleared his throat. "I didn't want to tell you the truth because I knew it'd do your head in."

She turned suddenly and shouted at him, "Why did you let me go there and make such a prick of myself, Liam? If they thought I was mental before, they'd—"

"I told you to stay away from them," he said morosely. "I told you, Mauri. I said stay away."

"Well, for fucksake."

"I said stay away."

Maureen looked out of the window. "Why did you lie to me?" she said.

"I didn't want you to know."

"You didn't want me to know what?"

Liam turned away, shaking his head.

"Tell me."

"Dad's back," he said flatly. "That's why Marie's here. Dad's back."

37

HUGH

SHE STOOD ON THE STEPS OF THE CHURCH AND TRIED TO WORK OUT where the entrance was. He had said Thurso Street but St. Francis was on Lorne Street. She walked down the hill to Thurso Street and leaned round the corner. A fence of high iron railings blocked the back from the road. She went back up the steps of the church and looked in through the open doors. A glass wall had been constructed five feet inside the chapel with doors on either side to keep out the cold and provide a soundproof area for noisy children.

The high altar was a white molded wall of saints on a background of pseudo-Gothic drapery. The front two pews were busy with penitents, sitting down awaiting confession or kneeling on the far side of the aisle from the confessional boxes with their heads bent intently, doing their penance. Just inside the glass wall, on the very back bench, knelt a white-haired woman wearing an old-style black mantilla. She was saying her rosary, her windswept arthritic fingers flicking through the jet beads wrapped around her hand, her lips quivering as she recited the "Glory Be," her pious head bent low.

Maureen looked to left and right. A small dark wood door on the right-hand side of the entrance was slightly ajar. She walked over to it and pushed it open, peering round the corner. It was a long, narrow corridor running the full length of the chapel. She walked halfway down it before realizing where she was going. "It'll hardly be in the fucking sacristy," she muttered to herself, cursing for badness' sake, because she was in a chapel and didn't belong there.

Rather than knock on the parochial house door and ask where the meeting was, she decided to walk all the way round the church until she found the entrance. She discovered a dark alley between the next-door primary school and the back of the chapel and put her hand in her pocket, wrapping it around her stabbing comb before stepping into the dark. Bright trip lights turned on as she walked down the narrow zigzag alley. She found herself at the top of a flight of steps. Straight in front of her was a small rickety wooden door covered in blistered brown gloss. A light shone out from under it. She trotted down the stairs and listened at the door. Someone was speaking—a woman was telling a funny story or something. Another voice interrupted her, a man's voice. Maureen knocked on the door. The voices stopped and the door opened. A tall blond woman wearing a smart black office suit looked out at her and smiled politely. "Can I help you?" she asked in a lyrical, upper-class English accent.

The room behind her was very shabby. The concrete floor was bare and the cupboard under the sink unit had lost its doors. Patches of plaster were crumbling on the wall and the thick layer of blue paint looked as if it were holding the wall up. Maureen felt as if she had stumbled on a coven. "I'm looking for a guy called Hugh McAskill."

The woman smiled pleasantly and leaned back into the room. "Hugh, love, it's for you."

Hugh McAskill came to the door, beaming when he saw her. She grinned back, overjoyed to see him and his gappy teeth and his gold and silver hair.

"Are you here for the meeting, then?" he asked.

"Naw," she said, trying to disguise her delight. "I just came to see ye."

"Come away in and get a cup of tea." He stepped back into the dingy room. The Englishwoman looked disgruntled. "It's all right," he said. "She's one of us, she just doesn't want to come up to the meeting yet, that's all."

Maureen walked in and shut the door behind herself. The floor was angled slightly, tipping toward a drain in the middle of the floor; she could feel her calf muscles compensating for the gradient. Some smoked-glass cups, a plate of expensive chocolate biscuits and a steaming urn were sitting on a wobbly table. Four other middle-aged women were standing around in a group at the end of the room, looking at Maureen with benign curiosity. They stepped forward one at a time and introduced themselves by their first names.

The door opened behind Maureen and a ridiculously tall man in his early twenties came in, dipping his head under the low doorway. "Hello, everyone," he called, looking around the room until he found the plate of biscuits. He made straight for them, picking up three and eating them whole. He looked at Maureen. "Who are you?"

"I'm Maureen O'Donnell."

"Are you an incest survivor?"

"Um, yeah," she said, frowning and wishing he'd mind his own fucking business. His manner was so insistently cheerful that Maureen suspected she was looking at a profoundly unhappy man.

"There's no need to be embarrassed about that here," he said, grinning through a mouthful of chocolate crumbs. "We've all been fucked by our families." He looked at her, expecting some sort of response, but she couldn't think of anything to say.

"Great," she said.

McAskill pulled her aside, turning her so that her back was to the happy-sad man. "What did you want to see me about?" he said softly.

She lowered her voice, talking into his chest. "I just wondered if Joe McEwan got a phone call of some kind . . . maybe from an exotic holiday destination?"

McAskill tilted his head back and laughed. She could see his fillings. "You don't give up, do you? D'you know Joe McEwan wants to throttle you? We've got a high-profile case and a nutter shouting about fire."

"Angus's prints matched the ones on Martin, then?"

"Yeah, perfect, he even had one of those big knives with him."

"Where?"

"In the leather bag."

She rolled her eyes and breathed, "Fuck."

McAskill sighed along with her. "You're a lucky wee bugger, you," he said.

She nodded. "Not half. What made McEwan think it was me?"

"Well, you slipped surveillance and your prints were all over the note. They were pretty smudged, though. The nurse at the cottage hospital managed to hold the note in about fifty different ways before phoning us."

McAskill smiled at her and she thought she might chance her arm. "Can I ask you something, Hugh? Something about the case?"

He looked uncertain. "Depends."

"Why did you stop looking for someone available in the daytime? Why did you start thinking it happened in the evening?"

He was stunned. "How do you know about that?"

"Auch, I just do."

He looked hurt. "Are you talking to someone else?"

"No, it's just . . . I noticed that ye were asking about the daytime and then, about the second time McEwan interviewed Liam, you started asking about the evening."

"Oh," said McAskill, thinking it through. "Right enough." He looked despondent. " 'Member the thing in the hall cupboard?"

"Yeah."

"It was decaying at a different rate from the rest of it. The timing was all messed up."

"Oh," she said, wishing to fuck she hadn't asked. "I see."

"Anyway," he said, "McEwan thinks you did it to wind him up."

"Yeah, everything I do is about Joe McEwan."

McAskill eyed her with earnest admiration. "You did it for her, didn't you, for your pal?"

Maureen didn't want to talk about her motive just yet. She had been doing it for Siobhain and the other women right up to the moment when she ran forward and nutted him. "Yeah. A bit. Anyway," she said, scratching her scalp, digging her nails deep into the skin, "Joe's annoyed but he's not coming after me for anything?"

"No, we couldn't prove anything. The guy's a mess but he's got LSD all over his mouth and in his throat. We can't say he didn't take it himself. All we had was a drunk man in a chip shop who saw three strange women. The prints on the note are useless. There's nothing we could do."

"God, I was lucky," she said, almost to herself.

"Aye, you're that, all right," he said. "He fell over by the way, smashed his nose."

A hot blush rose up the back of her neck. "I'm sorry to hear that," she said perfunctorily.

"Do ye want a biscuit?" He leaned over, snatched the plate away from the young man and held them out to her. The chocolate was bitter and dark and so thick that when her teeth sank into it they caused a tiny vacuum. "God in heaven," she said. "They're lovely."

"Aye," said McAskill, looking lovingly at his biscuit. "We get these every week."

"Where is he now?"

"Who, Joe?"

"No, the guy from the exotic holiday destination."

"In Sunnyfield."

"The mental hospital?"

He shook his head solemnly. "It's not a mental hospital, it's a state mental hospital."

"What's the difference?"

"The public gives a damn about people in mental hospitals."

"Didn't think it would last that long. It's been five days."

"Yeah," said McAskill, "ye can't tell how long LSD'll take. Anyway, he's been charged, so he's going nowhere."

The Englishwoman in the black suit opened a little door in the wall. It led to a wooden spiral staircase. "That's us, everyone," she said. "That's eight o'clock."

The waiting crowd picked up their cups of tea and made their way, single file, up the stairs. "Sure you won't come?"

"Naw, Hugh, another time."

"You might enjoy it."

"Yeah, there's some stuff going on in my family . . . If I come upstairs I'll just have to think about it and my head might burst."

McAskill looked at her respectfully. "I doubt that somehow. Come back though, eh? If only for the biscuits."

She poked him softly in the ribs. "I'll come back to see you."

He grinned. "You do that."

He watched her as she walked out into the brightly lit alley and pulled the door closed behind her.

38

ANGUS

SIOBHAIN HAD BEEN SHOPPING WITH HER ROLL OF DOUGLAS'S MONEY and bought a television with a thirty-two-inch screen. It had a video machine built into the body, detachable stereo speakers and its own matching matte black stand. It dwarfed everything else in her living room. Even the gas fire on the wall looked like a toy next to the monster telly. Leslie uncoiled the flex and plugged it in. Maureen stepped forward to turn it on. "No," said Siobhain. "Watch."

She took the remote control out of the plastic bag, fitted the batteries into it and pressed a button. The magnificent television came to life. They stood back and looked at it.

"Wow," said Leslie. "I'm not mad keen on TV but that is a thing of fucking beauty."

"Don't swear," said Siobhain, reading the instructions for her remote control.

"Eh?"

"I said don't swear, not in my house. There's no need for bad language."

She played with the remote, skipping backward and forward

between channels, increasing and decreasing the volume and color at each stop, oblivious to Leslie, who was flicking the vickies at her behind her back.

"And it goes like a five-bob rocket, as well," said Maureen, trying to keep the peace. She looked at Siobhain, not knowing if it was the right time. She reached into her bag and pulled out the corner of the video-tape, showing it to Leslie. Leslie nodded softly. "I'll just go for a quick hit-and-miss," she said jauntily, and disappeared into the bathroom.

"Siobhain," said Maureen, "I want to show you a videotape. It's something I got off the telly last night. D'you want to see it?"

"Okay."

Maureen took out the tape and put it into the machine. "It's got a picture of Angus on it," she said.

"Angus who?" said Siobhain, still absorbed by the remote.

"Angus Farrell."

"Oh."

Maureen was expecting a bigger response, tears or a fit of mute-ness, but not this casual disinterest. She put the tape in anyway.

"Is it rewound?" asked Siobhain.

"Yeah, just turn it on."

Siobhain changed to the video channel and pressed Play. The woman newsreader looked nineteen eighty-fourish on the enor-mous screen. The footage showed slow-motion detail of Angus being led from a big stone doorway into a waiting police van. He was handcuffed to a police escort. His nose was flattened to the side like a boxer's and he didn't have his glasses on. His mouth was hanging open. The voice-over said he had been charged with murdering Douglas Brady and another man. He was to be held at Sunnyfield state mental hospital on a temporary basis for further treatment. Carol Brady came on and said tearfully that she was grateful to the police for all their sterling work and she just wanted to be left alone with her family now. The report ended and a black line rose swiftly up the screen, wiping the picture away.

"It's broken," said Siobhain, and banged the remote with the flat of her hand, changing the channel to a documentary about skiing.

"No, Siobhain," said Maureen. "That's it. I stopped taping at that point."

It took a minute for the information to register. "Oh," said Siobhain. "Is it all there is on that tape?"

"Yes, that's the end of the story."

"But if I put on a different tape it will be all right?"

"Yeah."

"All right, then."

She took the full instruction booklet out of the big box and started reading it. Maureen coughed. Siobhain glanced over at her feet and went back to her reading. For a long shaky moment Maureen thought she'd got the wrong guy.

"So," said Maureen. "How do you feel about Angus now?"

Siobhain shrugged. "He can't hurt me now."

Maureen breathed a sigh of relief. "That's right." She smiled encouragingly. "He can't hurt you because he's in a prison hospital and he'll be staying there for a long time."

"No," said Siobhain disagreeably, looking at Maureen as if she were stupid. "He can't hurt me because I have friends now, because I have you and Leslie to look after me."

"Well, yes," nodded Maureen, "yes. There's that too."

Siobhain went back to her reading.

"Hoi, Mauri," called Leslie from the hall. "Let's get tae fuck out of here or we'll miss the police changing shifts."

"Yeah." Maureen stood up. "We're away, then."

Siobhain said good-bye without looking up.

Out on the street Leslie handed Maureen a helmet. "Did you get water?" she said.

"Yeah, it's in the tub," said Maureen, tapping the plastic pot of paste in the open luggage box. Next to it were the posters.

"That's shit paper," said Leslie. "It'll melt like toilet paper if it rains."

"Yeah, but it cost next to nothing and it doesn't need to last forever."

"Far be it from me to say this," said Leslie, slipping on her helmet, "but Siobhain's a prick."

Maureen scratched her head miserably. "Leslie," she said, "you're right." She did up the helmet strap under her chin.

"To be honest," said Leslie, "I liked her better when she was scared shitless and couldn't talk."

"She thinks we're her big mates now. She said she knew she'd be safe because she's got us to look after her."

"Oh, fuck," said Leslie, and bit her lip.

Maureen sighed. "I wanted to make a single heroic gesture. I didn't want to be her mum."

Leslie laughed and swung her leg over the seat, knocked the stand away with her heel and kick-started the bike, revving the engine. "Annie taught me an effective technique for dealing with needy people like that."

"Yeah?" said Maureen, pleasantly surprised by Leslie's tolerant attitude. "What's that?" She slipped onto the back of the bike and wrapped her arms around Leslie's waist.

"Tell them to fuck off," said Leslie, and pulled into the stream of traffic in Duke Street.

ACKNOWLEDGMENTS

With thanks to the Media and Information Service of the Strathclyde Police Department, Glasgow Women's Aid Collective and Ian Mitchell and Jon Redshaw of the Durham Constabulary for their invaluable help in researching this book. Further thanks are due to Rachel Calder, Marina Cianfanelli and Katrina Whone for their encouragement and guidance, without which I would have given up. Most of all to Stephen Evans for his grace, patience and good humor during months of early-morning typing feet away from the bed in which he was trying to sleep.

BACK BAY · READERS' PICK

READING GROUP GUIDE

GARNETHILL

A NOVEL BY

DENISE MINA

A conversation with Denise Mina

The author of *Garnethill* talks with
Margy Rochlin of *LA Weekly*

You started writing crime fiction because you were, and I quote, "fed up with big men solving crimes with women in the background."

Yeah, absolutely! I don't know how it is in L.A., but everywhere I go in Glasgow, there are wee guys shouting abuse at you. "Show us yer tits!" That just doesn't happen to male protagonists at all. I think it's a very different landscape if you're a woman.

Had you always been a fan of the genre?

[I'd read] a lot of crap, really right-wing fiction, particularly Patricia Cornwell. [In her books,] people who commit crimes are different from us, and the central character is right about everything. The very first Scarpetta book is lovely. After that, it's fascinating: Her central character gets more and more divorced from reality, and [Cornwell] gets more and more right-wing and more glamorous in the author's photo.

Do you see crime differently in Glasgow, where you've set all your books?

Glasgow has the highest per capita imprisonment rate anywhere in Western Europe. If you're working-class or lower-middle-class, you'll know somebody who's been in prison. There's a kind of socialist assumption in Glasgow. Everybody assumes that sticking it to the man is a good thing. They have a real respect for criminals. Criminality is not someone else, someplace else, in Glasgow. It's part of the culture.

Because of your father's engineering job, you were raised all over the world—Paris, Amsterdam, London. What made you decide to call Glasgow home?

I have a huge extended family there. But, also, Glasgow is a nice place to be poor, because everybody is. In Glasgow, instead of saying to people, "What do you do for a living?" and judging them on their job, everyone says, "Do you have a job? Have you ever worked?" In 1986, the recession was at the tail end. I'd come from London, which at the time was very Tory and very money oriented, to stay with my mum to get enough money to go back, and I just fell in love. It was a different world: Everyone at bus stops would introduce themselves to you. It was like the war had just finished.

How did you come up with using murder mystery as a device to explore complex social issues like alcoholism, sexual abuse, mental illness and battering?

I was doing a PhD on mental illness and female offenders, and I realized that six people would read it. I thought if I could write a crime novel with the same stuff in it, hundreds of people would read it. I never realized that it would be, like, thousands.

What was your thesis about?

The judicial system ascribes mental illness in a different way for men and women. If a man asserts himself in an antisocial way, he's regarded as very bad and is sent to prison. But if a woman behaves in an antisocial way, she's regarded as irrational and is sent to a mental hospital. But what could be more rational than a woman who is failed by the judicial system and her family, who decides to take her life into her own hands and impress her will on the world?

You used your PhD grant to support yourself while writing Garnethill. *Did you have to pay it back?*

No! I'd gotten stuck in a theoretical cul-de-sac. It was a nightmare. I'm sweating just talking to you about it. I did say to my academic supervisor, "I don't think I'm going to finish my piece. Do you think I'm going to run off and be a crime writer?" And he said, "If I were you, I would."

You have an infant son. Has motherhood changed how you think about violence?

People said to me, "Once you've had a baby, you'll never write about violence again." What shite! I'm very happy—and I write much quicker. Your time is very precious, and the best toy in the world is right next door.

The complete text of Margy Rochlin's interview with Denise Mina originally appeared in the issue of *LA Weekly* dated September 17–23, 2004. Reprinted with permission.

Questions and topics for discussion

1. Maureen O'Donnell is the youngest of four seemingly different children. How do the lives of each of her siblings—Marie, Una, and Liam—reflect their troubled upbringing? How does Maureen's personal history affect her relationship with the family?

2. Early in the novel Maureen's friend Leslie paraphrases Doris Lessing when she says "men are frightened of women because they think women'll laugh at them and women are frightened of men because they think men'll kill them." Do Denise Mina's male and female characters adhere to this observation? Does Maureen?

3. *Garnethill* takes on several cultural epidemics—child abuse, alcoholism, mental illness—while seeking to tell the crime story of Douglas's murder. Do you think Mina succeeded in striking an effective balance between the suspense narrative and the societal issues?

4. Maureen confesses that "having been brought up Catholic it seemed that she had always been passing her inner life in front

of someone or other for approval." How does Catholicism shape
the actions of Maureen and her family?

5. Scottish detective fiction, or "tartan noir," is often described
   as more brooding and grisly than traditional mysteries. In what
   ways does *Garnethill* adhere to or differ from these charac-
   teristics?

6. Maureen and Leslie have experienced significantly different
   childhoods. How do their respective upbringings shape the pre-
   dicaments they encounter throughout the novel? To what extent
   is Maureen responsible for her behavior?

7. *Garnethill* contains multiple scenes of intense violence, but much
   of the book—especially Maureen's dialogue—abounds with
   humor. Did you find either—the violence or the humor—to be
   inappropriate in light of the other?

8. Maureen returns in two more of Denise Mina's novels, *Exile* and
   Resolution. What do you hope is in store for Maureen? What situ-
   ations would you like to see her avoid?

ABOUT THE AUTHOR

Denise Mina is the author of the Garnethill trilogy—*Garnethill, Exile,* and *Resolution*—as well as the acclaimed novels *Deception, Field of Blood, The Dead Hour,* and *Slip of the Knife.* She lives in Glasgow with her family.

. . . AND HER FOLLOW-UP TO *GARNETHILL*

In October 2007 Back Bay Books will release a new edition of *Exile,* the second novel in Denise Mina's Garnethill trilogy. A new edition of the concluding volume, *Resolution,* will be published in November 2007.

An excerpt from the opening pages of *Exile* follows.

1

POSTIE

IT WAS MINUS FIVE OUTSIDE THE BEDROOM WINDOW AND MAUREEN'S
face prickled against the cold. She wanted to get out of bed,
wanted a cigarette and a coffee and to be alone, but his leg was
pressed tightly against hers and his hand was under her thigh. The
cumulative heat was itchy and damp. She peeled their skins apart,
trying hard not to wake him, but he felt her stir. He peered around
at her through sleep-puffed eyes.

"'Kay?" he murmured.

"Yeah," breathed Maureen.

She waited, watching her milky breath hover above her, listening
to the wind hissing outside. Vik's breathing deepened to a soft,
nasal whistle and Maureen slid into the bitter morning.

She flicked on the kettle, lit a cigarette and looked out of the
kitchen window. January is the despairing heart of the Scottish winter and black clouds brooded low over the city, pregnant with spite-
ful rain. It came to her every morning now; it was the first thought
in her head when she opened her eyes. After a wordless fifteen-year
absence, Michael, her father, was back in Glasgow.

They only found out afterward that their elder sister Marie hadn't bumped into Michael in London. She'd gone looking for him, contacting the National Union of Journalists and putting adverts in the *Evening Standard*. She found him living in the Surrey Docks in a high-rise council flat carpeted with empty lager cans. He was troubled with his health and hadn't worked for a long time so Una paid his fare home. Maureen told them she wouldn't see him but her insistence was needless. Liam said Michael never mentioned her, had never once spoken her name and ignored it when anyone else did. Even their mother, Winnie, was starting to wonder about that. Maureen couldn't get over the injustice of it. Michael was back in the bosom of the family and she was outcast.

The moment she heard he was home everything changed for her. It wasn't like the breakdown: she wasn't flashing back all the time and she knew it wasn't depression. It was a limitless, aching sadness that marred everything she cast her eye over. She couldn't contain it: her eyes had become incontinent, dripping stupid tears into washing-up, down her coat, into shopping trolleys. She even cried while she slept. When she stood at the window in Garnethill and looked down over Glasgow she felt her face might open and flood the city with tears. Grief distracted her entirely; it was as if her life continued in an adjacent room—she could hear the noises and see the people but she couldn't participate or care about any of it.

Vik snored loudly once and stopped. He was the only thing in her life that wasn't about the past but it was the wrong time for a fresh chapter and coy new discoveries. Maureen was seeing her father everywhere, grieving for Douglas and missing Leslie desperately. Vik knew almost nothing about her, nothing about Douglas being murdered in her living room six months ago, or Michael's late-night visits to her bedroom when she was a child, nothing about the schism in her family. Telling about Michael was the worst moment with new boyfriends: she saw them change toward her, saw them feel confused and implicated. Douglas had been different because he was a therapist. She'd never had to explain away the nightmares or the irrational phobias. Douglas was as soiled and melancholy as herself and Vik was a big, jolly boy.

She looked out of the window, took a deep draw on her fag and heard the swish of paper scraping through metal, followed by a light thud on the hall carpet. She recognized the blue hospital envelope at once—Angus was keeping busy. She picked it up and went back into the kitchen, sat down and lit a fresh cigarette from the dying tip of the old one. The envelope was made of cheap porous paper, her name and address written in a careful hand. She leaned across to the bills drawer and pulled out the pile of blue envelopes, laying all fifteen in chronological rows on the table. The writing was changing, becoming more controlled. He was getting better. Some of his letters were threatening, mostly they were gibberish, but the threats and the gibberish were evenly interspersed, regular and anticipatable. She knew the voice of random insanity from her own time in mental hospital and this wasn't it. He was a rapist and a murderer, but she wasn't afraid of him and she didn't give a shit. He was locked away in the state mental hospital. It was like being challenged to a dancing competition by a brick. Wearily, she gathered the unopened letter together with the old ones and shoved them into a drawer. She could read it later.

"Maureen?" Vik called sleepily from the bedroom. "Maureen?"

She stubbed out her fag and tried to find her voice. "Yeah?" She sounded tense.

"Maureen, come here."

She stood up. "What for?" she called.

"I've got something for you." Vik was grinning.

She brushed the hair off her face. "What sort of thing?" she said, forcing the playfulness. If she could act normal she might feel normal.

2

DANIEL

LONDON IS A SAVAGE CITY AND SHE DIDN'T BELONG THERE. SHE MIGHT never have been found but for Daniel. She would have disappeared completely, a missing splinter from a shattered family, a half-remembered feature in a pub landscape.

Daniel was having a good morning. It was a sunny January day and he was on his way to his first shift as barman in a private Chelsea club favored by footballers and professional celebrities. The traffic was sparse, the lights were going his way and he couldn't wait to get to work. He slowed at the junction, signaling right to the broad road bordering the river. He took the corner comfortably, using his weight to sway the bike, sliding across the path of traffic held static at the lights. He was about to straighten up when he saw the silver Mini careering toward him on his side of the road, the wheel-trim spitting red sparks as it scraped along the high lip of the pavement. He held his breath, yanked the handlebars left and shot straight across the road, up over the curb, slamming his front wheel into the low river wall at thirty miles an hour. The back wheel flew off the ground, catapulting Daniel into the air just as the Mini passed behind him. He back-flipped the long twenty-foot drop to the river, landing on a small muddy island of riverbank. The tide was out, and of all the urban rubble in the Thames he might have landed on, Daniel found himself on a sludge-soaked mattress.

He did a quick stock-take of his limbs and faculties and found everything in order. He thanked God, remembered that he didn't believe in God and took the credit back for himself. Staggered at his skill and reflexive dexterity, he pushed himself upright on the mattress, his left hand sliding a viscous layer off the filthy surface. Gathering the mulch into his cupped hand, he squeezed hard with adrenal vigor. A crowd of concerned passersby were leaning over the sheer wall, shouting frantically down to him. Daniel waved. "Okay," he shouted. "Don't worry. Other bloke all right?"

The pedestrians looked to their left and shouted in the affirmative. Daniel grinned and looked down at his feet. He was sitting on a corpse, the heel of his foot sinking into her thigh.

He scrambled to his feet, shaking the mattress, making her arm fall out onto the muddy bank. She was wearing a chunky gold identity bracelet with "Ann" inscribed on it. He staggered backward toward the river, keeping his eyes on her, trying to make sense of the image.

He could see her now, a bloated pink and blue belly and a void of a face framed by stringy gray hair, drained of color by the rapacious water. A ragged handful of custard skin was missing from her belly. Daniel called out, a strangled animal cry, and flailed his left hand in the air, scattering her disintegrating flesh. He crouched and splashed his hand in the brown water, trying to wash away the sensation. Panting, he turned back and pointed at the rotting thing hanging out of the mattress.

A man shouted to him from the high river wall. "Are you injured?"

Daniel looked up. His eyes were brimming over. The man's head was an indeterminate blob floating above the river wall. Daniel's eyes flicked back to the corpse, startled afresh by its presence.

The well-meaning man was shouting slowly, enunciating carefully. "Can you hear me?" he yelled. "I am a first-aider."

Daniel tried to look up but each time his eyes flicked back to her. He imagined she had moved and fear took the breath from him. He started to cry and looked up. "Are you the police?" he shouted, in a voice he barely recognized.

"No," shouted the man. "I am a first-aider. Do you require medical attention?"

"Get the fucking police!" screamed Daniel, his eyes streaming now, his nose running into his mouth. He shook his hand in the air, his skin burning with disgust. *"Get the fucking police."*

Also by
Denise Mina

DECEPTION

"Stunning. . . . An elegantly engineered novel of psychological suspense." —Marilyn Stasio, *New York Times Book Review*

"A shocker that's exhilarating in its energetic, witty sordidness." —Ken Tucker, *Entertainment Weekly*

FIELD OF BLOOD

"This mystery enthralls. . . . *Field of Blood* keeps you gripped and guessing right up to its thrilling end." —Joe Heim, *People*

"A fast-paced book. . . . If you liked *Trace* by Patricia Cornwell, or other gritty mysteries with smart female sleuths, try *Field of Blood*." —*Glamour*

THE DEAD HOUR

"An intense and entertaining work of crime fiction that feels so real it'll leave dirt underneath the reader's fingernails." —Dorman T. Shindler, *Denver Post*

"*The Dead Hour* is arguably the most gripping, surprising and satisfying thriller in many a season. . . . Some kind of magnificent." —Tom Nolan, *Wall Street Journal*

BACK BAY BOOKS
Available wherever paperbacks are sold